JOHN MCFALL was born in 1950, educated at Limavady Grammar School, Queen's University, Belfast and St Luke's College, Exeter. He lives in Cornwall where he taught in a local primary school for twenty-eight years.

He started writing his first novel, *Chosen*, in the summer of 1999. Recently retired from teaching, he and his wife live in their home overlooking St Austell bay.

CHOSEN

To Kate
Enjoy the Read
love John
xx

CHOSEN

John A McFall

ATHENA PRESS
LONDON

ISBN 1 84401 546 7

First Published 2005
ATHENA PRESS
Queen's House, 2 Holly Road
Twickenham TW1 4EG
United Kingdom

Printed for Athena Press

To my closest family and friends, especially John Williams who always believed Lizzie's story would be published one day.

Contents

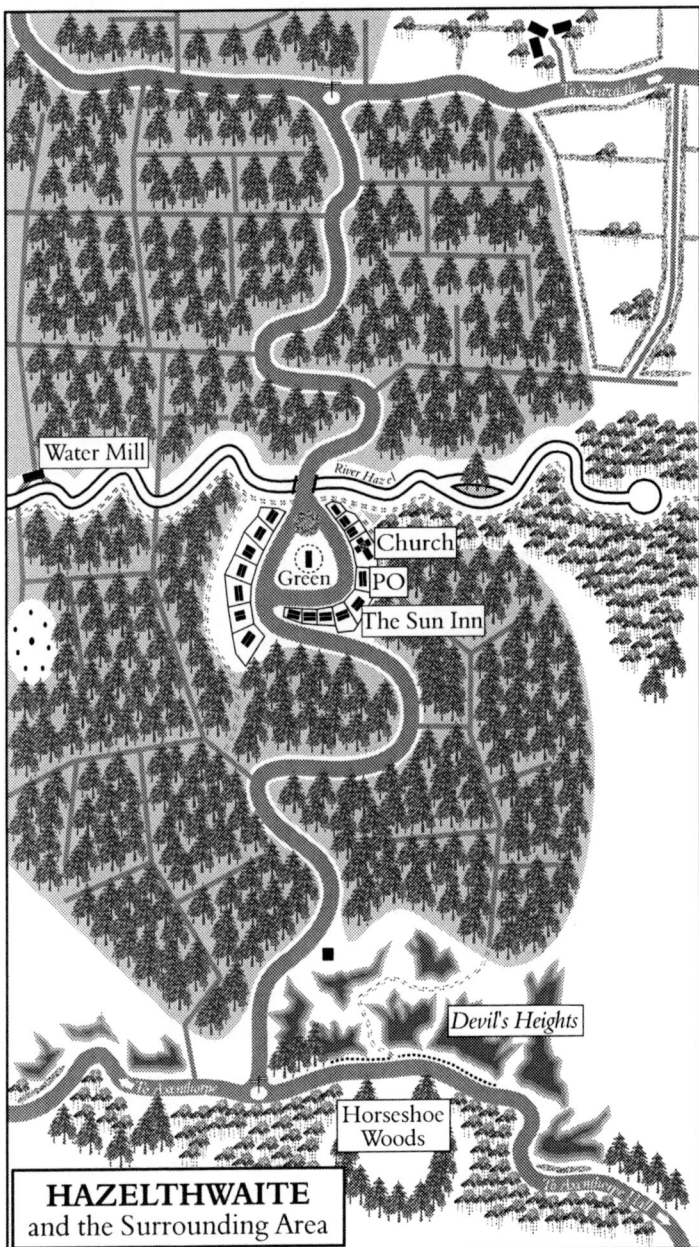

Water Mill

River Haz e

Church

Green

PO

The Sun Inn

Devil's Heights

To Ascnthorpe

Horseshoe
Woods

HAZELTHWAITE
and the Surrounding Area

'That was that!'

To her knowledge, she'd never had any fear of heights, never had fear of water and no real fear of the dark. So why did the scene before her terrify her so?

Hands on hips, she stood there still and silent, silhouetted against the silvery glow of the full moon. The roar of the falling water was deafening. Slowly, she peered down over the side of the rocky shaft. An unnoticed pebble beneath her right heel suddenly moved causing her to stagger, and she screamed but managed to stop herself falling over the precipice. Regaining her balance and composure, she moved her left foot forward inch by inch towards the edge of what looked like a huge black gun barrel. The silver light coming from the full moon couldn't penetrate far enough down the shaft to show where the bottom might be.

She didn't know why she was prompted to do so, but she turned round, bent down on one knee and carefully lowered herself over the edge into the black void. Feeling for foot and handholds, she started to climb down the treacherously slippery, moss-encrusted walls that formed the craggy sides closest to the opening of the falls. One last look towards the path that led to the village showed that no one saw what she was about to do.

At first the going was fairly easy as she could grasp small bushes and clumps of grass highlighted by the moon that grew near the top, although several times she felt her foot slip on a particularly slimy stone, making her scream in panic.

As she progressed further down into the darkness she now had to feel for hand and footholds. Where was she going? What in hell's name was she doing there? The crashing water swirled around her, saturating her clothes and spraying her face with its icy spears. She was cold and scared – scared to death! She was going to die, she knew it, and there was no one to help her! She felt her handgrips beginning to go, and at the same time one foot slid off the smallest of rock footholds!

Her fingers finally lost what little grip they had. My God, she thought, I'm beginning to fall... Slowly at first, her body started to slip downwards and out into the raging waters. She raised her head towards the opening which she had so foolishly decided to enter a few minutes earlier.

As she plummeted downwards she could just make out the full moon filling the gap like a great yellow plug. Moonlight and water poured in to her screaming mouth, choking her. She could feel the pain from the droplets stinging her eyes. She couldn't breathe, she was drowning and falling and the torrent threw her body against the jagged sides of the rocky shaft. God, the pain was unbearable she wanted it to be over.

A last look up. He was there, looking down at her but she couldn't see his face.

There was nothing he could do. He could just see her arms unsuccessfully trying to claw at the sides of the shaft. He closed his eyes and turned away from the horrific scene.

Lizzie sat bolt upright. She was screaming but there was no noise. Her body was bathed in sweat. Her pillow and sheets were damp with perspiration, as if she'd fought the cascading water in the darkened shaft. She immediately thought that she'd wet the bed again, but this time – thank goodness – it was just the sweat from her exertions during the nightmare! God, how many more of these dreams and bedwetting episodes would she have to put up with before she'd 'grow out of them', as she was continually told that she would by her mother? She reached out for her glasses, which were on her bedside table, and put them on. She continued to breathe heavily for a few minutes, then she lifted her hands to her face and arched her head back, at the same time flinging her long blonde hair back out of her eyes.

Who was the dark stranger she'd seen yet again, who always turned away and seemed to refuse to help her before she'd woken up? She couldn't remember but he didn't look as if he came from her world. What the hell! she thought. Lizzie got up and threw her duvet back to let the bed air and dry out. While she was up she popped to the bathroom, hoping that she wouldn't wake her parents. Explaining to her mum once again the problem of the dream was becoming a nightmare in itself.

When she'd crept back along the hall to her room, trying to avoid creaking floorboards, she changed into clean pyjamas and stood by her bedroom window, staring at the silent street below her. She took off her glasses and gave them a huff and a polish. She shoved them back on her nose and pushed her hand through her long blonde hair.

Why this dream? It came back to haunt her again and again, night after night, till she was heartily sick of it. The crashing water – why did it frighten her? After all, she swam like the proverbial fish. She even dived from the high board in the local swimming pool, and that had given her a real daredevil, tomboy reputation. She knew that something was worrying her, but supposed it was one of those 'girlie' growing-up things. Dare she tell her mother of the dream again, or would that start her mum worrying about her daughter's well-being again? Truth of it was, she didn't know what to do! At least her mum hadn't heard her get up and go to the loo, and as there were no bedclothes to wash, she'd give telling her mum about the dream a miss this time.

The bed-wetting was a problem at her age, but her mum had told her that she'd grow out of it over time and there were pills that might help if the problem persisted. Her mum had reassured her that it happened to lots of people, and whereas she knew that Lizzie didn't want to tell even her closest friends about this, she must continue to talk to her about it, and perhaps consult the doctor. She respected Lizzie's embarrassment about the problem enough to keep it from her father!

Lizzie's thoughts drifted back to the inexplicable nightmare. Why wouldn't – or couldn't – the stranger help her from her impossible position? All he had to do was stretch out his arm to her at the start of the fall and she would have been safe. Lizzie called the stranger a 'he', as she assumed it was a man watching her fall. Perhaps it wasn't a person at the top of the shaft looking down at her at all; maybe it was a branch silhouetted against the moon that looked like a human form. She shrugged her shoulders. She didn't know, and was it worth the effort trying to analyse it? It was a frightening dream and thousands of people had those every night. Why should she be so different? However, before she went to sleep for the second time that evening she thought that if the dream occurred again, which she hoped it wouldn't, she'd try hard to get a better look at that 'stranger' and try and make some sense of what was going on.

The two girls watched as Lizzie took off her glasses and gave them a huff and a polish before shoving them back on her nose. Next she pushed her right hand through her long blonde hair, which immediately fell into the same position as before. God, Lizzie was *so* boring and predictable!

David Webster sat totally still on the huge black horse. He was dressed in the style of a highwayman. From where he sat, at the top of Devil's Heights, he could see the village lights twinkling below him in the darkness. The church clock struck midnight. He would give someone a God-awful scare tonight. The question was – who?

Tom Bennett sat on an equally large black horse watching the Highwayman from the comparative shelter of Horseshoe Woods. He too was dressed in the style of a highwayman, but unlike the man he was watching he waited in absolute silence, as did his horse!

When Lizzie Miller came to live at Hazelthwaite, she was so upset and depressed that her mum and dad constantly threatened to send her away to a private school if she didn't buck her ideas up. She moaned about the village, the cottage, the dull life and the fact that she had left her two best friends behind in South London.

Life had been wonderful, so why should it change? She even liked her school and the teachers. Normally, children in their right mind detested their teachers; they're the enemy, so really they've got to be disliked – even if you secretly admire them! Lizzie hated the thought of leaving Dalebridge High School for Girls.

Lizzie and her friends, Brenda – nicknamed 'Bendy' (due to her unreserved love of things sweet, hence her rather full and rounded shape) – and Donna had been chatting, more like gossiping, in Lizzie's bedroom on that awful Saturday morning. They'd heard the phone ring, and Lizzie's mum answer it, talk to someone (obviously fairly important) and by listening in to the one-sided conversation picked up that 'if we had to go', she supposed 'that was that'. They'd all looked at one another in a rather distressed manner, quickly followed by Lizzie shrugging her shoulders. Then she trotted downstairs to see what the rather distressing 'that was that' was all about.

Jane Miller had said in a matter-of-fact voice to her daughter's less than positive demand about what was going on, 'Your father has the opportunity to take over a post office in the North of England, Lizzie, and really we have no choice but to accept the offer and go.'

Lizzie hadn't known what to say at first. She'd stood looking at her mother blankly, Her bottom jaw dropped wide open for fully five minutes before she half closed her left eye, drew her lips together and hissed between them, 'But we live here! I like it here, my best friends are here…' And at that point she couldn't say anything else, because she could feel the tears welling up in her eyes. She'd turned round disconsolately, shuffled upstairs to her bedroom, slammed the door, and much to the surprise of Bendy and Donna had promptly started to fall apart. Lizzie, hard as nails, was crying! Her friends freaked. Lizzie never cried – they thought she couldn't. Hell, Lizzie must have a heart somewhere after all!

Bendy and Donna were so upset when they'd heard the news they went home crying too, and it took Lizzie a fortnight before she could talk to them properly without filling up hankies, Kleenex and anything else that absorbed tears!

Naturally, her parents, Jane and John Miller, were upset because Lizzie seemed so inconsolable. They'd said she'd make new friends very quickly and that she could write and phone

Bendy and Donna whenever she wanted to, and that they had no doubt that the two girls could come up and stay in the school holidays.

Lizzie had quite bluntly and uncharacteristically told them that they couldn't possibly understand her feelings, that they'd never been young, ever – and she didn't want to leave London. She hated going north, even when her dad took her to see Arsenal play at Highbury. Crikey, it was cold up north, and from some of the TV programmes she'd seen they didn't even speak understandable English. Didn't the Romans live up there or something – and build a wall to keep out the bloody Scots? Or had her teachers been lying to her? Oh God, the whole thing was worse than her own worst nightmare, and that was bad enough! Jane and John had had a bellyful from her, and in the end for their own sakes had started to ignore Lizzie's ravings and tantrums.

Lizzie hated the countryside. She couldn't ever...*ever* like the quiet of living in some isolated backwater, and it was so...so far away from any shops. She'd even said to her father what he thought she and her mum would do for retail therapy when they got low. Lizzie thought she'd be low all the time; in fact she'd make it her business to stay permanently low. Dad told her that Newcastle had lovely shops, and Lizzie had thought it was getting worse!

They had many arguments, and Lizzie even sneaked off one evening and hid in the shed at the bottom of their courtyard. She'd burst open the lock, then jammed the door tightly shut and retreated to the back of the shed, covering herself with old sacks and a stinking tarpaulin. After half an hour in the quiet, she plucked up courage to switch on her torch to check the time and see what the rustling was around her feet...only to be confronted by a huge rat sitting on its back legs looking at her! Lizzie's blood had run cold. She was so frightened that the scream she'd let out was stifled as her hand was virtually stuffed down her throat. The rat was totally surprised that the fresh meat it was about to start nibbling for an evening snack had come to life, and took fright. It took a flying leap straight up Lizzie's legs, sprang off her chest and became momentarily entangled in her blonde hair before freeing itself and exiting through a broken window in the roof of the hut. Lizzie had been totally terror struck by the event, but had luckily not made enough noise to create any suspicion about where she was hiding. The whole episode had been over in a jiffy.

Mum had called the police when Lizzie hadn't shown up, and when she'd been finally found all sorts of horrid things were said, and huge amounts of groundings had followed that little episode. Everybody told Lizzie off. She thought it amazing that when things went wrong, how so many different people slid out from under stones to tell you off! Perhaps a Government Department existed, ready to dash into action to let your school, your granny, Auntie and the goldfish know that you'd done something wrong. The last straw was the aggro she'd got from Bendy and Donna; telling her that everything would work out well, given time, and that in the end she'd settle down. They'd told her to give her parents a chance. Lizzie told them she was trying to make a point but no one wanted to listen.

Lizzie's mum said she was attention-seeking – fat chance! Whatever she said or did wasn't going to make the slightest difference. They were going and that was final – 'that was that'. She didn't even know where Hazelthwaite was. She didn't need to. Hazelthwaite sounded like one of those murder mystery places that you saw on the telly, with interfering old busybodies with blue rinses who rode bikes with baskets on the handlebars in a wobbly fashion and picked roses for excitement. Lizzie was determined to hate it. Bendy, in one of her 'Lizzie comforting sessions' again said she had to give the move a chance. She then went on to tell Lizzie that her parents had told her that on no account would she be allowed to visit her, unaccompanied, in the holidays…and that set the tears off again.

Three months after putting their house in London up for sale, and her dad doing this and that transaction with the Post Office, coupled with several speedy excursions up north to look at the new property (that Lizzie didn't go on, because she said she really wasn't interested) and the Miller family were on their way to their new life – for good!

All the arrangements had slipped by so swiftly. No more suburbs, no more popping down the shops, no more nipping to the local swimming pool and bowling alley, no more noise. It was the end of life, as Lizzie saw it. All those things were replaced by the peace and quiet of village life. Lizzie told Bendy and Donna, much later, that she'd have swapped her autograph book (and there were some good signatures in that) for a whole lot of noise and bustle on many occasions, when she'd first arrived in Hazelthwaite. Lizzie had truly hated those first couple of months in the back and beyond! Hence her parents continual threat of private education.

Lizzie's new school was situated in the local town of Axenthorpe. Well, the locals called it a town, but Lizzie thought you could have put it into the middle of any one of the bright and trendy new shopping malls in London, it was so small. Axenthorpe was half an hour's bus ride from Hazelthwaite.

She'd found it very difficult to make friends, mainly because she didn't try and was stand-offish. The local village kids were friendly enough, but they spoke in a foreign language as far as Lizzie was concerned. To try and interpret what they said she had to watch their mouths very carefully and hope that when she said 'yes' and 'no' or 'whatever', that it was in the right place. They, in turn, reckoned she had a posh accent because she came from London – joke! If only they could've seen the street and house that she used to live in!

Anyway, one girl whom Lizzie sat beside on the school bus, called Mabel (bloody awful names up north, Lizzie had thought), took Lizzie under her wing, so to speak, and along with Mabel's friend, Amy, showed her the ropes: going to school, local shops and cinema, things like that. Mabel was quite sweet, she wanted to know what Harrods was like and how many times Lizzie had seen Prince Harry. When she said she'd only been to Harrods once to see the Christmas lights and that she wasn't keen on any of the Royal Family in particular, Mabel had gone quiet. Lizzie quickly realised that Mabel considered her rude for speaking her mind. When Lizzie had said she was an Arsenal supporter, Mabel had looked at her wide-eyed and terror struck, and said that everybody in Hazelthwaite supported Newcastle United and that if you even mentioned another team it was considered an offence. Lizzie never spoke about her beloved Arsenal again after that, and would never have dreamed of wearing her favourite Arsenal shirt for fear of being beaten with knotted 'Toon' scarves with 'Shearer' written on them. She had asked Mabel in passing if this Shearer ever had anything to do with sheep rearing, but the question had fallen on deaf or thick ears, so she hadn't pursued that line of sarcasm again.

Hazelthwaite was not a hive of activity. It was a sleepy sort of place. 'Excitement' was a word that hadn't seemed to have reached that far north yet, or so it seemed to Lizzie. The village was situated in a sort of pudding basin valley surrounded by hills covered in pine forests, which were steep and craggy. Trees lined both sides of the narrow road that snaked down to the village, then up the other side and on to Axenthorpe. When you got to the bottom of the valley there was a large triangular village green which had a low, white-painted picket fence surrounding it. At one end of the triangle was an enormous tree. Mabel confidently informed Lizzie that it was an oak tree and was literally hundreds of years old. A bench seat had been built around the base of the trunk and over the years lots of stupid names and messages had been carved into the slats on which you sat. Mabel also said that it had been used for hanging people about two hundred years ago, but Lizzie didn't believe a word of that.

The bench was built in a pentagonal style around the base of the oak, and your level of comfort depended on which portion of the pentagon you sat on. Mabel had ensured that Lizzie (much to her annoyance) had been placed on each bit that would give Mabel and Amy the maximum fun at Lizzie's expense.

For instance, on one side of the pentagon there were two slats of wood that gave way when you sat on them. Lizzie had managed to sit on the offending slats, ending up in a most unladylike position that had showed her legs and most of everything else off to the world. Several village boys who were around at the time for the set-up (and who all secretly fancied this blonde Londoner to death) had given her massive applause – much to Lizzie's embarrassment.

Another section, which had a rather nastily broken slat, would bend alarmingly, twanging up your bottom and giving a most uncomfortable 'wedgie'. Each time Lizzie was caught out, Mabel and Amy totally freaked. It was like they were giving this southerner her initiation to village life. Lizzie always huffed and puffed at their ridiculous antics, but the more she spent time with them the more they grew on her.

Along two sides of the green were the most perfectly built cottages you have ever seen, each with beautifully tended gardens, and along the third side were more houses, John Miller's post office and adjoining cottage and outhouses, the church and the pub. In the surrounding hills and dales were smaller villages and hamlets whose occupants used Lizzie's dad's post office and general store for any local shopping that they needed.

The trade was regular but quiet in comparison to London. John Miller had said that the summer tourists who came to the region would certainly buck his trade up, but added, 'God help us in winter when we're snowed in!' Lizzie had looked at him wide-eyed and repeated, 'Snowed in? Nobody had told me about being snowed in!'

He had continued that often the snow in these parts drifted so deeply even the snowploughs found it difficult to keep the roads clear. So, winter in Hazelthwaite sounded like a barrel of laughs; but then Lizzie thought, The school bus won't be able to reach us. And Mabel had backed this up when Lizzie had quizzed her about it.

Mabel had told her that all the kids got together on Devil's Heights and skied and tobogganed and had good fun. The children from Axenthorpe still had to attend school, but the downside of being trapped in the village in winter was that the teachers ensured that the children who came from the surrounding districts had extra homework, so they could keep up. Lizzie had remarked that she'd believe the fun in the snow when she saw it, but she didn't like the sound of extra homework! Lizzie considered herself decidedly non-academic.

Devil's Heights sounded slightly worse than it really was. Although there were some steep rocky outcrops on the northern slopes of the basin, the name, according to Lizzie, was slightly overdone. Lizzie walked up to the top of the Heights one

Saturday morning and found the going wasn't too difficult. True, there were some formidable rock and boulder outcrops near to the summit, but she'd stayed well away from them. There were plenty of well-worn paths through the bracken and gorse that got you to the top without any real climbing at all. When she reached the top and looked back over towards Hazelthwaite, even Lizzie had had to admit that the views across the valleys and hills were spectacular. But there was still no real noise and all the fun and bustle of London. While she had sat looking at the view and thinking of 'home', she thought of Bendy and Donna and had had a little cry. Alone on the top of the Heights she was very aware of the quiet of the countryside. She could hear the strong buzz of a million insects going about their business in the sunshine. There wasn't a breath of air to disturb anything. She picked a long piece of grass and chewed on it. She leant back on her elbows and closed her eyes, letting the sun warm her face and dry her tears. Maybe this wasn't so bad after all… Then the tears came flooding back again.

It was while she was dabbing the new fall of tears away with a very grubby hankie, and feeling very stupid with herself for having these feelings, that she had felt suddenly uneasy, as if someone was watching her. The quiet at the top of the Heights became less friendly. Why should she suddenly feel like this? The sun still shone. The insects still buzzed relentlessly in the gorse flowers. How odd! Lizzie didn't like the feeling, and wished that Mabel or Amy were with her.

At the top of Devil's Heights the land was fairly flat and the road to Axenthorpe curved quite close to the precipitous edge. Black and white pillars with sets of red reflecting plastic eyes were set into the rock floor to prevent vehicles from disappearing accidentally over the edge. Closer to the edge were large pieces of reinforced metal that would help keep cars from plunging over the edge if they were unfortunately involved in an accident, or in case their brakes failed. Lizzie noticed that there were one or two quite nasty crumpled areas in the metal, and several of the black and white pillars were leaning at weird angles, which certainly indicated that there had been accidents up on this dangerous bend. Black skid marks in the roadway certainly confirmed this.

God, it must have been frightening for the drivers and passengers! She hoped nothing awful had happened here.

On the other side of the road was a small wood of mixed broad-leaved and coniferous trees that had grown up in the shape of a horseshoe. The narrow part of the horseshoe faced the Heights, and then the trees opened into a large glade. As it was early summer, the leaves had grown thickly and shrubs had sprouted unattended between them, so that the glade was almost invisible from where Lizzie sat overlooking Hazelthwaite and the panoramic views of the surrounding area.

Suddenly, she thought she saw a movement; but it was nothing – perhaps a momentary breeze on a totally still day. She shivered. She took off her specs, gave them a huff and a polish before putting them back on. She looked again, but there was nothing to see and definitely no one about. However, she definitely detected a chill in the air. Lizzie still felt uneasy, and because there was no sign of life around, no farmers on tractors, and no sounds of buzzing chainsaws from the forestry workers, she quickly got to her feet and ran down the grassy slopes to the village. By the time she'd got to the village green, she felt totally stupid and completely puffed out.

It was some time later that day that she found out a bit more of Hazelthwaite's more sinister history. The part about Devil's Heights had interested Lizzie the most and certainly made the hairs on the back of her neck stand up.

Mabel, Amy and Lizzie were sitting on the bench under the 'Gallows Oak' which overlooked the village green. Lizzie chatted to them about her walk to the Heights and how she'd spooked herself. She felt silly talking about her concerns, but you know what they say: a problem shared is a problem supposedly halved. What she was about to hear made her even more concerned about her earlier afternoon happening.

'Lizzie, did you know that someone accidentally died on the 'Heights'?' said Mabel in a conspiratorial way.

'First I've heard of it,' Lizzie replied, trying to sound disinterested.

Mabel continued, 'Oh yes, it was a few years ago now. This tourist went out for walk after tea. It was still daylight, but by the time he'd got to Devil's Heights it was getting dark, and a thick mist had come down. He just lost the road or the pathway at the top and nose-dived onto a rock that jutted out. He was splattered everywhere!' Lizzie could see that Mabel relished telling her this gruesome part of the tale.

'That's horrible, Mabel!' replied Amy. 'We didn't see anything – she's just adding to the story, Lizzie.'

'No, I'm not, I heard the local policeman say that, and he should know because he was first on the scene. His head came off and…'

'Stop it, Mabel!' remonstrated Amy, 'Lizzie will never go up there again.'

'Anything else other than the blood and gore?' inquired Lizzie. Mabel went quiet. Amy looked away.

'Oh, for goodness' sake, tell,' begged Lizzie. 'Tell me, Mabel!'

'Well, it's silly, but a friend told me that the night the man died, about the time he would have fallen, she swore the mist had swirled away just long enough for her to have seen a light flickering. Like a torch being waved or a lamp flickering. But you know what we're like when we're chatting and we want to frighten one another with ghost stories, it was just that – a good story.'

'Well, you've made my skin crawl, 'replied Lizzie, 'especially as I felt something strange up there myself. Next time I go up to the Heights I won't be going on my own. That's for sure!'

*

At the end of July school broke up for the summer holidays and Lizzie received the best news ever. Bendy and Donna were being allowed to travel up to Hazelthwaite after all to stay for a fortnight or so. It meant that they could keep her company while John and Jane Miller looked after the post office and shop during the busiest period of the year.

Lizzie excitedly told Mabel the good news. Mabel, however, reacted as if her nose had been ever so slightly put out of joint.

'Listen, Mabel, you and Amy have become my friends, and just because Bendy and Donna are coming, I'm not going to just push you two aside. I'm not like that. I thought I'd hate it here, but you two have made it bearable for me; when the others arrive I know you'll all get on like a house on fire – so to speak,' Lizzie declared.

Once she'd cleared the air as to the position of the relationships, the three girls couldn't wait for Bendy and Donna to arrive.

Hazelthwaite could get extremely busy at times during the peak weeks of the summer holidays. One cottage, with a particularly beautiful garden, was opened by its elderly owners as a tearoom, and was very popular with foreign visitors (especially Americans and Japanese) who'd stumbled on the quaint little village.

On Saturdays and Sundays during the cricket season the local cricket team played on the green. It was great fun when one of the batsmen hit a hard shot through a car windscreen that had been parked too close to the boundary. The girls – well, everyone watching, with the exception of the unfortunate car owner – liked that. As the ball sailed through the air all the home supporters would suddenly begin a low *ooh* sound that would reach a terrifying crescendo finishing with a great *aah* as the ball hit glass, any type of glass!

Sometimes a really big hit might carry across the boundary, over the road and towards the cottages. Then you'd hear the sound of breaking glass as the ball went through a front window, or better still would sail into a back garden and smash into a greenhouse. Everyone liked that too! There was always great applause for the batsman, as he had to stand a round of drinks at the pub after the game was finished. Even the kids got Cokes or lemonades on these occasions.

The best story that Amy told was one about a very fat batsman who'd played for the Hazelthwaite team for years. He'd once given the ball such a wallop that it had landed in the garden where people were having their afternoon tea with scones stacked high with strawberry jam and cream.

The fat batsman had hit the ball so high in the air that when it had finally come to earth, it had smashed through a cake stand, squirting cream and eclairs and fancy little sponges everywhere. The lady who had been sitting at the table received a direct hit in the face with a large cream apple puff! Her husband had ended up with an éclair moustache and her dog, which she had tied to one of the table legs, had received a painful blow to his head from an ornate but very heavy silver teapot!

The dog, a Rottweiler, had arrived in the garden and unceremoniously cocked his leg against an ornamental fountain, so you couldn't tell which jet of water was which for thirty seconds or so. Then, before settling down to sleep with one eye permanently open, it had apparently growled threateningly at everyone occupying adjacent tables to its owners. This ensured that nobody dared to move from their now most uncomfortable deckchairs through sheer fright, until the dog received its untimely whack on the skull due to the effect of gravity.

The dog had been frightened to death when the teapot landed on its head. It had taken off at a rate of knots (ensuring that it bit anything it could surround its jaws with, while still pulling the now wrecked table) scattering tables, chairs, teapots and broken china all over the garden. It caused chaos. It rampaged through the flower beds, which were reduced to beds of bare stalks. It bit the head of a gaudily painted garden gnome fishing in the fountain pond. And, before leaping the garden hedge, table and all, like a demented tornado, it gave one final ear-piercing howl.

Well out of the sight of its owners, and to the relief of the mortified tea garden customers, the Rottweiler skipped across the boundary rope surrounding the cricket field. Now it could get down to some serious dog-biting business. It looked round for a postman: nothing, not a uniform or postbag in sight! The dog checked for a second, eyeing up the petrified cricketers. Slowly it pawed the grass like an angry bull, lowered its rear leg, did a quick wee and then dashed onto the village green. After all, a man with a large stick in his hand must want to play throw and fetch! At full pelt, the dog bit the fat batsman in the short mid-wicket area, and for a grand finale cocked its leg against the stumps before trotting back quite docilely to its masters with the middle stump tightly clasped between its ample jaws. The girls really liked this story, and Lizzie wished she could have seen it happen!

However, this story was the exception rather than the rule, and under normal conditions nothing much happened in the cricket matches. But with the second week in August getting closer, Lizzie couldn't wait to see Bendy and Donna. Then something quite strange happened to her…no, bizarre… In fact it was quite beyond belief!

Moonlight

As the time drew nearer for Bendy and Donna to come and stay, Lizzie noticed that Mabel grew more distant and sometimes didn't see her for a few days at a time. In a place like Hazelthwaite, that was difficult! But as Mabel seemed not to want to talk to her, Lizzie decided that she'd use her time alone to look in all the local so-called 'sites of interest' around Hazelthwaite, and perhaps find something vaguely interesting to show her friends when they arrived.

It was on the following Tuesday that Lizzie decided to go and look at the church. It was very old, originally built in Norman times, or so they said, with a couple of newer extensions that had been built on as time had gone by. She walked up the well-raked, crunchy gravel path to the double wooden doors. Anybody who approached the doors would almost certainly be heard arriving on the pathway from the interior of the church.

One of the arched doors was slightly open and she could hear voices coming from inside the building. A large sign outside the door advertised the 'Flower Festival' – 'donations kindly accepted on the way out'. Good, Lizzie thought, because she didn't have any money on her and she thought she might be able to get out undetected without making a donation. Lizzie pushed on the round metal door handle and went inside. There were parish notices neatly displayed in a glass-fronted display case. Slatted seats each side of the porch led to inner double doors. All the woodwork had been freshly painted. A nice old lady, whom Lizzie recognised as Agnes Smith, said 'hello' to her and hoped she would enjoy the flowers. All the displays were brilliant; even Bendy and Donna would appreciate the time, love and patience that had gone into constructing them, she thought.

The sun poured through the stained glass windows in rainbow-like shafts of light. It was very peaceful. She could hear one or two murmurs from other visitors looking at the floral displays.

Funny isn't it, you're not expecting anything out of the ordinary, when, suddenly a shaft of brilliant, white sunlight hit a dingy corner and picked out a brass plaque that Lizzie would normally have just passed by, as if magic dust had been sprinkled onto it. She supposed it was the dust in the air, highlighted by the light. She knelt down and read the inscription. It said:

David Webster 1958–1997

In Loving Memory

Victim of Devil's Heights.

That was all that was written. It was very much to the point. Almost too obvious, but of course Lizzie didn't pay too much attention to the inscription, except to think back to what Mabel had said.

This must be the tourist that she'd told her about. How strange that she should stumble on the plaque! As instantly as the plaque had been lit up, the shaft of light disappeared. Perhaps the sun had gone behind a cloud. Very strange, though, the rest of the church was still lit with bright coloured light.

'Are you enjoying the displays, my dear?' said a squeaky, quivering voice.

Lizzie jumped.

'Oh! I didn't mean to frighten you,' said the voice again, in the same strange high tone.

By this time Lizzie had turned around and saw it was Agnes Smith.

'I'm Mrs Smith,' she squeaked again.

As their eyes made contact, Lizzie noticed that Agnes had the lightest of blue eyes. The sun glinted off them like two lasers.

'This year's theme is, "Scenes of the surrounding countryside near Hazelthwaite". The one you've been admiring so studiously is of Devil's Heights. Cleverly made, isn't it? One of my favourites,' she added.

'I'm not sure,' Lizzie murmured.

Agnes ignored the reply Lizzie had offered her. 'Well, Mrs Webster designed it,' she explained, 'in memory of her son who died on the Heights, two years ago. Terrible accident…'

'Didn't he know the area very well?' Lizzie suggested.

'Oh yes! He was born and bred here in Hazelthwaite. Some say it was Tom Bennett the highwayman who lured him to the precipice with his lantern.' Her smile was like a grimace. Lizzie thought the tiny-framed woman looked more like a walking skeleton, and felt she definitely wouldn't like to meet her on a dark night!

It was getting too much for Lizzie. She thanked Agnes for her time and walked back down the aisle. As she walked out, Lizzie pretended to put some money into the collection box. Actually she had managed to find a couple of Coke tops in her bag. They'd made a rattling sound like money when they fell in the box. She'd wished she hadn't put them in it, the moment she'd done it because Agnes was bound to realise Lizzie had put them in there when she counted up the contributions at the end of the day. You could bet your bottom dollar that Lizzie was going to be the only kid who would have visited the flower festival that day on their own!

Lizzie reached the gate, and as she stepped onto the road she saw Mabel chatting to Amy underneath the 'Gallows Oak'. Lizzie waved and walked over to them.

'What had Agnes to say to you, then?' enquired Mabel.

'Not much,' Lizzie replied, 'she spooked me a bit, crept up behind me in the church and made me jump – weird eyes.'

They both laughed at her. It was a conspiratorial type of laugh and Lizzie didn't ask why.

'The man who died at Devil's Heights was called David Webster,' Lizzie said.

There was a short silence and then Mabel muttered, 'It was awful. Terrible conditions. He lost his way and fell. We told you that before, though.'

'Agnes told me...' Lizzie began, and then fell silent.

'Told you what?' asked Amy.

'Oh, nothing, it's too silly for words. I think she was having me on,' said Lizzie.

'Go on!' said Mabel. 'You've started now, so you've got to tell us. We reckon she's weird too.'

'Well!' Lizzie began. Then she told the two girls about the strange shaft of light and the silly story of the Highwayman and the flickering light.

They were both totally white and speechless when she'd finished the tale.

'We try not to talk about the Highwayman here,' said Amy. 'Mention his name…and it seems to bring bad luck. Something always strange happens or goes wrong. He's almost like Hazelthwaite's own Jonah.'

Lizzie was gobsmacked. 'I didn't know anything about that until today, did I? I wish I was back in London – I'm not ready for the countryside,' she muttered.

Mabel looked at Lizzie with her funny rustic look. 'Nobody's told you about your house and its history?'

Lizzie nodded 'no', puckered her mouth and shrugged.

'Meet Amy and me here tonight at ten, and we'll tell you a creepy story.'

'I'm not sure I can get out at that time. My mum will want to know where I am,' Lizzie replied.

'You'll have to sneak out. It'll be fun, and you have to do these things in the right atmosphere, otherwise the story loses its impact.'

Lizzie said she'd try but she couldn't promise anything. She said it might be difficult and left it at that.

At nine thirty, Lizzie told her mum that she was going to have an early night as she thought she'd go for a walk the next morning to Devil's Heights. She popped to the loo and brushed her teeth. She made sure that her parents heard her close the bedroom door.

Gently, she eased the sash window open. Lizzie's bedroom was at the gable end of the house, and from it she could see the lights of the cottages on the other side of the green. By the window there was a large horse chestnut tree, which she had tried to climb up in daylight, but certainly not as high as her bedroom. Now, she had to reach out and try and ease her way across a narrowish, well-leafed branch to the trunk. She could just about make out the ground. It suddenly occurred to her, perched on the window ledge, if she could get out without any difficulty at all, then it would be dead easy for a burglar to get in!

She was just plucking up courage to reach out for the branch when she was suddenly aware of a flickering light by the Gallows

Oak. No, definitely a trick of the light, a silly mistake; it's mind games. This is Hazelthwaite in summer – highwaymen went out with Dick Turnip or whoever it was…but there it was again, a flickering light. The moon was suddenly drowned in cloud and she could see the light quite clearly. Then it was gone.

As the moon reappeared, her mum called, 'Night, dear!' and Lizzie replied, 'Night, Mum!'

Thank goodness she hadn't left a few seconds earlier, otherwise she would have been rumbled.

She gently put her weight on the branch. It hardly gave at all, which surprised her. Lizzie carefully picked her way between the smaller leaf-covered twigs to the relative safety of the large trunk. From here it was quite easy to climb down, with lots of places for her to put her hands and feet. An owl hooted from somewhere. Bats dashed this way and that. She froze solid against the trunk when she heard two voices from the direction of the pub saying goodbyes; then all was quiet.

The light, if there had been one, had disappeared. Lizzie was shivering with fright by the time she'd walked across the village green…but not as frightened as when she got to the mighty oak itself! Lizzie approached very quietly and sat down facing the village green. She took her glasses off, gave them a huff and a polish and put them back on. Apart from the lights twinkling from the cottage windows it was dark and quiet. The owl hooted again; this time it seemed nearer. She pulled her fleece up to her chin for comfort.

Suddenly, both her arms were grabbed from behind. Lizzie nearly wet herself in fear, and she gasped out loud when she saw two horrific faces staring at her. One was wearing an old-fashioned tricorn hat and mask. Then the giggling started. She realised it was Mabel and Amy.

'You rats – I nearly…!'

'Wet yourself!' chortled Amy, 'Oh, what a laugh. We told you, you had to have the right atmosphere for ghoulish and ghostly stories.' They waved their hands in front of her face and cackled.

'Don't be so ridiculous, I could have fainted or something. I suppose it was you with the light?' said Lizzie.

'One of my garden lanterns,' said Mabel matter-of-factly.

'Sorry, we didn't mean to scare you to death, but you should have seen your face this afternoon and now.'

'Thanks, Mabel. Now, what about this story, before I'm grounded before Bendy and Donna arrive?'

Mabel looked thoughtful and then began the tale.

Apparently, in the early 1800s Lizzie's house had been a coaching inn, which is why there was an archway leading from the road to the inner courtyard. On several occasions an evil highwayman had robbed the Edinburgh to Newcastle stagecoach. On one particularly stormy night the owners of the Newcastle stagecoach had set a trap and caught him red-handed. The coach driver had been wounded in the arm but the militia, who were hiding in the coach, captured the man – Tom Bennett. He was brought to Hazelthwaite, bound up and actually stayed in one of the outhouses that had been stables for the changeover horses. While Bennett was asleep, the guard who had been posted to watch over him that night conveniently got drunk. The villagers broke in, dragged Bennett to the oak and hanged him without a trial. The story kind of got lost over time then reappeared again. It was embellished to make it more spicy, and then occasionally local people from other hamlets and Hazelthwaite would say they've seen or heard Bennett's ghost riding Devil's Heights and the surrounding district. It was thought his ghost might have been responsible for David Webster's death, luring him through the mist by the flickering of his lamp.

It was a good story but nobody really believed it. Old wives' tales, that sort of thing. But Mabel did add that she wouldn't want to cross Devil's Heights on her own on a cold and wild winter's night. Amy agreed wholeheartedly, and so did Lizzie.

When Mabel finished, Lizzie looked at her for several minutes. 'Why didn't mum and dad tell me the story?' she asked.

'Perhaps they don't know about it, or perhaps they didn't want to scare you, if they knew about the ghost.'

'So what did this highwayman do that made the village people want to hang him themselves?' Lizzie asked.

'He stole the six jewels of Axenthorpe Hall, or the jewels that surrounded the Icon there, and they've never been found. He had several lairs where he used to hide while he was waiting for things to cool down after he'd successfully carried out a robbery, and people reckon that they're still in those hiding places, probably not far away from here. The Axenthorpe family had given the Icon (with the jewels surrounding it) to Hazelthwaite Church in 1803. The icon stands in a granite niche in the church. It doesn't look much, just an old wooden frame with a picture on it that has faded with age. Anyway, it's said that he killed the vicar who had disturbed him with the very dagger that he'd hacked the jewels out of the icon with.'

'Nice bloke, this Tom Bennett,' Lizzie commented thoughtfully. The church clock struck midnight.

'God, is that the time?' Amy whispered.

'We'd better go,' said Mabel. Moonlight suddenly flooded Lizzie's face that was frozen in terror. 'What's the matter Lizzie?'

Lizzie pointed over Mabel's shoulder towards the Heights.

As the girls looked round, a distant flickering light could be seen on the top of Devil's Heights. Christ, it was him! They broke and ran back to the respective cottages.

On the highest outcrop of Devil's Heights the horse grazed on the grass while the dark stranger carefully studied the Gallows Oak. The lamp that he held in the air flickered in the light breeze, showing off his eye mask and tricorn hat. As his black cape flapped across his chest, the pearl handles of the brace of pistols tucked into the black belt glinted in the moonlight. The girl called Lizzie would have to be dealt with sooner or later, he could feel it!

From the shadow of Horseshoe Wood at the summit of Devil's Heights, a more sinister rider, in clothes matching the Highwayman's, watched as the horseman pulled his mount round and thundered off towards Axenthorpe Hall.

He followed the Highwayman at a gallop, but with no sound at all…as if he were floating over the moor land.

The Axenthorpe Icon

Lizzie had managed to sneak back to the post office without being seen. But she'd found it slightly more difficult climbing back up the tree and then pushing open the sash window of her bedroom without making a great deal of noise. Clouds had bubbled up and covered the moon and this had added to the ordeal, but at last she was back inside. She looked across at Devil's Heights one last time but nothing was visible. Mabel and Amy had really got to her. Lizzie got undressed and climbed into bed, pulled the duvet up to her chin for more comfort than warmth, and immediately fell into a dream-filled asleep.

'Lizzie! Lizzie!' In the dream, she heard her mother calling. She woke up with a start. Morning sunshine was pouring through the window. Her curtains were pulled and her mother was pushing up the bottom half of the sash window.

'Lizzie, you must put the catch across on the window latch at night before you go to sleep, luvvie. Anyone could climb the tree and get in.'

'Yes, Mum, sorry. I must have gone out like a light last night, but I do remember shutting the window. Just forgot the catch I s'pose,' she added.

'I've brought you a cuppa and a couple of bikkies. You'll have to make your own breakfast this morning as I'm going to the wholesalers for nine o'clock while your Dad stays in the shop. And remember, the girls arrive this afternoon,' she continued. 'Make sure you're around to meet them.'

'Mum – as if I'd forget! I'm shaking with excitement. It's been such a long time since I've seen them. God, I wonder how big Bendy is now. She'll have been eating like a bloody horse with the worry of the travel and all.'

'I don't think three months is that long, and you have been able to phone and write…and for goodness' sake curb your language, Lizzie,' her mother replied, smiling.

Lizzie looked idly out of the window and said in half-whispered tones, 'Yeah, but it's not face-to-face, wall-to-wall pure tripe gossip.'

Lizzie had missed her friends tremendously but had not pursued the issue with her parents. After all she had made two new and good acquaintances whom she hoped would become friends in the future.

After seeing that her father didn't need her help in the shop – and she did double check – she made her way to the church again. She stopped at the lychgate. It was too early for visitors to the village, and there were no cars parked in the church lay-by, but the flower festival was still in full swing; as announced by the board propped by the gate and another by the main church door.

A couple of crows flew lazily by cawing loudly, and landed on a high branch of a horse chestnut tree. A magpie cackled between the gravestones... What was the rhyme? One for sorrow! There was the heady smell of honeysuckle in the hedgerow and the faint buzzing of insects busying themselves as they moved from one flower to the next. Apart from these sounds the village snoozed under the morning sunshine.

Lizzie thought, what she'd give for a jolly good old dollop of hustle and bustle. She felt like yelling out, 'Get a life, Hazelthwaite!' – but it just didn't seem appropriate. She walked up the gravel path. Again the slight crunching from the gravel warned of her approach. The doors were slightly open, as they had been yesterday. The porch was cool. She pushed the doors open.

'That'll be seen to,' said a squeaky voice, which Lizzie recognised as Agnes Smith's.

'Good, because I feel we're close, very close,' replied a man's voice that Lizzie didn't recognise.

Now, listening in to people's conversations is rude. Lizzie's mum and dad had habitually told her that and could get you into trouble. It was while the man was replying that Lizzie accidentally leant against the ice cream container that was being used for collecting the donations for the flower festival. The whole thing tipped over, spilling the entire contents onto the flagstone floor of the porch. Funny, isn't it, that if you do knock something over, there are times you can catch it before it hits the floor and then there are other times when every last thing falls to the ground and makes a huge mess or breaks into a million pieces!

This was one of the latter, and Lizzie was mortified at the noise and mess. Every coin and note and Coke top......Coke top! Oh, heavens, those were hers from yesterday. They jumped and spun, up and down, round and round. It was like watching a slow motion video replay. The last coin spun, rattled, toppled over and lay still. Lizzie watched, her hands covering her mouth. She took off her glasses, gave them a huff and a polish, and pushed her hand through her hair.

Agnes and the man turned round sharply.

'Who's that? How long has she been listening to us?' he hissed in a loud whisper. Well, it was loud enough for Lizzie to hear.

'Oh, it's only Lizzie. She's a new girl come to live in the village. Moved from London, didn't you, Lizzie? Her mother and father run the post office. Have you come to see the floral displays again, dear?' squeaked Agnes.

There was no smile this time. Her lips were a straight line. She seemed to say the words without opening her mouth at all. In fact, she reminded Lizzie of one of the witches from *Macbeth*.

'Yes, Mrs Smith,' Lizzie lied.

The man half walked, half ran up the aisle past Lizzie. As he did so he pushed her shoulder and glared into her eyes as if taking in every detail of her face. Creepy, Lizzie thought. She smelt an aftershave that she would always remember.

'Out of my way, kid!' he said, and then he was gone.

'Some people – so impatient, aren't they?' squeaked Agnes, all smiles once again. 'I'll leave you in peace to look around the displays.' She shuffled away into the transept out of view.

Lizzie was drawn to the David Webster floral tribute that represented Devil's Heights. The sunlight that shafted through the stained glass played on the plants and rocks, and then a particularly dazzling beam forced her eyes upwards. There, above the cascading plants in small granite niche, was the Axenthorpe Icon. It didn't look very precious to her. A sort of picture made out of wood illustrating a person or persons in a landscape, but the paint was so faded and cracked that you couldn't really see what the artist had originally tried to depict.

What you could see was that the surround of the icon's frame had six holes of different shapes carved into it. The holes were splintered as if something sharp had been forced into them to poke or dig the jewels out. They must have been like that for nearly two hundred years. Lizzie thought that a dagger must have been used to rip out the jewels. In her minds eye she saw the Highwayman carrying out this vile deed; she saw him throw his head back and howl with satisfied laughter… Old wives' tales, she thought. Knickers!

'You seem to be very interested in the Icon, my dear – perhaps too interested for your own good!'

This time Agnes really did make her jump. Lizzie cried out loud and ran from the church. She didn't stop until she reached the large arch at the post office. She leant against the cool wall, panting madly. The church clock struck twelve. Blimey, she thought, they'll be here in a couple of hours – things to do!

★

Axenthorpe Hall was ten or so miles from Hazelthwaite. The road was almost single track with passing places every now and then. Mostly, the countryside was moor land and forests of conifers. A sign said, 'Axenthorpe Hall, open to the public 10 a.m. to 5 p.m. Monday to Saturday and from June to the end of September'. A single car was parked at the rear of the sprawling building. From the front it looked as if nobody was at home. The gravel drive had large conifers on either side, making a dark and forbidding approach.

The library was one of the main features of the Hall, and it was possible to look at certain books there if you wanted to make an appointment. The man with the strange smelling aftershave was deep in thought as he looked at some old manuscripts that were carefully placed on one of the antique desks.

One of the wardens who looked after the rooms came in.

'Is everything to your satisfaction, sir, or can I get you anything else? Coffee perhaps, or tea?'

'No, everything is fine, thank you. Just fine,' the visitor replied with a grimace that passed for a smile. He tidied the documents away. Then he left the building and drove to the estate cottage deep in Axenthorpe woods.

At three o'clock Lizzie was beside herself. She had been waiting by the pillar box at the front of the post office since two! A car appeared at the top of the hill. She could make out the taxi sign on the roof. It disappeared behind some woodland that snaked along the side of the road, and a couple of minutes later it came to a halt outside the post office after negotiating the village green.

The noise was deafening! Lizzie's dad paid the taxi driver, who gave him a nod that said, 'Sorry, mate, you look like you're in for a good summer,' and the taxi then duly disappeared up the road it had come.

Lizzie looked at Bendy and shrieked.

Bendy looked at Lizzie and shrieked.

Donna shrieked at anything and everyone.

They went into the post office, still shrieking, and from there into the house. 'So much gossip, so little time!' they all said at the same time. So it all had to be said again. 'Brilliant!'

Mum and Dad took the three girls to the pub for a meal that evening. Unbeknown to Lizzie they'd also invited Mabel and Amy and their folks to meet the girls. It was doubly brilliant! Everybody got on with one another and when the meal was over the five girls went to the Gallows Oak to chat.

'Lizzie, we've missed you so much,' said Bendy, 'but we're really glad you've found two more brilliant friends.'

'Even though they're Newcastle fans,' added Donna.

Lizzie purred, 'And I'm so glad to see you two, but I must say these two are great fun…' Then she stopped in mid-sentence. Her mouth dropped and her glasses fell off.

'It's there again,' she whispered, '*the light!*'

Mabel and Amy looked towards the Heights. 'Can't see anything,' said Amy hesitantly. 'Are you sure?'

Mabel tried to soothe the situation, 'Lizzie we were only kidding last night, and perhaps we all imagined something that wasn't there!'

Bendy looked at Lizzie. 'We've just arrived and something weird is going on. How can anything weird happen in a place like this?'

Lizzie forced the story out. The two girls listened, amazed at what she said. Even Mabel was astonished about the man in the church. 'I wonder what's going on?' she remarked to anyone and no one.

Lizzie looked at Mabel, 'We can't tell anyone. No one would believe us. But that man is strange, so is Agnes – and now Bendy and Donna are here I think we're all gonna get into big trouble.'

Bendy cooed, 'Luvverly.'

'Tomorrow we meet here and discuss what we are going to do. We have to find out about the stranger, Agnes and David Webster. It's all to do with the Icon, I'm sure!'

'What about the Highwayman?' Mabel continued, 'he can't be a figment of our imagination! But he's got to be, hasn't he?'

Secrets at the Post Office

When the three girls had left Mabel and Amy they walked back to the post office. Brenda and Donna walked slightly ahead of Lizzie, chatting about the day in general. Lizzie looked at Bendy's back and decided that she'd put on a lot of weight in the last couple of months or so. Bendy had the cheek to call it full-on roll muscle; everybody else knew different. It was as if someone had stuck a bicycle pump in her belly button and blown her up. Lizzie smiled at her wicked thought because Bendy, whatever you might say about her was a real good, loyal friend whom you didn't meet every day of the week.

Brenda looked round and said, 'What you thinking about, Lizzie? You're very quiet.'

'Oh, nothing, I was just thinking how good it was to have you two here. We're going to have a ball,' she replied, 'I've missed you guys heaps, and "home" for that matter.'

'But you've made two good friends in Hazelthwaite, and that's important,' Donna added. 'At least we know you're not alone.'

'I know. But it's not like it used to be,' replied Lizzie and the tears started again, soft sobs which she pushed away with the back of her hand after removing her specs.

Bendy put her arm round her shoulder.

'It's not like you to cry, Lizzie. Is there something bothering you? Something in the village…this old Highwayman cra…rubbish.'

'I've seen strange lights at night, even with you two here. Tonight I saw them. And there's this old lady and a stranger who frightened me. Mabel and Amy told me a most peculiar story about the village and our house – oh, everything – and I'm not sure what to believe.'

'Tomorrow we'll talk to this old lady. Try to get some sense out of her,' said Donna authoritatively. At least she thought she sounded authoritative. Bendy looked at Donna in an old-fashioned way.

'She'll smile and say, "I don't know what you're talking about, my dear," in her sweet and sugary voice. She'll just say the story about the Highwayman is made up...helps bring in the tourists, more like would keep them away if they knew what I knew – you wait,' continued Lizzie.

Then they were at the post office. Lizzie's mum welcomed them in, and after refusing something to drink the three girls went upstairs to bed. Very soon the cottage was quiet. Bendy and Donna were fast asleep, as the long journey, the meal, the country air and chat had thoroughly tired them out.

Lizzie leant against her bedroom window. What was out there?

It was about three o'clock in the morning when Bendy woke up. She could hear the regular breathing of Donna, who was obviously fast asleep.

What had woken her? Something had disturbed her light sleep.

They had been given the bedroom at the back of the cottage. It was directly over the large archway that led into the post office courtyard. From the window you could see the outhouses that surrounded the yard on the other three sides. Many years ago, one of the outhouses had been used as stables for the horses and the temporary prison of the Highwayman. Bendy looked out over the cobbled courtyard. It was filled with strange shadows as the clouds passed across the face of the moon.

John Miller had spent a lot of time filling the courtyard with beautiful ceramic and terracotta pots full of ivy-leafed geraniums, fuchsias and lobelia, potted palms and elegant grasses. There was a beautiful set of wrought iron table and chairs with thick cushions and an elegant beige coloured sunshade that looked like a far eastern parasol when it was in the up position. Both Bendy and Donna had remarked how nice it looked when they had arrived in the afternoon.

Then something moved. It wasn't a plant or a palm waving in the breeze.

Something, or somebody, was walking very slowly by the stable door, but keeping very much in the shadows. She rubbed her eyes to try and get the sleep out of them and looked again.

A figure with a triangular hat and long cape was trying to force the stable door! A shaft of moonlight suddenly caught the figure's face. Her heart missed a beat when she saw the mask. She bent closer to the window, and the figure turned and looked up towards where she stood. She looked away quickly, and by the time she plucked up courage to look down into the courtyard again, the figure was nowhere to be seen.

'Donna, Donna,' she whispered – pulling at her friend's shoulder.

'What?' replied Donna, startled. Bendy clamped her hand over her friend's mouth. 'It's the thingy, the wotsit, the duberry…the Highwayman in the courtyard. I've just seen him!' she blurted out in a loud whisper. 'I've got to tell Lizzie.'

Donna turned over. 'They've got you too! There isn't a Highwayman, I'm tired and want to go back to sleep.'

'I'm not sleeping while I'm terrified,' Bendy continued. She slipped on her dressing gown, which fitted where it touched, left the room and crept to Lizzie's room. She knocked very quietly.

'Lizzie, Lizzie, wake up! I want to go home!'

'What's the matter?' said the voice from the dark room. A lamp was clicked on; Lizzie was sitting up in bed, propped up on one elbow. 'It's ten past three, Bendy.'

'Lizzie, I've seen something in the courtyard. I was sleeping lightly and heard a noise, I crept to the window and this thing looked up and saw me. It was horrible! All black and sinister with a funny hat, cape and mask.'

'The Highwayman!' gasped Lizzie. 'He was here? What was he trying to do?'

'It looked as though he wanted to get into one of the courtyard buildings.'

Lizzie pulled on her dressing gown. 'Right, let's go look.'

'You're going to look? You must be mad. Tell your dad. Phone the Police!' Bendy argued.

'Who'd believe us? Lizzie said. 'Come on, quietly now.'

Lizzie led the way down the stairs, avoiding the creaking bits by hugging the wall. Quietly she opened the back door to the courtyard. Everything was still. The moon still cast shadows from the plants and garden furniture, and a breeze caught the frill of the umbrella, making it flap. The church clock struck the half-hour. The two friends made their way to the stables. Sure enough, by the little light they had from the moon they could see splinters of wood around the lock.

'This was no Highwayman, this was a burglar!' said Lizzie. 'Look at the door.'

'Well, it looked pretty strange to me,' Bendy snorted.

From the rooftop, and hidden by the tall chimney stacks, a silent figure watched the girls. The black mask hid the scarred face – the eyes were fierce slits. He undid the top shirt button, revealing the rope burn on his neck. In total silence, he climbed down the drainpipe. The he mounted the black horse, turned to face Devil's Heights and galloped off without making a sound.

Lizzie turned to Bendy, 'Not a word of this to anyone. We'll tell the others in the morning. But say nothing to mum and dad, or I'll kill you!'

The following morning they sat on the slatted bench at Gallows Oak, saying very little. After Bendy explained what she had seen, Donna scolded her for not making her stay awake; the other girls looked scared and said that they thought it was time to tell an adult. Lizzie again said nobody would believe them – just wild 'girlie' talk. Adventurous stuff never happened in real life. No! Whatever was going on in sleepy Hazelthwaite they would have to find out themselves, and take a lot of care about how they went about it! They all had to agree in the end, but how were they to start? Who could they see? Who could they trust?

Lizzie said they could trust nobody except themselves. Lizzie thought that as Bendy and Donna were on holiday, they could visit the church and chat with Agnes. After all, Agnes had not seen Lizzie with them yet, so she wouldn't be suspicious of two new girls showing interest about the village and the church. Mabel and Amy said they'd climb up to Devil's Heights to see if they could find any clues to shed light on the evening's peculiar occurrences.

Lizzie decided that she would go to Agnes' cottage and have a snoop about. The girls didn't like this idea at all, and reminded her that if she was caught on Agnes' property it would be trespass and the police would be called in and she might be grounded for ten years. Bendy thought she'd end up in a young offenders' school. Lizzie was adamant. She was going to take a look. She promised that she wouldn't do anything wrong.

The four of them looked at her in bewilderment. None of them believed a word she said, especially about not doing anything wrong. Nobody disagreed with what was about to happen again because Lizzie could make herself look very fierce and determined when she peered over the top of her specs at people. When her mind was made up, she took a great deal of dissuading!

Trespass in the Morning

It was another beautiful day in Hazelthwaite. The sun shone brightly over the village slumbering peacefully beneath it. The row of cottages on the far side of the village green opposite to Lizzie's cottage seemed to be resting so well that they all looked as if they'd sunk two feet into their gardens.

Lizzie walked across the flagstoned courtyard behind the post office, down the garden path, looked over her shoulder to check that no prying eyes were watching her, and gingerly slid between some broken fence slats. She followed the pathway that bounded the small stream that gurgled and bubbled its way over small boulders and stones until it curved almost at a right angle to join the River Hazel. As she approached the far end of the path she cautiously picked her way into the undergrowth that spilled down the bank to the edge of the stream.

She purposefully did this in case she met a jogger or dog walker. She walked on until she came to several large trees that grew close to the old stone bridge that was situated at one corner of the village. She peered round a trunk towards the village. Everything was quiet. Lizzie could see the odd person going about their business and she could see a delivery of beer being made at the pub. The vicar appeared at the lychgate and turned towards the post office. It seemed to be a very ordinary start to the day in Hazelthwaite.

'Good,' Lizzie heard herself say in a low voice, which definitely had a tone of menace in it.

Instead of walking over the bridge, Lizzie scrambled down the bank and walked underneath the arch. She could do this quite easily because the spell of recent good weather had reduced the depth and flow of the River Hazel. Taking this route kept her well out of sight of any onlookers walking in the village, which seemed few at this time. She climbed the bank at the other side and instead of following the path she kept to the shadows of the woods between the path and the Hazel until she was opposite

Agnes' back garden. She found a way into the vegetable patch through a broken piece of overlap fencing without damaging anything, and from there made her way towards the twin opening patio doors that led to the lounge at the rear of the cottage. As she made her way towards the cottage, she used large shrubs and bushes to conceal her progress.

Agnes Smith had a beautiful garden. Wonderful shrub and flower borders surrounded an immaculately mown lawn with two-tone green lines like you see on bowling greens, and this led to a patio that was almost hidden on three sides with clematis and wisteria-covered trellis. Lizzie looked at the tranquil scene. On the patio was the usual table and chair set, but Agnes' was made from dark stained wood. An expensive-looking parasol shaded the table and chairs. The chairs all had thick, soft, brightly coloured flower-patterned cushions on them. Lizzie thought it odd that a strange old bird like Agnes had such good taste. Everything she'd seen so far stank of money. How did she do it?

From her hiding place behind a large clump of pampas grass, she could make out that the table had one of those posh plastic glass and jug sets on it. Lizzie liked those, but her mum hadn't got round to buying them yet for their patio set. There was also a telephone and a couple of other things that she couldn't quite make out on the table's surface.

A chair, with its back to her but facing the patio windows, had a high back to it, and it wasn't until the phone rang that she realised that someone was sitting in it. Had the doors been closed she might have seen the person's reflection, but then again whoever was sitting in the chair might have seen her approaching. She saw a man's hand reach out for the phone, pick it up and press a button, and then she heard someone speak in whispered tones – but not so quietly as not to be recognised by Lizzie as the voice of the stranger Lizzie had seen with Agnes in the church. He was here in Agnes' garden! 'Now there's a coincidence,' Lizzie muttered under her breath. She crawled on all fours until she reached the nearest bush she dared to the patio, trying to gain a better chance of listening in on the stranger's conversation.

But it was no good; she could only make out the odd word or two. The person to whom the stranger was talking must have been foreign, because some of the conversation was conducted in German, or that was what Lizzie thought it sounded like. The man would then lapse back into English and it was then that she heard him say, 'The research is almost at a conclusion…and yes, things are looking very good.'

Finally, the man clicked the button and put the phone down. Then he got up, stretched and went into the cottage. Lizzie stayed very still. He turned, closed the Georgian-style patio windows, and a few minutes later Lizzie heard a car start up and drive away.

Lizzie looked at her watch: elevenish… Then the church clock chimed the hour confirming this, Agnes would still be at the church, probably chatting to Bendy and Donna at this very instant.

She plucked up courage and from her hiding place, crossed the patio and gently tried the handle of the patio doors. They wouldn't budge; presumably the man had locked them when he'd gone inside. Bummer! She moved round the side of the house. The pathway, which was edged with shrubs, all tidily trimmed and shaped, covered her every move from the cottage next door, so no one could see her progress. Suddenly, she saw what she was looking for. Halfway down the cottage wall a small window stood just open. It had frosted patterned panes of glass in it. The loo or bathroom – just the job!

Lizzie looked round to see if there was anything to stand on, to stretch up to the beckoning gap. She found a plastic bucket which she upturned and put on the seat of an old cast iron garden seat that had certainly seen better days, and then by standing on tiptoe she could just manage, with a lot of wriggling, to get her head, neck and shoulders through the fanlight window. She looked down into the little room. Sure enough, it was the loo. Typical, the seat was in the up position. She wriggled her body even further through the narrow gap until she could just put her fingertips on the porcelain cistern of the loo.

It was then that she lost her balance on the bucket. It was thrown backwards from under her feet with great force, and down she tumbled. Well, it was more of an uncontrolled slip. Her forehead whacked against the loo, one hand and arm went clean down the bowl and the other arm unceremoniously caught the flush handle.

The loo gave an almighty rumble and Lizzie's arm was covered in a swirling mass of water, which seemed to go on forever. The loo then gave an enormous belch and the cistern began to quietly refill. 'Oh God, why me?' she whined. The several litres of splashing, gurgling water had thoroughly soaked her T-shirt, arms, and anything else you care to name. The floor was soaked too! Lizzie fished her glasses from the bottom of the pan and gave them a huff and a polish dry using the perfectly ironed and pleated towel that hung by the little washbasin. She used the towel to dry herself as best she could. When she'd finished doing this, she tried to mop up the floor, but only succeeded in making things worse.

Well, if anyone else had been in the cottage they sure knew they had company by now. Lizzie had certainly made a complete dog's dinner of her 'Royal' entrance! She left the towel on the rail by the sink, dripping as much water back onto the floor as she had mopped up. Then she very carefully opened the loo door a few centimetres and peeked out.

What greeted Lizzie's eyes was a beautifully decorated hallway. She could see from the open doors that it led to tastefully furnished cottage rooms with sun gleaming in from the little windows. She looked into the dining room and front lounge but nothing seemed out of place. But wait! Agnes had a number of photos in various frames on a side table. Several of the snapshots she swore looked like younger versions of the mysterious stranger. One photograph, in a particularly ornate silver frame, showed two babies sitting on a shawl. Family? Lizzie asked herself.

If the photographs were of the stranger when he was younger, why had Agnes spoken to the man as if he was only another visitor to the flower show?

She didn't like this strange man and she was beginning to have a nagging dislike for Agnes, whoever she was. And this cottage was too perfect by half – well, not the loo, at this particular moment!

A key rattled in the front door lock. Lizzie looked at her watch; it said 12.10. She'd missed the church clock strike midday. Agnes always left the church at twelve to have her lunchtime snack.

She ran into the rear lounge and over to the patio doors. She turned the key and ran out into the garden, leapt across the patio and dived into the nearest shrub for cover. Lizzie looked back at the house. She could see Agnes approaching the door. She looked ahead with frosty disapproval, just as she had stared at Lizzie in the church. Agnes peered outside.

Lizzie heard her say in her squeaky tone, 'Coming here, leaving the door unlocked. I'll have to have words with the stupid fool!' Lizzie heard her tut loudly, then heard the door slam shut and the key, which she had turned to open the doors a few seconds earlier, being turned back again in the lock. She lay back and sighed, 'Too close for comfort, Lizzie luvvie.'

Lizzie backed out of the bush and made her way to the broken fence. She was just about to step through the gap when she heard an almighty shriek from the direction of the cottage. *Oops*, she's found the mess in the loo! thought Lizzie. That bloke's gonna get it in the neck good and proper. Serves him right! Then she thought, When he tells Agnes it wasn't him and really does convince her that it wasn't, what are they both going to think? Perhaps put it down to a chance burglary… Whatever, she and the girls would have to be very careful from now on!

They all met at the Gallows Oak at one o'clock. Lizzie was starving, so she ran across to the Post Office shop where her mum gave her a selection of fresh sandwiches and some cans of Coke to take back with her for all the girls to veg on.

While Bendy scoffed a prawn and mayo sandwich (sideways, virtually), Donna told them what had happened at the church. Which counted for very little as it turned out… Yes, Agnes had been very pleasant… Yes, she'd told them some of the local history, including the bit about the Highwayman, and that was it.

Bendy, halfway through an egg and cress sandwich, echoed Donna's story and then put her hand over her mouth to emphasise how bored they'd both been.

'Bendy if you continue to eat like that you'll end up fat as a pig,' Lizzie chided her.

'I eat loads when I'm excited or scared, and I'm tons of both right now,' Bendy chortled in reply.

'If we get into a spot of bother you won't be able to run very fast or squeeze through small gaps,' Mabel pointed out.

Bendy looked at them and laughed again. 'But I'll be able to bash into things and knock 'em down with my belly!'

And with this she gave a demonstration of what she might do, causing the other four to dissolve into fits of laughter with her.

Next, Mabel told them what she and Amy had found when they had climbed to the top of Devil's Heights. They'd seen some fresh hoof prints in the mud by the road. Certainly, if a person had been on the Heights last night and had had a light they would definitely have seen it from the Gallows Oak. They had picked up the tracks in Horseshoe Wood but then lost them again when they had disappeared on the bridle path on the other side. The track, which led through forestry commission land, finally came out at Axenthorpe Hall several miles away.

The most frightening thing was that as they had crossed the glade in the middle of Horseshoe Wood, although the sun was out and it was incredibly warm, the glade at one particular point was freezing cold. There seemed to be a kind of a scorch mark in the grass. Well…not a scorch mark that was black and had been made by a fire, but more of a discolouration of the turf. However, when you looked at it from a certain angle it appeared like the outline of a horse rider. Nothing else was out of place, though. The two girls had gone quite white and quiet. Lizzie looked thoughtfully at them.

When Mabel stopped talking, Bendy ate two cupcakes and a packet of beef flavoured crisps. This was real terror! She went back to the sandwiches and yet more cake when Lizzie started speaking.

They'd looked at her aghast when she told them about the stranger and the phone call. They roared with laughter when she explained the bit about falling in the loo and it flushing. (Bendy had butted in at this point and told them that some Year Ten girls from her school had flushed her head down the loo, but they'd been expelled because her dad had gone in, seen the Headmaster and given him hell.) They'd watched her open-mouthed when she told them about the untimely entrance of Agnes.

When Lizzie had finished they all chorused as one, '*Lizzie, you promised!*'

They went quiet for a few minutes while the information they had shared was digested. Bendy brought them all back to reality by belching loudly. She said this was a sign that she'd enjoyed what she'd eaten and didn't have anything to do with being rude.

Amy suddenly said, 'There's something I've forgotten. While we were up at the Heights a car drove quickly down the road heading towards Axenthorpe Hall. I caught a glimpse of the driver. He had blonde—'

And before she could finish, Lizzie said, 'Hair!'

'It was the stranger at the church, the same person at Agnes' cottage this morning. What colour was his car?'

Mabel answered, 'It was a green Ford Mondeo, but I didn't get the registration number. Didn't think it was important.'

'I couldn't, but it was certainly driven away quickly as if the driver was in a real hurry. I wonder what's going on at Axenthorpe Hall?' added Lizzie, talking to no one in particular. Her eyes looked up towards the Heights.

After days of hot weather, and quite unnoticed by the girls, it had started to rain. Small drops, then very quickly, huge droplets of rain started to fall heavily on the Gallows Oak, the village green and Hazelthwaite in general, out of a darkened, angry sky that had filled with clouds.

Before the girls could reach the shelter of the post office archway leading to the inner courtyard, there had been one large flash of sheet lightning, a huge report of thunder and torrents of rain. Five very bedraggled teenagers stood watching the coming storm from relative safety.

Discovery in the Afternoon

When Lizzie had first arrived at post office cottage, she had quite naturally looked around the outbuildings and barns that surrounded the courtyard. She'd glanced in at the stable block, and although she'd seen various old farm implements and hay wagon (that had been left by the previous owner, as they'd no use for it) she hadn't shown any real interest in the building and its contents, until now.

Lizzie asked Bendy about what she had seen again but Bendy wasn't too forthcoming, as she was still a little worried about the ordeal. So Lizzie suggested that they play 'hide and seek' in the stable block, as it was large inside with lots of interesting places to hide and out of the rain.

A game of 'hide and seek' had been met with a chorus of derision from the others, and Lizzie had blushed at the thought of her even thinking of such a stupid childish game.

'S'pose me mobile goes off in the middle of full-on hide! What ah me s'posed to say? I'm playing a kiddies' game,' Amy had wittered.

They pushed open the stable door, which was in two parts. The top half of the door could be left open separately while the bottom half of the door could remain in the shut position if you wanted. The door at the moment was bolted together and it creaked and groaned open, as the hinges hadn't had any oil on them for years. The small windows looked as if they'd never seen water on them at all, and the stable was quiet, dark and eerie inside.

'Bloody place stinks, Lizzie,' continued Amy. 'Are you sure this is a good idea, pet?'

'You wait till you get some straw stuck up your knickers,' laughed Bendy. 'And with a skirt that size it won't take long. You'll soon see the funny side of playing kiddies' games. Specially if I land on you from up there.' She was pointing to the upper floor.

Lizzie told the girls that the previous occupants had kept a couple of horses in one of the village fields which backed onto the property, and that explained why there were hay bales still stacked in the stable. Both Mabel and Amy confirmed this, adding that it had been the lady and her daughter who used to ride. They'd seen them frequently riding on the country lanes around Hazelthwaite.

In the middle of the building was a large wooden staircase that led to an upper level. It was rather like a broad, internal balcony and there was a rail leading all the way round except for an opening that had a block and tackle, which had once been used for pulling up bales and other heavy equipment to the second floor.

From the walls, rusty old farm tools hung on dangerous-looking hooks. To Bendy and Donna's delight, a wooden farm cart was parked in the corner with its hitching yoke left on the floor at an angle, just like you'd see in a museum tableau. On the cart, more straw bales had been stacked in piles of two or three high.

'What a place for a game of hide and seek, Lizzie,' cooed Bendy. 'You are lucky to have all this, Lizzie,' she added.

'Never really thought about it like that,' replied Lizzie. 'Didn't even think that Mabel and Amy would be interested to see it, let alone play in it. I must just mention there's hide and seek and there's the bloody rough version we used to play in the disused power station.' Bendy and Donna looked sheepishly at one another.

'What?' said Mabel.

'Well, just down from where Lizzie used to live was a power station that had been left derelict. She broke in one day and had a nose and found out that it was excellent for hanging out. Bit dangerous, but nothing much. Anyway we thought it would be a good place to play hide and seek. As we were heck of a lot younger then. Even Bendy could squeeze through the narrowest of gaps,' related Donna.

'Till the police found out, that is. Ruined a bloody good place to hang out in. Lizzie fell down this really dark passage one day when I was chasing her and we had to get help. Got grounded for ages after that,' Bendy said, matter-of-factly.

Amy looked at Mabel. God it was beginning to sound real bad! Mabel raised her eyebrows. What had they let themselves get talked in to?

Bendy said, 'Right, you lot, I'll be on. And –' she looked around the stable – 'the cart, just here by this straw bale, will be home. And if anyone reaches home, to release the rest before I see them, shout "One, two, three, *in!*" by the bale, then you can only be "it" three times on the trot, before someone else is on! Oh, don't worry, girls! This place is like a big girl's blouse to play in after what we've known.'

They then spent some minutes explaining their version of the rules of hide and seek to Mabel and Amy. When everything was sorted Bendy told them to buzz off while she started counting in ones, fairly slowly, to one hundred.

'No peekin'!' shouted Mabel, 'else we'll stuff your knickers with straw and chuck you out in the rain, and you really will look a big girl's blouse, as you say.' And they all bustled about looking for the perfect hiding place.

The interior of the stable was dark. The fact that the windows hadn't been cleaned for ever didn't help matters, and that made the barn appear even more gloomy. The occasional flash of lightning which lit up the interior, and the thunder crashing in the distance, made the old stable block a sinister place to be playing anything in!

The barn had gone quiet as the girls finally decided on, and settled into, their hiding places. All that could be heard was the rain hammering against the windowpanes and onto the slate tiled roof, and Bendy coming to the end of her extremely long count to one hundred.

The top half of the stable door had been left open by the girls for a little extra light to filter in. It also meant that a large amount of rain had gushed into the barn, which had soon developed into a fair sized puddle on the flagstoned floor.

After what seemed like an age to those hiding (especially Lizzie, who thought that Bendy's slow count was just being awkward), she finally finished counting.

'Coming, ready or not! Specially if you're not! Is that a bum I can see sticking out of the straw over there?' Bendy shrieked!

The girls could hardly contain their excitement. Hide and seek is a simple game that generates a lot of anticipated fun. After all, you don't really want to be "it", you want to hide! Although the girls were well aware of their ages, they were still getting quite a kick out of the thought of being found or trying to outwit Bendy, who was definitely trying to make them laugh to give away their position.

Bendy crept to the stable door and managed to close the top half of it with very little noise. All the girls, even though they were quite well concealed, felt the interior of the building darken even further. What was going on?

A flash of lightning suddenly filled the stable. None of the girls saw the evil, masked face staring in from the upstairs fanlight. But the Highwayman had seen all he wanted to see…

Bendy crept slowly towards a stack of hay bales with a small gap between them. She tried to control her breathing, but she was so excited that she giggled, and this set off giggling in the middle of the stack somewhere. She decided she couldn't be sure yet which one of them it was. She looked back at 'home', which was by the hay bale, ever conscious that one of them might make a dash for it to release the others. One of them might be at this very second trying to move behind her, trying to cut off her run for home while she was at the other side of the stables. Bendy couldn't see anyone in the bales, so thought she'd chance climbing the wooden staircase to see if she could look down on their places of concealment from the upper level.

It was then it happened. As she rounded a corner by a wooden wall that supported the roof, a tremendous flash of lightning lit up the whole interior. Terrified by the flash, Bendy stared at the fanlight window – and saw the tricorn hat, the mask, the piercing eyes and the evil smile.

She screamed and jumped back in the same movement. As she fell backwards and lost her balance she grabbed at something – anything – to stop her fall. This turned out to be one end of the rope linked to the block and tackle. As she descended, yelling at the top of her voice, the large bucket, more like a plastic rain barrel, carrying the hidden Donna ascended to the second storey. Donna, not understanding what was going on, leant to one side of the bucket and made it unstable. It, in turn, tipped over, spilling her out. Fortunately for her, she landed upside down in a high stack of bales, which started to totter over, ever so slowly at first then with increasing momentum as they crashed to the floor. Bendy had descended fairly rapidly due to gravity (and her mass) on the rope, and landed on the end of a badly secured floorboard, the nails of which had gone rotten over the years. The other end of the floorboard had then sprung upwards with such force that an earthenware pot, which had been placed on it, gently arced into the air. With all the shrieking and confusion going on, Mabel, who had popped her head out to see what was going on, was unfortunate enough to receive the pot (which was now on its way down) on her head. The urn almost knocked her senseless.

Mabel reeled dangerously round the balcony, hands clamped on the handles of the pot. Unbeknown to her, she came dangerously close to falling over the balustrade. Finally, she ran blindly into a wall, breaking the urn into a hundred pieces. Her skull received a severe jolt.

She was left with the neck of the pot and the handles hanging round her shoulders, giving a totally new meaning to the phrase 'jug ears'.

The block and tackle now swung on its hinge freely. It swayed dangerously back and fourth, at about head height, across the dark stable interior. Each time it moved from left to right, the large plastic container dragged it lower, until it smashed into the upright floorboard with a splintering crack. The end of the broken board was propelled into one of the hooks jutting out from the stable wall, which clicked down to reveal a hole in the wooden wainscoting.

By this time, quite naturally, the girls were shrieking and screaming enough to waken the dead. But with the door closed, the noise was not quite loud enough to attract Lizzie's parents' attention. They were still busy in the shop dealing with drenched holidaymakers eager to get out of the rain buying postcards, ice creams and anything they could get their hands on.

A flash of lightning lit the stables again. Lizzie stood motionless, looking straight ahead at the hole in the wall. She'd raised her arm and her finger was pointing at it. The others followed the arm and finger and slowly, very slowly, the five girls approached the gap. Another flash, more fierce than the ones before, lit the gap, which they could now see more clearly. In the splintered hole, just revealed, a tightly rolled document could be seen. And it looked as if it had been there for years!

As the long, last flash of lightning had revealed the wall's secret, the masked face at the window, if it had been seen, would have shown eyes that were now very contented, and a head that gave a little nod of approval. But no one saw him this time, for the girls were too busy concentrating on what they had found.

'Lizzie, do you think that the person I saw last night and just now, might have been looking for this, whatever it is?' whispered a wide-eyed Bendy.

'What do you mean just now?' replied Lizzie.

'I saw a face in the window when there was a flash of lightning. It was horrible, that's what started all the confusion, and things going up and down and Mabel almost falling over the balcony!' wailed Bendy.

Mabel said, 'Well, I didn't see a thing. I think you're making it up.'

'You were hiding. I didn't make it up. I wouldn't have caused all that commotion for nothing,' Bendy continued in hurt tones.

'I think you did see something, Bendy, but what? – that's the question. Do you really think that the Highwayman would have the nerve to come here in daylight?' asked Lizzie.

Lizzie reached up. She put her hand in the gap, and very carefully so as not to scratch herself on the splinters of sharp wood, lifted out the fragile parchment. It was rolled up tightly and bound with what looked like faded string or ribbon.

'Lizzie,' said Mabel, 'you might be the first person to have touched that since it was first written on and then hidden in there…maybe years ago.'

'*Hundreds* of years ago,' cooed Donna.

They all looked at the document with reverence, and then Lizzie plucked up courage and ever so slowly undid the ribbon, and started to unroll the thin paper.

'There's a light switch over there by the door – turn it on, someone!' Lizzie commanded. There was no 'please', so the command was immediately complied with by Amy. She'd detected that Lizzie was becoming quite distant about finding the document. Before she reached the switch, Mabel said, 'Do you think it's all right to turn the light on in the middle of a thunderstorm? It can be dangerous,' she added.

'Turn it on!' Lizzie shouted. 'What's the matter with you?'

The other girls looked uncomfortable. It was the first time that Mabel and Amy had seen Lizzie angry. Bendy and Donna, however, had learned to live with her tantrums over a long period of time!

'Oh, for goodness' sake I'll do it myself!' remonstrated Lizzie.

'No, I'm already here. I'll do it, Lizzie. But remember the little word next time,' said Amy quietly, but just as threateningly as Lizzie had been.

Lizzie dismissed the comment, overturned an old crate and they all pulled up some bales of hay to sit on. The parchment was yellow with age and torn at the corners. The other four girls gently held a corner each, as Lizzie scanned the contents.

'It's an old map of this area…looks a lot different. The houses and cottages have changed as there are more of them now, but the church, this place and the inn are all in the same position. Look, the Gallows Oak and Devil's Heights, the road to Axenthorpe Hall and surrounding countryside are all marked. Wow! I bet the Highwayman himself drew the map. There's crosses here and here. I wonder what they mean?' hissed Lizzie. She took off her specs and gave them a huff and a polish and pushed a hand through her hair.

Bendy said quietly, 'Anybody got anything to eat? I've become stressed with all the excitement again.'

'Perhaps they show where the jewels for the Icon are hidden,' suggested Mabel.

'But why would the Highwayman draw a map for someone else to find?' quizzed Lizzie.

'I wonder if he knew he was going to die that night, and this was the last thing he ever did. It was his legacy to the villagers of Hazelthwaite. He wanted them to find the jewels for the terrible crime he committed. People do strange things when they're faced with…' Amy was interrupted.

'Too fast, too fast!' said Lizzie getting irate again. 'The stranger said he had almost finished his research to the person on the phone. What research? Where would he look? And if finding this document was part of the research, we've got to ensure he doesn't get his hands on it. I hope that Bendy didn't see anybody a few minutes ago, and more to the point if there was someone at the window we've got to hope that they didn't see this!'

Mabel, who'd been listening very carefully to what Lizzie had been saying, finally spoke up. 'Axenthorpe Hall has a large historical library. It's quite famous in this area. There are hundreds of old books on its shelves which have been collected by various Axenthorpes over the ages. If anybody wanted to do research on the local area, that's where you'd go. Mind you, pet, you have to pay for the privilege.'

'The Hall is open to the public though,' added Amy. 'Let's go and take a look tomorrow. My mum's got the day off, and said she'd like to take us all out. Anyway, I've never been. We'll see how the other half live.'

'Sorted,' said Lizzie, 'Axenthorpe Manor, and maybe some clues. Oh, and I think I owe you all a little apology for being short-tempered.'

They told her to forget it, heat of the moment and all that.

Lizzie smiled and then said to Mabel, 'In answer to your statement, the little word that always drives mum mad is "now"!'

And they all burst into a fit of giggles.

The Highwayman's Perch

The following day was showery, ideal for a trip to somewhere where you weren't going to get too wet. At breakfast, Lizzie's mother had asked the three girls what they'd been up to the previous day. All she had received as an answer was… 'Not much, Mum, just chatting and hanging out with Mabel and Amy… And oh yes, a brilliant game of hide and seek in the stable.'

Jane Miller had told them that she and John had heard all the shrieking and carry-on and realised they'd been enjoying themselves. The girls looked at one another and grinned in that knowing way that said, 'Yes…but that's all you're getting out of us.' Jane dismissed the look; she'd seen it before.

Lizzie's mum had wondered what the girls might do in the village for a fortnight with not much going on, but judging by what they had said, they seemed to be occupying their minds. And exploring the stable block at the height of the thunderstorm, along with the hide and seek, had obviously kept them busy.

Jane Miller reminded them about being careful, considerate and polite when out with other parents, and after them promising to behave and telling her what on earth she thought they could get up to at a stately home, it was almost time to go. She had replied, with her knowledge of Lizzie's luck with ornaments and other precious things, that perhaps it would be safer if Lizzie had her hands tied behind her back, with all those priceless antiques about. Lizzie always played this game with her mum before she went out, and raised her eyes heavenwards and mentioned how embarrassed she'd made her feel. Bendy and Donna knew this patter well, and both of them laughed.

Then they heard the doorbell ring. Jane Miller went to answer the door and found Amy's mum there on the doorstep. They smiled, exchanged hellos, and with Lizzie's mum's 'Be good!' ringing in their ears, the three friends dashed to the car, waving and shouting hellos to Amy and Mabel.

Amy's Mum followed them to the car.

Donna shrieked, 'Ooh, a people carrier with lots of seats…brilliant!'

They all piled in and got comfortable, and with a final chorus of 'goodbyes' and waves to Lizzie's mum, they set off.

Unbeknown to any of the girls, Amy's mum had rung Mabel and Lizzie's mother to have their permission to take them all to Newcastle for a morning's shop and browse, taking in Axenthorpe Hall in the afternoon. The morning's activities, sightseeing and lunch (on Amy's mum) were brilliant! They all said so, and even Lizzie enjoyed herself. They all posed for silly photos, looked at upmarket shops, and the girls from London were well impressed with the variety of things to do and see. Lunch was whatever they wanted, wherever they wanted, and Amy's mum really enjoyed their company. She had thought that girls together could be wicked, and had her suspicions confirmed. She was sure at their age she hadn't had their sense of humour and fun!

Coming home, they took a different route, and arrived at Axenthorpe Hall at about two o'clock, which gave them ample time to look round the house and the large formal garden. The gardens had a wonderful maze in the centre of them, constructed with beautifully trimmed, dense privet hedges, ten feet high. When you finally arrived at the middle you could climb to the top of a wooden turret, complete with spiral staircase, to try and plot your way out. And they all thought that they'd enjoy doing that after seeing round Axenthorpe's interior.

As they approached the Hall, they found several tourist buses and twenty or thirty cars already parked in the extensive car park. The girls were on the lookout for a green Mondeo, and although there were a number of this type of car in the car park none were green. This had been disappointing. They were all quiet and contemplative when Amy's mum brought her car to a halt and turned off the engine.

She asked them if all was well. When they said yes, she then said that she didn't want to cramp their style, and after she'd paid their entrance fee to both the Hall and garden (which included the maze), she went off on her own to look round the various rooms.

When Amy's mother had disappeared from the main entrance vestibule, where there were information stands stocking explanatory house guides and maps, literature about other attractions in the Northumbrian region, and a shop counter where you could buy postcards and other expensive gifts, the girls split up to cover as much of the house as they could. To make sure that she had really gone, they followed her to where she had passed through the ornate doorway that led from the magnificent hallway to one of the reception rooms, saw her pause to look at some antique clocks, and then move out of sight into another room.

'Right,' said Lizzie, 'we split up – but we're very careful. If any one of us sees anything suspicious, we find help. This man could be dangerous, and he'll certainly recognise me!'

'In that case I'll check the library,' said Mabel. 'The sign on the cashier's desk said it is the only room not available to the public for viewing…something about being booked for research purposes. It could mean he's still here.'

Lizzie looked thoughtful, 'If he is still here, I mean still researching, it would certainly be useful to know what he was looking at, give us more of a clue as to what he was after. Problem is, no one here is going to let you into the library, Mabel, and if you were caught, well…'

Amy piped up, 'It's got to be the jewels, hasn't it? There are lots of stories that suggest where they might be, but mostly they're hearsay. But just supposing that he's found an old book, manuscript or map like we've got, he may be able to fit the bits and pieces together and find a location for them.'

'If he was after the map in the stable, I don't know where it would fit into the information he has already found out. I couldn't make head or tail of it. Perhaps it's got nothing to do with the Highwayman at all,' said a disheartened Lizzie.

'We're wasting time!' said Bendy, 'I'll go via the kiosk to buy a chocolate bar or something. I'm feeling an excitement moment about to happen.'

As you moved through the house, which had very impressive and well-decorated period rooms, you would sometimes meet a group of tourists being shown round by a guide. The guides explained the important characteristics of each room in rather boring, monotonous voices, and occasionally there would be several groups in one chamber at a time and you'd have no room to swing a cat or you might find yourself completely alone. However, you were never really alone for the Axenthorpe's employed quite a number of people whose task it was to oversee a couple of rooms to ensure things weren't touched or taken. These house guardians would patrol up and down, but in such a discreet way that you weren't really aware of them. If you wanted some particular information they were more than willing to oblige. In fact, they were often better informed than the guides about the portion of the house that they were responsible for patrolling. After all, they did the same job day after day for the time it was open to the public. The girls knew that if they were to gain any information at all, they would have to avoid the guardians, and that would be difficult.

It was while walking along a thickly carpeted corridor, which had rooms leading off to the left and right with signs and arrows indicating 'The Snooker Room', 'Indian Room' and so on, that Mabel saw the sign for the library. The door was a ajar, but there wasn't any sound of talking coming from it; no sound of pages of books being turned over or maps being folded and unfolded…only quiet. Mabel, mindful of what they had all promised, still felt the urge to take a peek inside.

The library at Axenthorpe Hall was very long and wide. The floorboards were highly polished and there were long carpets about two metres wide running its length. They looked foreign, Middle Eastern or Indian, but definitely expensive. But most impressive of all were the bookcases. They ran down each side of the six-metres-high room from floor to ceiling. Mabel took in the scene and heard herself say 'Wow!' under her breath.

Down the middle of the room, and at perfect intervals, were six huge desks with red leather inserted into their tops. A slanted, polished, wooden shelf was placed at the back of each desk so that you could prop very large and heavy books up to study them. And if you needed extra light, there were ornate brass reading lamps that could be positioned however you wanted them. It was a room in which you hardly dared breathe, let alone speak!

The bookshelves were enormous, with large collections of literature on every subject under the sun. Blimey, Mabel thought, who'd want to read all these? On the two long walls, every three metres or so, there was a tall, thin window with an old-fashioned radiator below it; but on the furthest wall of the room was an enormous arched stained glass window. At that moment the sun was shining through the panels casting beautiful coloured light on to the wooden floor. The library was utterly quiet and peaceful.

One or two of the bookcases had tall ladders on wheels in front of them. The wheels fitted into rails so that the ladders could be pushed back and forth for people to select books from any height. At the top of each ladder there was a small platform with wooden sides, so that you could actually sit at the top and read without descending. Clever.

Mabel looked over her shoulder. There was still nobody around in this section of the house, not even a guardian. She moved quickly from desk to desk checking to see if anything had been left out. Nothing!

But wait! On the last desk, where the stained glass window threw light to all corners of the library, was an open book. As she approached she could also make out a large map carefully unfolded and spread out across the desktop. Mabel could see the map had a reference on it…more of a title…1806…something… something…not important. What was important was that it showed the Axenthorpe district, including Hazelthwaite. The book was…

Too late! She heard men's voices coming from the direction of the corridor. At the moment the voices were still at its far end, but approaching quickly! She looked around for somewhere to hide. They'd see her under a desk, there were no curtains… Mabel tried to hurry herself up. She looked at the bookcases. That was it, her only chance. She dashed up the steps of the nearest ladder and flattened herself down behind the wooden support. It was hardly adequate as hiding places go, but no sooner had she done this, than two men had entered the library, walked its length and were standing directly below her!

'Will that be all, Professor Van Vebstriche? Have we managed to solve all your problems?' the voice said.

'Yes, yes, I sing zo. Ze quality of your reverance mateeril, maps and so on, ise ver' comprenzive. I vill be recommend you to our department at ze University of Rotterdam ven I am returning zer,' the stranger replied.

'You are most kind, Heer Professor. I will ensure your compliments are passed on to Lord and Lady Axenthorpe,' the voice said.

'Det pleasure was all mine,' the Professor replied.

Mabel chanced a peek at the two men. One she recognised as an Axenthorpe employee whom she remembered when Amy's mum had paid for them. But this foreign 'gentleman', if he was a foreigner, was definitely not what they were looking for. Lizzie had said the person they wanted was English. However, he did have blonde hair, of sorts. She lay there hardly daring to breathe. The employee bade him goodbye and left.

She could hear the Professor gathering his things together, closing up the book and shuffling papers together. A briefcase was opened, then clicked shut.

As she lay there on her precarious place she shifted her head to the right. Her eyes focused on the books next to where she lay. There in front of her was a gap in the neat lines of books! The book the professor had just closed fitted in the gap. Mabel's mouth dropped open. She looked at the gap. The gap looked back at her and smiled! Then it screamed at her and said… 'Mabel, in a minute you're going to get caught!'

She heard him move towards the ladder. She felt the ladder slightly tremor as he mounted the first then the second rung…she tried to make herself shrink backwards and smaller.

'Professor! Professor Van Vebstriche! A phone call for you in the private office in reception,' said the voice. 'Oh and don't bother yourself with replacing the books and maps. I'll do that for you before I go home.'

'Ver' vell, an' dank you,' Van Vebstriche replied.

Mabel looked at the gap where the book should now be standing and let out her breath very slowly. How lucky can one girl get? Then she thought of Lizzie. Lizzie would kill her instead!

Bendy never did anything exciting in London. Back and forward to school, going swimming, going to the cinema – all very ordinary. But since she'd been in Hazelthwaite she'd had more fun than she'd ever had in her life. In fact she'd been scared witless several times and couldn't tell an adult because no one would believe her. And the more they dug the deeper the hole became...brilliant!

So the next thing that happened to her was even more wonderful. Well, she thought that she ought to take it in her stride with everything else, but all she wanted to do was yell and shriek, in reality. Whilst walking down a rather long and boring corridor on the second floor of Axenthorpe Hall, she happened to glance out of a window onto a garden-cum-courtyard area in the grounds. And there, parked on the gravel chipped road that completely surrounded the Hall and under some trees that partly hid it from sight, was the green Ford Mondeo!

More importantly, a blond-haired man was getting into it. She watched him reverse into the middle of the drive, and then quickly drive off down the tree lined avenue, in the direction of a wooded area in the grounds. As she looked in the distance she could see what looked like a plume of smoke lazily drifting into the air. A cottage or lodge of some sort? she thought.

Bendy rushed down the corridor, making for the main staircase. She was politely told by a guardian, who had just come round the corner, to take her time and stop running as you never knew what might happen, and so on. Bendy made her apologies, walking backwards and bowing, and once she'd rounded the corner dashed to the stairs and descended two steps at a time to the ground level.

Amy's mum had told them to be at the tearoom about three for an ice cream and then they could go off round the garden and maze for another hour, which would then mean they'd be back at Hazelthwaite about four thirty. She didn't tell them the final treat of the day would be a BBQ at the cottage with the three families, around sevenish.

Lizzie could see that Bendy and Mabel were bursting to tell them something, but she had to be patient until they'd finished their ice cream sundaes and had made their way into the gardens.

'All right Bendy, give! What did you find out?' said Lizzie.

Bendy so excited blurted everything out as soon as possible and had to be told several times to slow down or totally repeat what she had said. Finally she sat down red faced but very content.

'Brilliant,' said Amy.

'Yeah, well done, Bendy. How did you manage to keep that to yourself for so long?' continued Donna.

'Dunno! I was bursting to tell you. But ice creams do take preference, even over that sort of news,' Bendy replied.

When Mabel told her story and how close she'd come to being caught, they could say nothing but give her a telling off.

'Too dangerous,' Lizzie said, 'if you'd been caught, who knows what this man might have done? Kidnapped you...' she tutted. 'We all promised...' Lizzie's sentence was never finished.

'I know,' said Mabel quietly, 'I can't apologise. I just did it.'

'Yes,' agreed Lizzie, 'and I'd have done the same.'

They all nodded and had a combined cuddle.

'Last one to the middle of the maze!' shouted Amy.

'Is a what?' shrieked Bendy.

'Yeah, a "what" will do!' replied Donna. And they all dived off into the maze in different directions.

Lizzie stopped and walked out. The attendant who looked after the maze to ensure no one got trapped inside, looked quizzically at her, 'All right, pet?' she asked.

Lizzie told her that the high hedges had made her feel uncomfortable. Touch of claustrophobia, the lady had thought. Lizzie nodded in agreement.

She ran to the back of the Hall, where Bendy had indicated that she had seen the car. There were the skid marks, just as she'd explained. Lizzie ran off as fast as she could in the direction of the wooded area. She had about three-quarters of an hour to find the mystery man, see what he was up to – if anything – and return to the Hall by four o'clock.

Some risks had to be taken. Firstly, the blond-haired man supposedly called Van Vebstriche would not be expecting anyone. However, he might be outside, and any noise, like a twig breaking, would alert him. Unlike the meeting in the church, a chance encounter in the middle of nowhere could not be explained. No, it could not even be contemplated.

So she could afford to be careless until…she didn't really know.

Lizzie kept to the footpath by the gravel road and as close to the tree line as she dare without snapping fallen twigs and branches. A bend and a widening of the track announced that perhaps the house or cottage was nearby. She could also smell wood smoke.

She thought of the girls having fun in the maze, and the new pact that they had just promised to one another… So much for that! How long does it take you to find your way through a maze and back? How long before they realised she wasn't there? They'd put two and two together when they all met on the wooden viewing gallery at the middle, and guess who wasn't around!

She stopped running, turned left and pushed her way into the undergrowth and pine trees until she reached the cottage clearing. In front of her stood another idyllic building. A green sign said 'Welcome to Highwayman's Perch – a National Trust Property'. The sign was written in gold paint in an old-fashioned style.

'"Highwayman's Perch" – how apt,' said Lizzie probably too loudly for her own liking. In front of the cottage was a round well-tended lawn with flower beds and the gravel drive sweeping round that, to return to Axenthorpe Hall. So, only one way in and one way out, good!

On the right-hand side of the property was a large Dutch barn where the Mondeo was parked out of the sight of prying eyes. To the left was a brick wall with a wrought iron gate in it, and some outhouses, one of which was a stable. It was then she heard the thundering of hooves. She just had time to duck back under cover as the blond stranger drew his pitch-black horse to a halt. He dismounted, patted the horse's nose, said something quietly into its ear and led it into the stable.

Lizzie dodged round the stable door, opened the gate, shut it and made her way to the rear of the cottage, which was similar to the cottages in Hazelthwaite. Both the patio doors were wide open. The man wasn't expecting anyone – why should he? – so Lizzie slipped inside. She half screamed and choked at the

Highwayman who stood before her. How had he got inside so fast? What would she say? What lies this time? The cottage remained still and quiet. When she'd pulled herself together she realised it was the most amazingly lifelike tailor's dummy dressed in highwayman's clothes. Fancy dress, she guessed. Fancy dress with a difference. Why would the stranger go to so much bother? The black horse, the outfit…why the need to scare people? How was Agnes linked to all of this?

She stood thinking, and the phone trilled loudly. Oh God, this was it!

She looked around for somewhere to hide – it had to be the curtains by the patio doors. She just managed to throw them round herself before the stranger entered. Surely, he must see them still swinging!

'Hello. Oh, hello, Agnes. Yes, all the research is complete now. One piece of information is missing but I think our young friend from the post office has found that. Yes. Yes I got lucky…it was in the stable…yes. What's that, no I haven't seen anybody at the Hall today…what do you mean, they're *here*?… Mind you, they could have been in the house without my knowing. Say again… No I've been in the library all day and I've just come back from taking Nell for a gallop. Okay, see you later.'

Lizzie heard the phone being replaced on the receiver. She heard him go out of the lounge. A few minutes later she heard the shower go on and the bathroom door close.

Lizzie exited fast. Van Vebstriche indeed! Agnes! She couldn't fathom why she was connected and involved with this man!

She ran back as fast as she could. Her watch said five to four. That was strange…the figures on her watch looked blurred. Oh no! Her glasses – where were they?

As she rushed up to the maze entrance, four people were whistling the 'Laurel and Hardy' theme tune. The ridiculous melody met her ears. The tune was coming from the direction of a high-backed park bench positioned next to the fountain garden. Four very stern faces peered over the top of the seat towards her.

Lizzie was going to have to do some pretty nifty explaining.

The Highwayman picked up the gold-framed spectacles by the patio door curtains. So, she'd been here. The green Mondeo quietly moved up the gravel road to Axenthorpe Hall, and from the front gate turned onto the road that lead to Hazelthwaite.

This girl, this Lizzie Miller, had become too much of a nuisance!

While Lizzie explained about the cottage, the blond-haired man and the Highwayman's costume, the girls did not interrupt her once, but listened attentively. Mabel was the first to speak after she had finished her story.

'So – for the second time in a couple of hours a telephone call has saved our bacon. We're dead lucky, Lizzie! If one of us tries to find something out on our own again, it might not be third time lucky.'

Lizzie nodded, 'Like you, Mabel, I'm sorry. It was totally done on the spur of the moment,' she lied, 'and I was scared to death when he came into the cottage to answer the call. But at least we know he's a human being and not a ghost or a foreigner. And I think we can handle that. But we don't know who he wants to scare in Hazelthwaite, unless it's me or our family, and why he's gone to so much bother with the disguise and so on…Agnes has definitely got something to do with him too,' she added as an afterthought.

Donna, who hadn't done anything dangerous yet and felt a bit out of it, turned to them and said, 'I think the blond-haired man is David Webster, and that Agnes is his aunt or some relation or other.'

Amy blurted out, 'But David Webster died that night on Devil's Heights, and there's a plaque in the church to prove it!'

'Proves nothing,' said Bendy matter-of-factly. 'In fact, if you wanted to disappear and then come back to look for something, that would be the perfect alibi.'

'But that still doesn't give the reason for all the secrecy,' said Lizzie. 'Why not just ask for the information?'

'Because he's hiding something,' continued Mabel, 'something in his past. He's pretending to be foreign, acting out a game, trying to frighten the villagers by digging up things that happened hundreds of years ago. People spook easy, Lizzie.'

'So how can we find out about David Webster?' asked Bendy, not sure that she really wanted to know any more about him at all!

David Webster

The evening's barbecue was excellent, and they all thanked Amy's parents for a great day out.

As they walked back to the post office, Lizzie's mum asked the three girls if they were happy just to stay round the village, relaxing. They said they were, but would it be all right if she let them catch the bus to Axenthorpe so they could have some time to themselves to wander round the shops? Although they had enjoyed Newcastle, Axenthorpe had several art and craft galleries that Bendy and Donna would like to browse around to look for ideas for presents to take home. Local crafty things would be more acceptable than a stick of rock or a tea towel.

Jane Miller thought this an excellent idea. They could catch the nine o'clock bus from Hazelthwaite and be back at about one thirty. This was agreed. And tomorrow would be as good a day as any to go on.

Naturally, the girls had a totally different agenda! The journey to Axenthorpe was uneventful, and when they arrived at the bus station they walked to the premises of the local newspaper and printers. In fact the print works weren't very large, consisting of a shop front announcing that it was 'The Axenthorpe Advertiser' in Gothic script over a window with back issues of interest in an ultra-modern window. The back issues were lit up with small but expensive-looking floodlights. A double swing entrance door was situated back from the pavement and the other window was in blacked out glass but with a very smart gold and red heraldic symbol surrounded by the newspaper's name. The newspaper offices were small but very well maintained, keeping up with the paper's successful image in the immediate locality.

They entered. A very attractive secretary, who sat behind a large desk equipped with a personal computer and modern telephone switchboard, greeted them. After explaining what they wanted, she let them browse through back issues concerned with the David Webster story. She told them that at that time it had been one of the biggest stories the *Advertiser* had covered, and the editor had run the story as front-page news in some form or other for several weeks.

Some of the most popular nationals had covered the story, and the journalists had stayed in Axenthorpe for a few days, using the facilities of the *Advertiser* while they were there. It had been quite exciting, she said, rubbing shoulders with some of the famous names that write for Britain's dailies. Well, she had continued the *Advertiser* usually dealt with marriages, deaths and pretty ordinary events.

She left them to read through the stories, and there was certainly a mountain of newsprint for them to look at: reports of the cause of death; police reports; pictures of the accident scene; views from local people living in Hazelthwaite, and reports from the rescue services. It was all pretty mundane stuff, and as they read and reread the articles it looked as if they were going to come to a dead end.

When suddenly Mabel piped up, 'Here – here it is! He'd been in prison for fraud, counterfeiting and robbery. Blimey, he was a nutter!'

Lizzie said, 'Let's take a look… please,' she added. Mabel smiled at her.

'Glad you remembered the little word, pet.'

Mabel gave her the paper and pointed to the column and paragraph she had just read. Lizzie scanned down the tightly written print. One of the contributors to this report was none other than Agnes Smith! As Lizzie read on down the report, Agnes had obviously got carried away with the importance of the moment and had informed the reporter that she had been married once but reverted to her maiden name. David Webster had stayed with her on several occasions when he had been on holiday in the district – and how awful the death had been.

Lizzie went up to the reception desk and asked if there would be any way of finding out Agnes Smith's married name. As it so happened the reporter who had written the story was still working with the paper, and yes, he was here today. When she bleeped his office, he had said he'd see them for a chat.

The reporter checked his notes and Agnes Smith's married name had been... He stopped and said, 'That's strange... a Mrs Van Vebstriche. She said that her husband had changed it to Webster when they had come to live in England. Oh well, you live and learn!' And after exchanging pleasantries, they thanked him for his time, and left.

'Do you think that David Webster was Agnes's son?' said Amy.

'Right,' replied Mabel. And they all chorused together, *'Why didn't she say? Why wasn't she upset?'*

Lizzie whispered, 'She almost gave the whole thing away when I was in church. She said his mother had designed the floral scene. But it must have been her all the time.'

Five very thoughtful girls arrived back at Hazelthwaite on the one o'clock bus. Jane Miller had lunch ready for them. They sat in the courtyard. Bendy munched her way through her round of sandwiches, plus half of Lizzie's and Amy's cake. She had said that she was very excited and needed extra energy. The girls had raised their eyebrows at her and made some comment about her weight again, but it had fallen on deaf ears.

While Lizzie's mum cleared away the plates, she mentioned to her that new glasses had been ordered on her old prescription, and was that okay. Lizzie had nodded in the affirmative.

'You really must be more careful, luvvie,' said her mother. 'They're going to set us back over one hundred pounds.'

'God, your sight must be appalling, Lizzie!' laughed Donna.

'That map, Lizzie, you know that you said that you couldn't make head nor tail of it. Don't you think it's time we gave it another look? If this Van Vebstriche, or whoever he is, wants it, perhaps, with the extra information we've got now, we could have a go at interpreting it. I think with our local knowledge we ought to give it one more go,' suggested Mabel.

The others nodded. There wasn't anything else pressing to do. Lizzie went indoors and returned with the parchment. The sun played on the old drawing and words.

'Hazelthwaite looks pretty much the same, a few more cottages and so on, field boundary changes, that sort of thing,' Amy remarked to no one in particular.

'What do the three crosses mean?' asked Lizzie.

'Haven't a clue,' replied Mabel, 'but they seem vaguely familiar. They're position rings a bell but...' she paused, deep in thought... 'I can't put my finger on it. These crosses here and here. Have you got an up to date map of Hazelthwaite in the shop, Lizzie?'

'I expect so,' she replied.

'Any tracing paper?' Mabel continued.

'Now you're pushing it,' replied Lizzie.

Bendy giggled. 'If you've got any of that really hard bog paper, that's good for tracing paper. If you put it round a comb you can play a tune through it too. Terrible as bog paper, though, as it tends to smear rather than clear,' she added.

'Greaseproof paper,' Donna piped up.

'Just the job,' said an excited Mabel.

Lizzie gathered all the bits and pieces together, then had to fetch a pencil which immediately broke, so a pencil sharpener had to be found.

Mabel was ready. She vaguely traced the old map onto the greaseproof paper and then transferred it so that it lay on the new tourist map of Hazelthwaite and district.

'Doesn't match anything at all,' moaned Bendy, who'd got very excited and was looking for something to eat.

And sure enough, the two pieces of paper sat on the white plastic top of the patio table showing nothing at all, or so it seemed to the girls. They sat back in the plush cushioned chairs, each in her own world, each with her own thoughts. Bendy had closed her eyes. Lizzie had put her feet up on one of the ceramic pots and leant back with her arms behind her back looking into the sky. The sun sent rays of light and warmth into the courtyard. It was peaceful, a beautiful summer's afternoon. The church clock struck the half-hour. Bendy flicked away a fly, that was irritating her nose. There was the sound of bees moving from flower to flower in the large pots.

You could feel the heat of the day. The greaseproof paper, due to the warmth of the sun, had turned up at the edges, rather like an upturned bowl. A gentle breeze played on the slightly torn edges. Very slowly, almost imperceptibly the breeze played with the paper and started to turn it round on the Hazelthwaite map.

When it had reached ninety degrees from where it had started, Mabel who had been watching the fluttering paper, suddenly gave an almighty, 'I've got it! That's it – of course!'

The slumberers woke with differing results. Bendy, who had now dozed right off and had been snoring through a wide-open mouth, fell backwards off her chair. Her mouth clamped down shut on an unsuspecting fly that was just about to inspect her tonsils. This threw her into a blind panic. Limbs thrashing this way and that resulted in her shoes becoming wedged just under the table, causing the patio umbrella to topple over. This in turn snapped shut on both of Amy and Donna's heads sitting on the opposite side of the table. Donna, who had been eating a very large jam doughnut, had shut her eyes for a few moments. Her hand hovered just in front of her mouth, as if in mid bite. The remaining seven-eighths of the bun squelched right up her nose, leaving sticky red jam sliding indelicately down her nostrils and slithering down the side of her mouth. Donna was Dracula with a severe problem for several seconds. Lizzie, leaning backwards already, just continued to sway back until she fell off the chair onto the hard flagstones, completing a full backward roll that left her sitting on a very large mature agave plant. The plant's rather vicious teeth dug into her bottom which purely through nerve ending contact propelled her painfully forwards into a grow bag full of ripening tomatoes that her father had painstakingly reared for the autumn chutney. When Donna's face appeared from beneath the umbrella, covered in what Bendy quite wrongly interpreted as blood, she quickly grabbed a large bottle of fizzy spring water and soaked poor Donna with its entire contents with the dexterity of a trainee fireman let loose with a fire extinguisher for the first time.

Mabel looked at the mayhem she had caused, and after uttering her extreme apologies, proceeded to tell them the result of her findings.

'Look, the two crosses here come to rest near the entrance and exit of the River Hazel. The other cross must have something to do with the Gallows Oak. The scale isn't quite the same, but that's it!' She paused. 'And the rhyme on the Highwayman's map goes:

"From here the Hazel bursts from Mother earth
to where she disappears in raging darkness."

The River Hazel flows from about halfway up the basin. It sort of changes position depending on the water table and it disappears...here...' at this point she indicated to the tourist map... 'on the other side of the valley.'

Donna said, 'You must have a good geography teacher, Mabel.'

'Joke! Nah, my dad told me about it; I knew it rang a bell,' Mabel replied.

'So what about the rest of the rhyme?' Asked Lizzie.

Without any more ado they all raced off towards the Gallows Oak, leaving the maps sprawled across a rather sorry-looking patio table.

Peace descended on the courtyard. The sun still shone strongly.

The Highwayman reached out his gloved hand, carefully rolled up the maps and put them into his tunic. Then, like a ghost, he stole out of the yard. He had just rounded the corner out of sight, when John Miller strolled into his little haven of peace and quiet for five well-earned minutes' respite from the never-ending queues of tourists. The scene of devastation that met his eyes would need just a little explanation! And he knew who would manage to wriggle out of it once again. Lizzie could always wind her father round her little finger.

Lizzie's Vow!

The girls raced across to the Gallows Oak. They broke unwritten village rules by running across the 'sacred' cricket pitch that had been recently mown and rolled, but not yet covered.

'Who's got the maps?' shouted Mabel.

They all looked at one another and with shrieks of, 'You did!' and 'No, I thought you did!' Then they realised the maps were still on the garden table in the courtyard. Lizzie ran back to the post office. She was quite breathless as she walked across the flagstones, but she could see they were no longer on the table.

'*Oh no!*' she wailed. She dashed this way and that, looking here and there, but they had gone, and she knew exactly who had taken them. David Webster, Van Vebstriche, or whatever he liked to call himself had the maps. The last pieces of the jigsaw were in his hands. She walked back to the girls and told them what she thought had happened.

That night, the crescent moon shone in a cloudless, still sky. Bendy and Donna had kept the sash window slightly open; sleeping lightly, Bendy must have heard a noise in her subconscious that woke her up with a start. She heard the clock strike eleven. She tiptoed to the window and forced herself to peek through the half-closed curtains. A black shadowy figure, wearing a tricorn hat and cloak, forced the stable door open and disappeared inside the building.

Bendy stifled a scream and ran to fetch Lizzie, who in point of fact was awake reading a book by torchlight under her duvet. Lizzie told her to keep a lookout from the bedroom window while she went to investigate.

Bendy was terrified and started sucking her thumb, as no food was available.

Using the moonlight through the windows to negotiate the

stairs and downstairs rooms, Lizzie gently unlocked the kitchen door. Taking advantage of shadows cast by the potted shrubs and palms, she crossed the courtyard. Her toe hit the boot cleaner by the stable door and her breath hissed out in a quietish 'Ooh!'

The highwayman heard the noise. He cursed, and pushed on a piece of wainscoting. A panel slid across, revealing a passageway that sloped steeply downwards. Inside the darkened corridor, he pulled a lever and the panel slid back to its original position. He waited before moving down the passage. It was pitch black.

Lizzie crept into the stable; everything was still, a little moonlight shone through the dirty windows. She looked and listened but nobody was there. Impossible! The stranger had entered the stable; there was only one door in and out, and she had her back to it – yet he had disappeared. She walked up to the second storey, the steps creaking loudly – too loudly for her liking – but again there was nobody there. Surely it couldn't be a ghost? 'No!' she told herself, 'this was human!' She walked around the stable one more time, passing the panel without noticing anything – except that smell – the aftershave. He had been here but where had he gone? How do you disappear into thin air?

Lizzie shrugged, then all of a sudden in a fit of rashness she said in a very clear voice, 'You're here! I know it and I will find you!' Then she left, closing the door behind her.

The Highwayman smiled to himself and murmured, 'Little girls should be seen and not heard!'

Switching on a powerful torch, the twentieth-century Highwayman followed the passage downwards. The old walls were crumbling. Rocks had dropped onto the floor and he had to take care as he picked his way along the torturous course. Finally the passage floor steepened as the Highwayman came to the end of his underground walk by a stone wall.

He bent down, pulled another lever, switched off the torch and a wooden panel in the parish church wall slid open.

He was walking quietly down a side aisle when the vicar suddenly popped up from the pulpit; he had been carrying out some last minute alterations to the PA system for the morning service to celebrate the flower festival.

'W–w–who on earth?' he stammered.

The Highwayman started to speak. The vicar, recognising the voice, gave a smile of acknowledgement and said, 'Where on earth did you spring from?'

The Highwayman didn't smile; instead he turned and started to run towards the exit. At the door he switched off all the lights.

The vicar looked in horror and started to run in pursuit. In the darkness he tripped on a stair rod that had not been secured properly on the steps leading to the altar. As he tried to halt his fall his forehead hit one of the wooden pews of the front row. The blow to his temple killed him instantly. Red blood trickled from the deep cut. The swift flow of blood soaked into the dark wine-coloured carpet that lay along the central aisle of the nave, up which the Highwayman had just fled.

The Highwayman heard the fall and the sickening sound of skull on wood. He stopped, switched on the torch and walked back to where the vicar had fallen. He checked for a pulse. On one knee, he bent his head as if in prayer and with the other hand removed the black mask.

Agnes Smith had heard the church clock strike 11.30 and told Lilli Froom that it was high time she went home to bed. She thanked Lilli for the tea and chat and that she would see her tomorrow. The crescent moon was still high as she made her way back to her cottage. But she saw a dancing light in the church. That's strange, she'd thought. Hope no vandals have broken in and are destroying the flower arrangements...

With no thought for her own safety, Agnes marched across the village green, crunched up the path and was confronted with an open church door. Very strange, she thought as she went in. There were no lights on. But at the end of the carpet leading to the altar was a crouched figure. She walked down towards it. As she approached the kneeling figure, it turned – she saw the face in the bright torchlight ... then she saw the body of the vicar.

'Oh no! What have you done?' she squeaked.

'No, no it's not what you think – it was an accident!' he stammered in reply.

Agnes ran off up the carpet. In her blind terror she saw an open door, ran through it and shut it with a loud echoing bang. Turning and thinking that she should seek help, she found that all that confronted her were the stairs to the church tower.

The Highwayman ran after her.

'Agnes, Agnes, don't be a fool, come back! We'll try and sort something out!'

But she didn't hear the calls. In total terror she started to climb the stairs. The circular stone staircase was marked with arrow-slit windows in the church tower that let in thin silver streams of moonlight.

The Highwayman threw the door open and started to run up the winding staircase. Agnes could see the powerful shaft of light from the torch getting closer as it glanced off the curved stone walls.

With superhuman effort she reached the top of the tower, pushed open the trapdoor and half fell onto the tower roof. She waited until the Highwayman pushed open the trapdoor and with all the strength she could muster thrust her slightly built body onto the door and onto his fingers. The trapdoor slammed shut. He screamed in pain. She heard him curse. He slammed the door open, and this time it threw Agnes to the floor.

She backed away towards the tower battlements.

'Agnes, dear Agnes,' he said softly, 'don't force me to do this!' He grabbed her arm and twisted it behind her back. As she tried to wrench free of his grasp, she fell between two of the upright stones that would once have given protection to defending archers. The scream came, but no one in the village heard anything as the church bell tolled midnight, drowning her last piercing shrieks! Agnes lay sprawled on the gravel path, dead.

The Highwayman fled down the stairs, back through the nave, passing the body of the vicar. Diving into the passageway, he then negotiated the tunnel at full pelt. He stopped momentarily at the stable end of the tunnel, listened and heard nothing. Then he walked through the darkened interior. He picked the lock on the door and exited. He found Nell still tied to the tree where he had left her and began the trek back to Axenthorpe Hall.

Lizzie saw him leave the stable. She had forced herself to stay awake.

In the church, nothing stirred. The vicar lay still, the blood that had flowed quite freely now beginning to congeal. The

Highwayman looked down at him. He turned away, his eyes thoughtful behind the mask. The last thing that Sexton, the church cat, saw as he lay curled up on one of the back pews – one eye still open – was a set of silent footprints slowly making their way up the carpet towards him. Sexton meowed loudly, arched his back, and hissed and spat at the strange sight – then the footsteps had gone. He looked around, licked a paw, which he brushed across both eyes, got up, stretched, turned round twice in his own length, curled up and fell into a deep and undisturbed sleep.

Murder at Hazelthwaite?

As the church clock struck eight, Mrs Golightly, the parish church cleaner, happened to be passing the lychgate and saw the main church doors standing open. She crunched up the gravel path, 'yoo-hooing' as she walked. Not receiving an answer, she walked round the path to the corner of the tower, to be met with the body of Agnes Smith lying on the ground in a gruesomely contorted fashion. Agnes' wide-open eyes stared at her accusingly.

Francesca Golightly could scream, and as screams go this one could have wakened the dead! Unfortunately, Agnes still lay there staring at her. The second scream brought several early morning villagers, going about their business, to her assistance. She was comforted by Lilli Froom, who just couldn't believe it; she said so over and over again like a record player with the needle stuck in the last groove of a record, while the postman used his mobile phone to call for the police and an ambulance. He asked Lilli about a doctor, and Lilli had managed to tell him that Agnes is with... 'Oh no, no... *was* with the local practice at Axenthorpe.' She told the postman that she must have been the last to see Agnes alive and said, 'My goodness...what will happen?' He tried to comfort her while making the calls, hoping that someone else would soon turn up.

Lizzie's dad had also heard the screams, as he put the refuse bags out for collection. He nipped inside to tell Jane Miller that he was going to the church to find out what all the fuss was. As he walked towards the lychgate, Fred Acheson, the landlord of the Sun Inn, joined him.

Shocked at what he saw, but grateful to the postman for what he'd already done, Lizzie's dad asked if anyone had seen the vicar. Had the church been checked to see if anything was missing? After people had shaken their heads in response, and could just about choke out a 'No, not yet,' he walked into the church.

A minute later, after exiting ashen-faced, a very distressed John

Miller told the assembled company that on no account were any of them to enter the church because of what he had found. Explaining the death of the vicar had not been easy, and the folk, still in shock over finding Agnes Smith dead, said nothing until the sirens of police cars and an ambulance jerked them back to reality.

The church grounds were cordoned off with blue and white police tape and very soon uniformed police, detectives and associated specialists wearing white suits and masks poured over the scenes of crime. An incident room was set up in the lay-by outside the church gate, and statements were taken from the first people who had arrived on the scene. Nobody could shed any light on why the awful crimes had been committed.

Lizzie and the girls were not questioned and didn't speak to the police, even in confidence. Well, 'A highwayman, you say'... 'You know it's wrong to waste police time'... 'Silly girlie stories'... 'Break-ins that couldn't be proved due to lack of evidence'... they just thought they'd better keep quiet, for good or bad. David Webster had a police record, but how could they prove he had anything to with the crimes...especially as he was dead! No, they wouldn't have believed them, so what was the point.

However, when they finally got together, the girls agreed that whereas in the not too distant past, when they'd gone their separate ways after promising faithfully not to put themselves in a difficult situation, and gone back on their word, they wouldn't do so again. The fact that they did know something strange was going on was to remain a secret amongst the five of them.

None of them needed a second telling about this; they knew that keeping information from the police was a grave offence. It just so happened that the information they did have was so far-fetched that it belonged on another planet! Because they'd put that slant on what they knew, they reckoned that withholding the information would be feasible. This would have to be a *secret* secret! Bendy became so excited that she managed to devour a large chunky Kit Kat in three bites. This was probably not a record for eating one, but must have pushed it pretty close.

The bad news happened later that evening. Bendy and Donna were telling their respective parents of the happenings in Hazelthwaite on the phone, and judging by the responses they were given Lizzie assumed that London was obviously a safer place than the violent countryside! Bendy's mum had told her so before she'd come, and the two of them were to return immediately. Jane Miller had tried to convince them to let the girls stay another couple of days but they had been insistent, and 'that was that'.

It was a thoroughly tearful couple of girls, and an even more tearful threesome from Hazelthwaite, who said their goodbyes the following morning. John Miller had arranged the taxi and train tickets and Bendy and Donna returned home to London.

The taxi had tooted all the way to the main Newcastle road, and the girls had waved until they couldn't see it anymore. They then made their way to the Gallows Oak to contemplate what they would do next. Whatever it was, it was going to be two-fifths less fun than they'd previously had.

The police were still carrying out extensive but sensitive enquiries, while the nationwide tabloid press had been buzzing around carrying out enquiries that weren't in the least sensitive, more like downright harassment of the local population. They were looking for the worst scenario they could find, and when they couldn't find it, they just made the news up to see who could print the direst banner headlines to sell their paper's column inches.

Not so the *Axenthorpe Advertiser*, which dealt factually but with sensitivity with the village folk about the murders. The reporter dealing with their lead story was Danny Grimshaw, the journalist who had talked to the girls at Axenthorpe.

Lizzie approached him while he was having lunch outside in the garden at the Sun Inn. He recognised her and the others and asked them how they'd got on with the information, and might they like to contribute to the story he was writing… 'the teenager slant sort of thing to such an occurrence'. But they said they didn't know anything that would help him. They'd all had a good laugh at the tabloid reporters' expense who seemed to make up anything to sell papers, present company accepted, and he'd replied that they'd probably sell their grannies to the devil if they needed a story.

'Mr Webster wasn't the person you were looking for, then?' continued Danny Grimshaw.

'No,' replied Lizzie, with the fingers of both hands firmly crossed behind her back.

Mabel and Amy exchanged glances. Not like Lizzie to lie.

Lizzie hadn't really thought of it as a lie and she'd crossed her fingers purely as a precaution. She had done so many things wrong in the past week or so that lying seemed to be almost second nature to her now. She could now see how one lie lead to another, and then you couldn't stop! Whatever might she do next?

Danny finished the pint of bitter he was drinking with one huge gulp and, without thinking, gave a large and satisfying belch. The girls looked at him and then creased up with laughter. The reporter apologised profusely and went scarlet with embarrassment. He said goodbye and disappeared into the police and media circus near the church.

It was Mabel that spoke first after he left, 'Lizzie you lied to him. I think he might be the only adult that'd listen to us.'

'No, Mabel, I don't agree – and what's more, I've decided that I don't like him. I don't trust him,' said Lizzie defiantly.

Amy said thoughtfully, 'He's got the look of Webster about him. Sort of family likeness. I expect he'll go straight to Webster and tell him we've been asking about him.'

Lizzie and Mabel looked at Amy in astonishment over this outburst. Danny Grimshaw had dark hair and looked nothing like this Webster man.

That night, and on her own for once, Lizzie had time to reflect on what had been happening and how she'd been inextricably involved with the 'Axenthorpe Icon' and its lost stones or jewels.

It seemed possible that David Webster had not died on Devil's Heights that night, but whoever had died had been given his name and lay buried in Hazelthwaite's churchyard, with a special plaque to commemorate him. Agnes Smith had family connections with David Webster, who Lizzie thought was the Highwayman, who in turn was trying to scare her and her family from the post office. He obviously wanted the clue to the whereabouts of the Icon's jewels that was on the map, which she had found and then immediately lost. Her fault completely! That made her blood boil. Why hadn't she been more careful? She was far to prone to acting without any thought. What was it her teachers said? 'Engage your brain first, Lizzie, and the rest will take care of itself!'

David Webster had a criminal record; he had come back to Hazelthwaite to look for the Icon's jewels. He'd come under an assumed name that would give him unlimited access to the information he needed in Axenthorpe Hall. He also had the audacity to act out the ridiculous dual roles, firstly as the foreigner 'Van Vebstriche', and second as the much more sinister and dark character of the Highwayman. He was either very cautious or very stupid and conceited. Lizzie thought she'd really like to pull a fast one on him. She still couldn't tell her parents, as she knew they would tell her to drop it, and leave her very fertile imagination to writing better stories in her English lessons. The police were a total no-no!

There was only one real plan of action she and the other girls could take, and that was to try and find the jewels themselves, even though it could be the most dangerous thing they'd ever do in their lives, and probably the most stupid! After all, David Webster had proved that he would kill to get his hands on the jewels, and three teenage girls would be no obstacle to him. She remembered her own words, 'The deeper you go…he could snuff them out like candles.' She sighed.

Lizzie looked at the time: seven thirty. The church bell chimed the half-hour. It was as if by magic it had known that she was looking at her watch. She told her mum that she was going to the Gallows Oak to meet Mabel and Amy and would be back in an hour. Her mother motioned her hand in a wave, told her to take care, and carried on with the ironing.

Lizzie looked over her shoulder. She'd lied again. No meeting with Mabel and Amy had been planned. The sun was going down over the western side of the basin and the crescent moon was already up, but hanging low in the sky. Some cottages had their lounge lamps on. They twinkled across the village green. Despite the trauma of the last day or two, Hazelthwaite seemed relatively peaceful. She sat on the slatted bench beneath the leafy branches of the Gallows Oak. The groundsman had trundled the covers over the cricket square and sidled off to the Sun Inn.

She could hear voices chatting in the pub garden and that made her feel safe and comfortable. A dog barked somewhere. Startled rooks cawed and chattered as they rose and fell back to their branches in a horse chestnut tree in the churchyard. Hazelthwaite settling down to a summer's evening. Lizzie could feel the heat from the day radiating into the evening sky. Small swirls of mist gathered on the village green in the fading light.

Lizzie looked up at Devil's Heights. What was that? She was sure she saw something. A dancing light…no, surely not. She popped off her specs and gave them a huff and a polish. They weren't very reliable, as she and her mum still hadn't picked up her new ones from the opticians yet and these were a pair she'd kept as spares. They were four years old and had scratched lenses. She looked again. There was a definite twinkling light moving very slowly back and forth. It looked like a signal – a signal directed at Lizzie? Was this going to be the challenge? But how would the Highwayman know she was going to be there? No matter, she wasn't scared. She knew this was not a ghost or spook, and come hell or high water she was going to find out who was up there. Lizzie was up for it!

For the first time, she was going to be the hunter, not the hunted. Not the one who was frightened.

When you start to be positive, you begin to get lucky too! One of the farmers who had been delivering some fresh vegetables to the Inn and to Lizzie's dad at the post office shop was just starting up the engine of his tractor to drive up the hill to Devil's Heights. She got up and raced across the village green, circling round behind the trailer as she did so. Unbeknown to the driver, he was going to have a passenger for the first part of his journey. The man eased the massive four-wheel drive machine into gear and gently pulled away.

He stopped at the junction of the village green lane. As he was looking left and right at the intersection, and just before he pulled away, Lizzie took her chance and scrambled unseen onto the back of the cart. There were a couple of straw bales and several stacks of old and rather dirty sacks to hide under, and she tried to cover herself up as best she could.

The driver, ensuring that it was safe to turn left, pulled out in a wide arc and started the climb up the winding lane to Devil's

Heights. Lizzie was surprised how quickly the tractor and trailer jumped and banged its way up the hill. Would the noise scare off whoever was at the Heights? She would have to be careful to time her jump from her perch when they got to the summit. If the driver didn't slow too much she could be injured just alighting.

The revolving reflector of the orange warning light threw strange shadows against the pine trees that lined the lane, turning them into hideous monsters. Suddenly, all the positive thoughts changed, and Lizzie became anxious at what she was allowing herself to get into. She might never see her parents again!

Near the top of the hill the driver let the tractor slow right down just before he came to the junction to negotiate a grassy mini-roundabout with a signpost in the middle that indicated the various village names, places of interest and their distance in miles. Lizzie decided that this would be her best chance to jump. She flung herself onto the road and rolled over to the grass verge and stayed very still.

She didn't feel that she had hurt herself and the canvas bag that she always kept with her when she was out seemed to be in one piece. She opened the zip and took out her glasses from their case, gave them a huff and a polish and put them on. She also took out a powerful torch. She zipped up the bag and slung it diagonally across her shoulder. Lizzie placed the torch into the grass and turned it on. The blast of light that came out told her that the bulb had survived the jump, but the beam was stifled by the thick clump of turf. This ensured that her present position wasn't given away to whoever or whatever was prowling Devil's Heights.

The tractor had now totally disappeared. No sound of the thumping diesel engine and no sign of the orange light. The night here was quiet, very quiet. It was dark too, save for the eerie orange glow coming from the low crescent moon. The flickering light was gone. The tractor noise must have disturbed whoever had been there – typical!

Lizzie still did not move but as her eyes became accustomed to the dark, she saw the dancing, twinkling light appear again as if by magic. He's still there, she thought, perhaps the light had been put out deliberately, disturbed by the tractor's engine. What he wouldn't be prepared for was her!

But the light wasn't coming from Devil's Heights; it was coming from almost directly opposite from where she lay, and that was Horseshoe Woods. Lizzie could just make out the silhouette of the trees, and the light was twinkling between the branches and undergrowth. She now realised that that was the reason why she could just make out that someone, be it David Webster, the Highwayman or whoever, was there from where she had sat at the Gallows Oak in Hazelthwaite.

So the light had nothing to do with luring her, or anybody else for that matter, to Devil's Heights or Horseshoe Woods. It had been pure luck that she had spotted it. The fact that she had acted on it was not so rational.

Whoever was there was searching for something in the woods!

Lizzie knew there was a bridle path to Axenthorpe Hall at the rear of the wood, so she quietly picked her way through the shrubs and smaller trees until she became aware of movement. She froze. Something in front of her in the darkness was moving around, making no effort to keep quiet. Lizzie eased herself forward. The moon came from behind a cloud, and there in front of her was a horse. The Highwayman was here!

The horse pricked up its ears when it heard Lizzie move towards it. She stroked its neck and side. It gave a little whinny of pleasure. She knew what she must do. Hurriedly she undid the girth securing the saddle, relocating the buckles so that it was loose. When the Highwayman, whoever he was, mounted the beast, the saddle would remain in an upright position long enough until he galloped fast or had to make a dangerous manoeuvre, and then the whole thing would shift and throw him. That was the theory, but she didn't know much about horses.

When the gloved hand covered her mouth tightly she realised the game was up! She shut her eyes tightly. Her thought about her parents flashed in front of her. All her planning was finished she'd never find the jewels. The Highwayman had won, and not only that – he'd got her! She would die a horrible death, like Agnes and the vicar. No one would know where she was buried...unless he threw her off Devil's Heights, in which case her body would be dashed against the rocks. The locals would put it down to a silly girl, out at night, being careless. Hazelthwaite would have its third death in as many days!

The gloved hand began to turn her round. As she was turned, she started to open her eyes, and although full of fright at that second, she thought she'd go with defiance blazing in them if nothing else.

The face she saw in front of her had a hand up with a finger over the mouth. It was saying, *Shh!* The mouth was smiling: it was Mabel, and she had Donna with her. Behind the two of them was Lizzie's dad! They were all wearing dark clothes. Now was not the time for explanations, but they all produced a very quiet but unforgettable high five. Lizzie took off her specs and gave them a huff and a polish and wiped the tears of relief from her eyes.

The horse gently cropped the grass in the moonlight. The four of them crawled through the long grass and bushes to the edge of the clearing. They could see a figure in the middle of the glade with a flickering lantern rigged up on what looked like a shepherd's crook. He was digging intently.

Lizzie, who had been lying in a bed of dandelions that had gone to seed, suddenly felt the urge to sneeze as the little white parachutes tickled her nostrils. She managed to stifle the first by holding her nose, thought she'd got over it and then quite involuntarily delivered the loudest sneeze possible. The sneeze echoed across the glade, across the basin that Hazelthwaite nestled in, and quite possibly all the way to the East Coast and beyond.

Time seemed to stand still. The Highwayman blew out the light and dropped to one knee all in one smooth action. They saw his gloved right hand dive to the wide, black belt and pull out one of the pair of pearl-handled pistols. He placed his hand with the pistol clasped in it onto the left forearm, which he had raised as a steadying platform.

Lizzie heard her father yell, 'Get down, down now!' As he spat the words out, the Highwayman fired. The lead ball sailed harmlessly into the trees above their heads. But they heard twigs breaking, and several frightened birds took off from hidden perches. The girls screamed. Lizzie's Dad told them to keep still. The fancy dress costume had become harsh reality. This person wasn't firing blank cartridges; this person meant business. The real world had finally reached Lizzie!

John Miller looked up. The Highwayman was gone. In those few precious seconds he had gained from firing the weapon he had dashed out of the glade. And by the time they had run to the middle of the wood, they could hear the sound of galloping hooves on hard grass. David Webster was making his getaway. Judging from the direction he was travelling, his destination was Axenthorpe Hall or the cottage called Highwayman's Perch.

'Let him go, Lizzie,' said her father softly. 'The police are waiting for him at the cottage, so he's in for a big surprise and a very long prison sentence!'

'Why did you come, Dad?' Lizzie asked.

'The girls here told me. Unbeknown to you, they were on their way round for a chat. While they were on the far side of the green they suddenly saw you dash across from the Gallows Oak and jump onto a farm cart. These two can be very convincing story tellers, especially when they said that my daughter would be in grave danger,' he replied smiling at Mabel and Amy.

A cold breeze suddenly prompted him to add, 'Let's make a move, we parked the car on the verge a couple of hundred yards past the Hazelthwaite turn; we can talk about things tomorrow. They'll be no arguments and no recriminations.'

'No what?' asked Lizzie.

'Well, no telling-off, no grounding. Just think and talk sensibly about what has happened over the last week or so, and how close you came to perhaps being...' Her dad didn't finish the sentence.

'I know what you mean, Dad,' Lizzie said quietly, 'there have been things that I've done that I know that you and mum would have killed me for, sorry...bad choice of words...well, if you'd known what we've all been up to.' Lizzie looked into her father's eyes, 'The problem was, we didn't think you'd have believed us.'

'Bits of the story, from what I've heard are hard to swallow, Lizzie, but you're safe and so are the girls – and that's all that matters,' he replied.

'Dad, you and the girls fetch the car. I'd like to be alone just for a few minutes. I'll catch you by the lay-by at Devil's Heights,' said a subdued Lizzie.

Her father nodded, 'I know how you feel, love, but only for a few minutes, eh? I want you safe at home, okay.'

A Promise to a Spectre

Lizzie drew her arms around herself and tucked her chin into the collar of her fleece. The coldness in the glade became more intense, yet there was neither a breath of wind nor the hint of a slightest breeze.

Slowly, before her eyes the white outline of a figure on horseback started to appear. It was dressed in a tricorn hat, cape and mask. Lizzie could make out pistols stuck in a belt.

'Oh my God, oh my God, the Highwayman!' Lizzie whispered in petrified wonder.

He looked down at her, 'Good evening, Miss Miller, Miss Lizzie Miller. Don't be afraid. I won't hurt you, I can't hurt you.' And after speaking, he doffed his tricorn hat in respect.

Lizzie was dumbstruck. The spectre faded back and forth from a whitish apparition to an almost solid form. Suddenly, the white was gone and Lizzie saw the Highwayman in all his glory.

If Lizzie could have dreamt up what a highwayman would look like, from the neatly tied velvet bow in his long black hair, to the immaculate silver spurs on his boots and the huge black horse, this would be it, perfection! The slight green glow that totally surrounded man and beast was weird.

'You've been here all the time, haven't you?' Lizzie asked quietly.

'No...not all the time. Even spectres can't be close all the time,' said a calm, deep voice, 'but there have been several occasions when I've seen what the Highwayman has been doing.' His voice wavered slightly.

'You do believe in me, don't you, Lizzie?' he continued. 'The more you believe in me, the stronger our contact can be, the more human I will seem to you.'

Lizzie paused. 'It's difficult,' she said, 'I always saw the lights but I didn't know whether there was a highwayman or not. I'm terribly confused. Can't ghosts be everywhere at once?'

'No, Lizzie. Ghosts have certain qualities, it's true, but I try and split my time between you and your safety and…Webster.' When he said Webster's name he almost spat it out.

As the spectre and Lizzie spoke she became aware that he had taken on the 'solidity' of a near human. He had said that the more she believed the better it would be. The greenish glow had almost disappeared.

He swung a long, black-breeched leg over the neck of the horse and slid neatly to the ground. The magnificent horse moved slowly about whilst munching grass.

Lizzie couldn't believe that the horse was still doing, well, horse-type things.

The Highwayman smiled. 'Listen, Lizzie, we don't have much time together, and I may not be able to summon up enough energy to appear to you again for a while—'

She interrupted. 'Oh, you've just shown yourself and now you tell me…'

He continued, 'I did wrong all those years ago, and I suppose my penance was to haunt the village and the surrounding area until the right someone came along for me to contact. Looks like you're that person, Lizzie. You're the one who'll search out the jewels and return them to the Icon – and hopefully give me some peace too.'

'I don't understand. I think I've seen a squadron of pigs fly by,' replied Lizzie icily.

'Pigs? What rubbish you talk, girl. You have no need to understand at this moment. But if I tell you the location of the first two jewels you must promise to say nothing of this meeting. I doubt anybody would believe you anyway. Then you must also promise to return the jewels to the Icon.'

Lizzie looked around for the laser light show that would prove this was all a wind-up. Nothing!

'Do you solemnly swear, Lizzie Miller?' insisted the Highwayman.

'Yes, I swear to do those things, but it'll be very difficult not to tell the girls,' she added.

'I know, they and your other friends have been strong, but my time is limited, and it is only you that I'm prepared to tell. Come nearer to me, Lizzie!' commanded the Highwayman.

Lizzie moved closer. He bent down towards her. His gloved hand pulled at the collar of his tunic to reveal a scar on his neck! The scar, which looked like a devilish grin, had been caused by the hangman's noose! To Lizzie, it resembled a second mouth and her blood ran cold with the thought of what it represented, a different time, different justice a different everything! She shook her head; it was too much to take in.

'Proof enough, Lizzie?' he whispered. 'Proof enough, my pretty?'

They both heard a car draw up on the lay-by near Devil's Heights. They heard Lizzie's father calling her name.

'I'll be quick, the first of the jewels is to be found in the caves where the Hazel leaves its valley. Do you know where I mean?'

Lizzie nodded, 'I lost the maps we made, but I think I can find it… And the second?'

'In the stable block of the coaching house. You must go to the wainscoted wall. Count along five of the upright panels of wood from the end and press gently just below the horizontal rail. You'll find a secret priest's way that leads to the church. When you enter, take care, for the passage is treacherous going. As you follow the passage, you'll find an iron bar set into the roof about thirty rods from the passage opening. Pull this down, and you will expose another passage that leads to a priest's hole. In this tiny room you'll find an altar set into the wall. Behind a little wooden cross you'll see a stone with the letter "A" carved on it. Behind this stone you'll find the second jewel. Have you understood all that I have said, Lizzie Miller? Remember, I'm relying on you!' She nodded slowly.

'Lizzie, take care, always beware the impostor!' And with that, he walked to his horse, picked up the reins and climbed onto the saddle. Looking down at her said, 'Do this for me, Lizzie, it'll help me find true peace.' And with that he galloped off soundlessly into the night.

As she watched him ride towards Axenthorpe Hall she saw him change from the near solid figure with whom she'd just spoken, to a white and ghostly spectre…then there was nothing!

It seemed a bit daft but she waved her hand as he disappeared. The glade was warm again. Turning round, she walked to the car. Her father was standing by an open door.

'Come on, Lizzie! Gosh, you're cold. Seen a ghost or something?' he said.

She looked at her dad and smiled at him.

'No, Dad, but everything's going to be good,' she said, 'cool.'

Mabel and Amy, sitting in the car, realised immediately that something strange had happened to Lizzie, there was no doubt in their minds that she'd just told a lie again. But for Lizzie as she sat gazing through the window as her father drove down towards Hazelthwaite life had changed. In a few minutes of being in the company of the highwayman she would grow up fast, faster than she could ever imagine!

David Webster? Sorry, no sighting at all!

David Webster galloped out of Horseshoe Woods, following the bridle path to Axenthorpe Hall, he had no intention of returning to Highwayman's Perch cottage, which he'd previously rented. His car was parked on a little used track a mile away in Forestry Commission land. It was for just an occasion as this that he had taken precautions. Things can go wrong. Didn't he know it! As far as he was concerned, the police would probably be lying in waiting for him at the cottage. Little did he realise just how right this was! He got to his car, which he had parked in the shadows of some tall pines, took off the branches that he'd laid across the back and roof for complete security, and unlocked the hatchback.

He changed quickly from the Highwayman's outfit into jeans and T-shirt. Quickly, he substituted the blonde wig for a black one and stuck on a moustache, using a wing mirror to check his appearance. He took the saddle off the horse and placed it under a blanket in the boot. The horse was given a hefty slap on its rump and the beast took off for who knows where. No doubt the police would find it in the morning.

Getting into the car, he switched off the interior light, started the engine and reversed the anonymous blue Astra onto the forest road. So as not to draw any attention, he now motored casually into Axenthorpe town. He booked into the local hotel, without as much as a second glance from the receptionist, and in his en-suite bathroom carefully put the final touches to his disguise. David Webster was no more!

Once Lizzie's dad had ensured that Mabel and Amy were home safely, he had phoned the police at Axenthorpe to find out about the arrest of David Webster. He couldn't believe what he heard in reply. Yes, he'd left on the horse...they'd seen him...no, they didn't follow him because he'd fired a gun of some kind at them!

What did they think they were? When he'd put the phone down, he looked at Lizzie and her mum and broke the news that David Webster had not been sighted. The police were extending their search to other parts of the county, and for that matter local and provincial airports and seaports, but they hadn't even found his horse!

Lizzie suddenly looked very frightened, 'He knows about me. He'll come after me, he's very clever.'

'Look, Lizzie, he won't come back here, there's still lots of police activity in the village. He will have made as much distance as he can from Hazelthwaite in the time he's had. It is my guess that he'll head for Scotland and then try and get out of the country. You won't see him again,' said her father, with more than a hint of authority.

There goes another squadron of pigs, said Lizzie to herself.

That night, for quite a while she lay awake thinking of the Highwayman, and the impostor...

The water was drowning her, she could feel the darkness but she couldn't scream. Her body was being thrown around and around. Her mouth and throat were totally full of icy water that she couldn't spit out; the strength of the deluge was forcing itself through her eye sockets and her eardrums. Die, Lizzie! Die, Miller! Let the pain be over! Now Webster's hands round her throat came to the aid of the water...

But she was screaming, and her mother shook her into reality. 'Lizzie, Lizzie, it's a nightmare!'

'It was horrible, I was alone, water pouring all over me, it was dark and there were shapes...' sobbed Lizzie.

Lizzie's mum held her in her arms until she drifted off into a dreamless sleep. Perhaps, she thought, she'd take her daughter to the doctor's to see what he said. She looked down at Lizzie, stroked her forehead, and before leaving, made sure the bedside light was on, the door left ajar in case the bad dreams invaded her sleep again.

For the next few days, the police presence in Hazelthwaite continued. The interest in the death of the vicar and Agnes Smith that had initially been shown by the national press died away. They became yesterday's news. The journalists and television crews melted away to bother other people in their moments of distress and left Hazelthwaite to deal with the mourning of their two beloved ex-residents. Even the *Axenthorpe Advertiser* dropped the deaths from the front page. Occasionally they would feature Hazelthwaite for a couple of paragraphs in the body of the paper itself, but interest in the story was waning. This was especially so as David Webster had obviously gone to ground or managed to slip out of the country. After all, there's only a certain amount of journalistic half-truths you can write, even on a serious subject. No doubt the interest would be restored as and when the police came up with some serious lead on the whereabouts of Webster.

The fact that Lizzie had not forgotten anything, and had had the recurring dream several times, prompted her mum to take her to the local surgery to see the doctor. A very sympathetic GP suggested that it would take a little time to get over an ordeal like the one Lizzie had been through, but he was sure that rest, rather than pills and potions would be a better aid to recovery.

When they'd got home, Lizzie had told Mabel and Amy what the doctor had said and they'd agreed with him. She'd looked at them old-fashioned like, but they had laughed it off when Lizzie had said that the only reason she'd go back to see him was because of his resemblance to Leo Di Caprio. Amy had said her mum would go with Lizzie if he was a 'looker' like that, and she was always complaining of aches and pains.

They asked her what she was going to do next about the jewels. Lizzie said they'd have to keep looking, but didn't think they needed to look in Horseshoe Woods, and certainly said nothing about the meeting with the Highwayman. She stayed true to the promise she'd made to him, especially about the whereabouts of the first two jewels!

That would come soon enough when the pressure on her eased and everybody had got back to some semblance of normality. Hazelthwaite seemed to be doing that slowly, and the wounds that would perhaps take years to heal for some families were beginning to mend for others. After all, life has to go on!

The tourists were still coming in thick and fast, the cricketers were still playing their mid-season games, and the post office/shop and the Sun Inn were extremely busy. Lizzie looked out across the village green. Her friends chatted about boys and music, often with reference to Lizzie, as several of the local village lads, as Mabel called them, had shown an interest in her. Lizzie had had boyfriends in London, but hadn't really had time when she'd come to live in Hazelthwaite. She'd been stand-offish to everyone at first, and that had put everyone off.

However, one of 'the lads', a rather nice-looking youngster called George, had plucked up courage, and after several dares, sat down beside Lizzie on the school bus. Mabel and Amy, who had just about managed to break the ice with this new girl from 'the Smoke', nudged one another when they saw what was happening. They'd normally sat beside her, but on this particular occasion they'd got out of their class late and had consequently arrived in the playground too late to join the queue. Lizzie, with George beside her, had asked him what the hell he was up to. George had come right out with, 'I fancies yer, pet! What about a date?'

The seats surrounding the two were full of 'lads' who were very eager to see how George would get on. They soon found out! Lizzie, who had her personal CD already on, had had to take one of the earpieces out to see what George wanted. Suddenly she slipped the other one out of her ear, ramming both of the speakers into George's ears and turning up the volume to full.

'Well, pet,' said Lizzie, emphasising the word 'pet', 'I'll call you if I ever want my dog taking for a walk.'

He'd retreated hastily to another seat with ringing ears and to shouts of riotous derision from the lads. Lizzie was sure she'd heard George mouth off a few choice sentences about her that had included 'bag' and 'cow', and if she had a dog it would definitely be a 'bitch', but to this day he hadn't tried to get to know her again. Lizzie had put it down to immaturity, but later Mabel had said he was the lad that most girls in the village would have given their right hand to get to know. Lizzie had quite hastily retorted that if that was all they wanted then she wasn't sure any of them had any taste at all! But that was all water under the bridge, and it was easy to see that they'd both been mightily embarrassed by the whole episode. However, Lizzie now had the reputation of a girl to avoid, because you never knew what she might do next. Lizzie wasn't like that at all, and as time had gone on, Mabel had seen her second glance George on a couple of occasions.

The sun shone. August had actually been a beautiful month weather-wise, when all was said and done. Lizzie thought about Bendy and Donna. She had phoned them on numerous occasions and had spoken to their parents. A vague promise had been made that they might come back for the last ten or so days of the holiday. But that was not a firm booking, and nothing to get in any way excited about. A lot would hinge on Brenda's father being able to get an extra week off work. 'If onlys' had a knack of smacking you in the face, so she decided to push the thought that her friends might come to stay to the back of her mind, for now at least.

The Cricket Match

Lizzie had detected that the whole of Hazelthwaite village was becoming very excited about the forthcoming cricket match against an eleven from Axenthorpe Hall. It would certainly help to take many minds off what had recently happened, and sort of bring the village together.

One Saturday in August, every year the Axenthorpe family and their staff put together a cricket team to play for the Axenthorpe Challenge Perpetual Trophy against Hazelthwaite. Depending on the availability of family members, some of whom worked in the City of London as merchant bankers, and others who lived abroad, the Axenthorpes could put together a very useful and competitive team.

James Axenthorpe, before joining the family merchant bank, had actually been a trialist for the County of Durham and could both bowl and bat. Mabel had told Lizzie that he was an 'all-rounder'. Lizzie had nodded at Mabel in an interested way, but with total disinterest in her mind.

Cricket, as far as Lizzie was concerned, was a long, dull game, played by slow-witted, dull people. Even the limited overs game that Hazelthwaite played was bound to be dull. To sit for a whole day from eleven o'clock in the morning till about eight in the evening watching 'still life' enjoy themselves seemed to make watching paint dry a much more interesting pastime.

For that matter, sitting in front of a computer screen, pretending you actually enjoyed surfing the net seemed more fascinating. Lizzie, however, would much rather sit with her eyes closed and listen to her iPod. Well, if the worst came to the worst, if she was going to have to support the game she could veg out in a deckchair, eyes closed listening to music, soaking up the sun. Sorted: that was what she'd do. Actually, she'd secretly pray for rain.

No, cricket wasn't for her, but she'd been assured that the whole village would be out to watch.

★

On the day of the cricket match, Fred Acheson, landlord of the Sun, had his bar staff set up a beer tent on the boundary. It was red and white and looked marvellous in the early morning sunshine. The sides had been rolled up and secured neatly. The men and girls had then busied themselves erecting trestle tables for glasses and the paraphernalia for serving the beer. There were deckchairs and tables with parasols advertising Martini and various beers set out in front of the tent's large awning.

To the left of this, Francesca Golightly, with willing helpers from Hazelthwaite, had put up the lunch and tea tent, not as colourful as Fred's beer tent, but everything added to the charm of the scene.

Lizzie watched the girls. Mabel and Amy were going to assist with serving coffee and sandwiches and had very short black dresses on with incredibly starched white aprons which Lizzie reckoned would stay clean for about ten minutes – if they were lucky – before Mabel quite certainly stained hers with tea and coffee dribbles. Lizzie was going to 'watch' the game from a deckchair that had a little frilly awning on it so that the sun didn't frazzle your neck while you paid attention to the music!

At about ten o'clock, people started arriving to claim their piece of space around the boundary. Lizzie was amazed. People came from all over the area to watch this very special event. Young and old sat chatting, picnic baskets were dragged from car boots, and more tables and chairs and parasols sprouted up like colourful mushrooms all around the village green.

A couple of boys (one of them happened to be George) had climbed the Gallows Oak to get a better view of the game. They then realised that the thickness of the foliage blocked the view they'd originally climbed the oak for. When they'd started to descend, one had fallen and had to be rushed to Casualty at Axenthorpe with a suspected broken arm. The boy's parents, by the time they'd dragged him this way and that, and thoroughly scolded him for ruining their day before it had even started, almost ensured that he had not only a broken arm but a broken neck into the bargain!

George, most unfortunately for him, caught his very baggy shorts on a branch, tearing a large hole in them. Not only had the offending branch ripped his trousers but his pants as well. He had to climb down with his back to the crowd, and with each stretch of his legs as he reached down for the next branch, the rip had got longer and longer until his bottom could be observed hanging out for all to see. Much to the boy's embarrassment (and much to Lizzie's delight) there were great cheers and laughter and shouts of 'Streaker!' as he rushed for home, hands covering his scratched, well-defined cheeks. Lizzie, along with other of the village girls, would remember that for a while!

Mabel had obviously taken note. As she stood watching, eyes on stalks, two coffees and a tea, tilting at a crazy angle on her tray were dribbling down her starched white apron onto a pair of knife-edged white trousers worn by Colonel Bright, who appeared to have steam coming out of his ears!

At a quarter to eleven the two umpires walked out to the middle of the green from the direction of the beer tent. That led to more screams of laughter and derision, as many of the locals knew full well the love the umpires had for a few glasses of ale. Lizzie thought that, even for them, it was a bit early for booze. What she didn't see was Blind Bob Bartlett – 'Blind Bob' to the local cricketing anoraks – put down his rushed and almost finished pint just before walking to the middle.

'Blind Bob' had earned his name through making awful decisions about leg before wicket. He had even been known to give batsmen 'out' when in fact the fielders had totally missed catches. Like Lizzie, he wore specs; his lenses, however, looked like huge round dollops of glass that are found at the bottoms of posh drinking glasses. They made his eyes bulge out like those of a frog.

Following the umpires were the two opposing captains chatting amiably about the game. The captain of Hazelthwaite was the fat man who had had the problem with the Rottweiler the previous year. Leading the Axenthorpe team was none other than James, their star player, and in Lizzie's terms a 'real looker'. Perhaps the game wouldn't be so bad and dull after all!

'Blind Bob' tossed the coin, which shimmered as it spun in

the air. When it landed, Lizzie couldn't make out who had won, but the two captains had shaken hands and walked back to the beer tent. (Later she found out that Blind Bob had even managed to bodge the call and the reason for the laughter in the centre of the village green was sorting out who had won what.) The beer tent was doubling up as a makeshift pavilion, and a couple of minutes later the Hazelthwaite lads emerged, to a spirited round of applause, onto the village pitch to field. They threw a couple of old balls to one another to loosen up. The opening bowler went through a few stretching exercises, and checked the length of his run-up to the stumps.

Five minutes after this, the two opening batsmen for Axenthorpe strolled out to the middle, to a ripple of polite applause. As they walked towards the stumps, they swung their bats around rather like one-bladed windmills to loosen their arms and shoulders.

After some nervous patting and dabbing at the grass on the wicket the facing batsmen asked Blind Bob to give him middle wicket as his guard. Bob shuffled him this way and that before saying, 'Thatalldoyathaatseet.' The batsman, nervous after all the toing and froing decided on one more quick prod at the grass and a glance round at the field placings before settling himself to look down the wicket at the bowler. The church clock struck eleven, and with great composure and assertiveness Blind Bob said, 'Play!'

Around the ground, villagers and tourists alike settled down for the morning's session under a cloudless sky. Lizzie's attention drifted away from the cricket to thoughts of the jewels. She had made up her mind that she would recover the jewel from the priest's hole that night. The Highwayman had made locating it sound fairly straightforward, but she knew she'd have to be prepared. Chilling out in the sunshine seemed just the way to train for the night's activities. But nothing was that easy, was it?

So deep in thought was Lizzie, and to be honest she really wasn't too interested in the cricket match, that she didn't see, sitting a good distance from where she sat dreaming in the summer sunshine, a very interested spectator. He wasn't, however, the least bit concerned about the cricket. David Webster studied her every move through a pair of binoculars. Lots of the spectators had binoculars of every size so they could see every facial grimace as the players went through the emotions of ecstasy and frustration, especially with the incredible stream of decisions that Blind Bob came up with. He was certainly having a wonderful spell of blunders. At one point a spectator had shouted across to him to take his 'ruddy specs off' as it didn't seem to make any difference to the game. Bob had replied quite seriously to the man that he was on top of the game, no problem!

Lizzie wouldn't have recognised David Webster anyway because of the amazing transformation he had done to himself with his disguise.

After forty overs, Axenthorpe had amassed a very creditable one hundred and ninety-five for seven. This had included an excellent seventy from James Axenthorpe, who didn't run once for any of his total, scoring everything in fours and sixes! All this without breaking any windows or car windscreens. Lizzie had watched James carefully…very stylish, but a bit old for her.

Lizzie, however, had been particularly interested in Robbie Axenthorpe. The fifteen-year-old had come in to bat at number five and had partnered his brother extremely ably. He had scored twenty-two himself, before being clean bowled by a nasty delivery that had caught the edge of his bat as he had ducked away, and the ball had sliced down onto the bails.

When he'd walked in, to a great round of applause, he'd smiled and winked at Lizzie. Lizzie had blushed, looked away and tried to show as much disinterest as she could. She'd had the odd boyfriend before. Robbie, quite tall for his age, took after his mother (an extremely good-looking lady) and obviously both he and James had the same blonde hair and fine, slim features that made them stand out in a crowd. Lizzie had noticed that all the village girls had yelled and shrieked when he'd first gone in to bat and that had made her sit up and be doubly interested. By showing indifference to the smile and wink, she thought she'd play hard to get!

After an earlyish tea, it was Hazelthwaite's turn to bat. Most of the chat at the interval had been about the Axenthorpe total and young Robbie Axenthorpe's innings. 'One to mark down for the future,' Lizzie had heard one old bloke say. The total, most people considered, was probably too much for Hazelthwaite to match this year; but you could never tell.

When the two opening batsmen had both been dismissed for a total of seven, things looked pretty bleak. But coming in to bat at number four was the captain, and the fat batsman who Amy had told the story about. He was a living legend! He actually came from the next village, but worked as a farmhand in Hazelthwaite, and that fact qualified him to play – or that's what the selection committee said. Nobody, but nobody, dared challenge them!

A buzz of excitement went round the ground. Something special always happened when the fat man was at the crease. He strode out to a great round of applause. He, like all the other batsmen, swung his bat in great windmill-like gestures. Here, however, the resemblance to the others stopped. The bat on a huge upward swing, that would have wrenched normal mortals shoulders out of their sockets, suddenly left his hand and arced upwards into the sky. It whizzed round and round like a boomerang. This was a boomerang out of control, though, and it wasn't going to return. As it continued upward at ever-increasing revs, it took on a backward direction aiming for the beer tent. The fat batsman looked horrified and shouted something quite unrecognisable.

From the direction of the beer tent there came shouts of…'Look out!'… 'Out the way!'… 'Duck!' …'Fatman's bat's in air!' Glasses and drinks went this way and that as frightened spectators tripped over one another to get out of the path of the rogue missile. The bat still hurtling through the air, just missed the beer tent, and finally came to rest in the windscreen of a Porsche 911, totally shattering it, after bouncing once off the bonnet.

The owner of the unlucky car had just settled down with a rather nice-looking bar maid who'd had a late lunch break and had taken a fancy to the car rather than the owner. The car belonged to the driver's daddy, and the unfortunate man was supposed to have been meeting his mother for lunch in Newcastle rather than pulling barmaids in Hazelthwaite. The young man was crying like a demented baby when the crowd surrounded the dented and bashed Porsche. How on earth was he going to explain the best part of three grands' damage to his dear father!

The fat batsman puffed and panted his way up to the inconsolable driver of the Porsche. He muttered his apologies and, 'Thanks to God that nobody's been hurt,' doffed his cork-fringed cricket hat to the tearful barmaid and waddled through the mayhem of the beer tent to the village green. A chorus of cheers and laughter soon turned to groans of fear when he started to wind up his bat again, but thinking better of it, ceased the swinging, and walked sensibly to the crease.

Lizzie turned to the direction of the tea tent where Mabel and Amy were standing with both thumbs up. She could hear Amy shout to her, 'And he hasn't even started to bat yet!' She laughed out loud and joined in a Hazelthwaite Mexican wave, which greeted the start of the fat man's innings!

He really did entertain the crowd throughout the afternoon. When he wasn't scuttling up and down the wicket running ones and twos, he was skilfully giving wrong calls to the other batsmen, managing to get three of them run out. All of this was carried out in total seriousness. It was if he'd never played cricket before. Lizzie understood what they were saying as they muttered oaths at him after being dismissed. 'Why do we put up with him?' was one of the kinder things said.

James Axenthorpe had bowled well, but he only had a certain amount of overs that he could deliver, and it was when he had completed these that the Hazelthwaite 'tail-enders', along with the fat batsman, started to cut loose. The fat batsman stayed in all afternoon, more by luck than judgement. He hit one of the Axenthorpe fielders on the head and the ball had just managed to drop to the ground before another could reach to catch it, and so it went on.

It was shortly before the last over of the day had begun when Lizzie for some reason turned her gaze to the Gallows Oak. The tree, which had been placed out of bounds by the club committee when the two boys had had their accidents earlier on, had been cordoned off with white rope and wooden stakes.

The Highwayman sat on the bench, watching the game. Obviously no one else could see him, only Lizzie. She got up and walked around the edge of the green. She had to negotiate cars and people who had spilled onto the road with their picnics and rugs, but she didn't take her eyes off him. Lizzie was totally oblivious to the fact that Hazelthwaite were close to drawing – or even winning the game.

She crossed the boundary rope and stood looking at him. Slowly the ghostly white shape took on a near-human look.

'Good game, Lizzie,' said the Highwayman.

'What are you doing here? All these people, they'll see you. Have you gone bonkers?' she blurted out.

'No, only you can see me, Lizzie. I thought you'd be around. I've come to remind you about the "impostor". You never know, he might be here even now,' said the Highwayman calmly.

David Webster's binoculars were watching Lizzie's every move. He could see her hand and head gestures. Why was she chatting to the tree? What on earth was she up to?

At one hundred and ninety-one for nine, the fat batsmen wanted to get the game over and done with. A particularly poor, slow bowler was in action, and he'd thought to himself, it was now or never to win the match. The next ball that was delivered was given the biggest swipe that the fat batsmen had ever made. The leather ball winged its way high into the early evening sky towards the boundary.

The crowd watched as the huge stroke was executed. Hundreds of pairs of eyes saw the ball make for the Gallows Oak. Then hundreds of pairs of eyes saw Lizzie Miller standing with her back at the point exactly where the ball would land.

Three pairs of eyes watched with particular attention.

The fat batsman watched and had already started to yell at Lizzie, but with seemingly no reaction.

David Webster watched in anticipation; perhaps he wasn't going to have to do his own dirty work himself after all. He actually started to rub his hands. Life could be good after all!

The Highwayman had seen what was happening too. He leapt up from the bench and just as the ball was about to hit a totally astonished Lizzie on the back of the head, he caught it.

The fat batsman, David Webster and the crowd were riveted as they all watched with disbelief the incredible scene that took place before their eyes. For a few seconds, the ball seemed to stand still in mid air, then it changed direction violently sideways before it flipped over the boundary rope.

Blind Bob put both arms in the air and shouted, 'Six!'

For a moment you could have heard a pin drop, and then there was an explosion of sound and cheering around the little ground. The fat batsman fell flat on his back in relief. David Webster slunk away in dismay at what had happened, and the Highwayman yawned in a bored fashion.

Lizzie looked at him again. 'You've saved my life,' she whispered.

'Now you must do your duty, Lizzie, but be careful. This time it was luck. Next time, I might not be there, my pretty.'

By this time, Lizzie's dad had reached his daughter.

'I ought to lock you up and throw away the key! What on earth do you think you were doing?' he said.

Lizzie shrugged and said matter-of-factly, 'I take it we won, then.'

'Don't be so flippant, Lizzie. For whatever reason, you were lucky out here today. You can't shed any light on what happened, I suppose, can you?' he continued.

Lizzie replied now slightly abashed, 'No, I suppose I got bored with the game…maybe the sun got to me. Who knows? I'm sorry.'

'*Sorry!* That's becoming a stock phrase with you. I'm getting fed up with it. I'll be glad when the new term starts and you're back to school with something to occupy your mind,' he remonstrated.

Lizzie remained silent. She followed her father back to the tea tent. She sat down beside Mabel and Amy, who stared at her. Neither dared speak.

A lot of people had made tracks home after the game, but many had stayed for Fred Acheson's 'Roast-a-pig' evening, everyone was welcome. While preparations went ahead for this, the teams had retired to the Sun for beers and a post-match chat. It had taken six members of the Hazelthwaite team to chair the fat captain to the inn's garden. Lizzie had watched them throw him unceremoniously into a large bush amidst good – humoured laughter. He was then sprayed with several bottles of champagne. She'd heard him shout, 'Dinna waste the stuff...you fools! Pour it doon me throoat!' There were hoots of laughter when someone mentioned the destruction of the Porsche, and even more when the fat batsman said he ''adna destroyed no poorch', to his knowledge.

While the girls sat nibbling crisps and nuts left over in the little bowls that had been provided on the tables outside the tea tent, Robbie Axenthorpe approached them and sat down on an empty chair beside Lizzie. He put his kitbag by the table leg and said 'hello' to them all. He had known Mabel and Amy from his time at the local primary school before moving on to his current very expensive public school. The girls introduced Lizzie to him. Lizzie took off her glasses and gave them a huff and a polish. It was nerves more than anything, but she remained cool and distant. However, he was nice, there was no getting away from it! Robbie chatted for ten minutes or so about this and that and how he'd really liked to have gone with them all to the local 'comp'. But then James arrived and he'd got up, said his goodbyes, dumped his bag in the very limited space at the back of the BMW Z3, and they were gone.

Lizzie watched them go. He had turned and waved and she'd given a half-wave back. Amy nudged Mabel.

'Oh, for goodness' sake!' said Lizzie.

'Cool, isn't he,' said Mabel.

'All right if you like that sort of thing,' replied Lizzie scornfully.

'We like all right,' they giggled.

They could hear the car accelerating up the road towards the Axenthorpe turn. Lizzie shrugged her shoulders, but the girls saw her flip her hand through her blonde hair.

Mabel winked at Amy knowingly.

Lizzie sighed at them. 'What?' she said.

They mouthed a silent 'what' back at her.

'If you're gonna be like that I'm going home, I'll see you later at the barbie. By then you both might have cooled slightly,' Lizzie said.

Mabel and Amy left their seats by the tea tent and wandered back across the village green. The groundsmen were pulling over the covers on the cricket square. It had been a good day, and apart from people tidying the beer tent and one or two folk getting things ready for the evening, calm had descended on Hazelthwaite.

Beware the Impostor, Lizzie!

The barbecue was in full swing when Lizzie joined Amy and Mabel. Several of the Hazelthwaite cricket team were quite merry by now, and groups of people chatted and laughed beneath the twinkling fairy lights that had been temporarily strung up between the parasols and the beer tent awning. Fred had hired a mobile disco from Axenthorpe, and the DJ was playing to an audience intent on eating and drinking at the moment.

He tried his hardest to entice people to dance, but he knew this would come later. However, three ladies (it's always three) had decided to have a laugh and were twitching like demented puppets to 'Dancing Queen' by Abba. Their handbags made suitable partners, as they did nothing, said nothing and occasionally got kicked. So the party sailed on into the warm summer's evening. The sun's rays had now dipped behind the surrounding hills. The crescent moon was already up and the stars twinkled in the darkening sky.

Lizzie left the proceedings at ten o'clock. The church clock struck the hour, she told the girls she was tired, and they said their goodbyes. Mabel and Amy were staying on as late as possible. People were starting to show some interest in the disco and they didn't want to miss out.

Lizzie secretly wanted to enter the passage as soon as possible, as she thought that she'd be less frightened with all the sounds of the evening going on, rather than to go into who knew what at midnight or the early hours, when she'd be scared to death. As it turned out, she couldn't have been more wrong.

The Jewel of St John

Lizzie paused when she got to the archway that led to the courtyard. She turned around. The village green looked wonderful, what with the fairy lights round the tables, the disco lights blinking on and off and the huge floodlight that had been placed at the foot of the Gallows Oak to illuminate the beautifully proportioned tree. She could see shadows of people dancing, and the sound of their laughter and chatting carried to where she stood.

David Webster saw her pause and look round. He had stayed for the barbecue after walking off in a nasty temper earlier that afternoon. He had chatted with people and had had a couple of very tasty bacon rolls washed down with a couple of pints of orange and lemonade. Now, he watched Lizzie, very carefully. The large double gates that were usually open during the day were closed and he saw her enter the right-hand one by way of a smaller door set into it, a judas gate.

She took another look, saw nobody was following her or taking any notice of her, and went inside. She didn't lock the gate in case her parents wanted to use it later. She opened the kitchen door, made her way to her bedroom and put on her fleece and the shoulder bag.

Although the evening was warm, it would probably be cool and damp in the passageway. She retraced her steps and stood quietly by the stable door. She could still hear the noise from the party drifting over from the green, and this made her feel better, safer. After opening the stable door and properly securing it open with the hook and eye catch, she made her way to the wainscoted wall. The moon made it slightly brighter inside with the door open, and Lizzie had earlier surprised her dad when she had said that she was going to clean the stable windows as they were so filthy, and this too helped to give more natural interior light. 'I don't think the windows will appreciate what's hit them,' he'd joked.

The side of the stable block had four individually sectioned stalls where horses were originally bedded down. She counted five of the upright panels from the far wall. She placed her hand below the horizontal rail of wood that ran round the wall at about four feet from the floor, and pressed very gently.

To her surprise, although the Highwayman had told her about it, a panel of the wall about ten planks wide moved inwards and slightly to the right. It moved just enough to the right to let you place your fingertips round the edge and push. She was surprised how easily the panel moved, as if it had been recently oiled or greased. It moved silently to reveal a black void, which smelt vaguely damp and fusty. She looked round once more but nobody was there, nobody watched her progress. Probably less than a hundred metres away the villagers continued to enjoy themselves. When she entered the passage and switched on her powerful torch, they could have been a hundred kilometres away.

She wedged a piece of wood in the gap to prevent the panel from shutting. It was one thing to pluck up courage and follow the passageway, it was another thing to get locked in and perhaps die an unpleasant death underground, nobody knowing where you were; but these were negative thoughts.

The strong torch beam showed her that the passage sloped down to start with and the floor, walls and ceiling were in good repair. She moved slowly and carefully. Whoever had built it all those years ago must have had a thought for tall people because she didn't have to stoop at all. But when the path levelled out, the bright beam showed her that up ahead was a curve in the passageway and that the walls and ceiling were lower, narrower and crumbling and that she'd have to watch where she placed her feet. She remembered the Highwayman's warning that she must take care in the passage, as it could be dangerous.

Before Lizzie had entered the passageway she had tied one end of a ball of string to a nail that was conveniently placed close to the panel entrance, and as she had made her way along its length she had carefully unravelled the string.

The Highwayman had said that the lever was thirty rods from the entrance. Lizzie had had to look up what a 'rod' was and had found out that it was an old unit of measurement of about five and a half yards. So she had carefully knotted the string at five-and-a-half-yard intervals thirty times. By the time the ball had unravelled to the last knot she would know that she was in roughly the right place to look for the iron bar lever that would release the door to the priest's hole passage.

It was amazingly quiet underground. She could hear her own breathing, and she could detect water dripping somewhere into a shallow puddle or pool. If she stood on a rock it seemed to make an awful clatter, but she couldn't hear anything from above. She felt as if the world had stood still and she was living in a narrow shaft of light. She wondered what worms and moles felt like with no light at all, but it didn't seem to bother them. It would bother her like hell if the torch beam suddenly went out. And she immediately put that thought to the back of her mind!

At ten thirty the party was in full swing, until quite unexpectedly, large anvil-shaped clouds built up, unnoticed, and covered the moon. Soon, huge drops of rain began to fall. An enormous flash of lightning and clap of thunder announced a thunderstorm. All the party goers fled to the safety of the pub. The DJ had tried to convince some of the beefier lads of the village to help him move some of his kit from the drenching it was receiving to his Transit van. But a ferocious bolt of lightning that had lit up Devil's Heights had sent even the manliest of them rushing for cover.

The 'Highwayman' pushed the church tower door open from the inside. He looked into the nave: nothing! Not even the cat was about. He moved round the font to the secret panel, pushed on it gently and entered. No second thoughts for this 'gentleman'; he knew exactly where to go, and how to tread. His flickering lantern light picked out the way as he followed the passage to the stable.

Lizzie had tied an extremely large knot to the thirtieth rod indicator and now held it in her hand. She shone the torch round, picking out the ceiling in front of her. There it was! In a gap between two old roof beams of wood was the iron handle. The Highwayman had been right, there would have been no way that you would have located it, if you hadn't been told exactly where it was. She reached up and with great care pulled the bar down. To her surprise once again, the handle moved downwards easily and a rock door opened to her left, revealing a passageway that was at virtual floor level. It looked as if she would have to crawl the rest of the way.

She wondered what it must have been like, to have had to have been hidden away in conditions like these. How long would you be able to breathe? She shrugged; that didn't worry her now. The air was stale and smelt awful. As she moved forwards, the torch suddenly went out. Hell! She panicked. Her worst nightmare had occurred, alone in the dark bent double with hardly any room to breathe. Stop it! Control yourself! She struggled with the switch. The torch beam flooded back into life. Thank God! She must have accidentally caught the switch as she moved forward. The tunnel widened above her head slightly and she found she could crouch. A few more crouching steps brought her into a small room, or so the torch beam told her. Black, shadowy shapes jumped out at her as she shone the beam of light round. Where was the altar?

Just in front of her was what looked like a black cloth or curtained area. She reached forward with one hand and pulled at the material.

What was left of the priest and his vestments fell on top of her, the skull resting on her shoulder. The eye sockets and the mouth smiled and winked at her in the torch's light! The arms fell round her in a ghastly, ghoulish cuddle, and it seemed that the rest of the body had broken and collapsed all over her. Some of the cloth from the vestments had become lodged in her mouth and she spat the evil-tasting material out.

The horrendous scream shocked the Highwayman. Where had it come from? He hadn't seen any light, yet she was down here! Where in hell's name was she!

It took Lizzie a few seconds to regain her composure. Her glasses had fallen off and she had to scratch around on the earthy floor to find them and when she did finally locate them she gave them an extra large huff and a vigorous polish before putting them back on. The Highwayman had forgotten to tell her that the priest's hole came complete with resident skeleton. She pushed the bones and material to one side.

There in front of her was the tiny altar. The priest must have died in the act of prayer, starved of oxygen and probably just as frightened as she was. She very carefully removed the little cross and put it in her bag. She shone the torch beam into the niche and there was the stone with the letter 'A' carved in it, in an early English style. She removed the stone, and behind it was a small leather pouch in remarkably good shape. The bag was fastened with a leather thong. Lizzie loosened the thong, and into her hand fell 'The Jewel of St John' – a beautiful emerald, the first of the jewels to be recovered of the Axenthorpe Icon!

She replaced the jewel back in the leather purse and secured this in her shoulder bag and zipped it up. As she turned to leave this awful little room with its hideous secret, she saw a gloved hand coming towards her through the shallow tunnel.

'The Highwayman – David Webster – this was certainly it! Nowhere to run. No dad to help this time! But the call from down the first passageway stunned them both.

'*Lizzie! Li-i-zie!*'

The hand disappeared back down the tunnel and she could hear him crawling backwards with great difficulty as fast as he could. She heard him swear and curse grossly, as he must have smacked his head against the stone ceiling. Then she heard the sound of running boots echoing down the passageway as he fled.

God, she was safe! But who was coming to meet her? She bent down, and crawled along the secondary shaft, emerging dirty and shaken at the passageway. No one was there. No friendly light greeted her. No Highwayman. Nothing!

Lizzie pulled the counterweight, and the bar slid back to its original position closing the door to conceal the ghastly secret. David Webster might know roughly where the priest's hole was located, but she was fairly sure he hadn't seen the lever to open it. She retrieved the end of the ball of string and made her way back to the stable. Nothing had changed. The panel was still propped open with the block of wood and the end of the ball of string was still tied to the nail. She could hear the rain pounding on the stable roof, and then a sudden flash of lightning revealed to her the intensity of the storm that had started while she had prowled the passageways.

Mum and dad'll wonder where I am. I'm sunk, she thought to herself. Lizzie pressed on the panel, which slid silently to the closed position. A quick clear-up here and there and nobody would ever know that a door had been opened or a person had been in the stable.

The church clock struck eleven. The house was still quiet, but she could see and hear that the pub was still full of the party goers. She climbed the stairs, went into her bedroom, closed the door and leant with her back against it.

'Lizzie Miller, you're one hell of lucky girl!' she hissed to herself.

The Highwayman had said the selfsame thing as he drove back to his hotel in Axenthorpe. The girl must have been born lucky. She must have a guardian angel protecting her every move. Each time he tried something, she countered it. It was almost supernatural!

'It's a Miracle'

Francesca Golightly had filled Agnes Smith's place as the flower festival hostess with great dignity. The villagers had thought that the show ought to go on, and Francesca would be a wonderful and sensitive person to look after the guests who came to visit the church in the wake of what had happened. So many new exhibitors had been booked to show their work that the new vicar had persuaded Francesca to rename the festival in honour of Reverend Mountjoy and Agnes Smith.

He was sure that they would have wanted it to continue until its termination on the last day of September. And so it was that a sign was placed at the lychgate and church door announcing the event was reinstated. This meant, to all intents and purposes, that the terrible weeks in August would not be forgotten but would be sort of 'put to bed for a while'. The vicar and Agnes could now be remembered in the nicest and fondest way possible by having the festival named after them, as a tribute to their lives.

Lizzie stopped at the lychgate. It was now eleven o'clock. The church clock rang out the hour. Nobody was around yet. No cars were parked on the gravel lay-by at the front of the church. She knew that Francesca had opened up the church and she'd seen the new vicar enter to do his daily chores.

The village of Hazelthwaite slumbered under the warm sunshine. It was going to be another beautiful day. After the previous evening's thunderstorm, the air was clear and the grass and hedgerows smelt fresh. She could smell the honeysuckle in the trellis that surrounded the gate.

A car drew up and an American couple and their two children climbed out.

'Hee-ell huun! The old guy in the hotel was dead right if this ain't the purrdiest of villages!'

'Sheor is, Frankleen,' the wife replied.

'Come 'orn, Paw, let's throw sum ball on the cute li'e park,' the boy drawled, 'they sure keep the grass reel short.'

'Hell, boy, we just plum arrived heeurr. Let's take us a look roun' the church. They got them a flower fee…estivaal,' the father replied.

The American, was wearing the most ghastly floral short-sleeve shirt with matching shorts, coupled with the biggest gut Lizzie had ever seen, started to waddle up the path. His wife, Jeenie, Nathaniel (the second) and Lucyianne babe followed in his more than ample wake. At every step, the largest photographic lens that could be attached to a camera body was pointed this way and that. The church was captured on film from every angle possible, and then some. Lizzie reckoned that this guy might be keeping Kodak in business himself. He was loading the second spool of film into the camera by the time he arrived at the church doors.

Lizzie heard him shout out to the family, 'Hey, huns, the church is Normaan!'

And Lizzie couldn't help but laugh out loud when she heard Nathaniel (the second say), 'Paw, neat name furra church! Theese Brits think of avrything!'

The American couple and their children would no doubt keep Francesca and the vicar 'happy' for the next hour or so. She hoped that Nathaniel (the second) wouldn't throw ball in the nave or go for touchdown between the altar rails! But she was sure that it would be amusing listening to their conversation about their links 'with the old country' and how 'quiaint efurrythoing' was.

When Lizzie entered the church, she could see and certainly hear the Americans as they shook hands with the vicar and Francesca as if they were near and dear family. Judging by what they said they were very near relatives of the Prime Minister, the Queen and practically the whole of Southern England, and it was only a matter of time before even Lizzie would become a fortieth cousin fifty times removed from the dreaded Nathaniel and Lucyianne babe!

They were mortified when they heard about the double murder, and she heard Nathaniel the first say, at the right time, 'Wallgettalodathat!' and 'Gettaoudaheeurr!' Lizzie felt sure he would crush them with emotion, if he felt that a hug was necessary.

The vicar muttered something to them, said 'Good day,' and hoped they'd have a pleasant visit. He retired at a brisk pace down the nave towards Lizzie. As he passed her, he smiled, asked her if she wanted any help, and when she said she was local and had just popped in to see the new exhibitors he bid her goodbye and left.

The American couple and their children were being taken to the top of the tower by Francesca as a special treat. They could then have a bird's-eye view of the village. She could hear their voices echoing as they climbed the spiral staircase. Then there was nothing. They'd reached the top, and Francesca had presumably shut the tower trapdoor to the roof.

All alone in the church, she made her way to the special plaque in remembrance of David Webster. She looked at the niche above it. The Icon looked even more faded than she remembered it. However, the shafts of light flooding through the stained glass windows suddenly lit it up, giving it life.

A green shaft of light had lit up an oval hole exactly the same size as the emerald stone she had in the leather pouch. She removed the pouch from her shoulder bag, untied the leather thong securing the neck and held the emerald in the thumb and forefinger of her left hand. Gently she leaned forward and placed the jewel into the scarred hole. It fitted perfectly! She pushed the shard of wood back into place where the knife had originally popped it out.

The emerald jewel shone in the bright green shaft of light!

The voices of the American couple could be heard returning down the spiral stone stairwell.

'Take reel good care, Lucyianne babe, yadonwanna fall down these steeairs right now, huh!... Nathaniel, pud that Goddam ball away, ya heer me!' This was quickly followed by, 'Beg pardon, ma'am, slip of the tongue – us bein' in church, an' all.' Then the Americans were back in the body of the church.

Lizzie was inspecting a beautiful floral display that represented the village green and the Gallows Oak when she heard Francesca Golightly's shrill scream. 'My God...it's a miracle, a miracle – look!'

The huge American bustled forwards, 'Whatinthehellama-lookinat, babe?' he drawled at Francesca. She in turn, already flustered at what she was looking at, almost swooned at being called 'babe' and pointed repeatedly at the Icon. He looked at her, then at Jeenie, and shrugged.

When Francesca finally explained to him about the jewel, his camera didn't stop clicking for fully ten minutes, as over and over again he said, 'Waid'llitellumbackome.'

Lizzie rushed to see what all the fuss was about, while Francesca rushed off to find the vicar to tell him the news. The American made Lizzie pose for photos with the family in front of the 'Icorn' and was amazed to hear from him that it had been involved with King Arthur ('You can call him Art, hun'), and that it was probably a part of the round table itself. When he'd told her this he'd gone very quiet and winked at her knowingly.

As Lizzie listened amused at the story, she watched the Icon. It was changing colour. Before her eyes, the section showing St John talking to someone with his hand raised was being restored to its former hues. Nobody else noticed this phenomenon taking place. A secret, just for Lizzie? She doubted it.

After the vicar had informed the Axenthorpe family and the local paper, the news of the jewel's return didn't take long to circulate round Hazelthwaite, and a crowd of eager admirers came to view the spectacle. One could only hazard a guess as to how it had appeared there, and more to the point, who had returned it! Somebody who'd found it years ago and now had had a massive twinge of conscience – a miracle, as Francesca had said – they were sure that they'd never know!

Mabel and Amy had hurried to the church when they'd heard the news. Lizzie was watching the proceedings and chattering and shrugging her shoulders like everyone else. Mabel sidled up to her.

'Lizzie, don't tell me you don't know anything about this?' she said inquiringly.

'Nothing, and that's the truth of it,' Lizzie replied, her fingers crossed behind her back very tightly. After all, she was in church.

'Oh, Lizzie pet, it had to be you! Apart from us, nobody knew anything about David Webster's secret identity,' said Amy. 'And where did you disappear to last night?'

'Yes, we came to the arch gate, but it was locked. We shouted your name but there was no reply. What were you up to?' Mabel whispered.

'The gate was unlocked,' Lizzie replied.

'No it wasn't, we tried it. We came to get you before the thunderstorm started. Robbie arrived with his brother and asked where you were. We told him you'd just gone home. So he persuaded us to fetch you back,' continued Mabel.

Lizzie's mind raced. The Highwayman must have missed the opening to the priest's hole the first time and gone straight to the stable. He'd checked the judas gate, found it open, so he locked it, and then just followed the string through the passageway. She'd led him to her! She'd been a doubly lucky girl, and no mistake. If Mabel and Amy hadn't had such loud voices he'd certainly have killed her… She'd be in the tomb with the priest right now. However, she was also positive that she hadn't heard anything in the tunnel when she'd first entered it. Perhaps the wind had carried the calls. Her thoughts then hurriedly turned to Robbie.

'Rubbish, I don't believe a word you've said. Why would he be interested in me?' said Lizzie.

Amy looked at her, 'Checked the mirror recently, Lizzie?' she asked. Lizzie took off her glasses and gave them a little huff and a polish. She looked at her specs. 'I wear glasses. He wouldn't be interested in me. He goes to a posh school. I expect the girls queue up for him,' she said.

'We're in the queue,' said Mabel. 'Anyway, if you're determined not to listen to us then we can't possibly tell you what he asked us to tell you.'

'I'm not interested,' said Lizzie, without conviction.

'Oh well, you can shove him in our direction any time,' added Amy.

'The jewel, Lizzie!' Mabel said again. 'Give!'

And Lizzie replied defiantly, 'I told you I don't know anything about it. So leave it out, the both of you!'

Lizzie looked at the two girls, desperate to tell them about the meeting with the Highwayman, her promise to him, her escape from David Webster and the jewel itself. She half gestured with her hand, thought better of it and let it fall to her side. They'd guessed the truth, but she still couldn't confide in them, which hurt her deeply. The Highwayman might not forgive her, might not appear to her again. If she got into a tight spot he wouldn't help her, and although she knew the whereabouts of the second jewel, he certainly wouldn't tell her anything more. She supposed that he could turn nasty again if she should let him down, although he had said that he couldn't hurt her. If she let him down, so he could let her down! It was as easy as that!

It surprised Lizzie how the return of the jewel had made everyone in the district so happy. It was almost the reverse situation of the two deaths. Bad things followed by good things; did that happen? It also surprised her that something that had been stolen and lost for two hundred years could be found by a total outsider in about two months!

What had made her so special? Was she special? She didn't think so, but the Highwayman had chosen her to look for, find and return the jewels. A quest, no? She was ordinary Lizzie Miller, who'd moved to Hazelthwaite from London. She'd hated the whole thought of coming up north, but now after ten or so weeks was beginning to love...well, perhaps that was a little strong...but she was certainly beginning to *like* her new surroundings.

Her new friends, Mabel and Amy, had almost taken the place of Bendy and Donna in the nicest possible way, but B and D would quite naturally and always remain her first, best mates. Sometimes she thought that it was nice to feel sentimental and emotional and she shed a few tears while her thoughts dwelt on the two girls in London. To comfort herself she went through the ritual of giving her glasses a huff and a polish. She pushed her hand through her blonde hair and wondered when she'd pluck up courage to look for the second jewel. She also realised that she was a total mug for not getting the lowdown on Robbie Axenthorpe.

So annoyed was she with this last thought that she shoved her glasses back on her nose so hard she almost caused the skin to split!

The Garden Party

It was just as well that Bendy and Donna hadn't returned to Hazelthwaite for the last few weeks of the summer holiday, as the weather took a turn for the worse. It was rather like a late monsoon season. Heavy rain poured from the heavens, often accompanied by a thunderstorm, which was then followed by an hour or two of bright hot sunshine. When it rained you could do nothing except stay indoors and be bored. When it was sunny you didn't dare go too far, for as soon as you started a longish walk or bike ride you got soaked to the skin in the next heavy shower. Typical stroppy British weather – no wonder it produced typically stroppy British people! In weather like this, Lizzie became the biggest strop bag in the north-east!

She found herself spending time in the shop, helping to stack shelves or sweeping up between the aisles or doing a bit of housework. Her mother said nothing about this, no sarcastic remark, no 'Oh, don't bother with that, I'll do it later' remark, just the odd 'Thank you' now and then. Lizzie had never been known to do housework of any kind, except to fill the linen basket to the brim with her worn-only-once clothes, take things out of the fridge without replacing them or generally ensuring that her bedroom was kept in a high state of untidiness.

Jane Miller remarked about this new wave of helpfulness to John, who agreed that maybe their daughter was finally growing up. He wondered, however, if there was someone she was trying to impress on the horizon!

On more than one occasion, Lizzie had thought about David Webster and his present whereabouts. Where had he disappeared to? He seemed to have just melted away. She hoped so. She knew the police hadn't arrested him, as her father made continuous enquiries about the current situation. They thought that he would be far away from the Axenthorpe area by now, but the case book was not closed on him, as someone might just recognise him from the photograph or description of him that had been circulated to all police stations. More than that, they couldn't say.

The police advised Lizzie's father to try and impress on her that she was quite safe and would come to no harm. If only she could have answered their queries with straightforward explanations. Well, they would have been pretty straightforward, if you had a direct line to the supernatural, and mere mortals believed you with any question or answer whatsoever. She had to grin and bare it for the unforeseeable future! Webster was out there. He was free, and she knew that she was his prime target. Lizzie felt she was almost a prisoner in the village, as for all she knew he was there right now, or very close by, able to keep an eye on her every move. She didn't doubt that he was never very far away, but you couldn't convince anyone else to think along the same lines. It was the same old story: 'Silly girl, it's all over now. Perhaps she should see the doctor again?'

Lizzie knew David Webster wanted the second jewel. He knew all he had to do was wait for her to make a move. She knew also that he wanted her to suffer! He had been thwarted once and she was sure he would not make the same mistake twice. The hairs on her neck bristled as she felt a panic attack coming on. 'Buck up, Lizzie,' she thought. You won't have the courage to walk down the street on your own in a minute, let alone go into dark forbidding passages…and she quickly shut the thoughts out.

The following day at breakfast, Lizzie's mother opened the post and found to her astonishment that the family had been invited to a Garden Party at Axenthorpe Hall. In fact, when Jane and John Miller opened the post office and shop that morning, they found through their customers' gossip that seemingly the whole village had been invited. It was a twofold thank you, really, one for hosting the splendid and successful cricket match that all the Axenthorpes had enjoyed, and secondly – but more importantly – as a celebration for the return of the jewel.

Lizzie had said in passing to Mabel and Amy she couldn't wait to go (not), and asked them if they thought that Robbie would be there.

'Pet, I told you you'd like him,' said Amy.

'That's not what I asked!' replied Lizzie.

'If you're not keen on him, why the question, Lizzie pet?' Mabel queried fully knowing what she really thought, but milking the situation as far as she could.

Lizzie thought for a few seconds, 'Because if he's there, I won't go. If he's gone back to school, and I can be sure of that, then I'll think about it.'

'You can't snub the Axenthorpes!' said Mabel. 'They're inviting everyone 'cos they want to!'

'Can't be sure of that, either,' Lizzie scoffed.

Amy looked at Lizzie. 'I'm surprised at you, Lizzie. We've tried to help you settle in, we've tried to take the place of your other friends and we've put up with your moods, but sometimes I just don't understand where you're coming from! Most people would jump at the chance to go to a posh place for free and have a nose.'

'I don't feel comfortable with them,' Lizzie replied.

'It's a thank you,' continued Mabel, 'but if you're determined not to go, then don't. Fine by us. If it was the teasing we gave you about Robbie, then we're sorry, but it was just a bit of fun.'

Lizzie wasn't used to somebody taking the blame for something. She wasn't sure how she should reply. So she leant over and they 'fived' one another's hands. Mabel and Amy understood this reaction. Perhaps they'd gone too far, and this show of affection was a reply that a thousand words couldn't begin to give.

★

The Garden Party was to be held on the second Saturday in September. It was something to look forward to after school started. Lizzie had been informed by a local lady who had a son at the same school as Robbie, that they would already have gone back to school the week before the Garden Party. There was absolutely no chance that Robbie would come back for a weekend when he had just returned to school! Private schools had holiday and term times that seemed quite alien to those of state schools – or that's how it seemed to Lizzie.

Lizzie was pleased to hear Robbie would be at school. She didn't really want to miss out on the Garden Party. Firstly, she was curious to see how Robbie Axenthorpe really lived, and secondly to perhaps have a chance to speak to one of the Axenthorpes about David Webster or 'Van Vebstriche', as he might be known to them. Perhaps they could shed some light on why he wanted information on the Highwayman story, and maybe the connection with Agnes Smith.

How she went about tackling them for this information was another thing. She imagined the scene: thirteen-year-old girl approaches large Axenthorpe in full riding gear, crop behind back, nose in the air and asks them about some family business. Thirteen-year-old girl politely told to get lost, and take your parents with you. Lizzie smiled at the thought. She liked the picture she'd created in her mind. In fact they probably weren't like that at all, and from what she'd seen of them at the cricket match, they were good fun and very approachable. Perhaps she might wait for the right moment and then do some polite, but discreet, digging.

The three days back at school went quickly and uneventfully. Lizzie even made a point of sitting by George, much to the envy of 'the lads'. She had apologised for her earlier rudeness, but had reminded him that now she and the local girls had checked out his 'cheeks', he'd better be extra nice to them. George had turned bright red, then laughed and told her that he reckoned his 'butt' was one of his good points.

The only problem with the week had been the weather once again, which had been lousy. They'd had so much rain that the River Hazel had risen quite high and had threatened to burst its banks on several occasions, but fortunately the channel just about coped with the extra water!

Saturday morning of the Garden Party was beautiful. The clouds had gone, the sun was warm and people in the shop talked about an 'Indian Summer'. The village came to life again. Gardens were still looking well tended, and it looked like there would be a late rush of tourists to the area. This meant that Lizzie's Mum and Dad might be busy till about one o'clock. They would then have just enough time to ready themselves for the Garden Party opening at three o'clock. They actually had a sign in the shop saying that they would close at one promptly.

Lizzie met Mabel and Amy at the Gallows Oak and then left them to see the jewel. Apparently the new vicar had installed a smart piece of security technology that allowed you to see the Icon and jewel, but had no glass front to the niche in which it sat. That was the clever bit. Lizzie hadn't a clue how it worked. What did concern her was how, if she did find the second jewel, was she going to replace it in the niche? Bells and lights and goodness knows wheat else now guarded the picture, which went off if you broke the beams or whatever had been fitted to protect it. Those things might prove to be insurmountable problems. Lizzie wasn't technical at all!

The church was quiet except for Francesca Golightly, who was still on duty as custodian of the flower festival. She greeted Lizzie and told her, 'Yes, there are still enough people passing through the village to keep the display open' …and, 'Yes, the jewel has been a huge attraction, and isn't it marvellous?'… and, 'Yes, I suppose that no more will be recovered, certainly for the remainder of my life.'

Lizzie had agreed with her, with fingers firmly crossed behind her back. She didn't like all these continual lies, and wondered why it was always in church that she found herself doing so. She silently asked to be forgiven, then immediately took it back when she said that what she was doing was for 'him' in the first place, sort of in his best interests, and that made her feel much better.

The Icon looked stunning with the emerald in it. Lizzie asked Francesca how the alarm worked, but she was told that it was all mumbo jumbo to her, but if anybody tried to touch the Icon they would be in for a nasty surprise!

The next few hours passed quickly, and when the Millers finally got into the car to drive to Axenthorpe Hall, they joined a cavalcade of vehicles going in the same direction. When they arrived, one of the Hall guardians had shown them where to park.

From the car park people were asked to enter the Hall by the main entrance, and from there, to follow the Garden Party signs. When Lizzie got to the entrance, she found herself actually tingling with excitement! Maybe Robbie would be there after all.

There was the sound of a band playing somewhere. People whom she recognised from the village chatted and laughed as they made their way to the Axenthorpes private wing of the Hall, and the garden. Lizzie was amazed when they moved from the old formal part of the house to a virtual ultra-modern home by just passing through two doors and a small adjoining hallway.

As she passed through the second door, the rooms that met her eyes were all beech-wooden floors and minimalist chrome and white with a splash of bright colour here and there. It was all very tasteful, if you like that sort of thing, and a far cry from the decoration in her own home. There were lavish displays of flowers and expensive-looking ornaments on their own in stark white niches and some very modern abstract paintings on the wall. They looked the real thing, not just reproductions. So this was how the other half lived!

She was incredulous when they passed through the last huge patio doors and they entered yet another beautiful lounge. One wall was totally constructed of glass sliding doors which led to an indoor and outdoor swimming pool. What do you say when confronted with something like that? Not much, because it was just too fabulous for words! The indoor pool was surrounded with marble tiles, and beautiful pool furniture with blue and white cushions and exotic indoor plants. Stunning! It looked like one of those dream rooms you see in upmarket magazines, but never think in a month of Sundays you will actually see yourself, or you wonder if they really exist at all.

The indoor pool was linked to the outdoor one with a short glass or thick Perspex tunnel with doors at either end. This pool also had plush furniture round it. Presumably you could swim from one to the other when the weather was good. The room that housed the indoor pool was warm, so the pool heater must have been on, and in the background there was the sound of trickling water. As Lizzie walked round, she could see that the water gently flowed over one end of the pool to create the sound and also the look of tiny waves across the pool's surface. Robbie certainly came from a totally different background to her!

In the garden, the village folk were milling about having food and drink, while at the far end of the outdoor pool a local rock band played very loud music. The Axenthorpes could really throw a party! They in turn were socialising with everyone, and Lizzie had to admit that there didn't seem to be any side to them. Well, with these wonderful surroundings there shouldn't be anyway... They seemed to be genuinely liked, and perhaps she'd made a terrible mistake in doubting their sincerity.

While she stood there taking in the whole the scene, Mabel and Amy walked up. She looked at them in turn and said, 'Looks like I've messed up again!' This was going to be fun! Shame Robbie wasn't going to be there...

'Van Vebstriche, meet Miss Miller'

Lizzie and the girls chatted with other villagers whilst Lizzie's parents mingled with people who they saw every day in the post office and shop but rarely had the opportunity to chat with socially. Some of the younger children had brought their swimming costumes with them and were allowed to swim in the outdoor pool. It had been made known on the invitation that any children who would like to swim could, and what was more if the adults wanted a dip they could use the indoor facility. Mabel and Amy went for a dip, but Lizzie had totally forgotten her bathers. Whilst the others jumped and splashed about, Lizzie sat on her own eating a huge plateful of potato salad, prawn cocktail and a large wedge of sun dried ciabatta bread. The band were playing a selection of music and were extremely good. Lizzie began to doze as the warm afternoon sun shone on the early autumnal scene.

The parasol that covered Lizzie's table was set at an angle to give a little shade. She sat with her eyes closed, totally relaxed on the high-back recliner sun bed. As she dozed she became aware that the sun had momentarily gone in behind a cloud. She opened one eye, only slightly though, shading it with one hand at the same time, just in case the sun came out from behind the cloud suddenly. Looking directly into the sun could do untold damage to the eyes. The sight that met her eye made her blood run cold!

Standing in front of her was David Webster. She just knew it was him, even with the heavy disguise he was wearing. Standing next to David Webster was James Axenthorpe.

'Van Vebstriche, meet Miss Miller, Miss Elizabeth Miller,' said James.

Lizzie gripped the sides of the sun bed tightly until her knuckles turned white.

'Van Vebstriche was most insistent about wanting to meet you, Miss Miller,' James continued. I'll bet he was, said Lizzie to her herself.

'I'll give you time to chat, but remember your plane leaves at six, Van Vebstriche. So when you have finished we will have to make tracks.'

'Miss Miller, I vill be quick anto zee point, as you zay. I know zat you hav on several occasions crossed my path, is it not?' He didn't let Lizzie have time to reply; in fact as he spoke to her it was as if he ignored her, having absolute confidence in himself. He nodded this way and that to others as he spoke. 'I cannot understanding how it is you hav managed to do what you do. Is almost you are being led by ziss ghost, how you put it, zing itzelf. But no matter, if we ever haff meet again it vill be ze last time for yourself. I haff put much time into ze research of ze Axenthorpe jewels and zer whereabouts. I vill zay goodbye now. You vill zay nothing to anyone about out little chat, is it not... I haff to go back to Amsterdam tonight, ze zentre of ze jewel vorld. I zink you vill understand vy I'm havvig to find the rest of ze jewels.'

She certainly didn't understand why he had to find the rest of the jewels! But he had spoken so directly and left so quickly that Lizzie had no chance to reply, or ask for help or seek the safety of her parents. It was a direct threat to keep her nose out of matters that didn't concern her!

A couple of minutes later, James Axenthorpe returned and asked how the chat had gone and what a charming fellow Van Vebstriche was. He'd met him at a party in London. He'd shown great interest in the lost jewels and the family affairs and fortunes. I'll bet he did, she said to herself.

On the way home, Lizzie was very quiet. When her mum had questioned her, Lizzie said she'd got an upset tummy, and put it down to eating a couple of bad prawns. She said she'd have an early night and hoped that she wouldn't keep them up going to the loo all night with a nasty dose of the runs! After saying goodnight, she waited a good three hours before she made a move.

Van Vebstriche...David Webster...whoever he was would be back, she was certain of that. He obviously had a very good idea where the second jewel was, because coupled with any other knowledge he'd gathered from his own research he'd also stolen their map. His first try in Horseshoe Woods to stop Lizzie had proved futile; his second attempt had been very close: third time he might just manage it!

The brass neck of the man, to have gone into hiding locally and then show up as a guest of the Axenthorpes! And she, Lizzie, had done nothing about it. Was it a race? Was she so taken by the quest for the jewels that she was becoming so obsessed with finding them that she was prepared to take actions above the law and her parents' wishes? But she'd been *chosen*, hadn't she? So was it because she was stubborn, thoughtless and downright single-minded? No: for good or bad, she'd been *chosen*. If she was going to be the one to make up for some great wrong committed hundreds of years ago, so be it. The Highwayman wanted to make amends for his actions, say sorry through her, and make good the bad, once and for all!

She heard her parents come up the stairs. Someone popped their head round her door to check she was all right, then the house fell quiet.

Lizzie quietly dressed herself. She put on her strongest walking shoes and her fleece, slung her bag over her shoulder and gave her glasses a huff and a polish. She was ready.

Eavesdrop, and you'll hear no good of yourself

Very gently, Lizzie eased the sash window up at the gable end of the house. Outside it was very quiet. A cloudy sky hid the moon now and then. She picked her way along the branch until she reached the semi-safety of the trunk. She heard a couple of people saying final goodbyes from the inn. She waited patiently. There was the noise of a car door slamming, the car starting up and then departing. All went quiet again. She climbed down the tree and went round to the back of the house, following the garden fence until she reached the graveyard. She had decided previously to skirt round the perimeter of the yard rather than creep through between the headstones. They could cause the most ghastly shadows, scaring you to death. She thought that she'd be scared enough that evening without starting off with a shot of adrenaline. Why is it that public places and churches can be perfectly nice when there's plenty of people around them during the day, yet suddenly turn into the most forbidding and unfriendly places at night or when there is nobody around? She pushed these thoughts to the back of her mind.

The moon appeared from behind the last clouds that were drifting to the north. Lizzie let out a relieved sigh. She was worried about using her torch near the village in case a late dog walker happened to see the beam and decided to investigate who was prowling around.

It meant going back on her tracks, but Lizzie had decided to make for the bridge over the Hazel as her starting point to be certain that she picked up the pathway to the 'Witches' Cauldron'. She'd used the bridge before when she'd 'visited' Agnes Smith, but tonight she'd be travelling in the opposite direction, away from Hazelthwaite.

She'd been in deep thought as she'd arrived at the well-kept fence and garden of Francesca Golightly. The dog jumped up from behind the fence, scaring her rigid. She could hear the

Doberman's claws pawing at the wooden panels. She could see the fence bowing under its ferocious attack. Lizzie froze. Then she heard Francesca open her patio doors. She heard her voice chastising the dog and calling it in.

'Trixie, what's the matter? Is someone there?' The dog growled menacingly, then threw its head back and started barking again.

The next thing that happened almost made Lizzie laugh out loud. There was a large bang against the other side of the fence as a rock or shoe hit it and a, 'Get in here, you stupid mutt, before I slap your ass!' rang out from a now clearly angry Francesca.

Lizzie heard the dog whimper all the way back down the garden. She then heard a very large painful yelp as it obviously received a slap around its rump as it entered the cottage. Poor beast had managed to get a wallop for being the guard-dog it had probably been bought for! Lizzie smiled with relief.

She moved quickly to the banks of the river. Before she could safely move off downstream she suddenly heard a car approaching the bridge. Got to get out of its headlights, thought Lizzie. Instead of moving off to the right she slid down the bank and out of sight under the bridge's arch. She got under cover none too soon. As she stood under the arch, the vehicle pulled up on the bridge. The voices of two men were speaking in subdued tones, but loud enough for her to catch the drift of their conversation.

'After what I said she'll try soon. I'll have to wait for a couple of days – even a week – to see if she'll appear.'

'You mustn't reveal your identity to her. If she gets an inkling of what's going on, I'm dead meat.'

'You sure are, Jimmy boy,' came the reply. 'You're in this up to your neck as much as I am. If the girl didn't know where to locate the second jewel, we'd have found it soon enough, and the others. We've lost one, but the rest are still worth a fortune on the market, even if it is the closed one, and I'm gonna make sure we get them. I know there are private collectors who'd give their right arm to own a bit of history like that.'

'Just make sure she doesn't see you, James,' said James Axenthorpe.

'Get on home, Jimmy boy, and leave the girl to me,' the other man said.

Lizzie now recognised the voices of both men. But James Axenthorpe mixed up with Webster…it still didn't make sense. And why had James Axenthorpe called David Webster 'James'? Who the hell was James when he was at home? she thought.

One of the men got out of the car and walked off in the direction of Hazelthwaite. The other started the car, drove over the bridge, turned around and retraced his steps up the hill. The vehicle was a 4x4 'off-roader'. Lizzie risked a peep as it drove up the road. She watched its lights turn to the right halfway up the hill and then disappear behind some densely planted Forestry Commission fir trees. She knew that the road David – no, James? – Webster had turned down finally led to the Witches' Cauldron!

Lizzie thought it was now safe to move off.

Webster stopped the car twenty or so yards down the forestry lane. He got out of the car and walked round to the rear. He opened the tailgate and took out a couple of warning signs stating that the road was closed, and a set of red and white painted boards which he set in slots of three heavy-based portable cones. The road now looked officially closed to any other vehicles. He doubted that the Forestry Commission would work in this area over the weekend, and now even the odd dog walker would be convinced to take another pathway. At least he had this angle sown up; all he needed do now was to find a suitable place to hide that overlooked the Witches' Cauldron. His plan was simple. He'd conceal himself, wait for the girl to show up, let her do the hard work and then take the jewel from her when she thought she was safe.

James Axenthorpe got back to the Highwayman's Perch twenty minutes after leaving Webster on the bridge in Hazelthwaite. Nobody had seen him go out and no one saw him return. For the moment he was off the hook. But he didn't like the thought that he now had to rely on someone else to help him totally escape, and Webster was too cocky by half! Something was bound to go wrong. He felt very uneasy – no, very scared!

The Highwayman had watched Lizzie's progress from her house to the bridge from a vantage point high on the church tower.

'So, Lizzie,' he muttered, 'tonight's the night, is it? Probably going to be a long one for me, then!' His eyes had narrowed when he'd seen her just miss being caught by the two men at the bridge. He knew exactly who they were, but of course he was powerless to intervene. Perhaps he could give them a nasty scare sometime? But now he must only keep an eye on Lizzie. He would have to summon up all his strength in case she needed him. For the moment she seemed to be coping with the challenge, but this was the calm before the inevitable storm. She'd face her worst nightmare soon enough!

Lizzie made good progress along the riverside. A reasonable pathway had been trodden by ramblers and dog walkers over many years as people had made the walk to and from the Witches' Cauldron. The moon, when it came out from behind light clouds, made the going even easier, and she was quite positive and pleased with herself when she saw Five Pines Holm outlined in the river. From here to the Cauldron would take about fifteen minutes. She took off her glasses and gave them a huff and a polish, pushed her hand through her hair and started walking again.

As she neared the Cauldron she could hear the water cascading down into the abyss as it dropped vertically about one hundred feet. The closer she got, the louder the crashing noise became.

As she rounded the last meandering bend of the Hazel, the moon appeared from behind the fast scudding clouds, and there in front of her the River Hazel suddenly left the land in a seething mass of white rapids into a huge hole in the ground. Over the hole on the opposite side to where she stood at the moment was an overhanging rocky crag. This was covered in thick trees and shrubs that all seemed to march downwards at crazy angles into the watery inferno. There were huge amounts of spray in the air. She hadn't thought about any of this. She hadn't even come to see it in daylight to suss out what she might do! Stupid!

How on earth was she going to get down? She hadn't thought of that either! If she did get down into the hole – where the hell was the jewel? How would she get back? The questions came at her thick and fast. The more she thought, the more she realised she didn't have an answer to any of them. This was the most ludicrous thing for a girl to do. Alone, in the middle of the night, in the middle of nowhere, with a madman out there somewhere ready to get her. She was beginning to get cold, and knew in her heart of hearts that the only way left was to retrace her steps home and admit defeat. She turned around, looking upwards – for some heavenly advice, presumably! The Highwayman's words came back to her. 'Do it for me, Lizzie, to give me peace.'

Lizzie unzipped her shoulder bag, took out her torch and shone it at the gap. Where the water poured down the precipice from ground level she could se no way to climb down. There were no footholds, nothing! It was just a sheet of water, flowing very quickly because the river was still swollen from all the extra rain they'd been having. If she were going to try and descend into the Witches' Cauldron it would have to be from the overhanging crag. She shone her torch upwards.

Webster saw Lizzie shine her torch from the Cauldron to the crag. From his vantage point on the hillside he could picture what was going through her mind. He imagined her fear. She was certainly a plucky girl. What on earth was driving her on?

Lizzie surveyed the trees that tumbled down the crag and down the hole on the opposite side of the Cauldron. She walked carefully round the mouth of the hole and started to climb onto an overhanging tree whose branches seemed to dip into the blackness. How was she going to manage the torch? She switched it off, putting it back in her bag. She would have to let the moon, which was now clear of the clouds, light her way. It sparkled on the crashing water.

She crawled along the branch until it started to bend. From this branch she managed to climb down to another smaller tree that was growing below the upper level of the ground, but which would still have had plenty of light during the day to encourage good foliage growth.

The water was now cascading directly behind her. She could feel the spray from it on her hair and fleece. The trunk and branches of the young oak were slippery, and more than once her hand slipped and she let out a little scream. She was more conscious of the huge drop behind and below her. One false slip with both hands, and she would be dashed on the unseen rocks below.

Webster had now lost sight of Lizzie. He couldn't even begin to imagine what hell she was going through.

Lizzie continued to make her way down the tree. How much further would she have to descend into the Witches' Cauldron? What was the clue she was looking for? No thoughts crossed her mind about getting out.

In one of those split seconds when things are taken out of your hands, and fate or someone from above takes control, the tree that Lizzie was climbing down, or rather clinging to for dear life, started to move. She screamed long and loud. The tree plunged down the hole. Her arms and legs gripped the trunk tightly. Her face was covered in the raging waterfall.

The recurring dream! She was drowning, falling…falling. Water filled her mouth and stung her eyes. She would die in the blackness; she couldn't yell for help as her mouth was full of water! She screamed inwardly for her mother. Then, as soon as it had started, the movement suddenly stopped – just as violently! Lizzie was totally unprepared for the falling to stop so suddenly and she was flung off the tree. The end of the trunk that Lizzie had been clinging to punctured the wall of torrential water and she was thrown onto a ledge behind it. As she looked at the wall of movement in front of her, she could see the jagged end of the topmost branches by her foot. The tree was wedged at a forty-five degree angle upwards. If she was to get out she would have to at least crawl up it. She would have to relive the fear of her face being pounded by the falling waters of the Hazel. Where would the tree take her? Would it support her weight? She looked around. The jewel wasn't here; there was no clue! God, this was the end! She started to cry.

Negative thoughts and deeds, Lizzie. Sitting there bawling her eyes out wasn't going to get her out! What had been that advice a teacher had given her once? 'Don't procrastinate, do it!'

At that moment in time, Lizzie didn't believe in anything. How could she? 'Desperate' wasn't a word that even began to sum up the situation she was in. She waited. She wasn't sure she had any courage left to summon up. She wiped her hands on her fleece, which was now so saturated it made matters worse, but it gave her something to do. She said out loud, in a voice that was drowned out by the raging torrent in front of her, 'I'm outa here!'

Shutting her eyes tightly, and gripping the trunk equally hard, she gave a mighty push outwards. Her head and shoulders broke through the wall of water. Slowly she moved up the tree, first pulling with her arms then pushing with her legs. The light from the moon that filtered down the shaft was the only thing that reassured her about what she was doing, and that the world was still there! When her head and shoulders were finally clear, she found that she could see the predicament she was in and realised just how lucky she'd been. The tree was wedged (she hoped) at a crazy angle against what looked like another ledge seven or eight feet above her. She pushed herself upwards. The tree started to give again.

'Oh, please no,' she prayed quietly. Lizzie waited again. She lay still, until the trunk stopped shaking, or she stopped shaking. She pushed again with her legs and pulled with her arms. Some of the broken branches jabbed her body and one badly grazed her face. She could feel the blood trickling from the cut. She froze, her eyes closed. She couldn't move. She didn't want to move. She was sobbing quietly and the tears mingled with blood from the gash on her cheek.

'Lizzie,' said a voice with quiet confidence, 'Lizzie, look up.'

She opened her eyes. From where she clung, on the narrow trunk over the chasm with water pulsing down behind her back and over her legs, this was the last person she thought she'd ever see again! He was sitting on the ledge three or four feet above her. He had one leg dangling over the chasm and the other tucked up with both hands clasped around a knee.

'Well, Lizzie, at least you're going in the right direction now,' he said, smiling. 'I know you're terrified, but look, you've only a few feet to go and then you're safe. What courage you've shown to get this far. You're not telling me a couple of pulls with your arms are going to stop you now! No; anyway, I've got total confidence in you.' The Highwayman smiled again.

'I can't move!' she wailed. 'You've got to help me, I can't get up there. I hurt all over, I'm bleeding and my side's started to hurt from the fall I've just had.' And she cried even more.

He waited for her sobs to stop, and between each of her deep intakes of breath said, 'Is that all? I thought for a moment you were in some sort of distress. I'll go now.'

Lizzie looked up again and wailed, 'Don't you go and leave me! I was only doing this for you. I've been through *hell* for you,' she said furiously.

'That's right, Lizzie Miller, get angry. You get up here and put me to rights! I deserve it,' said the Highwayman, in his most mocking of tones.

As he spoke, Lizzie had been inching up the trunk towards him. She'd get him all right! Very slowly her fingertips gripped the edge where he sat smiling at her.

'I hate you!' she snarled. She pushed up on an arm and then managed to swing her leg over onto the ledge.

Suddenly, with the extra down force of her body on the trunk exerted to push herself up onto the ledge, the trunk disappeared down into the blackness. She screamed and rolled over onto her back.

'There, Lizzie. Easy, wasn't it? Did I ever tell you the story when I robbed a stage full of—' But he never finished the sentence.

'If you were real you'd be dead meat!' Lizzie screamed at him, 'I've never been so scared in my life! I wanted my mum and all you did was laugh at me and say that I was hopeless.'

'Getting angry sometimes helps us to do things that we would normally find impossible. I couldn't help you physically, but I knew how to motivate you. I just got you angry a bit. Worked quite well, I should say. You're here on the ledge alive. What more do you want, girl? Anyhow I don't think I could stand being hanged again, do you?'

Lizzie suddenly laughed out loud, and then let all the tension out by crying bitterly.

The Jewel of St Matthew

The Highwayman sat looking at her. When she'd finished sobbing he pointed. She followed the finger. It was only now she realised that there was a shaft of light on the cave floor.

'Where is this place?' Lizzie asked.

'It's an old hiding hole I used to use when… well, let's say when I wasn't too popular in the local community. The shaft leads to the hillside above the crag. Even to this day, nobody knows of its existence. It's very well covered by undergrowth. But as you can see just enough of a hole to let a moonbeam in. When you reach halfway up the shaft, which isn't difficult to climb, I promise you, you'll see an exposed clump of tree roots. I suggest you stop there for a few moments, Lizzie…to catch your breath. All the best, my dear,' he said and disappeared. The cave that Lizzie crouched in suddenly became a few degrees warmer.

'I wish he wouldn't do that,' she whispered. She looked back momentarily at the Cauldron, turned away and started to climb up to the surface. The going was easy as he had said, and halfway up she was able to use her torch to pick out the large clump of roots. She jammed her back against the earthy side of the tunnel and rummaged around with her hand. Her fingertips suddenly picked up something soft. She pulled the little leather bag with the thong that secured it from behind some stubborn and twisted roots. In the light of her torch she undid the thong and emptied the contents into her hand, and there was the second jewel.

The Jewel of St Matthew shone ruby red in the shaft of light!

'It's beautiful!' Lizzie gasped. She placed the jewel back into the leather pouch, unzipped her shoulder bag and put it in. By the time she'd reached the brambles and nettles at the shaft's entrance she'd completely forgotten the ordeal she'd just been through. As she neared the top, Lizzie turned off the torch. She knew that David Webster or whoever he was might be watching; so from now on, no light, and hopefully as little sound as possible.

The entrance of the shaft to the cave had deposited Lizzie on the opposite bank of the Hazel, so instead of crashing through the undergrowth, which might give her position away, she decided to follow the opposite bankside path. She'd have to take special care not to stumble on anyone, as this side of the Hazel wasn't well known to her. She had walked the route to the Five Pines Holm several times with Mabel and Amy, but always from the other path.

The moon had clouds scurrying past it once more, and occasionally she had to stop for a few minutes before it lit the way for her again. She was now very cold. Her clothes were wet through and covered by earth and mud from the climb up the pipe. She knew her face was a mess from the graze she had. Her side hurt a lot now from the enormous jolt she'd received when she'd been thrown from the tree onto the ledge. But apart from those things life couldn't be better.

At night it's amazing how sharp your senses become to sound, light and smell. What was that? She heard a scratch, or was it a quick rasping sound, then she smelt – smoke! Someone had lit a cigarette. Where were they? She was opposite the holm, the little island in the Hazel. Is that where he was hiding? She supposed he had some kind of dingy or inflatable so that he could row to either bank. Quite clever, because he could keep an eye out on each bank. Lose a little time rowing across but if the unsuspecting person didn't know he was there, no problem. But if your gonna play commando games you don't light up a fag, mate. Lizzie said all these things to herself to pluck up courage to move on. Very carefully and quietly she made progress past the island until she was sure she was clear of human danger. She stopped and listened for a good five minutes. Nobody came. No one was following her. She quickened her step, when the moon allowed her to, and finally arrived at the bridge.

The church clock announced that it was five o'clock. Already there was the faintest glimmer of the approaching dawn. Soon the earliest workers would be going about their business, even on a Sunday. The jewel had to be replaced before the vicar arrived for the first service.

The vehicle moved quietly along the road. He hadn't put on the lights and had coasted the 4x4 down the hill. By pure chance he'd seen Lizzie half-crouching in the undergrowth by the bridge. Then she'd slid out of sight down the bank, and presumably waded across the river, even though it was flowing fairly quickly. She'd reappeared on the other bank and run off behind the gardens in the direction of the church. Webster drove the car across the bridge. He parked it in the church lay-by and climbed over the graveyard wall with a canvas bag slung over his shoulder.

Lizzie decided that she'd risk going home. It would be great to have a wash and change of clothes. Certain things she would be able to explain to her parents, like her filthy kit, but if her mum actually found her in her sodden and disgusting state…well, explanations only went so far. She could explain away the graze by saying she'd had another nightmare, fallen out of bed and bashed her cheek, but she didn't want to disturb them.

She climbed the tree and opened the window. The house was silent, thank goodness! She used the cold water tap to fill the washbasin, which the previous owners had had plumbed into the bedroom, to clean herself up. This was a stroke of very good thinking on her part, as the hot water system when it was used caused an untold racket. The gash wasn't too bad but needed a plaster. The bruise on her side was another matter. Not only was it painful it was turning nasty shades of black and blue.

She made a pile of the dirty wet clothes and shoved them under her bed. These could be dried and brushed later, out of her mother's sight and then put in the dirty linen basket in due course for a proper wash.

Now that she had washed and dried herself and put on fresh jeans and T-shirt she felt a different person. Lizzie took the little leather pouch from her shoulder bag and put it in her right-hand jeans pocket. She then shoved the shoulder bag into the deepest recess of her wardrobe. That would have to be dried and cleaned later as well!

Before she went downstairs, she remembered to shut and lock her bedroom window and gave her bed a good rough and tumble so that it had looked slept in. She threw her duvet on the floor in a heap. If either of her parents came into her room now, they'd think that she'd woken early and gone for a walk. Lizzie had done this before and they'd think nothing of it. She looked around one more time. Everything looked fine; a typical untidy Lizzie room. She peeked round her bedroom door. The house was still quiet. Well, not quite. Was that really her Dad snoring? God, what a noise – worse than a diesel engine at full blast! Carefully, she crept quietly downstairs, keeping close to the wall to avoid the creaking treads, and let herself out of the kitchen door.

Cat on a Red-hot Ruby

Lizzie paused for a few seconds at the door. The house remained quiet. She made her way around the courtyard using what shadows she could to conceal her from any prying eyes and arrived at the stable door. It was silent when she entered. Only a mouse, from a tiny hole in the wainscoting skirting, witnessed her press on the secret panel. It stood on its hind legs, rubbing its front paws across its whiskers as it watched her pass into the passageway and silently disappear. She allowed the panel to shut behind her this time, and switched on her torch. Lizzie started to make her way confidently down the passage following the bright light beaming out ahead of her.

On the previous occasion she hadn't used the passageway all the way to the church, and consequently hadn't realised how many twists and turns there were to negotiate. She passed the priest's hole, concealing its grisly secret, and remembered vividly her escape from the Highwayman's clutches. It seemed like an age ago now. When she neared the end of the passage she saw in the torch beam the slope as she approached the church. The torch picked out the lever that opened the panel. It was immediately to the right of the wooden wainscoting and set into the wall.

Lizzie heard the church clock strike six. She should have about an hour to replace the jewel before anyone arrived to open the church for the early Communion service. She listened at the door panel. Nothing stirred inside the nave.

It was a quarter to six when the vicar, the Reverend Martin Leonard, arrived at the lychgate. It was already a beautiful morning. He had seen a couple of people having an early morning jog and they'd waved and exchanged hellos. He opened the gate, and crunched up the gravel path, pausing to look at the parish notice board. He gave himself a mental reminder to update the information that was displayed on the rather faded pieces of paper, unlocked the door and went inside. He strode down the aisle, bowed before the altar and crossed to the vestry.

He unlocked the door and went inside. The snib didn't catch on the locking plate as he closed the door, so it swung back on its hinges to lie open by five or six inches. The vicar sat down at his desk and began to make some alterations to his morning service notes.

A few minutes after the Reverend Leonard had opened the church, Sexton, the church cat, appeared at the door as if by magic. He rubbed the side of his nose and head against the door, almost pushing it closed, then with a front paw he made a gap just big enough for his head then his body to slip round into the interior. He did this on tiptoe as only cats can. He looked around and then picked his way under the rows of chairs to the pews in the front few rows. He sharpened his claws on a footrest, dislodging it in the process and then jumped onto the seat. He walked down the red-cushioned pew and settled himself just under the niche that held the Axenthorpe Icon. The green jewel glowed in a shaft of early morning sunlight that slanted through the stained glass of one of the narrow windows.

Sexton raised an ear at the noise coming from the vestry but didn't show any signs of moving to see what it was. After all, a long night's prowling deserved some real rest. He got up, stretched, turned round twice within his own length to reassure himself that nothing was there and lay down. He shut his eyes, let out a contented sigh-cum-purr, flicked his long tail over his front paws and head and fell sound asleep.

Lizzie pulled the lever. The panel slid aside. Her mouth dropped open and her eyes widened. There with his back to the panel stood the vicar. She stepped back, pulled the lever and closed her eyes. When she opened them she was standing in pitch black. She let out a sigh of relief.

The vicar turned and looked at the wall, then around the church. What had made the noise? He looked across at the Icon. The jewel was still intact and he could just make out the slim beams of light criss-crossing in front of it. As he paced back to the vestry he told himself that even he was starting to feel the strain of the past few weeks and not to be so silly!

The 'Highwayman' watched the vicar's progress to the vestry from where he stood concealed behind the door to the tower steps.

Lizzie heard the vicar walk across the flagstones to the vestry. She pulled the lever once more. The 'Highwayman' looked in utter astonishment at Lizzie who stood crouched in the doorway.

That was it, she was going to replace the jewel! The little fool didn't realise the niche containing the Icon was alarmed! He'd have to stop her before it was too late! He moved forward. She couldn't see him for the moment.

'Yoo-hoo, Vicar!' cooed a woman's voice, 'are you they-ah?'

Lizzie recognised the voice as Francesca Golightly's. She stepped back into the passage and pulled the lever. The panel closed again. Didn't anyone sleep in on a Sunday morning in Hazelthwaite? she thought.

The 'Highwayman' also had to retreat hastily back to the tower. He pulled the door close to him, leaving just enough of it open for one of his eyes to follow Francesca's progress down the aisle.

The Reverend Leonard came out of the vestry to greet her. 'Hello, Francesca, you're up bright and early,' he said.

'Yes,' she replied, 'I've brought the flowers for the eleven o'clock service. Can I leave them in water in the vestry? I'll arrange them after Communion. I always like to take the dog for an early walk, thought I'd kill two birds with one stone.'

The Highwayman also considered killing two birds with one stone and then thought better of it.

'Of course you can, Francesca. I've finished what I want to do so I'll walk you down the road,' he replied.

Lizzie heard all of this, and heard Francesca fiddle around for a few minutes in the vestry. Then they both left. The door of the church was given a firm bang to shut it then there was silence. Lizzie pulled the lever. She waited, to make sure everything was still. After a quick look all around she confirmed she was alone. She saw Sexton lying sound asleep on the pew just below the Icon, so she wasn't quite alone!

She smiled as he moved both of his paws to cover his head. He twitched his back legs as the dream he was having obviously involved running away from a very large dog! A bad dream? Lizzie could teach him a thing or two about those.

As she stood wondering how she might replace the jewel, the decision was suddenly made for her! The shafts of light from the stained glass window that fell on the Icon dimmed and clouded over, as if a shadow had been thrown over them. She looked around. The 'Highwayman' was advancing up behind her, his hand outstretched to snatch the ruby jewel that she held between the thumb and forefinger of her right hand!

In his hurry to grab the jewel he tripped on the prayer hassock that Sexton had earlier dislodged and his hand hit Lizzie's bruised side. She uttered a piercing scream, at the same time throwing the jewel high into the air as her hand was thrust upwards. As she stumbled backwards, her left hand jabbed through the security beams that protected the Icon in the niche.

The 'Highwayman' looked aghast. Lizzie didn't even know what she had done until all hell broke loose. Sirens howled. Bells rang and lights were triggered off outside the building. Before either of them could react (which could only have been for a fraction of a second), they both felt extremely cold. It was as if someone had trodden on their graves.

The 'Highwayman' turned and fled as fast as he could towards the vestry.

Lizzie threw herself across the front pew and rolled over sideways into the passageway. Her hand fumbled for the lever as her side caught yet another bang from the fall and hurt immediately. The panel slid shut just as the vicar dashed back into the church to investigate why the alarm was ringing.

The jewel reached the top of its ascent and began dropping towards the floor. It was just about to crash to the floor when an unseen gloved hand gently caught it. The Highwayman thought that were he to live again, perhaps he would try cricket as a living, as he was making quite a habit of catching things at the last second!

Now Sexton knew all about danger, and the cold grip that had suddenly lifted his slumbering body alerted all his senses. He felt himself rising from his comfortable seat and then being replaced on the pew. This was too much for him! He suddenly reared up, arching his back and spitting violently. He reached upwards on his hind legs towards the niche's beams.

The Reverend Leonard threw open the interior doors just in time to see the cat, standing with his paws outstretched, back bowed against the niche containing the Axenthorpe Icon.

'I'll swing for you, Sexton, one of these days, I really will!' he shouted at the confused puss. 'Look what you've done – set off the alarm! We'll have the world and his wife here in a minute. What are you like?' He picked up Sexton and gave him a hug. Sexton returned this show of affection and purred loudly in his arms.

Whilst stroking Sexton he suddenly realised that something on the cushion was sparkling at him. There, where Sexton had lain, was the Ruby of St Matthew!

The Reverend Leonard looked at the cat. The cat looked at Reverend Leonard, and they both looked down at the jewel.

'Sexton, what have you been up to?'

At first the vicar wasn't sure what he'd found. But after picking up the shining object and raising his eyes to the Icon, he realised that he was holding the second very precious stone!

The bells and sirens had only been ringing for a minute or so when he finally came to his senses, rushed to the vestry and tapped in the code to silence the alarm. A phone was already ringing on his desk. He knew who would be on the end of the line. Picking up the phone, he answered the questions from the security firm correctly, got the new code numbers and punched them onto the keypad. He also said that there was no need for any further action to be taken… and no, they didn't need a police car to come to the village. The church cat had triggered the alarm! He thanked them for their prompt attention and rang off. Before retracing his steps, he switched off the alarm, giving him access to the niche.

He walked back into the nave and pressed a button that was located in the pulpit. A double piece of security that only he knew about and only he would transfer to a new vicar.

By now, most of the village had reached the church to find out what had set off the alarm. Could they help? Was there any damage? Was he hurt? Anything anyone could do?

He lifted down the precious little picture from the niche, turned to the assembled crowd and announced, 'I really have no explanation about what has happened in Hazelthwaite these last few weeks. Many things seem to have no answer at all. The vicar and Agnes Smith's death can only be guessed at, the sightings of a Highwayman around the locality can only be hearsay or wives' tales, and apart from the odd educated theory, even the police don't have any clues.' He cleared his throat, struggling for more words. Usually he had no trouble picking the right thing to say; it was what he was trained to do. 'Finding the emerald in the Icon was, we all thought, a miracle, but', and at this point he held up the ruby to the villagers, 'words really fail me for what I've just found on the pew here under Sexton.'

There were quiet gasps. Faces were completely astonished.

Reverend Leonard continued in subdued tones, 'I literally picked him up, and there it was on the seat!'

Very carefully he placed the jewel in its rightful place, and slowly, whether it was a trick of the light or whatever, the painting showing the area of St Matthew slowly recovered its original glory.

On seeing this, the Highwayman, who'd come back to watch the proceedings, moved off from where he had been standing close by the vicar.

'That's strange,' said the vicar. 'Is it me, or has the temperature gone up in here? I suddenly feel warmer.' He failed to notice the slight discolouration of the church carpet where the Highwayman had stood. (Much later he would try and have the patch cleaned, but with no success at all.)

All this time Lizzie had kept still in the passageway. She hardly dared breathe. She heard the vicar say that the Communion service would be half an hour late, as it was such a special morning. He said he would try and advertise a special dedication service for eleven o'clock. Lizzie heard voices say that he had no need to do that, as they would soon spread the word... No need to worry at all!... And the church would be full that morning.

As she heard people start to move around, she switched on her torch and made her way back to the stable. Nobody was in the courtyard or kitchen. So she slipped across to the gates in the arch and opened them. When she got into the kitchen she made 'getting cups of tea' noises that would let her parents know that she was up and about. She took them tea and biscuits in bed. They both seemed very tired, and Lizzie was surprised that they hadn't heard the alarm. He'd heard something, her dad had said, but had rolled over and gone back to sleep.

Lizzie told them that she'd got up early and been for a walk as it was nice, and then had heard a racket coming from the church. She didn't know what it was about, and didn't go to investigate, as she thought they'd appreciate a cuppa in bed as they rarely got the opportunity to do so. However, she'd seen lots of other people dash to the church, and assumed that all was well.

As he rushed from the nave to the vestry, the 'Highwayman' had started to take off his disguise as he made his escape. He realised the danger in this, because at any moment he might be seen, but had taken a gamble that anybody rushing to help would make for the front porch door. The bag that he'd left in the church tower was a common enough design and certainly untraceable to him, so would no doubt be thought to have been left behind by a careless child who had visited the Flower Festival. People left things all the time, and he was sure that it would fetch something or other at the next church fête. An event, *he* would definitely be missing!

He had opened the loo window adjacent to the vestry, finished taking off the rest of has disguise, rolled everything into his cape to make it look like a backpack and climbed out through the window. As people had rushed up the path to see what was going on, he'd slowly slipped through a gap in the honeysuckle hedge, made his way to the 4x4 and driven off. Nobody had noticed him. If they had seen the vehicle, he'd have gladly bet that they wouldn't be able to describe the make and colour, let alone the registration!

Again, he and the girl had had lucky escapes. He wondered how James Axenthorpe had made out. Well, no jewel, no source to finance his gambling and the huge debts he had run up – that was his lookout! He, the 'Highwayman', had risked enough for him already. It really was time for him to look after himself and to do a serious long-term vanishing trick. Let everything cool down. He would be back in good time.

The Highwayman story was always a good way of scaring the locals. Keeping them away from things that did not concern them. When the Highwayman was around, people died, and he knew that that fact alone would help him secure the other precious stones in the not too distant future.

Except for Lizzie! Now, she was a challenge. How had a teenager managed to recover two of the most important artefacts of the area with seemingly no assistance from anyone and virtually no knowledge of the area or the background of the Highwayman's story? Very strange! But thwart him she had done – twice, and in only a couple of months of moving to Hazelthwaite. It was as if, unseen forces were leading her! He halted this train of thought; surely she couldn't be in contact... no, it was impossible, it was too preposterous... With a little information she'd got lucky, dam lucky. But there were still four more jewels to locate. Lots more research to do. Once done, that would leave him well placed to recover them. To hell with the Axenthorpes! He'd look for the stones himself. Yes, the jewels would wait a little longer in their hiding places until he returned...

And Finally…

Lizzie and her parents walked round the corner to the church. It seemed as if the whole village had turned out for the service. It was a beautiful September morning.

A silver-grey Mercedes Benz, parked in the lay-by, announced that the Axenthorpes were already in the building.

Mabel and Amy were standing by the lychgate. Mabel eyed Lizzie. 'You've done it again, haven't you?' she said, her face sparkling.

Lizzie returned the look. 'No,' she lied, 'I know as much about the jewel's return as you do.' Her hands were in front of her, so she couldn't cross her fingers. Another lie – and just as she was about to go into church. Well, what's new? she thought. What else could she say?

If the other stones were to be found and returned to their rightful resting place, she would have to do certain things on her own. The Highwayman had demanded as much, and she believed that he would not appear to her again if she broke her word. She wouldn't let him down, but she hated the deceit, even though she was helping the church, the Axenthorpes and the Highwayman find his final peace. She decided all the other things on the opposing side of the equation, which included Webster, would be bridges to be crossed as and when, until the last jewel was found!

They went in together and sat down near the back of the church on three vacant wooden chairs that had hassocks set in to a little shelf near the floor. The hour's service was punctuated by a wonderful sermon delivered by a self-assured and happy Reverend Leonard. Lizzie could see by the nods and smiles of the congregation that they agreed with everything that was said. He even mentioned the Highwayman, and wondered what he would have thought almost two hundred years further on. Perhaps he would be pleased to think that some of the things that he'd done wrong had been put to rights, and that the jewels' return might help his soul by counterbalancing for the brutal murder of the vicar so long ago in Hazelthwaite.

At the end of the sermon the congregation had prayed, and after singing the final hymn, and receiving the Blessing, had started to drift away in small groups or in family parties.

As Jane and John Miller thanked the vicar for a lovely service, they turned to Mabel and Amy's respective parents and asked them for lunchtime drinks.

The girls left their folks and walked down to the Gallows Oak. Its leaves were beginning to change colour, and some had already started to fall. Mabel remarked about this and said that this was an indication that they could be in for a long, cold winter. Lizzie wondered if Bendy and Donna might be allowed to come to Hazelthwaite for Christmas, but after the summer fiasco maybe not. One could but ask...

Amy remarked that not only were the leaves turning brown and falling, but she was also feeling exceptionally chilly, even though the sun was quite strong. Mabel nodded in agreement.

Lizzie looked up in to the mighty oak and there, sitting on a still quite leafy branch, was the Highwayman. He was looking down at her, smiling. He touched his tricorn hat to her and winked. She in turn took off her glasses and gave them a huff and a polish, pushed a hand through her blonde hair, and the four of them settled down to watch the final cricket match of the season. It could be interesting, as the fat batsman had been promoted to opener!

Stand and Deliver!

The Highwayman had waited patiently in a small, straggly copse of Scots fir trees, which stood beside the rough, rutted track that was the old road from Edinburgh to Newcastle. He had lain crouched under a flat slate rock, which had been placed on top of two large boulders, thousands of years ago. He'd been waiting for several rain-lashed hours. The shelter had afforded him little or no protection from the torrential rain that seemed to totally engulf this desolate piece of moorland.

He'd chosen this particular spot to wait for the stagecoach for two reasons. Firstly, it would come from a northerly direction, and would have to slow to a snail's pace to negotiate a sharp bend before the steep slope that the track followed over the hilltop; and secondly, because he'd used this exact spot to hold up three previous stagecoaches. He thought the local militia would not expect him to use this location for a fourth time, as it was so near to the next village. One of the larger cottages had been converted to an inn by the current stage company, so that passengers could sleep for the night and to allow the driver to pick up fresh horses for the following morning's journey onward to Newcastle.

The passengers would be feeling happy and relieved to have travelled so far without interruption. When they realised they were only a mile or so from the hamlet of Littledale-on-the-Water, they would be breathing huge sighs of relief, to think that their coach had not been held up. He could hear them in the cramped confines of the carriage saying things like, 'Not long now'... 'Weather too bad tonight, even for highwaymen'... 'No one in their right mind would try anything so close to the inn, now would they?' He smiled to himself: little did they know!

He looked at his pocket watch; still no sign of the stagecoach. He could just make out the time, half past ten. Half an hour late, but anything could have happened: a broken wheel, horse gone lame, passengers been sick! This section of the road, if you could call it that, was notorious for all sorts of things going wrong with a stagecoach, especially across this moorland waste. The parish overseers were bad enough at maintaining the roads in the towns and villages, let alone desolate stretches of forbidding countryside like this.

Then, through the driving rain, which now seemed to be blowing almost horizontally into the Highwayman's eyes, he saw two twinkling lights in the distance. They disappeared then reappeared again as the stagecoach made its slow and jolting progress between the stands of pine trees along the rutted track across Littledale Moor. The driver would soon have to rein in the horses to a walk to negotiate the bend.

Tom Bennett pulled down the mask to cover his upper face. His eyes now looked like fierce slits. He tied his black scarf round his mouth, adjusted his tricorn hat forwards over his head and mounted his coal black horse. Just for now he stayed hidden in the copse of trees. He could hear the voice of the driver, shrieking above the noise of the wind at his horses to keep moving. He heard the crack of the whip, the clatter of the wheels as iron treads hit stone and shingle, and the squeaking and jolting of the heavy springs.

The two forward pointing lanterns came level with the Highwayman. He could barely make out the outlines of the driver and guard, whose bodies were almost bent double against the weather. The carriage moved slowly past. No rear guard, thank God, and no one riding the cheap seats atop the coach. All he could make out on the roof were the shapes of the luggage and one large trunk lashed to the rails. He had no doubt in his mind that he could deal with the two at the front. After a journey like they'd had this night, they'd do anything to carry on peacefully.

The guard and driver weren't the problem. But he wondered if anyone would be brave enough to take him on from within the stagecoach's interior. Some young pup eager to seek the affection of some silly wench he had met on the journey... or perhaps an old army officer stupid enough to think he could relive some former glory... or, more frightening to Tom, four or five of Lord Axenthorpe's militia in the coach, just in case he should rob it! That certainly did not bear thinking about!

The stagecoach was slowing for the bend on the incline. The noise from the wind and rain was deafening, mixed with the curses from the driver and the noise of the horses and the wheels clattering on the stony path. The Highwayman rode casually past the coach, behind a row of pine trees that grew parallel to that stretch of the track, rounded the end of them and at the steep bend, where the stagecoach would be moving at its slowest, brought his horse to a halt.

He sat waiting patiently in the middle of the road until the stagecoach drew close enough for him to shout the time-honoured words.

As the driver looked up for a brief glimpse of the road (for in this weather he tended to let the horses follow the track by instinct) a huge flash of lightening lit up the sky. There, before the lead pair of horses, was the Highwayman. The two frightened animals not expecting to see anything, reared up, wild-eyed. They moved about in an unsettled fashion. The driver tried to settle them but the fear of the lead pair had spread to the others, and the driver was finding it difficult to keep them under control.

Both mother-of-pearl handled pistols were raised and cocked. Above the sound of the wind and the constant beat of the rain, the Highwayman calmly announced, 'Good evening, gentlemen! Not a pleasant night for this, for me or you, but all the same, stand and deliver!'

The driver held on to the sodden reins tightly. He could almost feel them biting into the skin of his hands through the gauntlets that he wore. The Highwayman didn't move. The two stagecoach company employees saw the sinister outline of the pistols poised and ready, and that was enough for them. The journey had been atrocious, what with the fat Scotsman they were carrying being more than scathing about their best endeavours to get him and his fellow passengers to their destination on time, in the weather the worst they'd ever known – and now this! Could it get any worse? One thing was for sure; they weren't going to die this night if they could help it! They both put their hands in the air and waited for the Highwayman's next command.

The Highwayman motioned with his pistols for the driver and guard to dismount from the high bench seat that offered no protection from the foul weather. They did so. The guard left his blunderbuss under the seat. He'd already decided not to play hero and the gun probably wouldn't have worked on a night like this anyway. The powder would have been soaked hours ago and it was more likely to have gone off in his face than hit a robber at ten paces. They stood, thoroughly tired and dejected by the stagecoach's front wheel. The driver wiped a drenched caped arm across his face and spat something foul to the ground.

A side window of the stagecoach opened, letting out a small amount of dimly lit lantern light from the coach's interior. A man's head appeared and looked round. The head was covered with a large powdered wig.

The man cursed the weather then said, 'Driver, what in hell's name have we stopped for this time? The inn can't be that far away. Not another problem with the accursed axle, is it? This coach is older than I am; I shall be complaining to your employers when we finally arrive in Newcastle. Ye've no heard the last of this, my man!' The driver shrugged his shoulders at him and raised his eyebrows.

'How dare ye?' the man continued, 'I'll not be looked at like that–'

The sentence was never finished, as a huge flash of lightning suddenly revealed the pistol that was pointing at the side of his head. His mouth dropped open and his eyes widened. The heavy rain had started to clog the wig, and a little of the man's white face make-up had started to run.

The Highwayman approached him and shut the man's mouth by gently pushing the pistol up under his chin. He beckoned the driver and guard over to him. He took the pistol from under the man's chin, and after asking them both to turn round, he pressed the guns into their backs most uncomfortably.

He then said very matter-of-factly, 'I want you, sir, and any other passengers who are inside with you to climb down and then face the coach, putting your hands behind your backs where I can see them.' He continued, 'Failure to comply with these very straightforward instructions will result in the driver, and then you, my fat friend, being shot.' He said nothing else.

The man almost fell out of the coach, missing his footing as he did so. A much older gentleman, helping down a strikingly beautiful woman who held the hand of a little girl, followed the large, loud-mouthed man. All four passengers were terrified.

The Highwayman apologised for the inconvenience, but explained to them of his need for a comfortable bed that evening as well as them, he would like to lighten the coach's load of any money, gold or anything else they thought that was precious to them. Of course, once they were unburdened of this extra weight they would arrive at their destination so much sooner!

The guard was forced to hold his hat out for the passengers to contribute to the Highwayman's 'wages' for the evening. He did so very willingly, as the pistol was now hurting his back and he cursed the loud-mouthed man for taking his time looking through his pockets.

Suddenly the Scotsman spoke up. 'Ye'll no get away with this! I'm Lord Sanderson from the Edinburgh Court of Session. Ye'll be hunted down and hanged like a dog, sah!'

'Bravely said, Your Lordship,' mocked the Highwayman, 'but I value my skin too much to be caught by the likes of you, the militia or anyone else for that matter. Incidentally, the rather large bulge in your waistcoat pocket, My Lord–' the Highwayman pointed to the lump– 'do you know, I think you're being less than honest with me, and you a judge!'

The driver and guard grinned. The judge threw a large purse on the ground. The Highwayman tutted and motioned with his pistols for the guard to pick it up. The guard did so hurriedly. He detected that the Highwayman was getting a little edgy with the judge's attitude and he didn't want to make matters worse. In fact, the way the judge was acting, he was going the right way to receiving a heavenly blessing, not before time and good riddance!

'Thank you, my good man,' said the Highwayman, 'and now, driver, unhitch your horses from the coach, if you please.'

The driver did as he was told. The Highwayman put the purse and the judge's other belongings into his saddlebag and gave the tricorn hat back to the guard. The guard was staggered to see the rest of the belongings returned to him. The Highwayman put his finger over his mouth so that the guard would say nothing.

'Give them back their belongings when you reach the inn. I suggest you do this discreetly, when the judge is out of earshot, perhaps when he's had a few glasses of the landlord's brandy.' The guard nodded. He then told them all to get back into the stagecoach, which they did without further ado.

The Highwayman mounted his horse and trotted over to the stagecoach door. He bent over and looked into the crowded interior. 'Friends,' he said in a pleasant voice, 'it has been most valuable doing business with you. Don't alight from the coach for fully five minutes. My colleague in crime, who is, at this very minute covering my every move from the rock outcrop yonder, will expect me to ride off without any hindrance or any thought of anyone watching my departure. To do so could be fatal. I'm sure you understand. I'll bid you goodnight and safe journey to Littledale. Gentlemen, mam, adieu.'

The fat judge shouted after him from the safety of the coach, 'We'll meet again, rogue. Of that you can be sure!'

The Highwayman rode off in the direction of Greywater Scar.

Five minutes later, much to the judge's annoyance, the driver got down from the coach's interior; recovered the horses, which had wandered up the hill and hitched them to the carriage. The Edinburgh to Newcastle service resumed its journey to Littledale-on-the-Water, arriving at the inn three-quarters of an hour late.

The innkeeper was not surprised that the service was late due to the terrible conditions, but he was horrified to hear that the Highwayman had held up the stage less than a mile away in exactly the same spot.

'He's getting too cocky by half,' he blustered.

'What can be done about it, even at this late hour?' whined the judge.

'Nothin', Your Honour, Your Worship,' the innkeeper replied. 'He'll be clean away by now, any tracks washed away by the rain. He'll know the area like the back of his hand, and probably have several hideouts. The local militia has tried to find out from local people who it is, but they all stay quiet when they mention the Highwayman. It's as if the ground just swallows him up!'

The judge replied, 'Who's the local landowner? How many troops in his militia, did you say?'

'That would be Lord Axenthorpe, owns Axenthorpe Hall. Lives about ten miles further on. He retains about ten full-time men and say, another fifteen or so who work his land. But they're not as good as…' The innkeeper went no further. Then he added, 'Folks 'roon 'ere don' take kindly to militia and do-gooders pokin' their noses in local affairs!'

The judge snorted. 'Seems like folk around this whole area are a lawless bunch. Weel, let me tell ye, my good fellow, he's met his match wi' me this night. No, he'll no get away wi' robbing Lord Sanderson.'

'I can see you're a stout and fine upstanding gentleman, an' no mistake,' the landlord mocked.

'That I am,' preened the judge. 'I will speak to Lord Axenthorpe pairsonally tomorrow. Driver, arrange a detour, as we make for Newcastle in the morn. No one will mind. I think we need to deal with this scallywag once and for all.'

As the judge chatted with the innkeeper and took large mouthfuls of chicken leg and vast gulps of ale, all accompanied by even vaster belches, the guard walked over to a table that had been placed near to the welcoming fire.

The old gentleman, the lady and the young girl had sat quietly eating their supper before retiring for the night. It was when the judge got to folk being lawless in this area that the guard very carefully placed his upturned tricorn hat in the middle of their table. The three passengers looked at him in bewilderment. Like the Highwayman before, the guard had his finger on his mouth. He slowly drew his handkerchief away from his hat. They looked on in amazement as they saw what the cloth had hidden; they all wanted to blurt out their thanks, but the guard had kept his finger jammed against his lips, shook his head in the negative, and winked. They understood!

The Highwayman had given back their personal treasures and only taken money and the judge's belongings. They didn't agree with stealing one little bit, but perhaps he'd got what he'd deserved. He'd been an awful travelling companion with filthy habits, despite his high and mighty position. It was the old man who recognised influence, and the judge had plenty of that! He was not a man to be meddled with.

The old gent had a sneaking respect for this upstart Highwayman: bad, yes, but not all bad! He'd also noticed that his daughter had blushed when he'd been near to her. He had cut quite a dash in his black attire even though he'd been soaking wet. Perhaps it was the cool, calm and assured tones of his voice that had captivated her. He would never know, because he would never ask her opinion about this night!

If the judge managed to have the Highwayman arrested, then he would be a dead man. The judge would have his revenge, most certainly. The old man lit his pipe thoughtfully. His daughter and granddaughter had said goodnight and had made their way upstairs to rest.

The inn did not offer the most comfortable accommodation, the rooms being small and smoky from the wood-burning fires, and the only thing that might make them sleep this night would be total fatigue. The old gent had told his daughter that he would go to bed as soon as he had finished his pipe. She had urged him one more time not to be too long, and he had told her not to fuss.

The judge was the last to retire, or rather stumble up the stairs to bed, as he had consumed half a bottle of brandy on top of all the ale he had drunk. When he had finally made his way to his room, he tripped over the chamber pot and fell straight onto the end of the bed in a bloated star shape and went straight to sleep. His snoring could be heard all over the inn that night!

The Villa at Greywater Scar

He had ridden, for most of the journey at full gallop, to Greywater Scar. The Highwayman had picked his way through the thickest pine forests with no bridle or cart tracks to mark the way.

The storm had ceased and now small, broken clouds scudded across the crescent shaped moon, driven by a stiff breeze. He was tired, wet and freezing cold. He rode slowly to where the trees thinned at the edge of the forest that led to Greywater Scar.

At the forest's fringe was a large open area of ground that dropped away to a vertical cliff of about two hundred feet. As you looked east of the cliff, there lay the meandering valley of the Greywater. A waterfall thundered down the cliff to fill Greywater Lake. The name 'Scar' had been given to this particular hidden place by the Highwayman as a tribute to the forbidding, rocky outcrops below it. It looked especially forlorn in the appalling weather he'd just experienced. Occasionally the whole valley would be filled with low mist, and then you might just see the tops of the pine trees, which ringed the margin of the lake and marched up the valley sides.

On the open stretch of ground, between the forest edge and the cliff, stood a perfectly kept secret – well, almost.

A Roman villa, perhaps the most northerly building of its type still in reasonable preservation, but dilapidated nonetheless, sprawled out in front of him, lit by the moon.

He watched the building carefully for a full ten minutes or so. It seemed that none of the traps he had set had been touched or triggered off. It was virtually impossible for anyone to approach the villa except from the direction that the Highwayman had taken. The cunningly hidden devices would have immediately alerted him had anybody tried to do so. However, after he'd been away for a few days he always waited patiently for any sign of life before entering the outer arched quadrangle.

All looked peaceful. An owl hooted somewhere from the

valley below. He dismounted, and led his horse to a post, where he tethered it. After quickly and quietly surveying the rest of the villa by foot and finding nothing disturbed, he returned to his horse, saw to its needs and stabled it for the night.

The front of the villa overlooked the valley and had been built in a semicircle with a large, intricately designed mosaic patio and a central colonnaded walkway that led to a large round pond. Many of the columns had fallen into disrepair due to the passage of time and weather. The results of this perishing had meant a number of the stone lintels had crashed down, shattering parts of the mosaic. This had also caused other columns to topple and break into several large pieces, which were left strewn about where they had fallen. The pool and fountain, which had once operated from a waterway that led from the stream that cascaded over the cliff, had long since ceased to function.

The Highwayman relaxed. It had been pleasant tonight, in a strange sort of way. He always experienced a surge of nerves and fear because of the unknown, but to have robbed the pompous Scottish judge had been a bonus, really worth the effort of the endless, rain-lashed wait.

He could imagine the faces of the gentleman, the lady and the little girl as they received their treasures back from the coach guard. Perhaps they'd been wide-eyed with wonder at the notion that a Highwayman, a common thief, would take the trouble to hand their things back. He smiled.

A fire crackled in the grate. The smoke from it rose lazily up the central chimney into the night sky. He felt safe, as his nearest neighbour was at least a good twenty miles distant. Tom Bennett crossed to a small room he used as a temporary bedroom. He lay down on a straw mattress. After pulling some thick, roughly woven blankets over himself he gazed thoughtfully out of the window.

He had stumbled on the villa purely by chance. Three years before, he had held up a stage, and unbeknown to him a small troop of militia had been following it less than a mile behind. Not in any way had it been a trap, just pure coincidence. The Highwayman, the coach driver, passengers and the militia had all been surprised. Fortunately for him, the Highwayman had been the first to react to the situation.

The militia, not known for their expert horsemanship or their desire to chase anyone into unknown difficult territory, had hunted him on this particular occasion like a pack of hounds chasing a fox. It wasn't until the Highwayman had turned into the deepest forest and literally hacked his way through the densest undergrowth that the militia had given up the chase.

He had continued on, not knowing where he might finish up until quite by accident he found himself at the place containing the villa. It had been overgrown with bushes and climbing plants. As he could go no further unless he jumped off the cliff, which he would have been ready to do had the militia followed him, prepared to take his chance on surviving the drop into the lake, he decided to make the villa his home.

If someone else should stumble over it during his stay, as the occupier he would have to deal with that situation when it occurred. Up to this moment in time he and the villa seemed to lead a charmed life, and he constantly reminded himself of his good luck. Why it didn't seem to appear on maps of the area he neither knew nor cared, but one thing was for sure: he would never let it go without a fight. Hence all the traps and snares placed strategically around it. Oh yes, if someone did fancy their chances playing games with the villa, then they would be in for some wicked surprises!

Tom Bennett had been lucky that day, and up to tonight, his luck still held out; but one day, through his overlooking the simplest thing or his own stupid carelessness, the hangman's noose would be there for him. Perhaps one last robbery and he might be able to live in comfort within the law.

He smiled at the thought of studying law himself: some hope! Then tiredness overcame him and he fell into a nightmarish and broken sleep that ended in him swinging from a tree, his breath rattling in his throat in front of a faceless crowd of people dressed in black. They were all laughing silently. It was this final ghastly image that awoke him. It seemed ages before he finally drifted into a dreamless sleep.

★

At breakfast the following morning, the judge had continued his whining about the previous evening's hold-up and asked how long it would be before they departed for Axenthorpe Hall. The driver and guard, who had eaten before the passengers, now made an appearance and were attending to the horses.

At eight thirty, the guard blew several discordant notes on the post horn that hung on the side of the coach. The driver released the brake, cracked his whip at the lead horses, and the judge, accompanied by the old man, his daughter and granddaughter, renewed their journey to Newcastle via a short detour to Axenthorpe Hall.

★

Tom Bennett had slept well in the end. He too had risen early, eaten a meagre breakfast and then fed and groomed his horse, all by eight o'clock.

He had decided that he would visit his brother, who lived at Hazelthwaite, in three or four days' time, to check if Lord Sanderson had been as good as his threat, or if he'd been all mouth. If Tom Bennett knew what was going on, he would be ahead of the militia – and anyone else for that matter. If the past was anything to go by, after a major robbery, the village would still be full of gossip and rumour about it and he would learn much from local opinion.

Before he left for Hazelthwaite, he reset all the traps round the villa, ensuring all the invisible snares were ready for any suspicious and not so suspicious characters that happened upon 'his property'. After saddling his horse, and packing his highwayman's attire into matching saddlebags, he set off on his journey to Hazelthwaite, picking his way carefully through the thickest parts of the forest.

The Highwayman watched Tom Bennett leave the villa from his perch high above the treeline. He pushed the telescope back into itself and placed it into a leather cylindrical pouch. From his prone position he pushed himself onto one elbow. 'Well, Mr Bennett, I wonder where you're off to now?' he said to himself in a whisper. The Highwayman had already decided that he would raid the church at Hazelthwaite that very night. He had to have those jewels, as his creditors were becoming intolerably impatient! Now, wouldn't it be a coincidence if Tom Bennett were on his way to the village at this very moment! No, it would be divine retribution for a very bad man! He smiled then laughed out loud. He'd show the local population what the word 'bad' meant, and not be caught into the bargain!

He followed Tom Bennett at a very safe distance across the bleak Northumberland moors and heavily pine forested tracks until it became obvious that he was destined to arrive at Hazelthwaite. When Tom Bennett turned down the track that passed as a road to the village, The Highwayman smiled behind the sinister mask he wore that covered all his face. Turning his own mount into Horseshoe Wood, he gently cantered down the bridle path to Axenthorpe Hall.

He didn't ride directly to the Hall but reined in his horse at one of the outlying cottages that had stood empty for some years. He dismounted marched up the gravel path, unlocked the door and disappeared inside. Twenty minutes later, he reappeared in the finery of Lord Axenthorpe's third and youngest tearaway son. He decided to walk the horse up the drive from the cottage rather than ride, which might draw undue attention to him. On reaching the rear of the mansion he tethered his horse in one of the spare stables in the block opposite the kitchen area. He stole into the dark, brooding house and made for his room, which was well away from his parents and any other guests they might have staying. He would make all his apologies for staying out late at breakfast the following morn. This youngest Axenthorpe had his parents eating out of the palm of his hand, although they certainly wouldn't like his gambling habits that had got him into the sort of debt that could quite easily bankrupt them, let alone their devoted son!

No Mercy for William Bennett

Hazelthwaite slumbered peacefully beneath the afternoon sun, as the church clock struck the hour of three, and apart from a herd of cows being driven by what looked like a very bored farmhand to the water meadow at the far end of the village, virtually no one was about. The cowherd had just managed to coax the last of the animals over the bridge with a rather brutal-looking stick, and it wouldn't be long before he sauntered out of sight.

As Tom Bennett approached the Old Oak tavern, situated at one corner of the village green, the guard from the Newcastle to Edinburgh stagecoach appeared from the coaching inn, fifty or so yards down the cartwheel rutted road, and climbed up to his seat. An ostler was chatting to him as he in turn held the lead horse's rein. The guard picked up the post horn and blew a few long, shrill notes on it. Passengers straggled from the thatched roof building and were helped courteously aboard the coach by the driver, who was dressed in a smart red overcoat to match the livery of the carriage.

Several poor souls were actually going to sit out the journey on the roof of the stage, and they had to climb to their roof seats via a little ladder that was located to the rear of the stage. At this particular moment they seemed full of cheer, but later when they were dusty, cold and at the mercy of all the elements, their tune would change! God help them, if it were to rain, as it had done the previous eve! Bennett smiled to himself. Well, they weren't going to be troubled by him this time.

However, there wasn't any hint of the previous day's storm in the air as the village slept under the hot sun. Tom Bennett gave the oak tree a cursory glance at the end of the triangular grassy area, its huge leafy branches rising high into the blue sky, glad that up to the present moment he wasn't realising the recurrent nightmare he'd been having recently!

He turned his horse to the right and let it walk up to the

hitching rail in front of the inn. Raising his right leg over the horse's back, he slid down from the saddle and stood idly for a few minutes to watch the three o'clock stage leave for the next torturous portion of the journey from Newcastle to Edinburgh. As he watched the passengers embarking he felt sure that he recognised one of them from the portly body and wig.

Tom gave the driver and guard a cheery wave as they drove towards him. They returned the wave, but the fat man sitting by the window, whose face was outlined in a curly powdered wig, certainly did not wave back.

Tom Bennett recognised the man. It was the judge, Lord Sanderson, and although he didn't know Bennett (as he'd worn a mask on their previous encounter) the stare that he returned seemed to pierce Bennett's skull. The bloated face scowled at him as the carriage drew level, then his hands pulled the two heavily laced curtains together and the judge disappeared from view.

The Highwayman wished him and his unlucky travelling companions a pleasant trip from under his breath. He was sure that by the end of the journey, especially if it was all the way to Edinburgh, the judge's travelling 'friends' would long to cheerfully string him up from the nearest gallows. He smiled, shrugged his shoulders and walked across the grass to the inn.

Several men were sitting on roughly constructed benches by the inn door drinking ale and making the most of the warm afternoon sun. They were local villagers, farmers, herdsmen and craftsmen from in and around the Hazelthwaite area. Bennett recognised all of them and they all acknowledged Tom as he passed them on his way to the bar. Bennett was a popular character in Hazelthwaite, as he was elder brother to the Reverend William Bennett, the local vicar.

Tom learnt much from his chat with the villagers and the innkeeper about the robbery. This Sanderson man had been a pompous ass just because he thought he had rank. They'd since learnt that an old man and his family, who'd been travelling with him, had had their possessions given back to them, making him look the fool he was.

Apparently this had made the high and mighty judge fly into an even worse fit of rage. Although they still had no truck with the Highwayman, they all had some sneaking respect for him, and if he continued to rob from ignorant rich people, and didn't harm anyone whilst doing so, then good luck to him. Tom agreed whole heartedly with what they said.

The inhabitants of Hazelthwaite went about their business for the rest of the afternoon and early evening. It wasn't until six thirty, when the church clock had rung the half-hour, that things became decidedly interesting. The assembled drinkers heard a horse gallop up and slide to a halt on the gravel road. Several seconds later, the rider ran into the inn and informed the open-mouthed audience that the afternoon stage had been held up and the driver shot.

The men, eager to hear all the news soon surrounded the farmer. Yes! It had been the Highwayman. Yes! It had been in broad daylight. No, no one was dead, but the driver had been badly wounded and was on his way at this moment to Hazelthwaite to be tended by the doctor. He'd lost a lot of blood and, oh yes, one more thing, there was one passenger who had demanded to be dropped off at Axenthorpe Hall, to speak with His Lordship himself – some judge or other travelling to Edinburgh.

Bennett's eyes narrowed to fierce slits. Trust Sanderson to put himself and his own personal glory before someone who needed urgent attention. His time would come! There was talk of the militia being involved, and with that, the overwrought farmer was forced into a seat by the hearth to calm down.

Tom Bennett listened carefully. Well, well, another highwayman – and on his patch of countryside. The very idea… He smiled; this would certainly stir up local feeling. What he didn't like, however, was the fact that this highwayman had obviously shown no mercy!

He would have to tread very, very carefully. Tom asked the farmer some questions of his own. Most of the answers he received were obviously hearsay, and exaggerated. However, he was sure that the Highwayman had ridden a black horse.

So why would someone want to hold up yet another stage so

soon after the last robbery? Definitely to stir up local feeling, but also to provoke some action from Lord Axenthorpe to use his private troops to give safe passage to the Newcastle–Edinburgh stage through this wild and 'lawless' area. It was known in London that this part of England seemed to harbour some rough, nasty types, and people asked when might it be made safer for travellers? Quite a number of the upper class were mumbling about Axenthorpe's authority in the North East of the country. Tom could imagine the court gentry relating stories at their fancy soirées and masked balls about the northern lord who protected business interests by doing nothing.

By now, the sun had set, and most of the villagers had arrived at the inn to hear the poor farmer telling and retelling his story over and over again, each time making it more outrageous than the last. Tom knew the farmer was secretly enjoying his moment of popularity; bad news always went down well. He got up, threw a few coins on the table and said his farewells. Leaving the building by the main entrance, Tom stood in the porch for a minute or two to deliberate on what he had just heard.

Next, he walked to his horse, which had been patiently cropping the grass tethered by the long rein that he had been given. Unwinding the leathers from the rail, he stroked the beast gently on its face. The horse moved its head towards him, shaking it up and down as it did so and whinnying. Tom whispered in its ear to stay calm and then walked it to a small cottage in the church grounds. He hitched it to another post, undid the saddlebags and threw them over his shoulder.

The cottage was in darkness. Strange, thought Tom, his brother usually finished his notes for Sunday's sermon on the Saturday eve, sitting at a desk positioned by the window of his study at the front of the cottage. The light from the lamp cast a warm glow across the path to the front porch, and Tom would often wave to William as he approached the front door. But seemingly not this evening.

The only light at the moment was coming from the full moon, which lit the path and to some extent the cottage interior. Tom banged on the door; no answer. He stepped back from the door's porched entrance and called his brother's name a few times. Still nothing stirred. He walked round to the rear, but this door like the front was locked, and there was no light coming from any of the tiny windows, or any sign of life. Tom presumed that William must be still in the church.

Bennett approached the parish church up the gravel pathway. He could just make out what looked like a flickering light inside the nave of the building. He would have to remind William not to be so conscientious and to have some rest. He could picture the man tidying and cleaning the nave or whatever jobs needed to be completed before the early service. The church was always a picture, and was beautifully maintained by the young clergyman who had such a wonderful career before him.

The first sign that something wasn't quite as it should be was when William didn't answer his brother's secret whistle. They'd had a pre-arranged signal since William quite by chance had stumbled on his brother's 'occupation'.

Of course, on the one hand William had totally disapproved of his elder brother's chosen calling, but he couldn't stop being his brother, and had pretended, quite wrongly, to ignore what he did by way of 'work'. Tom had never harmed anyone, and local folk said that the Highwayman stole from the well-to-do; and now, since he'd been known to return some items to their owners, respect had built up for him.

William would often impart to his congregation during sermons that it was quite wrong to respect law-breakers, full knowing that his brother committed such crimes. On Sundays, however, he would pray for everyone's soul, as if this would make a difference.

Tom had from time to time given incredibly generous donations to the collection when he'd attended his brother's services, and William would find himself having to make double or even treble blessings on these 'special' occasions.

With the pre-arranged signal not returned, Tom moved very cautiously forward along the remaining few steps to the porch. He could just see that one of the double doors leading to the church's interior was ajar. He looked round to see if anyone had come into view. Everywhere remained silent. Bennett slid into the church crouching as he did so to make use of the cover provided by the rear pews. The church was uncomfortably silent. Near the altar steps a lantern was flickering where it had been placed on the floor. From where he crouched he could see nothing out of the ordinary, but he sensed somebody had entered the church nonetheless.

Tom moved off to his left and followed the aisle that led to the altar, furthest away from where he could see the lantern light, using the pillars that supported the vaulted ceiling for cover. As he neared the front row of pews and looked across to the right of the church where the pulpit was positioned he froze in absolute terror.

There on the floor, in an ever-spreading pool of blood, lay William! He moved swiftly to his brother's side. He saw the dagger that had been plunged deeply into his brother's stomach. Both of William's hands clasped the knife. His eyes were shut but they flickered open when he heard Tom run to his side. They bore the same look of terror in them as Tom's had done seconds before, but when the figure had become less blurred to him and he realised who the new person was they relaxed and he forced a smile that obviously hurt him, as he cried out in pain. The eyes closed again.

'William, William.' Tom choked the name out.

William Bennett reopened his eyes. Tom could feel tears welling up and he wiped the back of his hand across his face. William seemed calm now and smiled again. He removed one of his hands from the hilt of the dagger and grabbed at Tom's arm.

'William, don't move,' said his brother.

William pulled him close. 'I haven't much time in this world, Tom, so listen, please listen,' he whispered.

Tom Bennett motioned to open his mouth. He wanted to fetch the doctor. He wanted to extract the dagger. Things looked so hopeless. Things were hopeless.

'I said listen. There's great danger. The Highwayman has been here. He's taken the jewels from the Icon…I–I– disturbed him…we fought…' William's speech faltered. His hand slipped down to his side.

'William!' Tom shouted, tears now pouring from his eyes.

'Tom, he used the old, secret priest's passage to escape,' William continued.

Tom Bennett was mystified. 'Priest's passage, what priest's passage? What are you talking about?'

'All vicars that are assigned to this parish are given the passage's secret. It leads to a priest's hole that was dug out several hundred years ago. I was sworn to secrecy not to tell of its existence. How John Axenthorpe got to know about it....'

At this point William just shook his head then coughed up a lot of blood. Tom could see that his younger brother's time had almost come.

'Lord Axenthorpe's son did this to you? How did you know it was him?' Tom, whose tone had changed to one of uncontrolled anger and hatred, spat out the words.

William replied faintly, 'I managed to pull his face mask off during the struggle.'

It then registered with Tom Bennett as he started to weigh up the situation in a cold and calculated way. 'William, do you mean he's still here in the church?'

William nodded, 'Push the wainscoting just below the rail by the first pew, then slide the panel back with your hand. When you go through there's a lever to your right that will close the panel from the passage side. The passage leads all the way to the coaching inn. The priest's hole is approximately halfway along the tunnel. Tom, be careful. I've never agreed with what you've done. But you will be forgiven one day. But now you must go and do what you think is right. I think you know what I mean by that.'

William's head fell to one side, resting in the crook of his elder brother's arms. His eyes were still open.

Tom looked at the dead figure and tenderly closed the eyelids. He could still feel his brother's warmth.

'Is that you, Reverend?' said the faltering, rather high-pitched voice.

Tom spun round, brought sharply back to reality. This had been too much even for him. But here was a new, deadly threat.

The nightwatchman was shuffling down the central aisle of the nave towards him. Tom crawled behind the altar. There was only one thing he could do. Quickly, he opened the saddlebags, took out the black cape, tricorn hat and half-face mask. He pushed the pistols into his belt and waited.

The old man seemed to take an eternity to reach the place where William Bennett lay.

'Is that you, Your Reverence?' he stuttered. Tom Bennett sensed the area towards the pulpit light up as the lamp was raised. 'What on earth has happened here?'

Tom, from his prone position behind the altar, imagined the man's contorted look on his face as it suddenly registered with him that the Vicar of Hazelthwaite was dead. The watchman suddenly cried at the top of his voice, 'Murder, murder, help!'

For an old man he could certainly shout, and this took Tom Bennett by surprise. He would have to act quickly if his business with John Axenthorpe was to be completed this night!

The Highwayman stood up from behind the altar. The nightwatchman's mouth dropped at the sight of such an apparition suddenly appearing from behind the altar. His eyes blazed with hatred. Not bothering with the fact that he was well over seventy years old, the old man attacked Bennett with as much ferocity as he could muster. Time was against Bennett; every second spent in the church meant that Axenthorpe got further away, and help would soon arrive to assist the old man.

Tom Bennett hit the old fellow hard in the face with his gloved fist. It was hard enough to knock him unconscious but not so hard as to do too much damage, he hoped. Always the gentleman, Bennett had said sorry as he thumped him.

There was the sound of running footsteps on gravel. The watchman's calls for help were being answered. Time to go!

Bennett grabbed the lantern from the altar steps, kicked over the old man's lamp which immediately extinguished itself, swooped down to the panel that William had indicated and started pushing at the wooden slats that made up the wainscoting wall. God, please move! He pushed again this time more urgently; the footsteps were now entering the church porch. He could hear the shouts of an angry group of men.

The panel suddenly gave way. Tom Bennett pushed the leading slat wide enough to slip through the gap, and had just enough time to locate the lever to seal the gap before the first of the men reached the night watchman. Tom rested his back against the panel; he didn't dare move or hardly breathe.

From the other side of the panel, Bennett heard the watchman stutter out the words, 'A-a-a-a black shape, I-I-I saw him down by the pulpit.'

'No one there now,' came a reply, 'he must've got out by the vestry window.'

'No. I've just looked in there; it's locked. He must still be in the church!' yet another voice shouted. 'Quick, search everywhere! Look in the tower, he can't have disappeared into thin air. He's not a ghost. Get a move on! Someone fetch some rope.'

Tom Bennett had never felt so scared in all his life. Even though he was fairly safe in the passage, certain death wasn't more than a few feet away. The villagers had turned nasty. They had become a frenzied mob. If they caught him they'd hang him!

He now knew that the Highwayman would be blamed for the death of the clergyman. If he'd stayed by his brother's body, the nightwatchman would have recognised him, and still he would be blamed with the killing. After all, he had blood on his hands and his clothes, what else should the villagers think? Murder was a hanging offence, and judging by what he'd overheard, a fair trial – or any trial – was out of the question. The locals wouldn't bother about a motive, Icon or no Icon; he was the one who would take the blame! He wasted no more time listening to them tending to his dead brother and preparing for the hunt.

Bennett now gave all his attention to the tunnel. The passageway smelt damp and fusty. He followed it as best he could with only the lantern's flickering light to guide him. He paused every so often to listen for signs of life. He couldn't see any other dimmed light up ahead, but the passage zigzagged so he might come up unexpectedly on Axenthorpe, who would be able to gun him down in the confines of the tunnel. He wouldn't miss, either, at such short range. Tom knew that his pistols weren't accurate over any distance but here…

He still sensed that the other man was ahead of him, but how far? What had William said about the priest's hole? Tom thought he remembered him mumbling something like, half the distance between the church and the coaching inn. It was difficult to tell how far he'd walked or stumbled, as the passage twisted so. A bend in the passage loomed up in front of him. He chanced a look. Nothing was there. He moved on a few steps. What was that?

There was a definite scratching noise. But from where? Tom held the lantern as high as the tunnel's roof would allow. Still he could see nothing, just hear the incessant scratching or digging. He brought the lantern down low. The noise seemed to be coming from behind him and near to the ground. He turned and bent down almost until his shoulders were at ground level. This must be it – another passage off the main tunnel with yet another secret door. This time the door was open! If it hadn't been for the door remaining open and him being alert to the sound he would have missed it completely. The lantern just didn't give off enough light. How had the door been opened. The scratching noises were definitely coming from inside the priest's hole. The Highwayman was in there! He obviously thought William was dead, and the passage was still a secret known only to him.

Tom stood up again and held the lantern up high. Yes! There was a handle carefully concealed between two wooden beams that supported the roof. Very clever, and impossible to spot by searchers who didn't look up. They would have thought the priest had well and truly disappeared into thin air.

Tom realised that he would have to extinguish his lantern to gain access to the priest's hole proper, but he assumed that the unsuspecting Highwayman would have his lit. After all, there was no reason for him to think that danger was a matter of paces away! He blew the light out. With his hands he felt his way down the wall until he reached the small aperture that indicated the entrance to the passage. Keeping very low lest he struck his head against the low rock ceiling, he gradually inched his way along the claustrophobic tunnel. After four or five yards of painful crawling he saw a flickering light. Axenthorpe's lantern! The sound of the scratching and scraping became quite loud in the confined space of the priest's hole. Then the ceiling of the passage slanted steeply upwards into the room.

Axenthorpe was so busy pulling a stone from a small niche that he didn't hear the Highwayman enter the room and stand up behind him.

The first he knew of the danger was when the Highwayman growled, 'John Axenthorpe, murderer.'

The 'Highwayman' spun round. He looked in terror when he saw what looked like his own reflection.

'The mask, take off the mask!' Tom demanded.

The two pistols that were pointed at Axenthorpe indicated that he should follow the instruction.

'Normally, I don't even wound, let alone kill anyone with these, just use them for a little friendly persuasion,' he continued, 'but tonight will be different. Tonight I will take great pleasure in killing you in cold blood, Axenthorpe.'

John Axenthorpe pleaded with him, grovelled in front of him and begged him for mercy.

Tom Bennett replaced one of the pistols in his belt and then took off his mask.

'*You*!' hissed Axenthorpe. That was the last word he spoke as the pistol ball ripped through his forehead, splattering blood and fragments of skull about the small room. The Highwayman waited. The crack of the pistol must surely have been heard! But there was nothing, no sound of footsteps or excited voices!

Tom pushed the body aside. What had Axenthorpe been doing? There were fresh marks in the niche, and the dagger he'd been using to scratch the soil with had fallen by his side. He held up the lantern. One of the stones had a freshly scratched 'A' on it, written in old English script. He moved the rock and there behind it was a small leather pouch held fast with a thin leather thong. He opened it and there was the emerald from the Icon. He replaced it.

This was an excellent hiding place. He'd leave it here and retrieve it later, to be restored to its rightful home when the present circumstances cooled down. So where are the rest of them, Axenthorpe? He searched the body. He soon located the rest of the gems hidden in five similar purses, in one of Axenthorpe's pockets.

Tom knew several other very safe hiding places for these. If he could only have the time to split them up, it might just help him out of a sticky situation in the future. Now he turned his thoughts to escaping from the priest's hole, the passage and Hazelthwaite.

Firstly he replaced the stone carefully, brushing away the dirt that had been scratched away by the dagger with his gloved hand. He put the little stone cross back in the middle of the niche's sill, and as a final ironic touch he placed John Axenthorpe's body in front of the 'altar' slumped forward, as if in prayer, his last prayer. Tom thought that if anyone should go to hell, this should be the person; but perhaps placing him like this would help his cause when he knocked at 'Heaven's gate'.

The rest of the pouches containing the stones he pushed into his cape pocket. Then, picking up the lantern, he crawled back down the passage.

Tom realised that it would be fruitless to go back to the church. There would be guards at every door and window, so he would follow the passageway in the direction of the inn and hopefully the other end. He closed the priest's hole using the roof-mounted lever, making the sanctuary a tomb that would never be discovered! After all, now that William had passed away, the next vicar wouldn't know of its existence and Tom certainly wasn't about to tell him. He held the lantern as high as the tunnel would let him and began to walk carefully down the narrow twisting passage to who knew where!

He seemed to walk for an age before the floor started to slant upwards, like a ramp. Then he saw the end of the passage. A wooden panel stretched from the floor to about four feet in height. The light from the lantern shone on the handle to open it. But where had he arrived? What was on the other side?

He knelt down on the earthy floor of the passageway and pressed his ear to the panel. He listened for a few seconds for any clue as to what lay on the other side. It came soon enough. There was the sound of soft whinnying and hooves moving on cobbled floors. Stables! Oh God! He suddenly remembered his horse left tethered by the cottage.

The villagers would know he'd been to the church and was now nowhere to be found. They'd have found his saddlebags by the altar, but from what he could remember there would be nothing left in them to incriminate him as the murderer. But they would be wondering where Tom Bennett was, and asking why he wasn't by his brother's side? And more to the point, where were the Axenthorpe jewels?

He had become a fugitive quite by accident, and from now on he would be able to trust no one, and would certainly have to live off his wits. Many things flashed through his mind in those few seconds as he knelt by the door that would ultimately lead to his 'freedom'.

Dare he stay in the area? He was sure that no one knew of the villa's location, and now that Axenthorpe was dead even Tom Bennett didn't know how 'safe' he was.

It's that feeling you get…

Lizzie Miller sat by her bedroom window overlooking the village green. Since she had recovered the second jewel of the Icon, life had become tedious and dull. She had her chin resting on her hands. Slowly, she leant back, yawned without putting her hand over her mouth, stretched and pushed her right hand through her long blonde hair and shook it. Life could be a real bummer, she thought.

She hadn't settled in at school very well either, and although Mabel and Amy had tried to involve her in after-school activities she'd just become more distant and troubled. It wasn't as if she was nasty or grumpy – just changed! Mabel supposed it was because Lizzie really did miss her best friends, Brenda and Donna, and had become withdrawn because of that fact.

Mabel couldn't have been more wrong. She really didn't know Lizzie and what motivated her at all! Despite the wrench from London and her friends (which she could always play on for sympathy if she needed to), Lizzie had put these concerns behind her. What had happened during the summer holidays she'd put behind her; she'd forgotten everything.

Forgotten everything – except, of course, the Highwayman… and he was different! She wondered where he was? What did he do? Where did he stay? What did ghost highwaymen do in the off-peak season, especially one who was about two hundred years old? She pondered these insoluble questions as she looked across the leaf-strewn village green. Might he sit on the tail of a jumbo jet and pop off to Orlando to holiday at Disney World? She tutted, took off her glasses, gave them a vigorous huff and a polish and shoved them back on again.

She resumed her position by the window, chin resting on her thumbs and fingers in front of her mouth as if in prayer, elbows on the window ledge, watching a grey Hazelthwaite day late in October. She looked but saw nothing.

The Highwayman, the thought of him drove her on from one day's end to the next. She'd been *chosen*! He'd told her that, so she'd just have to wait until he gave her another sign, whatever it might be.

Lizzie slunk downstairs, slamming the door.

'Oh, there you are, luvvie,' said her mum. 'Your dad and I are going to walk up to Devil's Heights. Do you fancy blowing the cobwebs away?'

Lizzie, apart from passing the Heights in a car, hadn't ventured near the place for weeks. She didn't have pleasant memories of it, and as soon as her mother had mentioned the name she'd shivered in fear. But...

'Okay, but isn't it getting late to walk up all the way? It'll be dark in about an hour,' Lizzie replied.

'Well, we might not make the top, but we can follow the path as far as we can then cut through the Forestry Commission land on one of their tracks to the road,' said her father.

'Sounds good,' said Lizzie unconvincingly.

She walked upstairs to get her coat, hat and gloves. It certainly got chilly in the late afternoon in the north-east of England, and there'd even been a severe weather warning for sleet and snow. The whole family had noticed how much colder it was than London – and it could certainly get cold there!

The three of them walked out of the kitchen, across the courtyard and down to the bottom of the garden. The apple and pear trees in the small orchard near the fence were almost leafless, and the flower borders were looking drab, provoking a comment from Lizzie's dad, about needing to do some tidying up, which Lizzie half heard.

Something she had heard him say was that come the springtime, he'd start to redesign the garden nearer the house, and smarten it up so that they could sit on the lawn rather than the courtyard, which lost the sun later in the day. Her dad had certainly worked wonders in the courtyard, and Lizzie, Mabel and Amy loved to sit and chat out there, as it reminded them of an Italian restaurant they went to in Axenthorpe. The owners of the restaurant had modelled the interior on a Venetian terrazzo.

They'd paved the floor with terracotta tiles and placed a fountain in the middle of the eating area. The fountain was surrounded with beautiful potted plants. Each of the black and white marbled tables with matching cane chairs had their own trellis around them. Large terracotta pots had been planted with creepers that snaked around the trellis to give the illusion of privacy.

The walls of the building had been painted in shades of blue, but done in such a way so as to make the restaurant appear very old. The girls loved eating there as the chef produced the best pizza special (with all the toppings on it) that they'd ever had! When you went in through the ornate patio doors there was always a wonderful smell of garlic bread, and the sound of real Italian waiters shouting orders at the top of their voices. How anybody received the correct order, Lizzie could never fathom. But the whole 'thing' of eating there was wicked!

'Dad?' she said.

'Yes, sweetheart,' he replied.

'Can we go to the Italian at Axenthorpe tonight?' she asked. 'Only I feel a pizza thing coming on.'

'Course we can. What made you think of that?' he replied.

'Oh, just what you were saying about the garden. I love what you did to the courtyard. It reminds me of Gianni's,' she continued.

They scrambled between a couple of broken fence slats (which prompted John Miller to say he really must get round to repairing those as well) and turned on to the bridle path that lead up through the pine forest towards Devil's Heights. There was a strong smell of pine needles in the air and the path was strewn with cones and old needles that had become detached from the branches. By the time they'd started the climb upwards, the light was fading and the path became a narrow dark aisle. The only noise came from their shoes and boots swishing through the needles. None of them spoke, all lost in their own thoughts, happy just to share each other's company in silence.

Without even consulting one another, when they reached the forest lane closest to the Heights they turned right along the Commission's track that lead to the main road.

The lane was well kept, but muddy from the incessant use of tractors and other forestry vehicles shifting logs to the main road and maintaining the firebreak area. The grassy verges were cut short, so you could see into the forest both sides for quite a distance. However, with the light going, it did mean that the forest took on a silent, almost eerie, quality.

It was disturbing enough to make Lizzie feel uneasy. She definitely felt uncomfortable when she found that her parents had disappeared round a bend up ahead and she was now alone. She'd dawdled as usual, lost in her own thoughts.

It was then that she heard it? Was it a breath of wind? Certainly a couple of roosting crows had been disturbed and had flown off, cawing wildly and making her hand shoot up to her mouth. Or perhaps it was the twig that snapped over to the right that made her stop and listen harder. Lizzie's senses started to overreact. She didn't cry out, although she knew she should. She stood rooted to the spot, unable to move either of her legs. Her parents had walked who knew how much further on? The light from the day was virtually gone.

Something or someone was out in the forest watching her every move. She tried to peer into the trees but it was impossible without any light. There were the distorted, grotesque shadows of the pines as they marched back into the forest. Nothing stirred. Whatever was there knew that she had stopped, and was trying desperately to see her. She'd imagined it, surely! Her mum and dad were just round the corner. One scream and they'd be there. But Lizzie couldn't scream. The silence was overwhelming her and she could feel the evil near her. Finally she overcame her inability to move and started off at a brisk pace, but not a run.

The sound started again. Something was keeping pace with her, stalking her just thirty or so metres away. Another twig snapped. Lizzie thought my God who can it be. Then she saw the flickering light, 'My God,' Lizzie whispered, 'the Highwayman.'

She started to run, but in the semi-darkness she fell in one of the deeper ruts, landing in a muddy puddle. She called out. A twig snapped in front of her.

She hardly dared look up.

'What's the matter, Lizzie?' her dad sighed.

'I-I thought I saw a light, over there in between the trees,' she cried.

'Lizzie, Lizzie, are you all right,' said a worried Jane Miller, as she ran up.

John Miller turned to his wife and raised his eyebrows.

'I'll go and check the place that Lizzie showed me. But I'm sure there's nothing there; perhaps it was a fox or something,' he muttered.

'Foxes don't stalk humans, Stop when they stop, move when they move. You've got to believe me,' spluttered a dejected Lizzie.

'I do believe you, sweetheart,' replied her father.

Lizzie looked at him, 'You don't sound very convinced, Dad.'

'I can't see a light. You two carry on to the road – Ill be with you in a few minutes,' her father said agitatedly.

Lizzie turned to her mother and then looked down at her feet. She could feel the tears starting to well up in her eyes.

'Sorry, Mum, I got spooked. I'm so stupid,' Lizzie gasped, between large gulps of breath. But try as she may she couldn't fight back the tears.

Lizzie and her mum waited by the Forestry Commission stile that lead to the main road, until John Miller ran up to join them. He had the high-power torch on that he had carried to help light their way home. As he approached them he still seemed edgy and agitated. He looked at them both. Then he patted Lizzie on the shoulder, reassuring her that he could find nothing; but when his eyes met Jane's, he narrowed them and shook his head as if to say, I'll talk to you later, but in private! Lizzie had seen the look pass between her parents. When later on came, and they thought they were on their own, Lizzie would make sure she listened in to the conversation. The look had said it all: something was wrong, and someone had been in the forest! She knew it!

The trio made their way down the winding road to Hazelthwaite. Lizzie said nothing, and her parents could feel the hostile atmosphere that was being generated by silence. Lizzie could certainly make you feel in the wrong, even if you weren't! The village clock struck six as they approached the green.

They had decided to walk round the green, stopping first at Mabel's, then at Amy's house to invite both sets of families around for drinks about eightish. Lizzie had decided the trip to Gianni's should be put off to a later date and would rather see her friends.

This would allow the girls an opportunity to have a chat on their own whilst the parents got together for the first time since the end of the summer holidays. Jane Miller also wanted to find out what the villagers of Hazelthwaite got up to during the long winter evenings, and especially what to expect when it snowed and how the villagers celebrated Christmas. After all, you couldn't start too early!

Lizzie was pleased that her friends were coming round and thought that it would give her the time to tell them of her fear in the woods. She didn't realise that she was going to receive the information she wanted so quickly about her afternoon's fright.

Lizzie popped upstairs for a bubble bath, and it was while she was lying in what can only be described as 'snowy water', which she had very naughtily filled almost to her chin, that she heard her Mum and Dad discuss the events that had happened earlier.

Lizzie had left the bathroom window open a fraction to let the steam out, and unbeknown to her parents it was open enough for her to hear the conversation going on in the kitchen. She'd deliberately left it open for the sole purpose of eavesdropping. Although they weren't talking loudly Lizzie caught the drift of what her father was saying.

No, he wasn't quite sure what he'd found. Well, no it was a feeling he got when he'd left the track and walked twenty or so metres into the forest, sort of cold feeling...stupid really, as if someone was watching. He'd shrugged it off, but thought they'd better monitor Lizzie's movements to be on the safe side.

Although the information that Lizzie was receiving didn't make her particularly happy, because she had bad memories of Webster, when she thought of her encounter in the priest's hole and the never to be forgotten adventure in the Witches' Cauldron, a little tingle of a thrill went through her body. Perhaps Webster was back; perhaps the Highwayman was ready to help her solve the whereabouts of the other Axenthorpe jewels. Who knew what lay ahead?

Of course it had been scary in the forest, but if it had been the Highwayman surely he would have appeared to her. If it was Webster, perhaps he was back to scare the locals again. It seemed too soon for him to make a reappearance. Surely he'd be pushing his luck as far as he could go, if he was back in the area! The police still had his file open. She knew this, as her father occasionally rang them to see if there was any news of his whereabouts. Each time he'd enquired they'd come up with a blank. So he was somewhere, but was he that close? She would certainly be on her guard from now on.

★

Tom listened, his right ear pressed hard against the rough wooden panelling. Apart from the sound made by the horses chomping on their feed, no other sounds came from the stable. He would have to risk pulling the handle, and hope that the door would slide silently to the open position without startling the horse that was stabled not more than two feet away from him. He still could not be sure that a groom or ostler wasn't on duty in the stable, but he presumed that the horses had been bedded down for the night and that the exterior doors to the double storey building would be locked anyway.

It was also sensible to presume that every available villager was either looking for him in the village and surrounding countryside or on guard duty around the church. Bennett assumed that Lord Axenthorpe had been sent for, but it would be a fair time before he and his militia arrived back at Hazelthwaite.

He mouthed a silent prayer and pulled the handle. The panel slid open silently. Fortunately, there was no horse in the stall adjacent to the passage entrance. So the beast he had heard a few minutes ago was a terribly noisy eater! Tom Bennett smiled to himself. There'd be no frightened whinnying or bucking and rearing in front of him to alert the innkeeper: hurdle one over.

As Tom stepped out of the passageway in a semi-stoop and had stayed that way just to get his bearings, he became aware of something or someone watching him. He looked up and from the little moonlight that penetrated the darkened building he could see the outline of a horse's head slightly angled to the side looking back down at him. The moonlight caught the horse's eye, which glinted at him and seemed to say, 'How the hell did you get there?'

Again Tom smiled. He stood up and gave the horse's nose a stroke and as the face lowered he whispered in its ear. It snorted its appreciation of Tom's loving touch and reassuring words. Tom told it quietly to shush, and it went back to eating the hay that had been put in its wooden manger.

The stable was free of any human life so, after gently forcing the stable door's lock with an iron rod, he risked a peep into the courtyard. There seemed to be plenty of activity in the inn as he could hear muffled voices and could see long shadows being cast by candle and lantern light as people hurried to and fro. However, no one was in the courtyard and it lay in darkness accept for the occasional shaft of moonlight peeping out between passing clouds.

He slid back into the darkened interior of the stable, unhitched the horse he had befriended, and slipped on a saddle blanket and spare saddle over its back. He tightened the girth straps carefully and slipped the reins over its neck, checking the bit fitted comfortably, and quietly led it to the door. Gently reassuring the beast all the while, he walked it through the shadows of the kitchen garden between rows of well-kept vegetables and flowers.

Slowly, very slowly, he continued to make his way between the apple trees that made up a roughly kept orchard at the end of the inn's grounds. Soon he reached the comparative safety of the pine trees and undergrowth that lined the bridle path leading up to Devil's Heights. When he thought that he'd gone far enough to be out of human hearing, he mounted the horse and gently spurred it up the incline. In a few hours he would be safe at Greywater Scar, and then he would be able to do some serious thinking about his future!

The further he rode away from the village the more careful he became. Tom realised that there would be villagers around scouring the countryside for him, and they could easily have got this far; after all they hadn't needed to be careful about making noise. Also, he didn't want to come across Lord Axenthorpe on his way to Hazelthwaite via a back route. So several times he stopped for a few minutes to listen for any strange sounds that might announce the presence of what would now be considered the enemy! Fortunately, nothing untoward happened and soon he was able to gallop the horse in the direction of the Scar without thought of anyone following him. This night had been the worst in Tom's living memory!

On arriving at the villa, he waited as usual. There was now little in the way of moonlight, and he was sure no one had tracked him, but old habits die hard and he wanted to be doubly sure that it would be safe to enter his home. The traps and snares were just as he had left them. After searching the villa, he dared to light a fire and a lantern. He cooked a rabbit that had been snared in one of the traps he'd set. While it roasted on a makeshift wooden spit, he stood in the moonlight, or what there was left of it, his left arm resting on one of the Roman columns that flanked the pathway to the fountain, staring down to the water in the valley below him.

With his brother murdered, and his murderer dead, Tom Bennett decided that life for him was more or less worthless. The return of the jewels to the Icon would be his priority, and this was going to be incredibly difficult. However, this was going to be the only way he, Tom, could repay John Axenthorpe's ghastly crime committed against William, against the villagers who had dearly loved the clergyman, and Hazelthwaite in general.

He would, however, need a plan of action for hiding the jewels, probably separately, so that were he to be caught, he might have some bargaining power for his life, and at least no one would find them in his possession.

Only he could be responsible for returning them to the Icon in the church! If that could be done, Tom reasoned his brother's soul would be freed as guardian of the jewels. It also might help him escape the gallows if he could prove his innocence, which would now be very difficult if not impossible. He realised now he hadn't made life easy for himself by making such an enemy of the Scottish judge, Sanderson. If he got his hands on Bennett with all the incriminating evidence against him there would be no such thing as a fair trial; there wouldn't *be* a trial. Tom was positive about that fact!

He knew of several very safe places to hide the jewels but getting them to the various hideouts, especially around Hazelthwaite, would now prove difficult. He could never go back to the village in daylight without some form of disguise, and it would be equally difficult being abroad by night. From now on it was 'tread carefully, Tom Bennett, or you're a dead man'.

His thoughts shifted to his brother. The villagers of Hazelthwaite would give him a wonderful funeral, as they, like himself, had thought the world of him. He had been the sort of man that had helped anybody, rich or poor, saint or sinner, without a moment's hesitation. Perhaps being too good had been William's downfall. He had hated knowing Tom's secret, and that was the only bad thing that the Reverend Bennett had ever done. Tom knew he'd prayed often to help himself live with his brother's 'sinful life'. Tom also knew full well that as keeper of the Icon he would have defended it with his life, and ultimately that was exactly what had happened.

Fireworks at Hazelthwaite

October dragged into November, and Lizzie was beginning to realise what winter in a small village was like! Mabel and Amy came round for her every Saturday, and they went on the local bus to Axenthorpe for a swim or to see a film at the local cinema. And God, and what a dump it was! In London, Lizzie and been used to multi-screen cinemas with surround mega-sound and anything else that the technical wizards of the cinema could come up with. But not in Axenthorpe, oh no. You were as likely as not to get a film break down or wonky sound or some twit spilling popcorn over your shoulder.

On one occasion Lizzie had been sitting minding her own business, when at a particularly quiet and memorable part of a film, one of the springs in the base of her seat had broken. It had spiralled up underneath her, causing a rip in her jeans and sending a nasty farting, boinging sound around the auditorium. Mabel and Amy had hurt from laughter over this, actually thinking Lizzie's predicament more entertaining than the film.

The other thing that they thought incredibly funny was when someone leant heavily on one of the ancient seat backs, collapsing it, causing the unfortunate person to land in the lap of the person behind. One night a seat twanged back so hard that two teenagers on the back row had the embarrassment of a half-eaten Mars bar stuffed between their noses whilst in the middle of an attempt at the local record for back-seat snogging. Even Lizzie had managed a gut-wrenching stitch, laughing at the unfortunate pair, who vowed never to come back to the cinema again! At school the following Monday they'd been ribbed unmercifully, and in fact they'd kind of never lived it down!

On another occasion the three were watching the latest movie to hit Axenthorpe, when all of a sudden a particularly dippy Year Eleven girl, accompanied by an even more stupid-looking spotty guy from another local town, were suddenly both tipped violently backwards. Their arms and legs were trapped together pointing directly at the ceiling. The boy's lolly had accidentally been shoved in Louise Baker-Smith's ear and her popcorn (which was very sticky) had been emptied over and become stuck to the daft boy's hair, which was smothered in gel.

Their combined screams of help had provoked the usherette and the manager to rush in, shining their high-powered torches into their faces, resulting in the two of them being ejected from the cinema – through no fault of their own. The girls had liked that!

The audience had given them a hell of a cheer and a chorus of wolf whistles as they'd left; especially the boys in the audience, as Louise's miniskirt had been inadvertently caught up behind her equally short coat, exposing her thong underwear.

This little episode had meant that Louise's life at school had been hell. Wherever she went she was given the smirks behind the hand and lots of practical tips about the right kind of sensible knickers to wear on dates. Needless to say Louise hadn't bothered to go back to the pictures, and no one had seen the boy since that unfortunate evening.

★

Mabel and Amy were becoming more excited about bonfire night. Lizzie told them not to get too overwrought about a few rockets and a small blaze. Once you'd seen some of the displays she'd attended in London, you'd seen them all. Lizzie totally missed the look of sheer derision that passed between the two local girls at her lack of tact. She'd turned her back on them and had proceeded to give her glasses a huff and polish and sweep her hand through her long blonde hair in an 'I've seen it all' sort of gesture. They had just replied, 'Wait and see!'

Hazelthwaite, because of its location at the bottom of a natural basin, was an ideal place to have a firework display. What they didn't tell Lizzie was that a large company in Newcastle always came to test their latest display creation before setting off on a large north-eastern tour of English towns and cities and some prime locations in the Borders of Scotland towards the Christmas period.

It just so happened, that November 5th fell on a Tuesday. When the apology for a bonfire was lit on the edge of the village green, and the villagers had let off their measly collection of rockets and Roman candles, Lizzie definitely thought that Mabel and Amy had been winding her up. She told them so, in no uncertain manner. Again, they'd retorted, 'Wait and see, Lizzie!'

However the villagers had tried to make the occasion as fun-filled as they could. The landlord from the Sun had erected a beer tent outside the pub, away from the fireworks and bonfire. The electric leads had been rolled out and the same lights that had lit the disco tent in the summer flashed on and off. There was no disco, but a very powerful sound system had been brought out and was pumping music out across the valley.

The fireworks hadn't been wonderful, it was true, but all the village folk had gathered on the green to chat, and when they could they'd oohed and aahed at the right times!

The only hilarious moment of the evening was the arrival of Hazelthwaite's one and only fat batsman. His name had been drawn out of a pint mug in the pub a week before to open the display. He had taken this opportunity very seriously, and even had a small speech prepared for the occasion. The ceremony was simple: he was to take an already smouldering taper and light the touchpaper to fire off the first rocket and then stand clear.

The fat batsman took the taper and very solemnly announced, 'It gives me great pleasure...' Just as he bent down to send the rocket on its way and then complete his speech, a dog had howled in one of the gardens on the opposite side of the village green.

Now everyone knows that you keep your pets locked away on bonfire night, but this clever Labrador had chewed its way through a piece of string that was holding a kitchen door shut. The lock had broken just the day before and was awaiting repair. The animal had then stood on its hind legs and pulled the handle down with its front paws. On escaping into the back garden, it had let out an almighty, 'Where are my owners?' howling woof.

The fat batsman, who had had a particularly nasty bite from an evil Rottweiler earlier in the year, panicked when he heard the howl. Thinking that the damned thing had returned to haunt him, he threw the lighted taper into the night sky, where it fell directly into a full and unfortunately open box of fireworks – with disastrous consequences!

The resulting scene was chaos. Rockets popped off on random flight paths, Roman candles had climbed into the night sky at crazy angles or horizontally, and sparklers seemed to create the largest fizzing bouquet you've ever seen.

The boy who'd left the box lid off his 'weapons' had also managed to sneak in some bangers and jumping jacks, which when ignited by some stray sparkler sparks made the corner of the green sound like a war zone.

One rocket that had taken a horizontal flight path had sizzled through the beer tent, causing startled customers in the queue to veer left and right in a perfectly swayed human 'V' shape.

Catherine wheels, like sizzling Frisbees, spun across the hallowed cricket square, and three rockets that had taken off simultaneously and all at the right trajectory winged their way in tight formation before thudding to a rest in the 'Sun Inn' sign, causing it to swing noisily on its chains like a demented dartboard.

The terrified boy who had watched the whole proceedings open-mouthed, now clutched his head in his hands as he saw the ladies from Hazelthwaite's crochet and knitting circle suddenly leap up and down like an aged morris dancing troupe, as they tried to avoid the jumping jacks! He realised he would be grounded from now to eternity!

As an astounded innkeeper surveyed the scene in front of him, he finished the fat batsman's opening sentence: '...to blow the place to pieces!'

Mabel observed, 'If you want some action, you can always rely on the fat batsman!'

Lizzie agreed, but after that the party had been decidedly flat.

★

It wasn't till Wednesday evening, as the school bus turned down the Hazelthwaite single-lane road, that things really did get interesting.

Mabel, Amy and Lizzie were sitting in a triple front seat that was positioned sideways on to the aisle of the bus. The bus suddenly sighed to a stop.

A few hundred yards down the road, huge lorries were queuing to turn onto the Forestry Commission road, and one was parked in a lay-by facing up the road towards the bus. Lizzie's eyes were wide open. Mabel and Amy exchanged 'told you so' glances.

'What on earth is going on Mabel?' said Lizzie.

'Oh, looks to me like it's the preparations for the firework display on Saturday,' Mabel replied.

'You didn't tell me it was going to be like this! You said that Tuesday... you've been holding out on me – made me look a proper twit!' continued Lizzie. She gave both of them a playful push, which meant that Mabel's elbow shoved Amy in the pit of her stomach, causing her to fall across the bar of the bus that passengers would hold to get up the bus steps to pay the driver. Lizzie took off her glasses and gave them a huff and a polish. Wait till she told Bendy and Donna this bit of news!

'These fireworks must cost a fortune,' said Lizzie, 'how do they get permission to use them in this area?'

'They take them right down the forest track almost to the Witches' Cauldron, and then you know the open ground behind that...' explained Amy. Lizzie nodded. 'Well, they plant all the rockets and whatever they're displaying up the hill, pointing away from the trees. It looks spectacular from the village.'

'Who opens the show?' asked Lizzie, giggling.

Mabel and Amy chorused together, '*Not the fat batsman!*'

For the next three days the village buzzed with excitement. The lorries carrying the huge fireworks and all the safety equipment associated with the display shuttled up and down the road virtually non-stop. Riggers had set up a laser light and sound show to accompany the fireworks, and it had been announced that Lord and Lady Axenthorpe would deliver the welcome speech on the village green before the display began.

Hazelthwaite had one problem for this sort of event: its size. The roads could not take the volume of traffic expected, which would include coachloads of people who came from all over the area, let alone people who lived locally coming to watch the display by car.

One answer was to direct most of the bus traffic to Devil's Heights, so that people watching there would get the maximum benefit of the display. Local people living in Hazelthwaite and a good majority of those coming by car, however, would be allowed into the village to park on a carefully constructed duckboarded car park on the green itself. The advantage of being low down would mean that your senses received the full advantage of the light and the sound show. According to Mabel and Amy this could be 'outasightmanpet'. Lizzie said she'd reserve judgement till after, but deep down she knew it was going to be just as they said, and probably better.

The police had total control of the situation, and many temporary constables and extra stewards would be drafted into the area to keep order and control and to advise people where to go and so on. The road to Newcastle would be closed for a couple of hours before the display and about an hour after, so that traffic could disperse. Plenty of advertising was in place so that people knew exactly what was happening on the evening.

Lizzie had phoned Bendy and Donna telling them of the coming display, joking that they should come up for the weekend, but that had been met with a chorus of 'I wish' and the like. Lizzie had mentioned to them that perhaps their parents might consider Christmas!

They both said they'd ask, but Christmas meant families being together, and what would their grandparents say… and by the time they'd put a whole string of excuses past her, Lizzie felt like saying, 'Get lost, forget it' – and worse. But she didn't, and she was glad that she hadn't said what she felt, as it turned out!

At 7.45 on the Saturday evening, Lord and Lady Axenthorpe (and to Mabel and Amy's delight, but to Lizzie's embarrassed anger) Robbie Axenthorpe, who had come home from school just for this special event, arrived at the Sun Inn (courtesy of a police escort through the traffic) to officially open the display. Actually, firework display was a limp and poor description for what was going to be a pyrotechnical masterpiece of sound and vision.

John and Jane Miller, accompanied by Lizzie, walked across to the green. It was a particularly clear and cold night. The moon was almost full over Devil's Heights, and even from the bottom of the basin you could hear excited if muted voices travelling across the valley as the hundreds, maybe thousands, of visitors who had earlier arrived in semi-darkness readied themselves for the display.

This time, when Lizzie had looked towards the Heights, the flickering lights had meant BBQs and lanterns of people who. though unknown to her, had every right to be there. The cars and coaches that had arrived earlier had provided their own light show as they had manoeuvred back and forth into their parking slots. A seemingly non-stop convoy of vehicles had driven head-to-tail like a twinkling snake slithering down the two roads into Hazelthwaite to park, cramming the temporary car park like sardines. Then everything was stopped. Hazelthwaite was gridlocked. It was time to start!

Lizzie was dressed for the weather in hat, scarf, fleece and trousers; she didn't look or feel trendy but she wasn't cold. Mabel and Amy were attired similarly but then so was everybody else, bar one!

Robbie was a revelation. Much to his parents annoyance he had a T-shirt with a wicked logo printed on the front of it, huge, baggy cargo trousers that looked as if they'd end up round his ankles because of the vast chain that drooped down from his waist, and thong sandals. His hair had been streaked with several colours of blonde, and instead of the upper-crust cricket-loving youth of the summer there stood the northern equivalent of a surf bum, without board or reef break! As soon as Mabel and Amy saw this vision they'd rushed off to find Lizzie. Lizzie flinched when she saw him, wondering what on earth he was thinking of! Obviously out to impress…but who?

Lord Axenthorpe delivered his short welcoming speech, which everybody thought was excellent. The exception being his offspring, who scowled through the whole thing and then wandered off disconsolately, head down, towards the Gallows

Oak. Lizzie watched him go with a thoughtful expression on her face. How could he be so rude? She'd go after him and tell him what she thought of him. Without any idea of how she'd strike up a conversation with Robbie, apart from vent her anger on him, she started picking her way in between the cars that were parked on the duckboarding, to the far end of the village green.

By the time Lizzie had managed to negotiate her way to the Gallows Oak, the pyrotechnics had begun. Fabulous displays of fireworks lit up Hazelthwaite to match music of all kinds. These, coupled with the laser lights that flitted on and off, gave a breathtaking display, better than anything she'd ever seen. For a little while she stood with her head raised towards the hills and sky watching the display.

Then she came back to reality with a bump, when a rough voice called to her above the bangs and cracks and music, 'What you doin' 'ere?'

Lizzie looked at the Gallows Oak. It was in deep shadow, even though most of the leaves had fallen. The large branches hung low to the ground. You could hardly see the bench that surrounded the huge trunk. Soon the tree surgeons would have to cut back the lower branches so that the tree regained some of its balance and shape and let in some light round the lower trunk.

Robbie was watching her, testing her reaction to his question. A particularly bright Roman candle display lit up the area from behind where Robbie was sitting, outlining the tree, and she saw his form sitting slouched on the bench. At the same time as she did this she looked up for a second.

She shut her eyes and looked again. About twelve feet up, sitting on a thick branch, sat Tom Bennett the Highwayman.

'Noisy evening, Lizzie,' he remarked with a sardonic tone.

'What do you want?' hissed Lizzie, frantic that Robbie would look up and see Bennett.

'I asked first. God, it's gone real cold all of a sudden, worse than before,' said Robbie.

'Don't be so rude,' Lizzie snorted.

'Sorry, I'm sure, milady,' mocked the Highwayman.

Lizzie, still looking at him, stuttered, 'Not you. *Him! You!*' She was pointing at Robbie.

Robbie looked up into the tree, 'Last time I saw you by this tree you were chatting to it. You're batty.'

Lizzie looked at Robbie over her glasses. A large set of Roman candles lit the basin.

Lizzie shouted, 'Your horse will bolt. Animals don't like fireworks!'

Robbie gazed at her in astonishment. This girl is seriously unbright, he told himself.

'He's deaf and dumb to all this,' replied the Highwayman, 'where there's no sense there's no feeling.' He shrugged.

'I came by car,' continued a bemused and now a trifle concerned Robbie.

Lizzie looked up again oblivious to Robbie, 'You've got something to tell me, haven't you?' she asked.

'Wow! You're quite direct, aren't you?' said Robbie. 'I thought you were a bit distant in the summer, sort of playing hard to get, but I see that...'

'Jeez, get a life, Axenthorpe!' hissed Lizzie.

On first seeing Lizzie at the cricket match that summer, Robbie had been really taken by her, but this constant whining about first one thing then the next had gotten to him.

'Well, give!' Lizzie said again, with uncontrolled curiosity.

'We will meet again soon, in less busy circumstances, Lizzie. Tonight is awkward.' He looked at Robbie below him, motioning with his thumb at the fireworks. 'Things have cooled down since the summer, and you dealt well with the first two jewels. It's probably time for your next test or series of tests,' said Bennett.

'Can't you tell me anything that might give me a clue as what I might have to do or where we will go together?' said Lizzie.

'This is ridiculous, you're not listening to anything I say, are you? I've dressed up in these ridiculous clothes, that I normally wouldn't be seen dead in, except maybe on Bali, because I thought you'd be here and this was the sort of stuff that might get me noticed. Talk about being embarrassed!' wittered Robbie to himself. 'I suppose girls of your age are all the same. I should have known better. I should've stayed at school.'

Lizzie looked at The Highwayman, 'All right, I'll wait for some sort of sign, I'm glad you've made contact... I've really missed you.'

Robbie, now totally perplexed, got up and left, shaking his head.

Lizzie grabbed Robbie's arm and spun him round, 'Hey you, Axenthorpe, I haven't finished or even started with you yet!'

At this outburst Robbie shook himself from her grasp and made a rapid break for freedom, dodging between the cars. The Highwayman smiled at her and started to disappear. Things change over time, but some things never change, and that was a good sign!

On her return to where Mabel and Amy were watching the display they quizzed her about what had gone on between her and Robbie. She told them that Robbie had been very rude, but she hadn't got much sense out of him, and that he was a typical boy, someone thoroughly spoiled who'd lost whatever plot had been installed in him at birth. Perhaps they all did at fourteenish!

'That's funny,' replied Mabel, 'because when he got back he seemed very subdued, went straight to his Dad's car – and you'll never guess when he got back he was wearing jeans, fleece and woolly hat, just like us! You never can tell, can you?'

'Yes, and when he went over to his folks, they smiled at him and his mum put her arm round him. As if he'd had a shock,' continued Amy. 'We thought he'd seen a ghost or something, or had been influenced by someone.'

'No, he didn't see a ghost,' whispered Lizzie, 'but...' Her comment was drowned out in the loudness of the display as it entered its last phase.

There was a brilliant finale of rockets of every variation and colour and starburst linked to the 1812 Overture. When it had finished, for a few seconds you could have heard a pin drop the silence was so complete. Then a wave of applause and shouting and car horns and headlights flashing from Devil's Heights erupted all over Hazelthwaite.

Lizzie wondered what Robbie was up to. Maybe he wasn't so bad. It was true, she had rather snubbed and ignored him during the summer, but surely he hadn't gone to all that bother for her. No – she wore specs, and boys didn't like that too much! And the way she'd looked this evening wouldn't have warranted one glance, let alone two.

All this had confused her and she took off her specs and gave them a huff and a polish. She'd set them back on the bridge of her nose so hard with a backward push that they had slightly grazed some skin. Typical!

A Blast of Winter!

Tom Bennett allowed two weeks to slip by before venturing away from the villa. He was expert at trapping and shooting wildlife. He had a ready supply of fresh water and fresh fish in abundance in the lake. He could exist here for good if he wanted to but the most important thing to him at that particular moment was news.

He was starved of news. He needed to know what the local folk felt about the murder. He needed to know whether he should contemplate fleeing the area for good and make a new start. He hated the thought of leaving his beloved Northumberland, but he'd travelled once or twice to Scotland, and although it could be a wild and inhospitable place he thought his 'talents' might be useful there. Certainly the border area was quite untamed and further north in the Highlands... He shrugged his shoulders. That would be in the future – a last resort!

Firstly, he would try Hazelthwaite for news; dangerous but necessary. He also knew of two other excellent places to hide the jewels. Pleased about making this decision, he made preparations for the trip.

His disguise would need to make him unrecognisable, even though he would mostly travel by night. Very slowly he transformed himself into a traveller, a soldier who was home from the wars and down on his luck. After all, there were plenty of them about.

After a fortnight, his hair was long and unkempt, and he'd grown a rough-looking beard and droopy moustache. He used dye to darken his hair. He ensured his hands were rough and calloused and bit all his fingernails until they bled and were uneven. Cutting his cheek with a knife produced the beginnings of a war wound, the scab of which he kept picking off to make it look angry. The patch over his eye finished the transformation, and Tom Bennett highwayman was dead for the while, and Corporal Weaver of the Durham Infantry was born.

He worked on the farm cart he had acquired. It had taken an age to transport it to Greywater Scar. He hadn't even known why he'd bothered to bring it to the villa, but he had, and now he was pleased with his act of forethought. Tom built a basic wooden box-like structure onto the cart, roughly put together but watertight. He added a small window and a door to the rear. The chest that he built into the interior of the caravan would act as his bed, and there was a little entrance door from the interior to the bench seat at the front.

The little extras built into the caravan might save his life later on. Small pots and pans, a knife grinder, water barrel and other bits and pieces were tied or hooked onto the exterior. The whole cart was then given a thin lick of paint to give the impression that he had been on the road for months. It was three weeks later, not two, as he had originally planned, that 'Corporal Weaver' hitched the horse (which Bennett had stolen from the stable at Hazelthwaite) to the cart's traces, and after seeing the traps and snares were all freshly set, ambled slowly forth to the town of Axenthorpe.

Now, depending on people's attitude to the kind of day they'd had influences their reaction to a newcomer to the area. Axenthorpe was a long way from London. News was scant concerning the war, and this Corporal Weaver, with his vivid stories and obvious injuries (especially that nasty limp, which needed a crutch for support) went down very well with the poor and well-to-do alike.

Some of the families had loved ones who were still fighting out in Europe and many would not come back. But this man, who'd taken the King's shilling, fought with courage and come back to England, with nothing to him save his little caravan, and whatever pride he had, was accepted into the heart of the community. Corporal Weaver loved it, even though it was a pack of lies, and God help him when he finally met up with his brother again!

However, he learned much about the murder of the vicar of Hazelthwaite, and the awful Highwayman, who at the moment had gone to ground like the coward he was, and about the Scottish judge who had put a price on his head. The locals said the sooner he was caught and hanged the better. So in the

Axenthorpe neighbourhood, Tom Bennett wouldn't have been welcome one little bit! Corporal Weaver assumed the same welcome would have awaited the Highwayman in Hazelthwaite. So a price on my head, he thought, interesting!

★

The first snow started to fall on December 1st. It just got colder and colder. The frosts in the Hazelthwaite basin were very hard. The roads were constantly salted and gritted and large mounds of sand and grit were strategically dumped on the verges, to help drivers who got stuck on the icy slopes. The hedgerows appeared white, and any low, watery sun that managed to reach into the village during the day showed up a million spiders' webs that turned the hedges into lace, and the grass on the village green seemed to be permanently tipped with white. In a way, Hazelthwaite was as beautiful in winter as it was in summertime. The church clock echoed across the valley when it chimed the hour, and generally sounds were keener in the cool, clear air.

Lizzie was not ready for the snow when it came. Mabel and Amy kept telling her to wait for the cloud to build up and the temperature to slightly rise, and then the snow would fall in bucketfuls! Lizzie had asked them how could the temperature warm up, when it was minus fifty at least, and they told her not to be so stupid!

Of course she'd seen snow when she'd lived in London, and there had been severe frosts as well, but this was different. In one day, Lizzie saw the village come to a grinding halt. The snow blocked the two roads in and out of Hazelthwaite in half a morning. In fact, the local farmers had large tractors with snowplough attachments on them that helped to clear most of the roads; but it was the late afternoon and evening that was the real problem. As the temperature plummeted the snow that had compacted during the day turned to sheet ice, and although the roads had been gritted, black ice was the danger to both vehicles and pedestrians.

Lizzie looked out from her bedroom window at the coming evening. There was a final display of bright pink and yellow from the west announcing that the sun had disappeared, and a deep blue-black took its place. The sky had now cleared and a crescent moon hung over the village, the stars twinkling brightly in the clear air.

Hazelthwaite was incredibly beautiful and peaceful. Lizzie opened her bedroom window. The cold air hit her face and stung it. The church clock chimed six. It seemed so much louder in the frosty air. The snow that had fallen during the day had rounded all the familiar features she had come to know since moving to the village, and she could make out footprints of people that had come and gone to the post office that day. There were black scars on the roads where the snow ploughs had cleared great piles of snow onto the verges. The black areas now deadly ice sheets. Lizzie shivered and closed the window.

Across the cricket green, two people dressed as skiers stumbled and staggered knee-deep in snow towards the post office. Mabel and Amy had decided to brave the arctic conditions to come for a chat with Lizzie.

Lizzie heard the doorbell ring and her mother ask the two girls inside. She walked out of her bedroom, looked over the banister rail and asked them both to come up. Before the two girls started up the stairs, Jane Miller asked them if they wanted anything to drink and they suggested that a hot chocolate would be good, but a bit later. They walked upstairs after taking off their outdoor clothes, which were left in a large heap by the front door.

'We don't think there will be school on Monday,' said Mabel. She sprawled across Lizzie's bed and waved her legs in time to the music that Lizzie had put on.

'How do you know?' replied Lizzie, 'There might be a thaw by then.'

'Because we reckon it'll snow real heavy tomorrow and they won't chance the bus on the hills,' Mabel continued. 'We've seen it like this before. You think it was bad today… just wait, it'll get worse before it gets better.'

Amy butted in, 'Only one prob, though.'

'What's that?' asked Lizzie.

'Well, if the buses can't get in to Hazelthwaite then neither can anything else. So I hope your dad's got lots of stock in the shop,' said Mabel seriously.

'He relies on deliveries of certain fresh things every day, but I suppose for a couple of days he'll be okay,' replied Lizzie. 'I wonder if he's thought about that… bound to have.'

Lizzie walked out of the bedroom to the top of the stairs and leaned over the rail. 'Dad!' she bellowed.

'What's wrong?' came the reply from the lounge.

'Amy and Mabel were wondering if you're well stocked up with stuff in the shop as they reckon it'll snow heavily again tomorrow,' she replied.

'Well, we've been promised a county snowplough to keep the roads clear, so I'm hoping that some deliveries will get through. I suppose you're hoping that the school bus won't make it!' He laughed.

'It damned well better not! These two have promised a riot in the snow,' she shouted back.

'Well, don't hold your hopes up too high. If we can get you to school, we will,' her father continued, 'and don't swear behind my back, Lizzie.'

Lizzie had already mouthed 'bloody hell' to Mabel and Amy through the open door.

Lizzie seemed resigned to the fact that she would be attending school on the following Monday. Mabel and Amy assured her she wouldn't: 'Trust us!' they said. That was what worried Lizzie.

On Saturday, even Lizzie couldn't contain herself when she woke up. She clambered out of bed, went over to the window and dragged open the curtains.

The weather had changed again. What met her eyes was a dull grey, almost black, sky with snow falling out of it heavily. It was almost a white-out. You could hardly see across the cricket green to the cottages opposite. They seemed like little grey oblongs, with the trees and hedgerows that showed the borders of their gardens totally engulfed in white.

There was no sign of movement anywhere in the village, and the footprints that were visible last night had disappeared. It was impossible to see the roads, but an orange light was just visible showing the very slow progress of a snowplough at work on the hill road; you could see nothing of the vehicle itself.

'So, Dad, do you think that we're going to school on Monday?' Lizzie muttered under her breath. She wondered if the snow would stop long enough for the tobogganing and skiing that the girls had promised her. She looked up at where Devil's Heights should be, but with all the snow falling at present it was invisible. It would either be totally stunning clothed in white when the snow stopped, or even more sinister than it usually was. Could be interesting, she thought.

Lizzie put her dressing gown on and went downstairs to make her parents a cup of tea. She was more than surprised to see them both sitting at the kitchen table, tea already made, looking seriously out the window.

'Hello, Lizzie,' said her mum. 'Guess you've seen the conditions.'

'Yes,' replied Lizzie enthusiastically.

'I'll have to start making some phone calls,' said her father, 'see if anyone is venturing out today making deliveries. Shouldn't think so. Dangerous driving today.'

'Mum, do you think when it brightens up that the snow will thaw quickly, or stay?' quizzed Lizzie.

'Looks like it's in for the weekend,' replied Jane Miller. 'If you do go out, you'll have to take care. It looks pretty grim underfoot. Snow on top of ice could be dangerous.'

No sooner had she got the words out of her mouth when she and Lizzie heard a crashing sound, then nothing.

Lizzie shouted. 'The snowplough – it was working on the hill!'

'Oh God!' her mother replied. 'John, did you hear that.'

Lizzie's father rushed in. 'Yes, I was on the phone in the shop and looking out the window at the same time. The orange light that was only just visible has disappeared. Perhaps the plough has rolled over.'

He raced down to the shed at the bottom of the garden. He pushed on his gardening boots, fleece, gloves and hat, and grabbed a shovel and the first aid kit.

'Ring for the ambulance, love. God knows if it'll get here or not, just try!' With that, John Miller opened the front door, letting in a gust of icy air and a huge flurry of snow, and went out into the whiteness. Lizzie watched him go out, losing sight of him almost immediately. She just managed to glimpse a couple of hunched figures plodding in the general direction of the incident, whatever it was. Lizzie could hear her mother on the phone, and by the sound of the one-sided conversation she could fairly well predict that an ambulance getting to Hazelthwaite was almost out of the question. But they said they'd try to be at the scene as soon as they could.

What happened next Lizzie would never be able to explain to anyone. She just felt that she should try and help as well. She put on her outdoor clothes and slipped quietly out. Her mother felt a sudden draught and wasn't sure where it had come from, but answering questions from the ambulance controller meant that she couldn't just leave the phone at that particular second. However, she did see a shape disappear into the driving snow where the post office car park used to be.

Lizzie trudged through the thick drifting snow towards the road up to Devil's Heights. The snow flurries came and went and just occasionally she saw what looked like a hedgerow or tree or light from a cottage window. She actually bumped into the inn sign and grazed her cheek. Eyes almost closed, she bent hard against the wind and snow. As she moved slowly along the road she could hear shouts coming from above her and as the snow flurries ceased for a few seconds she could make out flashing lights. Now she was aware of a dull orange glow, which was rhythmically flashing between the pine trees that flanked the roadside on the way to the Heights. She could hear her father shouting orders above the roar of the wind; then the snow flurries came again but this time stronger.

One last effort and she was right by the incident: God, not an incident – a terrible accident! The snow flurry stopped and she could see the full extent of the crash. She could make out the lorry with the plough attached to the front overturned at a crazy angle in the ditch. She could see her father balanced on top of the lorry with the driver's door half open. The driver was inside the cab, slumped against a shattered windscreen.

Lizzie stumbled to the rear of the vehicle so that her father couldn't see her. How could she help?

The Highwayman watched Lizzie. He had seen what had happened and although he didn't know exactly the extent of the driver's injuries he knew he was badly hurt. He'd seen that the impact had rammed the steering wheel into his stomach and seen the blood that had come from a vicious cut in his leg. He knew that the driver should not be moved, but he had also smelt something that he knew the rescuers had yet to discover. When he saw Lizzie, he sensed this as his chance to warn the others through her!

'Lizzie,' he said, 'always in the right place at the right time.' Not loudly but in a voice that she recognised as authoritative.

'You're here! Where have you been? Why haven't you spoken to me? I need to talk to you!' Her words gushed out almost intelligibly.

'I'm here now, and you need to listen to me carefully without interrupting. I don't know anything about these noisy machines, but I do know when someone is badly hurt, and I do know danger when I sense it. The smell Lizzie, what's that smell? Look at the back of the vehicle in the ditch – perhaps you might know what is wrong,' said the Highwayman.

Lizzie looked at him, then worked her way across the back of the lorry until she was virtually underneath it, in the ditch.

'Oh my God,' she whispered, appalled. 'The fuel line has broken and it's leaking fuel and it won't be long before it touches something hot and explodes in a fireball.'

Lizzie crawled under the lorry and fuel spurted onto her clothing. She screamed. She wriggled under the front axle and a helper pulled her out.

'What the hell are you doing here, Lizzie?' screamed her father.

'Get him out quick, Dad!' Lizzie pleaded.

'He can't be moved. He could have internal injuries,' he said through the howling wind.

'The fuel line's been cut,' she blurted out, 'you've got no choice – he has to be pulled out now, regardless! I've seen it!'

John Miller had no choice. Fortunately, the driver was unconscious, so he wouldn't know what was happening anyway. Carefully, and to Lizzie's thinking far too slowly, John Miller grasped the driver below his armpits and hauled him up out of the door. Two willing helpers eased him out and down to the snow-covered road.

'We've got to get him clear of the plough quickly!' urged Lizzie.

'We're doing our level best!' shouted her father. 'The man's in a bad way.'

No sooner had he said this than there was a huge explosion that ripped the truck apart. Large pieces of metal were pitched into the air like confetti, and it was pure luck that none of the rescuers were hit.

Lizzie was hurled into the verge on the opposite side of the road. Her father and the other rescuers were scattered this way and that like rag dolls being thrown out of a toy trunk over a toddler's shoulder.

John Miller picked himself up and felt for a pulse on the driver's neck. Nothing... Wait, yes, there was one, but oh so faint... The doctor took over from him just at that second, and never was John so pleased to see someone as he was then to see the village GP.

Lizzie – Christ, where was Lizzie? He looked around. Suddenly he saw her lying face down in a snowdrift. 'Lizzie!' he howled, and rushed to his daughter's side, not knowing where to touch her in case he hurt her even more. She opened her eyes when she heard her name called and tried to move, but he told her not to.

'Don't move, Lizzie. The doctor will be here in a moment. You'll be okay,' said her father softly. I wonder how you knew about the fuel line leaking?' he went on.

'I got lucky,' lied Lizzie. 'What about the lorry driver?' she continued.

'In your words, love, he got lucky too,' replied her father.

'I'm glad,' said Lizzie.

She shifted the position of her aching body to try and support herself on her arms. It was at that moment she let out a heart-rending scream. In the darkness he'd missed it, but now as torchlight was aimed at Lizzie, her father saw the long, jagged piece of metal that was embedded in the back of her shoulder blade.

As he shouted for help from anybody, but especially the attention of the overworked doctor, Lizzie lay slumped in his arms. John Miller looked around at the awful scene, which was now lit by flashing blue, orange and green lamps and powerful torch beams penetrating along the forest road. Then he glanced back down at his daughter, and wondered if this was reality or just a few minutes of an improbable nightmare!

The last words she heard before she lapsed into unconsciousness were those of her father pleading for the doctor to hurry up and see to her.

The last face she saw was that of a worried Tom Bennett, who managed a half smile and nod to her before he too disappeared.

★

A couple of days later she woke up in hospital. She could feel the pain in her shoulder. When her eyes flickered open she saw her mum and she cried. It took her a while to realise that she had been very close to death once again, as the shard of metal from the tanker had pierced her shoulder like a javelin and gone extremely deep. She'd lost a lot of blood, but the team of surgeons who had operated on her to remove the metal had said she was very strong. Given time she would make a full recovery, although there would be some scarring, which they might be able to be put right at a later date. Little did they realise how strong and determined Lizzie Miller really was!

Mabel and Amy were allowed to see her, along with their parents on the following Tuesday, and Lizzie had been overwhelmed with cards, flowers and gifts from lots of her friends and acquaintances from both the village and her school. One of her teachers had even been cheeky enough to write a card that had said that when she was feeling better she'd send her some school work to do, as she appreciated that Lizzie would be devastated to get behind in Maths!

Favourite cards and phone calls had been from Bendy, and a card from Robbie Axenthorpe. (Now there was a turn-up for the book! How had he known about her accident? Perhaps his mum and dad had told him about the incident... or two conniving girls she knew had been on to him.) Lizzie smiled.

When Mabel and Amy first saw Lizzie in bed in a side room reserved for people who were considered very poorly by the nurse in charge, they didn't really know what to do or say to her. The scenario was made so much worse because of the various tubes stuck into her arms, which in turn were connected to monitors that regularly bleeped and beeped. They were only reassured that all was well when she beckoned them over to her for a very gentle cuddle. Lizzie actually winced with pain when they did this and they jumped back in horror in case they'd hurt her, but she said that with every move she made everything seemed to hurt. Then she giggled, and that hurt too. She confided in them that she didn't know why she thought she had to help on the fateful night, and with her fingers crossed below the bed covers she added that she didn't know why she had intervened at the time she did. The first time they had visited they couldn't stay too long, but they were promised longer visiting hours when Lizzie grew stronger.

The nurse who had been assigned to look after Lizzie had told her that the driver of the lorry was a patient in the same hospital. He was making an excellent recovery and wanted, at some time in the not too distant future, to thank her for saving her. This made Lizzie feel wonderful. To think that she had saved someone's life (even though the Highwayman had helped) and done something right for a change – not forgetting that it had almost cost her her own life.

At nine o'clock, the main children's ward and special side wards in Axenthorpe General were almost quiet, save for the odd bout of coughing and spluttering, or a child crying for the nurse on call for some attention. The doctors had finished any rounds they might have had to make, the last visitors had long gone, and the last evening medications had been dispensed. The wards in the hospital in general went quiet. The lighting was dimmed and staff went about their evening duties quietly and efficiently.

Lizzie was in that half-asleep, half-awake stupor when she thought she was aware of the handle of the door to her private room being opened. She thought she saw a shadowy figure dressed in long green overalls and a gauze mask tiptoeing towards her bed.

Before she realised this was reality and not a dream, and before she could bring herself to press the panic bell for nurse supervision she felt a pillow being forced over her face. She tried to wrestle her good arm free, which set off huge amounts of pain shooting into her injured shoulder, but she couldn't yell because of the pillow. Fortunately in her bid to free her good arm, a tube ripped free from her wrist setting off an alarm in her room and at the nurses' station.

The man, caught off balance for a second, tried to steady himself by grabbing hold of one of the moveable monitors, which fell, spinning him around. Lizzie managed to pull the face mask from him. Her body froze. His eyes blazed. She yelled again but no sound came from her mouth.

David Webster looked at her. Total hatred was in his gaze.

'I've been waiting for the right opportunity to thank you for saving my life, Lizzie!' he spat. Then he was gone before the nurse could do anything to apprehend him. None of the security staff could locate his whereabouts. The police were again baffled by the ability of Webster (if that was who it had been), to come and go as he pleased, especially in a public place like a hospital, and manage to torment Lizzie and her family at will!

Lizzie didn't say a word for days after the attack, so totally traumatised was she by the events. But she knew from the words that he had spoken that the man who had attacked her was indeed David Webster. So! The lorry driver who she had saved was her sworn enemy and he'd do anything to get his hands on the remaining items that belonged to the Icon. Presumably the attack had been meant to frighten her and let her know that he wasn't far away. After all, if he'd killed her there wasn't a chance of him finding the remaining jewels, was there? Or was she missing something? Whatever happened, she would never tell anyone what had been said during the vicious attack, and the sooner she was better, the sooner she could pick up the threads of the search for the rest of the precious Axenthorpe stones.

He was still around Hazelthwaite, haunting her. No wonder she'd been frightened in the woods that evening. It must have been him stalking her and her parents, and her sixth sense that had picked up his bad vibes from the darkened forest track. Hideous man, she thought. She wished that the Highwayman would come and take her away – rescue her.

At least she now knew she would never be rid of Webster, and that she would always have to be on her guard, not only in what she did and where she went but certainly what she said. She really couldn't let anything slip to anybody, except having total confidence in the Highwayman.

After Lizzie had resolved to start the search for the jewels, under the guidance of the Highwayman, if he ever appeared again, she made a miraculous recovery, to everybody's astonishment. The treatment she received for the shoulder injury and the mature way she knuckled down to her physiotherapist's exercises impressed her consultant enough to say that she would be able to go home for Christmas. He also mentioned to her that it was the promise of her taking it easy and not under any circumstances doing anything to aggravate the injury that made him allow this to happen. Lizzie double promised him, ensuring that her fingers were crossed under the bedclothes, just in case the Highwayman asked her to find a jewel – well, just a small jewel – with not too much danger involved!

And after the consultant had moved on down the ward she had been able to push her hand through her hair and with great care huff her specs into some kind of cleanliness, and she liked that.

On December 21st she was released from hospital. She hadn't an inkling of the welcome she was to receive when she got back to Hazelthwaite. Her mother and father picked her up from the hospital at about one. They had had to have words with the doctor about her medication and exercises, and after much fuss and goodbyes from the ward staff, Lizzie and her parents got into the car and journeyed back to the village.

Lizzie looked out at the snow-covered hills. The roads were now mostly clear, and slush and grime had made the verges dirty, but where the sun hadn't touched the fields the countryside looked beautiful under its duvet of white.

She turned to Jane, her mother. 'Mum, I'm so glad to be coming home for Christmas. I'll take it real easy, I promise.'

John Miller half turned to his daughter sitting in the back. 'You bet you will. And we're not going to let you out of our sight,' he said.

'That's a bit over the top, Dad. I've got to have some space,' Lizzie replied.

'You know what your dad means. No wondering off and thinking that you can save the world on your own,' said her mother.

'Have you heard from Bendy and Donna, Mum?' asked Lizzie. 'I'd have thought that I'd have had a phone call or text message or something by now, especially as I'm coming home today. I'll give them hell when I speak to them next! It's always me that has to do the contacting! Perhaps they're too busy with Christmas and stuff, I suppose. I wish we could go and see them.' She sighed.

John and Jane Miller exchanged knowing glances. Lizzie missed this, as she was sitting in the back looking wistfully out of the window at the countryside while she spoke. The car turned down the Hazelthwaite road just before Devil's Heights. Lizzie looked at the forbidding clump of trees and thought back to the first time she'd met the Highwayman. She shivered. This road down to the village, in fact this whole 'perfect area', had changed her life forever!

At a curve in the road where you could see the village green, John Miller gently braked. Lizzie looked between the head restraints out of the windscreen and there etched into the snow in huge letters was the simple message, 'WELCOME HOME LIZZIE!'

She brushed away some tears that had started to fall down onto her cheeks with the back of her good hand and arm. She forced out the words: 'That's beautiful, I really don't deserve it.'

By the time the car had pulled up outside the post office, what seemed like the whole village had turned up to greet her. Mabel and Amy rushed forward to cuddle her and then stood back when they realised they might hurt her shoulder, but she dragged them in again and said that it wasn't that bad and she could certainly put up with a smidge of pain for such a wonderful homecoming.

'Oh God,' said Lizzie, 'I never thought...'

'That we all cared, pet,' said Mabel softly, 'You'll never know how much we all bloody love you – you're a very popular girl, Lizzie Miller. Look at all the local blokes that have come to see you.' Amy added, 'Yeah, even the spotty ones!'

Lizzie was overwhelmed. It was perfect. The village dressed in white, The Gallows Oak, the little cottages nestling in their gardens. This really was home!

Now she was back safe and sound, and she'd acknowledged all of the well-wishers, she turned towards the cottage. John and Jane had already gone inside with her small suitcase of clothes and things she'd used in hospital, and Lizzie followed slowly and painfully, arm-in-arm with Mabel and Amy. The three of them wittered on about nothing special, just pleased to be back together.

The next surprise really did knock Lizzie for six! As she walked through the kitchen door and across into the corridor that led to the lounge, it was surprisingly dark. Mabel and Amy lagged behind her as she pushed open the wooden door into the oak-beamed lounge.

A lamp in the far corner was on, but it was dark apart from that. In an instant all the light switches were thrown on – and there were Bendy and Donna and their respective parents. Everyone shouted, 'Welcome home! Lizzie could be emotional, but this was too much, and she broke down and wept like a baby. Then all the girls broke down and cried as well. John beckoned to the parents to accompany him to the dining room for drinks.

The girls were left to calm down. They then cried again, and at last, after talking all at the same time about nothing in particular for a good half-hour, they joined their parents.

'What a Christmas this is going to be,' cried Lizzie, 'I can't believe it!' Then she looked serious, 'Where in the hell are we all going to sleep?'

'Lizzie, your language hasn't improved,' said her father, with a wicked grin on his face.'

Sorry,' she whispered, head down.

He continued,' Well, Lizzie, the quick answer to that question is we're not staying here for Christmas.'

Lizzie looked on in silence.

'While you've been away convalescing in hospital, we've all made arrangements to go to the Greywater Scar Hotel for Christmas Eve through to the New Year. Are you coming, or would you rather stay here on your own? You'd certainly have enough space!'

Lizzie's mouth fell open. 'What, do you mean all the families going to the Scar! Jeez – brill! Oops, sorry, Dad.'

Bendy shouted, 'Come on girls, upstairs! We've got loads of catching up to do!'

' Just once, I might have done something right for a change,' muttered John Miller to himself, with a smile.

The Hotel at Greywater Scar

Owing to the lack of accommodation at the post office (and the fact that the Millers knew that Lizzie was going to need some rest, especially at night) Mabel and Amy were going to have Bendy and Donna's respective families to stay with them, until they all set off for Greywater Scar. This meant a not too tearful goodbye at about 9.30, as all the families had had tiring days, either preparing for Lizzie's homecoming or travelling a long way by car from London.

By ten Lizzie was in bed. Her mum and dad had said goodnight to her and she had given them a special thank you for making the forthcoming Christmas celebration such a brilliant surprise.

Her curtains weren't totally drawn and the moonlight shone into her bedroom, creating a silver sheen on everything it touched. She very hesitantly climbed out of bed and stood by the window. Hazelthwaite was incredibly quiet. The church clock rang out the half-hour. She could make out her welcome home sign in the snow. As she turned to go back to bed she felt as if someone or something was watching her. Something close by!

As if by a magnetic force she slowly turned to the window. On a branch of the tree just by the window, she could make out a shape appearing. Oh God, it's him, it's the Highwayman! She slipped the bolts of her window to the open position and pushed the bottom sash upwards.

'Cold night, Lizzie,' said Tom Bennett with his twisted smile. 'I've been waiting for you to return. Are you better?'

'Much better, thanks. I've been dreaming about you. Willing you to appear. Do you know who,' Lizzie stopped for a second, 'you saved that night?'

'Yes,' said Bennett, 'I also know that he attacked you in hospital. I don't think that he wanted to kill you, just give you a severe scare. He realises that you're no good to him dead.'

'Gee thanks, that makes me feel so much happier,' Lizzie replied sarcastically. 'Why didn't you visit me in hospital? I prayed for you to come,' she whispered.

'Don't do hospitals, Lizzie. Can't stand the sight of blood and gore. Probably why I was such a terrible highwayman; I never could kill anyone, not on hold-ups anyway,' he mused.

'Trust me to get mixed up with a highwayman who's a bloody wimp,' she hissed.

'Language, Lizzie! Not sure I know what a "wimp" is. I'm sure I could make an educated guess, though. In actual fact you couldn't be further from the truth. I'm just a modest, honourable, old-fashioned sort of fellow,' he continued.

'Honourable, my ass!' said Lizzie, 'What do you want? I need my beauty sleep, or so my therapist tells me.'

Bennett smiled the wicked, crooked smile again. 'You're a terrible girl, Lizzie Miller. I suppose that's why I like you so much!'

Lizzie blushed.

'I hear you're going to spend Christmas at my villa – or rather the hotel by my villa,' he continued in a matter-of-fact voice.

'Your *what*?' said Lizzie.

'My house, my villa at Grey Scar. Where I live.' Bennett turned away for a second and stared over the green. 'Or rather, where I used to live,' he muttered wistfully.

'Explain, please,' said Lizzie softly. There was something strange here. Tom Bennett, her Highwayman, was never emotional like this.

'Hope you've got half an hour,' he replied, looking into Lizzie's puzzled eyes. This time he smiled.

Lizzie blushed again and ran her good arm through her hair.

Jane Miller crept up the stairs to bed. She'd heard Lizzie murmuring; bad dreams, possibly. They'd go away in time. She wouldn't disturb her, as that might be bad. Time was a great healer, wasn't it?

After the Highwayman had explained about Greywater Scar, Lizzie was amazed and excited. She had wanted to know everything, each little detail. Tom Bennett went through his discovery of the villa to the minute he executed John Axenthorpe.

'God!' said Lizzie when he'd finished. 'So the skeleton in the priest's hole was an Axenthorpe, one of Robbie's ancestors! But why tell me all this?' said Lizzie.

'Well, while you're on holiday, you might as well collect two more of the Icon's jewels,' he said with a shrug of his shoulders.

'You're joking! You hid two of them at the Roman villa?' she could hardly get the words out, but Roman villa was loud and clear.

'Ssh! Not so loud, Lizzie. Yes, I did, but there are problems in retrieving them,' he replied.

'Oh, I didn't think it would be a cakewalk. So, a holiday that isn't a holiday. Brilliant,' she added.

'There's that arm to be considered,' whispered Tom.

'Oh, that's nothing, it'll be as right as rain. Jeez, I can't wait!' she said.

'Language, Lizzie, language,' said the Highwayman, smiling.

With that he started to fade away.

'Next time I'll see you, it will be at my old home, in a few days' time,' he said.

'What about Webster?' she whispered, but the outline had disappeared. The Highwayman had gone, but he had heard her worried words as he sat on the branch before jumping onto the saddle of his horse.

We'll cross those bridges together when we come to them, Lizzie Miller! he thought.

★

The Greywater Scar Hotel was a late Victorian building constructed in the grand manner of the time. It had been built on a rocky point that looked back up the valley towards the Roman villa. The architect had also placed it opposite the waterfall.

Benjamin Tillsley, a wealthy mill owner, had had the hotel originally built to celebrate the discovery of the villa and its subsequent restoration. It was said at the time, quite nastily, that the whole project might have been what Tillsley wanted future generations to remember him by. It was Tillsley's answer to leaving a library or town hall or suchlike! However, Victorians flocked to the North of England in the late nineteenth and early twentieth centuries to take in the country air, the landscape, and especially to view the villa.

The hotel had a beautiful conservatory that had been built along the front of it overlooking the villa and falls, which doubled as a part sitting room, part dining room known as the 'Veranda Room'.

Other features that made the hotel so special were the turret bedrooms, all of which had a different interior theme, and the number of comfortable public rooms for guests.

The families had booked separate rooms for each of the girls, with seemingly no expense spared to give them the best of everything the hotel could offer. Lizzie had one of the corner turret rooms. This gave her two wonderful views, one across the valley and one looking towards the villa, both of which were stunning. She had pushed her head out of the window and from this position she could almost see up to the other end of the valley: wonderful. She pushed her hand through her hair and gave her glasses a very careful huff and a polish.

She looked again at the villa. Just imagine, two or so hundred years ago Tom Bennett had lived there. God, what a man!

The restoration may have changed it, but by all accounts Tillsley had ensured that any restoration was faithful to the original plan; he'd even got the fountain back in operation.

Lizzie's room, next to her parents', was on the third floor of the building. The Scar lay below the hotel, and so the drop from her floor to the lake glistening in the valley below must have been close to a couple of hundred feet.

Again she looked out of the window. There were quite broad ledges that ran round the building which seemed to connect all of the windows, and for some of the most expensive rooms the ledge broadened to form wide balconies overlooking the valley. Lizzie could see that some of them had tables with parasols to shade them and expensive-looking recliners on which to sunbathe when the sun caught that side of the building. Very nice, she thought.

All of the drainpipes and gutters looked very solid, but she didn't fancy the drop, so she breathed a sigh of relief when she saw several metal fire escapes. At least she wouldn't risk hurting her shoulder climbing in and out of her room, especially at night. (Little did she realise that by night the building was lit by subtly diffused garden lamps that helped with security, as well as making the grounds of the hotel a beautiful place to stroll in, especially in the summertime.)

They all went for an early meal in the conservatory, which was excellent. The band that played later in the evening was definitely aimed at adults, but apart from that, Lizzie enjoyed her first evening with her friends very much, and kept telling them so, till they told her to shut up about it! However, she did get tired and her shoulder was aching, so she said her goodnights and went to bed about ten thirty.

Half an hour later she was dressed in jeans, fleece and hat, ready for action!

She had felt cold in her room and turned up the thermostat on her radiator, which didn't seem to do any good at all. She put her pyjamas on over her outdoor things, just in case anyone called and she could quickly jump into bed, and was just brushing her teeth when Tom Bennett appeared. He sat silently on the end of her bed, waiting for her to finish. When she turned round, she nearly died.

'God, don't do that!' she hissed. 'Can't you appear when I'm looking in your direction?'

'Not always possible, Lizzie. Listen, we've got to move fast. Do you remember, as I disappeared last time you said something about Webster?'

Lizzie nodded and was about to speak when the Highwayman lifted his hand as if to tell her not to interrupt.

'Well, he's here tonight at the hotel. I don't know his disguise – maybe a waiter or something. I saw him arrive and he was looking pretty mean. But since then, nothing. I don't know where he's disappeared to. So you've got to move tonight – preferably now – to get the jewels.'

'I got dressed to go, but now I'm not so sure if I-I'm ready,' stuttered Lizzie.

'You said you were dying to get the jewels,' replid an astonished Highwayman.

'Well, I was but, my shoulder's sore. I don't know if...' she stopped.

'Very well, if you don't want to go, I can't force you. Goodbye, Lizzie Miller, for ever... and I thought you were my chosen one!' He smiled, pushed his tricorn hat on his head and began to disappear.

'You're going to make me very angry again!' spat Lizzie.

She pulled off her pyjamas, and just as he was about to fade away, she was ready.

'Got your torch?' said the head – which was now just a mouth, nose and two eyes.

She patted her bag. She'd been ready, then had second thoughts, but now the thrill of the chase had given her third thoughts that were all positive. Anyway she couldn't let him down, could she!

'See you at the fountain, one hour from now,' said the mouth, and the left eye winked at her before vanishing. He was gone.

Lizzie walked across her bedroom, unlocked the door and opened it, so that she could just glimpse down the corridor. All was quiet. She could hear the band playing some tune that she thought she recognised, and she could hear the muted murmur of voices coming from hotel rooms along the corridor, perhaps from televisions sets, but no one to her knowledge was around.

She could see the fire door that led to the escape. She closed her door and locked it – or so she thought – from the outside. However, closing it gently had caused the catch not to click properly.

Voices. *Damn*!

Across the hall was a door with a sign saying 'Linen Cupboard'. She crossed the hall and hoped that it would open. It did!

'We need a whole set of linen for number 53. A girl has been sick in her bed,' said the voice.

'Hell!' said Lizzie through clenched teeth. She unzipped her bag, switched her torch on and dived into the furthest, dirtiest linen basket at the back of the large cupboard.

Seconds later the room was bathed in corridor light. She could hear the maid lift things from shelves and then the cupboard was dark again. She prayed that the maid would not lock the door. She didn't; Lizzie sighed.

She opened the door, looked left and right, and sprinted down the corridor and slipped through the fire escape door.

Only the maid's rather butch-looking eyes, peering from a face showing six o'clock shadow, saw her depart. Lizzie wasted no time descending the fire escape. Her rubber-soled shoes made no noise. She did have one nasty moment when a window opened and Bendy's dad's hand flicked a cigarette butt into the grounds. She made a mental note to say something provocative about smoking and littering the place next time she saw him.

She reached the foot of the fire escape and stared up at the building to check if anyone was having a last look at the view. When she saw and heard nothing, she dashed across the gravel path to the security of the bushes, which marked the edge of the garden to the Scar's drop. The drop itself was flanked with a strong fence, thank goodness. She had a quick look through the chain-link, and it sure was a hell of a long way down. To be avoided at all costs!

Lizzie followed the path from the cover of the bushes to the edge of the villa. She could make out the covered walkway and the fountain in the moonlight. There was a gentle trickle from the water splashing in the pool, and further away to her right the crashing of the waterfall.

Certain areas of the villa were lit with lights that pointed out particular features. They looked beautiful from the hotel, but now each shadow that was cast seemed sinister, and Lizzie began to feel distinctly uneasy!

The fountain seemed very exposed to everyone's view, so she followed one wall of the villa until she reached the covered colonnade. From within the confines of the marble pillars, she moved from one to the next until she was a dozen or so paces away from the fountain. The Highwayman appeared. He was sitting on the ledge surrounding the pool, gazing into the distance down the valley.

'I'm here,' whispered Lizzie from her place of semi-concealment.

'Good,' replied Bennett, 'hope you weren't followed.'

'It was difficult, but I think I got here without being seen,' she replied.

David Webster watched her mouth and hand gestures. He looked carefully around. What the hell's going on? he asked himself. Who's with her?

'Lizzie, I'm afraid things have changed drastically since I lived here. Everything has been put back to its original state. I knew it as overgrown and derelict. The jewels are hidden in the hypocaust system,' said Bennett.

'Hypo-*what*?' hissed Lizzie.

'The underfloor heating system. Rich Romans fitted their villas with what you would know now as central heating today, but when they built it, it was underground. They built a raised floor on brick columns and then sort of sent hot air from fires through the spaces until it warmed the villa's rooms. Very clever, you know. Unfortunately, you've got to crawl under the floor of the villa to get to the jewels,' explained Bennett.

Lizzie looked at him in disbelief. 'You mean I've got to go under the bloody villa!' She turned away hands on her hips. 'Go on, then, how do I get there? Dig a hole in the mosaic? I knew it. It's going to be dark, dangerous, and I'm going to end up in hospital again.'

'Well, there's a little more to what you said, but I'm glad you're so positive about the quest,' he replied.

'How can it get worse?' Lizzie wailed.

'You have to get into the villa via the bottom of the fountain's pool. There's a grate in the bottom, which you have to pull up. You can crawl along the drain, which is quite roomy, from what I remember. You will be able to keep your head above the level of the water all the way. When you reach the end of these columns–' he pointed back towards the house– 'you'll see another grill that you'll have to open to gain access to the underfloor heating system. Only then will you be under the villa building itself.'

'Well, it sounds dead easy, doesn't it?' Lizzie sneered. 'First I get soaked. God knows how long I'll have to hold my breath before I release this grill thing. Then I swim or crawl about thirty metres along a pitch-dark drain, only to be confronted by another grill. And still you haven't told me where the bloody jewels are! Don't you think this is just a bit too difficult for me, having just recovered from a spell in hospital?' she asked, now in total control of herself.

'Just out of curiosity why can't I just go through the front door? Don't tell me it's alarmed!'

'It's alarmed,' replied the Highwayman.

Now totally ignoring her, Bennett explained that after she'd got through the second grill she would have to follow a dead straight line for about twenty feet until she came to the largest of the underfloor pillars. This would be her marker. She would then be at the centre of the building. She must look for a brick with an 'A' on it and behind this would be a pouch containing the two stones.

'Well, I've been there, done that,' said Lizzie.

'It's the best help I can give you, Lizzie,' he replied in very earnest tones.

'I feel most reassured,' she mocked back.

He gave her a wicked smile. 'You'll be there and back within half an hour, I wager!'

Lizzie could only laugh back at the audacity of the man.

The knock on Lizzie's door came ten minutes after she'd departed for the villa. Bendy's voice whispered loudly at the door, 'Lizzie, Lizzie, are you awake? I've got some chocolate surprise for you from the dining room. This nice waitress gave it me for you!'

There was no answer. Bendy tapped on the door. 'Lizzie, we're going to have a midnight feast in Mabel's room. Come on, I've got this choccy surprise for you.' Still no reply!

Bendy, exasperated at receiving no answer, tried the door handle. To her consternation, it gave way with little force at all. She saw that the lock should have caught, but hadn't.

'*Lizzie!*' Bendy hissed again.

The only light in the room was coming from the moon, which shone directly into Lizzie's room. She could see quite clearly that Lizzie's bed was made up and she wasn't there.

'Oh God!' Bendy moaned. 'Where's she got to this time? And her shoulder still poorly.' As she said this quietly to herself she moved towards the window. Lizzie certainly had a fab view from here. She looked again and thought she saw a figure making its way between the bushes towards the villa. But what really grabbed her attention was what looked like a maid or waitress following the distant figure.

When Bendy looked again the first figure had disappeared. 'Oh,' she whined, 'I hope that isn't Lizzie! Her folks will go spammy if they think she's up to something. I'd better not say I've been here. Oh God!'

With that Bendy made her way back to her own room. No midnight feast for her; she would have to say she felt a little poorly, and didn't go to Lizzie's room but went straight to bed! She closed Lizzie's door quietly behind her, this time making sure it clicked shut. She checked by pushing it. 'Wherever she is I only hope she's got the key and knows what she's doing!' she said to herself, and hurried back to her room, unseen by anyone.

Webster had now reached the shadows of the colonnade, and there he waited. Nothing stirred. Lizzie was nowhere to be seen. No other person was about. He crept up to the fountain. She'd seemingly disappeared into thin air.

The Highwayman was still sitting on the fountain's retaining wall watching Webster. He shook his head slowly and smiled his crooked smile. What a pity he couldn't raise the alarm right now! However, ghosts were only capable of so much, then they had to sit back and enjoy what went on around them! He watched Webster pad around in his stockinged feet. He could see that he'd shoved the heeled shoes he must have been wearing into the waitress's belt. Bennett thought that if he'd ever had to run in such high heels he could do himself quite a mischief, and smiled again.

Tom saw the hatred in Webster's eyes, heard him mutter an oath about Lizzie and how she seemed to be able to evade him so easily. What happened next certainly took him by surprise. Webster suddenly turned round, walked up the mosaic path between the columns and disappeared round the corner of the Villa.

Bennett ran after him, arriving at the same corner just in time to see him turn to the front of the building. What was he up to? Tom was at his shoulder when he realised exactly what Webster was going to do. He'd obviously managed to get hold of the villa's alarm code and was going straight in through the front door. Why hadn't he thought that this would happen? The man was capable of anything. Well, almost anything: he hadn't got his hands on any of the jewels yet, but Lizzie was certainly in danger now. She wouldn't be expecting anyone in the villa and would probably make a fair amount of noise under the floor getting to the central column. Webster was bound to realise where she was, and what she was up to! All he had to do was wait, and when she didn't appear in the villa itself it wouldn't take him long to realise that she'd entered via the fountain, and the jewels were somewhere underground!

Lizzie, watched by the Highwayman, took a couple of very deep breaths. She was standing knee-deep in freezing cold water. She'd already bent down and lifted the grating, which had yielded to her pulling quite easily, as it was regularly serviced. Next she had pulled it to the side of the hole in readiness for her 'swim'.

She ensured her torch was on but shielded from any prying eyes (which she was sure there weren't), and knelt down. The cold water caught her by surprise. She managed to hold the air she'd breathed in spite of finding it difficult to wriggle through the opening. She also caught her bad shoulder on the side of the grating, which made her wince. Once she'd got her body through the gap and had swum no less than three or four strokes, mainly kicking crawl-like with her legs, she was able to surface. She hoped that Bennett was right and the drain went dead straight to the villa.

In fact it proved quite easy to negotiate, and she managed to crawl on arms and knees through the water, and with the drain being so large she didn't even catch her back on the roof. At one point she went a little quickly and frightened herself by being dragged under the freezing water; but the torch stayed on and this reassured her.

She reached the grill that led into the villa, and it came away with a fairly hefty push, which again hurt her shoulder. It banged against the wall and she cursed the sound. Why? She didn't know. No one was there to hear her make the sound. What a fool! She forced herself up and over the lip in caterpillar fashion and sat on the floor of the hypocaust system to catch her breath and get her bearings with the torch.

The pillars supporting the villa floor were regularly spaced, but the corridors between them were fairly small. However, there would be enough space for her to crawl along. She could see the middle pillar from where she squatted with the torch beam, but she was going to ensure that she could find her way back by using the string method. She opened her bag and dragged out a sodden ball of twine. She tied it round the nearest column. Now, if her torch let her down and the second one she had also failed, then at least she'd be able to get back to the first grating. Everything was in straight lines, so she thought she'd even find her way back to the fountain. Of course, it was easier said than done. Think positive, Lizzie. Nothing will go wrong!

Tom Bennett had told her that the grill she had just crawled through was approximately in the middle of the villa wall. The villa had been built to exacting symmetrical demands by the original Roman owner, and that if she moved forwards and tried to keep in a dead straight line with the grill she'd eventually come to the middle of the building and therefore the widest pillar, where the jewels were. So far he had been dead right. The string was her safety valve!

Webster crept silently across the mosaic floor. Rooms radiated off the central reception area where he stood, and in the middle of the mosaic floor was a large marble statue to one of the Roman gods. A grill was set into the floor beside it.

He had frozen solid when he'd heard the metallic ring or crash. It had seemed to come from below and towards the rear of the villa. Somewhere outside, perhaps, in the garden? No, someone was in the building! Christ, the girl was in the building, under the floor! In the hypocaust system – she couldn't be – and yet there was a definite scratching sound coming from beneath the floor. Why would...? Of course, the jewels must be somewhere in the villa, but surely not under the floor! Why would she come that way? To avoid the alarm, that was it! She'd never have been in the position to get the code, but how in hell's name did she think to come this way? So she knows where they're hidden. Let's wait and see!

Lizzie, unaware of the danger virtually above her, was beginning to ache. The cramped conditions hadn't helped her shoulder, and once she had given it another nasty knock on some quite sharp bricks that made up the pillars. Finally she'd reached the largest of them. She sat down to regain her breath. Her torch seemed to be dimming. She felt in her bag for new batteries, not daring to use her reserve torch just in case. The batteries were wrapped in plastic to protect them from the ducking earlier. She now sat in the dark replacing them. The torch came back on with a crisp beam. Right in front of her was the stone marked with an 'A' scratched on it.

She dug out the cement, which flaked all over her. Then the stone became dislodged and fell into her hands. She put it down carefully and then felt in the hole behind. Yes, there was the purse. She lifted it out, pulled the leather thong apart, and into her hand blazed the jewels – two whopping great diamonds. She gazed into the incredible light that was being reflected from them.

It was then that she noticed that although she was cold and soaking wet the atmosphere in the maze of pillars was definitely getting warmer, decidedly so!

God, she thought, the heating is on! Surely I can't be that late. She checked her watch; the luminous hands showed midnight.

The heating wouldn't come on until the morning, as a demonstration to the public. Somebody has turned it on, on purpose! *Webster*! Here! *Oh no*!

Lizzie realised that she'd have to get out quick. The way she wanted to escape was now cut off. Bennett and she had discussed that if she got the jewels she would climb out of the hypocaust system through the grill that led into the villa and find a way out, even if it meant breaking a window and setting off the alarm. Lizzie had been sure she'd find her way back into the hotel without too much trouble, but now there was only one way of escape – and that was to go back the way she'd come!

Lizzie pushed the pouch into her bag and carefully zipped it up. She put the brick back in the hole. The spaces between the pillars were now rapidly filling with a hot steam, and she found that crawling had become difficult. She followed the string back to the grill and pushed herself through. Next she had to replace the grill, which proved more difficult, as she tried to rush things. The freezing water in the drain soon brought her senses back to life, and by the time she reached the fountain end of the drain she was frozen and petrified. She didn't know what to expect when she surfaced, but she couldn't stay here all night. She took a huge breath of air and swum the few strokes to the grill. She wriggled back through it and very slowly surfaced. She looked over the fountain's retaining wall cautiously. All was quiet!

The hotel, gardens and villa were still bathed in the soft lighting. The villa however was shimmering in a heat haze, rather like an early morning mist. She decided to leg it back to the hotel before a night porter or someone noticed the haze.

Tom Bennett couldn't understand why Lizzie hadn't shown up in the villa, and neither could David Webster. He felt sure the heat would have flushed her out through the inside grill, and Bennett was worried that she might stay down there in the hope that the problem would right itself. Both of them were jolted out of their thoughts when a siren was heard coming up the gravel road towards them.

Webster, turning quickly, slid on the mosaic floor and crashed into the statue. In getting up and brushing himself down, he didn't notice one of the high-heeled shoes fall from his belt and become lodged in the grating. He pelted out of the building and ducked down the colonnade. Running past the fountain, he found cover behind one of the bushes on the way to the hotel. Five minutes before this Lizzie had used the same bush to hide behind while she caught her breath and gathered her thoughts.

Lizzie reached the fire escape. She looked up; it seemed a long way up to the third floor. She moved as quietly as she could. This time, no window opened and she was pleased to see that the fire escape door that she had pulled to but not shut was still open. If the bar had been down she'd have certainly be sunk! Running down the corridor, she felt for her room key in her bag.

She heard the fire escape door open. God, why hadn't she bothered to thump it closed? Noise, she supposed. She fumbled with the key in the lock. Open, open, please open!

Click went the lock. She threw the door open and then closed it equally as quickly.

Webster fled down the corridor. Just as a guest door opened, he slipped into the linen cupboard. Webster and Lizzie stood with their backs to the closed doors, eyes shut, hands on the handles, not daring to breath – no less than four metres apart!

Webster looked down at his belt, and to his horror he saw that one of the shoes was missing! Although running in stockinged feet had been painful on the gravel, and the fire escape had dug into the soles of his feet, the fact that he'd lost a shoe was doubly agonising to him. God knows where he'd lost it!

The following morning the police arrived with a size nine high heel shoe in black leather that had been found wedged in the grill by the statue in the villa.

The detectives assigned to the case were looking for 'Venus' Cinderella. Happy Christmas!

When the police had been entirely satisfied that no one from the hotel – guests or staff – had had anything to do with the break-in at the villa, which in the end they put down to high spirits, they left to continue with their own festivities.

Bendy knocked on Lizzie's door at about eight. 'Lizzie! Lizzie Miller, open this door at once!' said an angry Bendy.

'Go away, I'm still tired,' replied Lizzie.

'Tired, my ass, Lizzie! I'll create hell if you don't open this door,' retorted Bendy in disgust.

The door was unlocked and Bendy was confronted by an awful sight. Lizzie's shoulder was swollen and angry looking under her T-shirt. Her bed was a mess and she could see clothes drying on one of the radiators. They were creased and filthy.

'Don't ask,' said Lizzie with a withering look. 'What you don't know, you can't tell.' She looked through the window with her arms folded, staring down the valley. The body language said it all.

'What's wrong with you, Lizzie?' asked Bendy, this time in a completely different tone. 'You've just come out of hospital after a terrible injury. You've been taken away supposedly to have a brill Christmas. We've all of us made an incredible effort for you, and you treat us like...' Bendy didn't finish the sentence; she turned away from Lizzie's back and started to cry quietly.

Lizzie looked at her. 'I can't...' she began, and stopped. It was no good. She had made a pact with herself. If they didn't like it because they didn't understand, they'd just have to lump it!

'I had to go out for a walk last night... felt my style was being cramped, needed some air,' she lied.

'Yeah, and I wonder how you got out, and how you look a mess, and how your clothes got like they are. Who was the walk with – a platoon of the SAS? What are your mum and dad gonna say?' Bendy spluttered.

'Nothing, 'cos they won't know, will they, Bendy,' muttered Lizzie threateningly, moving closer to her friend. 'Let's forget about last night and just go and enjoy Christmas, okay?'

Bendy was not convinced but nodded her agreement. Lizzie didn't even see her friend's look of despair, as she was already planning how she was going to get the jewels back to the Icon when they got back home. Tom Bennett was wondering about that too!

Two of Diamonds

The holiday turned out to be truly amazing. Bendy did try to forget Lizzie's 'outing', although it was always at the back of her mind. Her best friend had overnight, or maybe over a longer period of time, changed. Perhaps she'd grown away from them, living in the North. She certainly seemed to be getting through life a hell of a lot faster than they were, and it didn't really seem for the better. Bendy never let Lizzie know her innermost thoughts, but she had been hurt after Lizzie had made her feel 'outside'; it was difficult to explain!

Lizzie, to give her some credit, did as much as she could do to enjoy herself and make the others and her parents believe that firstly she was getting better and secondly was doing all that was possible to put David Webster behind her, make them feel that a new Lizzie was emerging. Bendy could have told them all that a new Lizzie had already emerged and she didn't like what she saw: hard, single-minded with a real hint of ruthlessness in her.

Saying the goodbyes from Hazelthwaite was every bit as difficult as the last time. But at least Bendy and Donna's parents had said unreservedly that the two of them could come back to see Lizzie during the summer. They'd acted rashly before, but now things were different. They certainly were sorry, but Bendy saw the crocodile tears that Lizzie shed as they left.

Hazelthwaite in early January was still very prone to heavy frosts, yet more snow and more time off school, which would be punctuated with good days on toboggans and work sent home to do. Not so good!

Lizzie kept the diamonds hidden in the little leather pouch waiting for the right time to get them back to the Icon. One Saturday afternoon in particular, when her parents had gone into Newcastle to shop and Lizzie had thought that Mabel and Amy would be around to hang out with, turned out to be a real bore. They had both had to go out with their respective parents to

Axenthorpe, or wherever, as Lizzie had said, for 'trivia'.

She walked across the village green, past the cricket square to the Gallows Oak. The huge tree, totally bare of leaves, stretched up to a cold and cloudless sky.

She sat on the bench kicking her heels. The church clock struck two. The vicar walked down the gravel path and turned toward the vicarage. She could hear sparrows chirruping in the hedgerows that still had bright green ivy growing in them. Jackdaws and rooks rose and fell, chattering and yelling, in the uppermost branches of the trees in the graveyard.

She looked up to Devil's Heights. A car was parked in the lay-by, by the bollards that protected the road from the drop. The low sun reflected on the windscreen. Someone was enjoying the view across Hazelthwaite!

The village was dozing in the afternoon sunshine. Quiet! What an opportunity! Lizzie walked back to the post office. She let herself in, and after getting her fleece, bag, torch, and the pouch with the diamonds in it, she made her way to the stable block. She looked around; the double doors and Judas gate were shut and bolted. To the back, the courtyard and garden were quiet. Nobody was walking their dog along the path at the rear of the garden.

She slipped inside the stable and walked to the far wall. She pushed gently on the fifth upright from the end below the dado rail. She pushed the panel across, turned on her torch and disappeared into the passage. The panel slid back into place. She flashed the torch to check the handle had snapped back into position.

Lizzie reached the other end of the tunnel in double quick time. She didn't even think about the skeleton slumped in the priest's hole this time; she had only two things on her mind – depositing the jewels and getting back.

On reaching the church, Lizzie paused to listen. Too many times she'd opened the secret panel to be confronted by someone's back or a voice or something. Care still needed to be taken. Just as she was about to reach for the handle to slide the panel open, a vacuum cleaner started.

'I don't believe it,' she muttered, 'every pigging time.'

She could hear the vacuum coming closer. Francesca was doing a last minute clean before Sunday service. The vacuum stopped and she could hear Francesca singing. Then the singing went muffled as she retired to the vestry to clean the silver and suchlike.

Lizzie pulled the handle and the panel slid open. She could hear Francesca singing quite well now. The phone went and she heard her answer it. 'Paula, how nice! We haven't spoken for ages. Well, well, well... how are you? No, I'm on my own, got all the time in the world. It'll be nice to chat!'

The words were like music to Lizzie's ears: 'long chat', 'all the time in the world'. She pressed the panel to close the passage. If she was caught now, at least she could explain she was looking for the vicar for... oh, she'd think of something. Lizzie stood up, her back to the nave and the first row of pews.

The gun dug into her back. She lifted her hands slowly. *Webster*. How could he know she was there, with Francesca so close? She remembered the car on the Heights. She should have realised!

'I'll scream, 'whispered Lizzie through her teeth, 'even if you get me, Francesca will get away and raise the alarm.'

Sexton meowed. The cat had woken from a deep sleep, stretched and pushed his tail into Lizzie's back.

Lizzie turned, 'God, Sexton, you moron!' She tickled his chin and he gave a sighing purr and pushed his face into her fist, which she had stretched out for him. 'Off you go, quickly.'

Now, Sexton never did anything quickly if he could avoid it, and he sauntered up the central aisle as if he owned the church. He stopped at the door, rolled over on to his back and promptly fell asleep again with all four paws resting in the air above his tummy. These he stretched now and then as he dreamed.

Lizzie moved towards the Icon. Parts of it gleamed as light from the sun's rays caught it. The emerald and the ruby shone out, and Lizzie was sure that the painting was getting clearer by the month! She wondered what would happen when the two diamonds were replaced in the frame?

She looked round the church. Where to put them so they'll be safe till tomorrow, that was the question. The Icon couldn't be touched because of the electronics. Sexton couldn't be used again; in any case he'd finally woken up and gone.

A beam of light falling through the window close to the altar had picked out a chalice that had been placed on it. In turn the beam had reflected onto Lizzie. Perfect; it would be used the following morning or even be checked tonight by Francesca or the vicar. She tiptoed up the three steps to the altar slipped the purse into it, so that the leather thong drawstring hung over the lip from the rear.

'Paula, lovely to hear from you… Yes, we will, dear. Cheers then, bye.'

Lizzie heard the receiver replaced. The call was over and Francesca had immediately stood up and was on her way. Lizzie dived behind the altar.

'Now what's next on the cleaning agenda?' she heard Francesca say. 'Where's me list? Plates, candle sticks, chalice… right!'

'Chalice! Oh God, she's going to find it now!' whispered Lizzie.

'Now what on earth is this dirty bit of material. What on earth…?'

Lizzie pictured what was happening on the other side of the altar. She could imagine Francesca's face as she pulled the thong back and looked inside the leather purse and then turned the contents into her hand.

Lizzie counted one, two th… She didn't get to three because the silence was broken by a scream that even made Lizzie quake.

'Vicar, Vicar come quickly!' wailed Francesca, as she made a bolt for the door. Lizzie heard the crunching of gravel as her feet rushed off down the path. Lizzie slipped from her hiding place to the passage and made he way back to the stable.

She closed the panel, and let out a long sigh of relief.

'Well done, Lizzie Miller,' said the Highwayman, smiling. 'Looks like we've – sorry, *you*'ve – done it again!'

Needless to say, the parish church of Hazelthwaite was brimming with congregation the next day. The vicar, virtually speechless, placed the two diamonds into their respective notches and blessed whoever had returned them to the church.

The Icon seemed to glow with the jewels of St Mark and St Luke returned to their rightful home.

Lizzie smiled. Mabel nudged her and said, 'Bendy told us that she thought you'd been busy while we were away at the hotel. Looks like she was right, eh, Lizzie?'

Amy smirked and winked, 'Lizzie, you're a wonder.'

Lizzie looked at them and remarked quietly, and because they were after all in church, that she thought the squadron of pigs had just flown by again. She also told them that if they spent time listening to Bendy they might as well listen to... The sentence was never completed as the vicar continued his sermon.

'However, the return of the jewels prompts me to wonder from where they were recovered and who was responsible. We were overjoyed to accept the last two stones, and most of us, me included, assumed some sort of divine intervention, some sort of miracle or miracles had happened. We must now be sensible, more down to earth about what has taken place. No miracle this,' he announced, pointing to the Icon, 'someone is returning the stones, and it could be someone local to the village, even in the congregation now present.'

A murmur went round the assembled people, and Lizzie was inwardly horrified at what he was saying. She continued to look interested, although her gaze was at the base of the pulpit, and she certainly couldn't bring herself to look at the girls. But she could feel their stares!

'Evidently someone or some people have unearthed information concerning the Axenthorpe stones, perhaps from old records or whatever, and as they seek out their whereabouts, they've found the goodness in their souls to return them to the church and not profit by them. I think everyone here knows the so-called story, fairy tale, call it what you will, about the highwayman, Tom Bennett. Personally, I don't believe a word of it, but if there is any truth in these old wives' tales about the murderer then I suggest they come forward, soon! We must all suppose that if the rest of the jewels are to be recovered, danger must accompany them, and it would be better for the correct authorities to help, than for Hazelthwaite to suffer another tragedy.' The vicar was referring of course to the deaths of Agnes Smith and his predecessor.

Lizzie still looked dead straight in front of her but she could again feel pairs of eyes boring into her very brain.

The Highwayman, standing in the pulpit behind the vicar, signalling to Lizzie to be still and quiet with a finger of his right hand over his lips; the other arm had his tricorn hat under it.

'So I say once more,' said the vicar, quite sternly this time, 'if the person or persons responsible for finding and replacing the Axenthorpe jewels are here today, consider sharing the information with me. Strictest confidence will be shown, if that be necessary. Let us pray.'

When Lizzie looked up after the Blessing, Tom Bennett had gone. After the service she remained in her place for a few minutes contemplating what to do.

'You look thoughtful, Lizzie,' said the vicar. 'Nothing I said worried you, I hope?'

'Oh no,' replied Lizzie, 'I just wondered who would be capable in Hazelthwaite of recovering the jewels. She got up slowly and a twinge of pain in her shoulder made her wince.

The vicar watched her thoughtfully as she walked down the aisle and disappeared out through the covered porchway. There was something, something very deep about Lizzie Miller. She wasn't what she seemed. He made a mental note to watch her movements, and where she showed up and didn't show up, if another jewel found its rightful home…

The Weaver of Hazelthwaite

'Corporal Weaver' tethered his horse to a post situated by the side of a square of grass at the rear of the inn in Hazelthwaite village. The hitching rail by the track at the front of the building, where he'd tied his horse several weeks ago, already had several mounts secured to it. This indicated that there were people already drinking in the inn.

He unhitched the caravan, entered the inn and sought out the innkeeper's permission to stay for a few days. He also asked him if he minded him having a small fire. The innkeeper nodded assent. Then, looking carefully at the tattered uniform and medals, asked him where he'd been and what had happened to him over the last couple of years.

Tom Bennett told him the story (lies) and then caught up with the latest village news and gossip, most of which still centred round the murder of the Reverend William Bennett.

Apparently, the vicar, according to the innkeeper, had a ne'er-do-well brother who was probably responsible for the crime. There was even the suggestion that he was the Highwayman. Regardless of whether he was guilty or innocent, the Axenthorpes, the local villagers and most certainly a Scottish judge called Sanderson, were going to see him hang. As soon as they got their hands on him the Gallows Oak would have a customer. When the innkeeper had said this, he'd laughed out loud and then spat on the floor. Tom agreed with him and said he'd keep a weather eye open for this scoundrel on his travels.

Tom retired to his caravan for the night after one mug of ale. He made up the fire with some wood that he'd cut to try and prevent it going out overnight. Then he set up some interesting alarm systems around his caravan that would alert him to prowlers, climbed the little set of steps to the split door, and went inside. He shut and bolted the bottom half of the door, took a last look round the front of the caravan and shut and bolted the top section.

The caravan was to all intents and purposes very ordinary from the outside. The inside, however, once the doors were locked and the interior shutters closed, changed. Although Tom knew he could be attacked from the back of the van he usually positioned it fairly close to trees if he could. Amazing how a wood could swallow you up if you knew what you were doing, and if you'd taken the trouble to scout around. A little knowledge can be a bad thing but on occasions it can save your life. Tom Bennett was a knowledgeable woodsman and could disappear at the drop of a hat if need be.

Next, he tucked the sacks of straw that he kept for the horse into the little side bunk bed to look as if a body was asleep in the bed. Quietly, he slid a panel in the central table across to the left and crawled inside, and down into a cleverly recessed bunk that he could drop out of onto the ground outside.

Effectively, Tom slept below the caravan floor. If anyone entered the caravan during the night up to no good, he would hopefully have a few seconds of valuable time to escape. Up to now he hadn't needed to use the escape route, but the innkeeper hadn't seemed that friendly, and he'd noticed a couple of locals leave furtively after he'd nodded to them. Something strange was going on, but he couldn't quite put his finger on it!

Bennett knew there was no use trying to move on that night, as the innkeeper would definitely suspect something. But on the other hand, if he acted naturally perhaps all would be well and his disguise would hold up here in Hazelthwaite – in the lion's den, so to speak.

It was about three in the morning when they came. He'd always slept lightly and he was immediately alert to the footsteps on the grass. Strangely enough, he'd been listening to a pair of foxes calling and an owl that had been particularly busy hooting. When they went quiet, the footsteps became obvious to him.

Two, maybe three, people had approached the caravan from the rear and from one of the sides. Well, they were in for a few painful surprises and shocks…

A hand that wants to open a door will grab the knob or latch fairly hard to gently move it. This door latch had along its rear edge one long dagger blade, and as the footpad suddenly realised his hand was being sliced an awful scream rang out over the cold night air. It was quickly stifled by the huge lead weight, which fell from the caravan's porch extension that protected Tom from the weather when it was raining, onto the man's skull.

They must have had a signal to attack at the same instant. For as the man's hand was being sliced on the front door, someone trying to climb onto the rear of the caravan by holding a wooden support realised that it had suddenly come away, due to a particular amount of force being applied to it. The support split a barrel it was attached to, revealing a large spike that entered the man's neck. The third man, slightly slow in reacting to the fate of the other two, suddenly realised that there was a vast problem and had run off. The bolt from the crossbow caught him before he had managed ten yards. The underslung bunk had small drop-down slots in the sides, just large enough for a crossbow to be aimed and fired. Tom Bennett smiled at his forethought.

The sharp scream that had rung through the night air would be put down to animals shrieking in the woods, if anyone heard it at all. Hopefully, no nosy locals would peer out to check, and if they thought anything else they'd be advised to stay indoors and mind their own business.

As the first rays of sun shone into the Hazelthwaite basin there was no sign of the attempted break-in at the caravan. The door latch had been replaced by a new one, and the lead weight had been drawn back to its original position to merge in with the roofline.

When Tom appeared at the inn for breakfast, the innkeeper stood looking at him open-mouthed. When Tom had asked him if anything was wrong, he'd just shaken his head and produced him ham and eggs and a large hunk of bread saying it was wonderful to serve an old soldier. Tom had smiled, given his thanks, and realised that the man he was standing before was as big a liar as he was! He'd also remarked to the innkeeper that he could catch a pheasant in a gap as large as he was showing him every time he stared at him. Was there something wrong, or not? He smiled.

Tom's smile faded when a voice barked from the top of the stairs. 'So, Corporal Weaver, is it? I dinna think so!' It was a leering Lord Sanderson. With that, about twenty of the Axenthorpe militia flooded in to the inn's dining room!

'I dunno what 'ee mean, Your Lordship, begging Your Lordship's pardon,' said Bennett in an apologetic tone, and giving him a mock bow.

'Oh, you don't, do you?' went on the pompous judge. 'Seize him. If he's telling the truth, he'll have nothing to worry about and can go on about his business. Oh, and search his cart. And find me the three who were supposed to bring him to me last night.'

Tom Bennett raised his eyes to the ceiling. He was fairly sure that his disguise, and the cart's for that matter, would pass even a close inspection; but he hoped the militia wouldn't pry too deeply into the woods behind the inn, otherwise he may have a problem explaining the grave – if they found it!

The judge flew into an evil rage when the militia came back with nothing to tell him.

'Let me tell you, Corporal Weaver, if that's your name, which I very much doubt. I'm very big in this area now,' said Sanderson, staring him right between the eyes. Bennett could smell his foul breath in his face.

Tom nodded vigorously. 'Oh, very big, Your Lordship, I can see that,' he replied, looking at the man's stomach. For this remark, and the way he looked at the judge, he got a musket butt in the back for his cheek. Tom fell to the floor from the force of the blow.

The judge continued, oblivious to the remark Bennett had made, 'If you so much as put one foot wrong while you're here, you'll be for the gallows – to hell with a trial, do you understand me? I dinna like ye, my man, and ye'll be none the worse for a hanging!'

Bennett staggered to his feet and looked Sanderson full in the face, but then backed down and nodded.

'You've got two days here, then we don't want to see you again. Understand?' added the judge. With that he turned on his heel and waddled out, followed by the officer and eight of the militia, presumably to make for Axenthorpe Hall.

Bennett didn't wait either. He hurried out of the inn and made his way back to Greywater Scar. He knew what he must do now!

A Customer for the Gallows Oak

The gravel driveway that led to Axenthorpe Hall was lit by lanterns on metal posts, which made the poplar trees that flanked its length look like giant sentry spears stretching up into the night. The lake in the gardens was a silver plate in the moonlight, and the island in the middle of it had a turreted folly, reflected in the water like a miniature castle. The moonlight bounced off the little arched windows and these too were reflected in the still water.

The Highwayman watched the guards at the gate very carefully. It being two o'clock in the morning, they'd not expect anyone to arrive at such an early hour, and it had made them sloppy. One was already fast asleep, his musket leaning against the wall, whilst the other shivered by a nearly extinguished fire. He would wait until both of them slept soundly before giving them the shock of their lives!

It was the sound of the hooves that woke him. The bleary-eyed soldier opened one eye only to see a huge black horse at full gallop coming directly towards him. Too late to shout, too late to shoulder and aim the gun: they were in trouble! By the time they had shouldered their muskets and fired, Tom Bennett was already approaching Axenthorpe Hall, still at full gallop. He swung the horse round the central grassy area in front of the elaborate doorway, pulled out both pistols and shot out two of the front windows. Then he took the bridle path towards Horseshoe Woods in the direction of Hazelthwaite.

The judge, Lord Axenthorpe and the militia took about twenty minutes to dress, saddle up and take up the trail. Tom Bennett made it easy for them. He waited in the little horseshoe copse of trees at the top of Devil's Heights, and when he heard the sound of their horses' hooves, he took off again. He launched his horse across the road, pulled up hard and turned left. He heard several screams of men and terrified horses as they plunged to their deaths over the top of the Heights!

When the rest realised what he'd done, he let them almost catch him before taking off again. He raced down the track to the village. He could hear the voices of Lord Axenthorpe and Lord Sanderson cursing at their horses and their men. At a breakneck gallop, Tom urged his horse into a right turn and crossed the village green.

He pulled up at the coaching inn and banged on the large double doors. Just as they were opened by a terrified owner, and he was forcing his way in at pistol point, a shot that was loosed off by Lord Axenthorpe hit and split his shoulder. Blood poured from the wound. Lights flickered on in all the cottages surrounding the village green in Hazelthwaite. Most villagers ignored problems, especially at night; but this sounded bad.

Bennett pushed past the innkeeper and made a run for the stable door. The second shot hit him in the thigh. He fell down, but managed to half hobble, half crawl to the furthest of the stables. His hand reached up towards the panelling, but then a fist knocked him unconscious!

When he awoke, he could see Lord Axenthorpe, the judge and all of the villagers of Hazelthwaite leering at him. Through a sea of pain, Bennett started to tell them about the passageway; but the words wouldn't come out and he blacked again.

Several hours passed and when he awoke again, a girl, dressed as a parlourmaid, was watching him. He tried to move, but his hands and legs were bound tightly, and the pain coming from his shoulder and thigh wounds was unbearable.

'What's your name, girl?' said Bennett in a whisper.

'Eliza, sir,' she replied.

'Well, Eliza, I'm going to tell you a story and I want you to listen very carefully, and if at the end of it you believe me, you can either tell someone or you can keep it a secret. It'll be entirely up to you.'

While she listened, Eliza bathed his wounds and got him to sip some water…

At dawn, they came for him. The whole village was there to witness the hanging of the murderer and highwayman, Thomas Bennett, at the Gallows Oak.

Thirteen-year-old Eliza watched his last breath on earth, and she swore that he'd given her a crooked smile and a wink before he died. She also would take his secret to the grave!

★

Lizzie's shoulder mended incredibly well. Occasionally she got an odd twinge from it, especially if someone accidentally whacked her with a hockey stick on a tender spot during games. She also felt it if she landed awkwardly on it in gymnastics, or if Mabel or Amy forgot how poorly she'd been and slapped her on the back. Apart from that, all was fine!

It was coming up for the Millers' anniversary of their arrival to Hazelthwaite. Lizzie was chatting about it to Mabel and Amy in the courtyard behind the post office one warm April morning. How much they'd been through and how much she enjoyed living in Hazelthwaite! The girls reminded Lizzie how much she liked Robbie Axenthorpe and that had led to a slanging match and a good giggle. Jane Miller had come out with drinks and a snack for them. After putting them on the table and returning inside, Mabel quite out of the blue said to Lizzie, 'So when do you get the next jewel pet?'

Lizzie looked livid but composed herself. In a fairly pleasant voice, she replied patiently, 'How many times do we have to go through this, Mabel? If I was the person responsible, do you think, knowing me the way you two do, I could keep anything back from you?'

Amy looked into Lizzie's face. 'So you're not a bloody little liar, then!'

Lizzie hadn't ever heard Amy swear; in fact she was rather shocked.

'A-Amy, I don't know what you mean. *Liar*, that's a strong word, and suggests that you really don't trust or like me,' she replied.

'Amy, that was uncalled for,' said Mabel. 'Before this gets out of hand, you'd better say the little word.'

'I have,' said Amy, 'she hasn't really denied it. You can't have a friendship when you believe there's deceit, that's all I'm saying.'

Lizzie looked at her drink and then at the two girls. She was so shocked at Amy that she just started to open her mouth, when his words filled her brain: 'Do you solemnly swear, Lizzie Miller?' She nodded.

Mabel and Amy looked at one another. What was she doing? Lizzie was in some kind of trance.

'She's off with the fairies again,' said Amy, 'I don't know why we chill with her.'

'Certainly getting chilly,' remarked Mabel. 'Think I'll nip home and get a thicker top.'

With that the two girls left. They were both disappointed by Lizzie's attitude, and Amy wished she hadn't said what she had. Half an hour later, she went back and put things right. Lizzie even promised her more effort in the future to be extra friendly. Amy just wished that she would confide in them! After all, didn't girls who have probs need the closest of allies to confide in?

The half-hour interlude had proved to be very disturbing to Lizzie. Mabel was right; the atmosphere had become chilly. Tom Bennett had arrived and had witnessed what the girls had said and noticed how close Lizzie had been to telling them the truth. He knew they would never believe her now. How else could anyone retrieve the stones so quickly? So he had given her a severe warning. If she told them, then the secret was gone and he would not, repeat not, appear to her again! Lizzie had been distraught!

What neither of them had realised was that Jane Miller, who had been vacuuming the upstairs corridor, had happened to glance out of the window only to see Lizzie talking and gesticulating to – no one! She thought that the girl was in severe shock and had deeper problems than any of them had imagined. She had even managed to catch most of the one-sided conversation. But it was the phrase, '...stone... tonight... Yes, I know where it is,' that had caught her imagination.

My God! Suppose Lizzie was the one retrieving the jewels, and supposing she was being led by a ghost, phantom or spectre… what could she do? Well, 'support her from a distance' sounded good to Jane Miller!

Three for The Watermill!

When did she go? How did she go? What clothes did she wear? What things did she take with her?

She was scared of the dark! Although she'd walk, she didn't overly enjoy it. She'd got lots of the right sorts of clothes but when had she got together the things she might need, like what? What were the things you took?

Too many questions, and virtually no answers, spun round Jane Miller's head!

God, what am I going to tell John? How am I going to get away from... Wow, she didn't know! How long might Lizzie be out for? Wait up, she was going too fast. She didn't know for sure that Lizzie was the culprit! The strange thing was, she was incredibly excited, and knew that she couldn't tell anyone, even John! It was the famous catch-22 situation... Now she understood that if Lizzie was responsible for retrieving the jewels she couldn't possibly have told anyone, because she just would not have been believed! Imagine, her daughter...

Story? What story was she going to make up? Nothing came to her. She was going to have to be deceitful, and John could never know, and whatever happened later she could not interfere or intervene with what Lizzie might get up to!

Lizzie's shoulder pains started to act up about ten. She kissed her mum and dad goodnight and went upstairs. Jane Miller carried on watching the box and told her to sleep tight, and dad did the bugs bite bit, which made Lizzie cringe, but she was always secretly pleased he did and would continue to do so.

Jane made a cup of tea for them both and added two sleeping pills to John's. Whatever happened, he must never find out about the evening's happenings!

She heard Lizzie going about things that she normally did

before going to bed and they both returned her final goodnight. Lizzie's bedroom door closed and upstairs went quiet. It wasn't long before her husband yawned and complained of tiredness, a long day that sort of thing and he too went upstairs. Same procedure as before; usual sorts of noises, then quiet. Well, quiet plus snoring! She really must get him to do something about that.

Lizzie had heard her dad retire for the night, heard her mum clink the cups and things in the kitchen, heard lights being switched off, toilet flush, and then the cottage went quiet. Lizzie waited by the already open window. The church clock struck half eleven: time to go! She locked her bedroom door from the inside. Lizzie was already dressed in jeans, fleece, hat and walking shoes. She threw her bag over her shoulder, made a last check that she had everything she needed, and after stepping out on to the chestnut's broad branch beside her window, turned and gently pulled the bottom part of the sash down.

So Lizzie had not gone to bed! No matter how quiet you are, if you are ready and alert for noise, you'll hear it. Jane Miller heard her daughter gently close the window and knew she had to be climbing down the tree.

She quickly ensured that she was equipped for whatever lay ahead. Well, she had the spare torch and huge amounts of rubbish in her backpack, which she threw over her shoulder before walking downstairs, avoiding the squeaks on the stairs by stepping close to the wall. One last listen to the snores. Um, like listening to a porker sleeping on a bad day... She smiled and let herself out of the kitchen door.

Jeez! She flattened herself against the wall. Lizzie was coming through the judas gate, back through the courtyard. In a way, this was a piece of luck, as she wasn't sure which way she'd be going, if she had stayed out at the front of the house. Out there, there were so many places she could have hidden.

Lizzie moved softly across the courtyard and exited through the garden gate down past the vegetable patch that her father had planted. Then she vanished through several slats of wood that she pushed aside.

The rapid movements of her daughter shocked Jane Miller. She was so quiet as well – it was like tracking a ghost. 'She's done this sort of thing before. Little madam!' she hissed.

The pathway led past the back of the churchyard and several gardens to the bridge that crossed the Hazel River. Lizzie moved fairly quickly along its length, and remembering the previous encounter with Trixie, Francesca's dog, she was very careful to be extra quiet at the foot of that garden. However, nothing stirred!

In fact she had slowed down so much that her mother almost stumbled into her in the darkness. Lizzie had at that moment switched on her torch to check the time, as she hadn't heard the church clock strike, and the moon had disappeared behind some clouds.

The Highwayman watched Lizzie's progress from the church tower. She was going to have get a move on if she was to finish her task by daybreak. He was just contemplating whether or not to have a word with her when he became aware of movement from down the path. Someone was following Lizzie. Webster! He needed to warn her fast... Then the moon came out from behind the clouds, and there was Jane Miller.

Now what was going on here? How had she found out about Lizzie? He was positive that Lizzie would not have told her. Somehow Lizzie had been discovered! When? It had to be that very afternoon, when Lizzie had spoken to him in the yard. Lizzie had become very animated. That was it; she had been seen talking to nobody and overheard. This was going to be a huge problem. Especially when Jane saw what Lizzie was about to do! If she tried to interfere... Well, he couldn't do anything about it now!

Lizzie peered round the fence. As she looked back across the village she could just make out the Gallows Oak in front of her. The bridge was just to her right. Half past midnight rang out. An owl hooted somewhere. Apart from the period village lamps that cast pools of light around the green at intervals, and the shafts of moonlight that poured a milky glow over the green and cottages, Hazelthwaite was in darkness.

She moved swiftly down to the bridge, stopped, looked back

once and then disappeared under the arch. The River Hazel was running low, and she came up on the other side without getting her feet wet. Now, she would follow the path that passed the rear of the cottages on the far side of the village green until she reached the old mill.

The path that followed the Hazel began to steepen. It had become fairly overgrown. Woods surrounded both banks, and the amount of moonlight reaching the path was insufficient to light the way. Lizzie switched on her torch. She tried to mask the beam as best she could but she presumed that she was safe now. She was far enough away from the nearest cottage not to be seen, even from an upstairs window.

Jane Miller felt ridiculous; well, worried and ridiculous. Here was her daughter, creeping about the village at gone midnight, getting up to whatever – and here she was doing the same. But bloody hell, it was exciting! The worrying thing right now was that she had lost sight of Lizzie when she'd rounded the fence near the bridge. Where the hell had she gone? She looked around. Lizzie wasn't heading back into the village, as she'd have seen her shadow. What was that dancing, twinkling light ahead on the other side of the bridge? Of course! The footpath by the Hazel River…where did that lead? The old watermill…surely not, but that was where the light seemed to be travelling towards.

'The Watermill it is, Jane,' she whispered to herself. And with that she too disappeared under the bridge, came up on the other side and hurried after her daughter.

The Highwayman had told Lizzie that the mill was being rented by a couple from Japan, but she would have nothing to worry about as he had seen them leave with what looked like an overnight bag the day before and drive off in the direction of Axenthorpe. Perhaps they were having a few days in Scotland!

Lizzie had said she hoped he was right and that no one was there. She might be breaking all sorts of laws if she was caught. Tom Bennett assured her the place was empty. In fact, Lizzie knew she was breaking all sorts of laws before she got to the mill!

The Watermill had been built in the seventeenth century to try and provide the area with some basic water-driven looms to produce cloth. However, what with icy conditions in the winter and the advent of steam power, it had quickly outgrown its use and fallen into disrepair through the eighteenth and nineteenth centuries. It was only in the late twentieth century that the farmer who owned the land decided to invest some money and convert it into top-class accommodation. Since this had happened, The Watermill was virtually occupied all year round, being very popular with American and Japanese visitors.

The undershot wheel had been completely renovated and the machinery overhauled, so that the owner could demonstrate to his visitors how the mill had actually operated. The accommodation was beautiful; the house had been tastefully decorated and furnished and the grounds had been landscaped. Visitors could walk to the village, which took about thirty minutes but it was usual to access The Watermill from one of the forestry roads by car.

Lizzie stopped walking when she was level with the mill's garden on the opposite bank. She could hear the mill wheel turning slowly on its axle as the water pushed it round. The water to turn the wheel was diverted from the Hazel further upstream, and then the mill race rejoined the main river below the house.

When Tom Bennett had hidden the sapphire at the mill, it had been disused and totally neglected. He'd placed the stone in a large hollow in one of the beams high up in the rafters. He'd had plenty of time to do it, and the surfaces of the building had made climbing into the roof area easy; today things were different.

Lizzie surveyed the scene in front of her. Firstly, she had to get across the Hazel River. She flashed her torch across to the other side. The water wasn't running particularly quickly, so wading across wasn't going to be very hazardous. However, you always had to be on your guard, because it was so easy to slip on a dangerous hidden boulder; but there were risks with everything. God – wet again! She stepped sideways down the bank, supporting her weight with some sturdy grasses and rushes.

Lizzie carefully put her foot, then her leg into the water, and she felt the current start to pull. Oh no! It was deeper than she had thought. She felt the water come up to her thigh. It was going to be a hard pull across to the opposite bank. She held her bag and torch above her head as high as she dared so that she didn't loose her balance. Feeling with her foot, moving it left and right, she tested the bottom and started to make for the mill bank.

A couple of times her foot slipped on a pebble or stone but she managed to keep her balance and the top part of her dryish. The water lapped around. Too noisy, Lizzie, she thought. It was a damn good job the Japanese couple were away, as she felt sure she was making enough noise to awaken the dead! As it happened, her progress was totally masked by the noise of the mill wheel.

Jane Miller watched her daughter's progress. She hasn't batted an eyelid about crossing the river. No thought of personal danger at all, she mused. No wonder you're home with bruises and God knows what, Lizzie!

The flashlight played on the water and the vegetation on the other bank. It would be her turn next, and she hadn't done anything like this since... Well, actually she'd never done anything like this in her life before. She knew it would be wet, cold, uncomfortable and dangerous for her anyway.

Lizzie made her way along the bank, found a tree that she could easily climb, hauled herself up and jumped from her perch into the mill garden. She ran up behind the fence till she reached the mill race where the wheel was turning. She couldn't see from this angle how she was going to climb up to the original roof space from this side of the building. She walked round to the front.

The old mill was almost split-level, being built on a hillside. There were wooden steps up to the front door and the first floor. Above this was an upper level – the loft – and below the first floor there was other accommodation and storage area. On the river side of the building was the wheel (of course) and to the rear of the wheel an old-fashioned hoist with a hook that could be swung into the old loft to raise and lower the original heavy machinery and sacks of grain. It was this that had given Lizzie an idea of how she was going to access the loft without breaking into the house itself, which was no doubt alarmed. Lizzie thought, Hell the bloody loft might be wired as well!

When Jane Miller had lost sight of her daughter, or rather the torch that had shown her position as she had crossed the Hazel, she'd had second thoughts about crossing herself. Lizzie would have to come back, presumably the same way, and she'd pick up her trail again then. For now she'd wait and watch. Little did she realise what Lizzie was proposing to do...

She walked further upstream until she could get a good view of the mill. Moonlight picked out the outlines. It was all very beautiful: the wooden planked exterior, the wheel, hoist... It was easy to see why foreigners would want to spend time in a place like this, with so much history! If only she knew the real truth of her own thoughts. It was then that she spotted Lizzie's outline again. She stood riveted to the spot! What on earth was she going to do?

Lizzie had managed to gain access to the rear of the waterwheel in the mill race. It was quite difficult to stand up unsupported, as the water that was being diverted was flowing quite quickly. Well, it would need to, to have the power to move the huge wheel. The wheel, on the other hand, was turning fairly slowly towards her. No good; she would have to paddle waist-deep to the other side of it. Only now as she looked up at the vast structure did it look what it was: pigging big, dangerous and slippery.

She pushed these negative thoughts to the back of her mind. The plan was simple: climb on to one of the vast wooden paddles as it came up from the water, hitch a ride to the top and just as it started its downward plunge to the mill race grab hold of the hoist and swing into the loft!

From his viewpoint on top of a shed overlooking the stream, the Highwayman looked worried. He knew exactly what Lizzie was thinking.

Jane Miller, from her viewpoint from across the stream, looked frightened to death, as she too realised what Lizzie was going to attempt to do.

From Lizzie's viewpoint, standing in front of the mill wheel that thundered in front of her, things looked daunting. She tried to count the seconds as each paddle appeared. Then one foot on, two hands on and the other foot up – and she was being slowly hoisted upwards. As she struggled to maintain a grip on the sodden, slippery wood her second foot suddenly slipped and she was flung sideways. Momentarily it looked as if she would be thrown off the side of the wheel. She screamed out loud, the sound piercing the night air. The Highwayman stood totally still, watching what would happen next.

Jane Miller, hand over her mouth, watched her daughter sway over the side and then regain her balance. She had heard the scream, and silently screamed herself at the same time! Lizzie, what are you doing? The sudden sideways lurch had driven a stab of pain through her newly healed shoulder and it was this, not the thought of falling into the race, that had made Lizzie cry out.

Fortunately the wheel was moving very slowly, and it had taken just a second for her to lose and then regain her balance. Now her gaze focused on the hoist. As the wheel reached the top of its journey, Lizzie stood upright and got ready to grab the hoist. She certainly wasn't ready for its reaction. For as soon as she grabbed it, the weight of her body travelling forwards caused the beam to swing violently against the side of the mill.

Lizzie felt the full force of the crash and almost lost her grip. She was now side on against the building, with the loft doors about three metres to the right. She got a really tight grip with her hands, on the hook, lifted her feet to her chest and gave an almighty shove with her legs.

The hoist flew out across the top of the wheel with Lizzie hanging to it, back towards the double doors, which were secured with an ancient, rusted padlock. There was a sickening crash of splintering wood as Lizzie's braced legs smashed through the old timbers, the padlock rendered useless against such force. She felt a searing pain in her shoulder, which really did cause her to scream in pain this time, and she was left unceremoniously dumped onto the loft floor. She lay for a few seconds on the buckled wood and splinters before moving.

The pain in her shoulder was awful. The pain all over her body was awful. But she'd done it, she'd arrived, and that almost made all the effort worthwhile. She realised that she must be well battered and bruised again. How would she explain this time?

Her mother had watched all of her daughter's actions in abject horror. She was watching the actions of a stranger. She'd given birth to and brought up a total stranger! This was not her little Lizzie, this was some kind of walking nightmare who was callous, hard and deceitful. Lizzie had lied to her time and time again; she must really hate her mother. Jane looked down and tears trickled down her cheeks. What she'd witnessed tonight at the mill was someone else, someone alien to her. From now on Lizzie ceased to exist, she was a Miller in name only.

'Couldn't have done better myself, Lizzie,' said the Highwayman. He was sitting in what looked like a quite uncomfortable position between two rafters ten feet above her. From across the valley, the church clock sounded three.

'You'll have to thread your way across the rafters towards me, and you'll find the stone is in its pouch in a notch over there.' He indicated with his thumb.

Lizzie stood up. Every part of her body ached, and as she brushed herself down bits of splintered wood from the door tumbled to the floor beside her. She looked around the loft for a place to climb up into the open roofed area where the exposed timbers were. It didn't take her long to reach the place where Bennett had been sitting. He now stood on the floor looking up at her.

'Just in front of you,' he said.

'I don't know what I'm gonna tell my mum when I see her,'

Lizzie moaned as she retrieved the bag. 'If she could see me now she'd have died, and I'd be dead meat too!' she continued.

'Oh, I'm sure she'd be very proud of you Lizzie,' he replied. 'Now a get a move on, dear, or it'll be light before you get back.'

'Don't call me "dear"!' snapped Lizzie.

Lizzie climbed down to where Bennett was standing. The little bag had been positioned exactly where he had indicated. She drew the strings and looked at the stone. She held it up to the moonlight. The rays hit the sapphire.

'It's beautiful, isn't it?' she murmured.

'Yes,' he replied.

'They've all been fabulous! The Icon must have been worth a fortune,' she replied. 'Oh well, back home – and then there's just one more to go,' she concluded.

'Lizzie,' said Tom.

'Yes?' she replied. She hadn't liked the tone in his voice when he'd said her name.

'Oh, nothing that won't keep. Well done tonight. Safe home and be careful. I've heard nothing about Webster for a while. You must be continually on your guard!' he continued.

'Thanks for being nice to me. Tonight's been real difficult. When the hoist swung out and back I thought I wasn't going to make it through the door. I was scared,' she admitted.

'I know you were. We were all concerned,' replied Bennett.

'*We*?' she said looking at him strangely.

'Oh, nothing,' said the Highwayman. 'On your way, Lizzie.'

Jane Miller could just make out Lizzie's outline sitting in the doorway, the hoist beside her. She could see her move her arms, and from her body language realised that Lizzie was engaged in an earnest discussion with someone. She couldn't see anyone and she couldn't hear anyone, but she sure was talking to something! Strange…

She still didn't know how she would approach her daughter in the morning, she felt so much anger towards her at the moment. She was so confused about her actions, yet understood that if Lizzie was for some unaccountable reason being led by this – this *something*, whatever it was, then she couldn't tell anyone. Gee, what a mess! Perhaps to do nothing was best. See how Lizzie reacted to her later on at breakfast. She knew that she could put her so-called daughter under a lot of pressure if she demanded to see how her shoulder was, because she knew full well there would be a mass of new bruises and God knows what on her body. Apart from this fact, how was Lizzie going to disguise how tired she felt from all her night-time activity?

Lizzie surveyed the damage; not much she could do about the ruined doors, but the Japanese couple would have to assume there was an attempted break-in that had gone wrong. She watched the waterwheel paddles come slowly up towards her. She lowered herself down and let the wheel gently take her down. She stepped off and onto dry land and retraced her steps back to the garden. She stepped through the fence, slid down the bank, waded across the stream and started back along the path for home. Every step she took was painful, wet and cold.

Her mother followed at a safe distance, and by the time Lizzie had cleared the bridge the church clock had struck four. Lizzie crept up the garden, crossed the courtyard, slipped through the judas gate and made her way back to the chestnut tree.

Jane Miller waited till she saw Lizzie pass through the gate. She then dashed indoors, ran upstairs, this time not worrying about the squeaky one, and opened her bedroom door – to a chorus of snores. She breathed a sigh of relief the sleeping pills had done their job! John hadn't woken up. No explanation needed on that front as to why she'd been out of bed for such a time...

Lizzie climbed the tree just as the first tinge of dawn lit the sky. She had even heard a car or van engine somewhere, probably the milkman on an early round. She pushed up the sash window and climbed into her bedroom. Lizzie took off her wet clothes and dried herself thoroughly. She got into bed, turned on her electric under blanket and dozed till about six thirty. She got up, popped to the loo, and walked downstairs to make her parents a cup of tea.

Ten minutes later she was back upstairs with tea and toast. She knocked on the door of her parents' room. She heard her mum say, 'Come in' – but that was all!

Lizzie entered, put down the tray and kissed her mum on the cheek, 'Morning, Mum, Dad,' she said cheerfully.

Jane nudged her husband sharply in the side with her elbow. 'Wakey, wakey sleeping beauty!' she shouted in his ear.

'God, I feel awful. I feel as if I've been asleep for a week! Feel dreadful… Oh, thanks for the tea, Lizzie. You are a good, thoughtful girl,' he continued.

Jane Miller regarded Lizzie thoughtfully. 'All right dear, are you?'

'Yes, Mum… Shoulder aches this morning, think I'll take a Paracetamol,' she replied.

'Bad dream, perhaps?' continued her mum. 'Maybe you were sleep walking and gave it a whack or had a heavy fall.'

'Give over, Mum! I slept like the proverbial log last night, although I did have a fall out of bed. Maybe I was dreaming – who knows,' she replied.

She turned round to go out, and as she did so she was aware that the door of her mother's wardrobe was slightly open, and she felt certain she saw what looked like muddied clothes lying in the bottom. Was that a boot that looked as if it had been carelessly chucked inside, in a hurry?

Lizzie pushed her hand through her blonde hair and gave her glasses a huff and a clean. She shut her bedroom door behind her and leant against it. What had the Highwayman meant when he'd said, 'We were all concerned?' Surely he hadn't meant her *mother*! No, it was inconceivable! Lizzie shook her head and went to shower away the pain she felt in every limb. Perhaps a bath might be the better option!

Batting or Chatting?

By the time she had had a bath, dried herself and her hair, got dressed and walked down the stairs to the kitchen, her father had finished his cereal and toast and was just sipping the dregs of his coffee.

'I'm off to get some bits and pieces from the wholesalers,' he announced, 'see you later, Jane. Don't do anything I wouldn't do, Lizzie.' He smiled and then yawned, murmuring, 'God, I feel real tired.' Then they heard the front door close and he was off. Lizzie smiled at her dad's 'don't do anything'... He was so predictable.

Jane Miller asked her daughter in an offhand way if she wanted cereal, toast or a cooked breakfast. Lizzie said cereal and a slice would be fine. Whilst Lizzie covered her bowl in Sugar Puffs, extra sugar and floated the lot in milk, her mother watched her.

'Sleep well?' she quizzed.

'I told you earlier, like a log when I finally got off. Took some time because my shoulder was giving me heaps,' she explained.

'Perhaps you should've had a pill,' said Jane icily.

'Didn't have any in my room – and in any case I wouldn't have wanted to disturb you and dad. You know what the landing is like – creaks and things. Once you get to bed you hardly want to get up for a pee unless you're bursting,' she added.

Lizzie's mum still eyed her. 'Would you like me to have a look at your shoulder, dear, and perhaps give it a massage?'

Lizzie didn't like the questions. She was becoming ever so slightly suspicious of her mother's intentions, but she wasn't going to be rattled.

'No, it's all right. Stop fussing, Mum,' she answered.

There were a few moments of awkward silence before her mother said,' Oh well, if you're sure, Lizzie. Like to come for a walk with me this morning? Perhaps we could go for a wander by the river, it's such a nice day.'

That was it! Lizzie had had enough. 'I told you I'm fine, Mum. Just leave it at that. You know I hate walking, and I can't stand water!' she shouted. 'And why all the questions? Don't you bel...?' Lizzie broke off, got up and walked out of the kitchen. She'd got rattled – what a fool!

Jane Miller didn't tackle her daughter again about the episode. What Lizzie hadn't said was enough for her; it condemned her. She'd lied from the start, and as far as Jane Miller knew Lizzie's life for a considerable time had been a lie.

Lizzie walked over to the Gallows Oak and sat down on the bench. She bent her head forward and rested it in her hands. Her long blonde hair fell over her face. Her glasses slipped down her nose a smidge. She used her right index finger to push them back up to the bridge. They slipped again. She swore silently to herself.

From across the cricket square, way over to her right, she heard her name being called. It was Mabel, and she was coming her way. Oh God, more questions. What had her teacher said about Spain in the old days? Something about the 'inquestion', 'inequestrianism'? She couldn't remember the correct word. Bloody history, she thought, just a load of long words and dates, and totally useless! The church clock struck the half-hour, nine thirty.

'Wad ah yeh up too, pet?' said Mabel.

'Norralot,' answered Lizzie.

'Hazelthwaite centre of...' mused Mabel.

'...boredom,' chimed Lizzie, finishing her sentence.

'Oh, I don't know, soon be the start of the new cricket season,' said Mabel, smiling.

Lizzie looked at her and grimaced.

'It sure was a wild and wicked weekly event last year,' said Lizzie in her most bored and sarcastic tone.

'Ah, but pet, this year Robbie will be playing permanently. He's coming back from school to help out our li'l ol' teeam,' said Mabel in a conspiratorial way.

'Meaning what?' said Lizzie. 'Don't try and match me, Mabel! You know what I think of him.'

'Outwardly Lizzie, yes, but me and Amy think you've got a real soft spot for him.' She winked and giggled as she said this.

Lizzie gazed up at Devil's Heights. Mabel of course was right, but she certainly wasn't going to let on to her. It would be round the village and school faster than... she couldn't think of a simile, but as quick as quick!

'Me mum is takin' me and Amy to Newcastle today. Wanna come?' continued Mabel.

Lizzie thought this would be an excellent idea. It would get her away from her mum, who was being a proper pest. It would give her some space to get over the stress she was in.

Jane Miller could think of no good reason why Lizzie shouldn't go. Well, she could, actually, but grounding her for six months without reason wasn't one of them! Although Lizzie had put herself and her mother through hell the previous night, she could never divulge to Lizzie that she'd followed her, and so it would be churlish of her to say no, now. Although things would probably never be the same between Jane and Lizzie, perhaps time might be a healer!

Nothing out of the ordinary happened for a month or so after the 'trip' to the mill. Easter came and went, and spring moved imperceptibly into early summer.

Hazelthwaite awaited the yearly rush of visitors, and Lizzie waited for the right time to address the problem of replacing the sapphire. She had more or less forgotten the argument with her mother and had actually got down to some half decent school work, much to the shock of the teachers, friends and parents!

The Highwayman had made himself conspicuous by his absence, and she often wondered what he was doing. David Webster had seemed to have dropped out of the picture although she was always wary, especially going to and coming from school. She always thought that she might be abducted, or even worse; but her worries proved totally groundless. The possibility of her leading him to just one of the stones was enough for him to stay at least a good arm's length away. Only she knew there was one left to find, and then 'that was that', so to speak. However, if he were anywhere local he would be sure to know that the fifth jewel had not yet been replaced, or for that matter recovered. So he would assume that there were still two to go, and either of them would still be worth a fortune, even in a closed market.

The cricket square and ground had been cut and rolled and obsessively well tended. The little wicket fence had been painted white and the rope that marked the boundary pegged in place. The Gallows Oak was in full leaf and the gardens around the village green were beginning to show early colour. It was just as Lizzie remembered it from last year, perfect.

As she sat with her brown legs dangling from the branch of the chestnut tree by her bedroom window, she heard the car coming down the Axenthorpe road before she saw it. The BMW Z3 came to a halt by the pub, and the two Axenthorpes got out. Lizzie watched them disappear in to the pub garden. She could hear good-natured laughing and banter going on with other team members.

This Sunday was to be the first team practice day. Nets had been erected at the corner of the green closest to the pub and already some of the cricketers were going through the motions of batting, bowling and fielding. Kit was scattered here and there on the grass.

Lizzie watched as Robbie emerged from the pub garden in his cricket whites and a large white pullover. On his head was a large floppy white hat and he carried a bat under his right arm and a head guard in his left hand. He let his head guard fall on the grass after skipping over the white fence.

She drew up her binoculars to see him more clearly. What she saw she liked! She swung the bins round in a slow sweep of the village. Mabel and Amy came in to sight. They were gawping at Robbie too! Cheek of it, and they were the ones that said she liked him! Lizzie was sure that Mabel couldn't have squeezed into a shorter skirt even if she'd tried, and Amy was wearing spray-on jeans!

She moved the bins on. Blimey, it seemed as if all the girls (if that was what you could call them today) in Hazelthwaite had come to view the younger Axenthorpe. Most of them were half-hidden, as she was. They were gazing through bushes, peeking over walls…what were they like? Competition, that's what they were like! Lizzie smiled.

Well, it would serve them all right. She climbed down the tree, pushed her hand through her hair and gave her glasses a huff and a polish and walked down to where the players were gathered. Robbie saw her approach. He left his fielding routine and jogged over to where she stood.

'Hello, Lizzie,' he purred.

He's got a very appealing smile, she thought.

'Hi,' she replied giving him the cutest smile she could muster. 'I wanted to thank you for the card you sent me when I was in hospital. I haven't seen you for yonks,' she continued.

'You wrote. That was fine,' he said, smiling again.

A player called across to the youngest Axenthorpe, 'It's batting, not chatting up practice you're here for, Robbie. Gerramoveon.'

Robbie went crimson at exactly the same time as Lizzie and they both laughed.

'Coming… Lizzie, I'll see you later. About an hour, okay?' he said.

'Okay,' replied Lizzie, saying a secret *Yes!* to herself.

She walked back towards the post office. Amy and Mabel ran up to her – well, as fast as their clothes would allow them to.

'Give, Miller,' said Mabel.

'Oh, I just wanted to say thanks for the card he sent to me,' she retorted.

'Spare us the excuses, Lizzie. What did he say?' said Amy.

'Well, he didn't call me a bloody liar,' said Lizzie not given to subtle answers at the best of times.

'Touché!' said Amy, 'I deserved that.'

Lizzie stared at her, then crossed her eyes and laughed. 'He said he'd spare me ten of his precious minutes after nets,' she told them.

Amy eyed Lizzie then turned to Mabel and said, 'She's done it! She's pulled Robbie, lucky little…' She stopped in mid flow.

There then ensued uncharacteristic talk about boys. Well, it was that way to Lizzie, as everyone knew her views on them. She finished with something like, 'It must be my subtle charms he's fallen for.'

Mabel almost choked. 'More like your *un*subtle ones Miller,' she retorted, eyeing her up and down. They fell about laughing. Needless to say, Lizzie was ribbed mercilessly for days after her 'meeting' with Robbie.

What she didn't tell them was that he had invited her for a swim at the Hall the following Saturday. Now, that was going to be worth waiting for, as the girls would be green with envy if they knew!

Return of Van Vebstriche!

Lizzie had 'sat' on the sapphire for several weeks before thinking about returning it. She had thought about using the passageway, but this usually ended in her having a minor attack of nerves. She didn't know why, but each time she plucked up the courage to return the jewel something cropped up or she invented something to stop her going.

Good fortune was to be with her, though, as the yearly flower show that had started all the business with the Icon was to give her the opportunity she needed.

Francesca Golightly had asked for additional help to oversee displays for an hour at lunchtime on a Saturday. This would give her time for something quick to eat and give the dog a walk. Lizzie volunteered for a couple of these sessions as it meant that there would certainly be a time when she would be in the church on her own. Her parents had thought this a good idea, but it had raised her mother's suspicions again. It had also raised the suspicions of the vicar. In fact, raised his suspicions so much that unbeknown to anyone he installed a basic CCTV camera concealed in the church overlooking the Icon. It also gave an all-round view of the church towards the altar and vestry end.

However, the vicar thought that it was unbeknown to anyone. Unbeknown to the vicar, the day he had the camera installed in the church, with TV and video linked in the vestry, he was being watched by Tom Bennett! The Highwayman silently agreed with the dear Reverend when at the end of the installation he said, rubbing his hands together, 'Now then, that'll learn ya, whoever you are!'

'Certainly right there, Vicar; it'll certainly learn ya, and no mistake!' said Bennett wickedly. He smiled the crooked smile.

Armed with his information, Tom proceeded to seek out Lizzie and tell her this rather disarming piece of news. He found her spring-cleaning the stable block for the summer. How she'd ranted and raved when she heard the news! He let her go on for several minutes then put his gloved hand across his neck, indicating for her to be silent. She stuttered and spluttered on.

'I've just organised some quality time to replace the sapphire!' she shouted.

It took Tom Bennett all of his patience to explain to Lizzie that the church was the jurisdiction of the vicar, and didn't she understand that he was just a little concerned about what was happening? Lizzie had gone on and on about it, until he turned round to her, said he'd warned her, and disappeared. This had annoyed Lizzie even more!

'You come and go when you like with seemingly no respect for what I'm trying to do for you!' she protested.

He stood in a corner watching Lizzie rant on at an empty wall. Finally she had calmed down and got on with the tidying. As he sat down on a step that led to the hayloft, he now realised that she certainly wasn't going to like what he would tell her on their next meeting! Even for a spectre he felt scared; she certainly had a wicked tongue and temper.

Perhaps he'd send his horse to tell her. She didn't know, even by then, that it spoke and could hold an extremely intelligent conversation on subjects as far apart as George the Third and the fighting capacity of a Stealth bomber. Damned good horse all round, thought Bennett. Oh well, things to do…

The first Saturday in May was horrific. Rain hit Lizzie's bedroom window like handfuls of pea shale being thrown at it. It was raining so hard that she could hardly see the other side of the village green. She showered, dressed warmly, as she knew the church would be freezing, and then went down to breakfast.

She helped her father get the shop ready for opening, then nipped up to her bedroom to see if the swim was still on at the Axenthorpe's. She used the text on her mobile and received quite a telling reply back from Robbie that made her blush. Cheeky pig! But she thought she'd just check the state of the size of her thighs in the mirror in case the new two-piece she'd bought for the occasion wasn't suitable. She then made her way to the church.

Lizzie remembered the first couple of times she'd walked up the gravel path, recalling Agnes and all the previous year's problems; it all seemed such an age away. The porch door was open. She walked past the notice board and down the central aisle.

Francesca was busily organising areas for the fifty or so displays and welcomed Lizzie with a hug.

'You're early, dear,' she said.

'Thought I'd come and lend a hand with the organising, then you can take an extra half-hour over lunch,' Lizzie replied.

'Lizzie, dear heart, you're the most thoughtful girl,' cooed Francesca. She directed Lizzie to do several tasks, and by the time Lizzie had moved this thing and placed that thing, sometimes the same thing several times over to Francesca's satisfaction, the time had moved on to eleven thirty.

'Thanks so much, Lizzie. I'll be off now, back around oneish, if that's all right with you, dear. Shouldn't be much happening, especially with the weather the way it is. Show doesn't open till tomorrow, so it's just a matter of having someone around in case of a late delivery. Okay?'

Francesca left. Lizzie watched her go, and then for the sake of the camera carried on with several jobs. She didn't go near the Icon, and made sure that she was in camera shot at all times.

She had the sapphire in the leather pouch in her pocket, and after half an hour of busying herself with polishing, she made a great fuss of setting out her lunch on the first pew by the altar steps.

'Oops!' she said in a loud voice. 'Must just go and wash my hands.' She walked as loudly as she could across the flagstones into the vestry. She popped into the loo washed her hands in the little basin, and while the loo was flushing, she dashed to the cupboard that housed the video and hung the pouch on one of the buttons. The whole process took just two minutes if that. Even a thief would have had to look for several minutes before he could locate where the video was hidden, as the vicar had concealed it behind some large religious scripts and books.

She walked loudly back to the pew and ate her lunch. She felt sure the short time lapse of her being out of camera view would be enough to persuade the vicar that it couldn't have been her. It had to be enough!

Robbie was waiting at the front door for Lizzie when she arrived for the afternoon. He'd told her dad that his father would drop her back to Hazelthwaite about nine thirty, after dinner. Lizzie felt worried: dinner at the Hall... Six lots of cutlery to deal with, best manners, oh hell! Robbie creased himself when she'd told him. He reassured her, that he'd never had to use six lots of cutlery for sausage and chips. What on earth did she think he was used to at boarding school!

It was when they'd changed and went through to the pool area that Lizzie was to receive an awful shock. Nothing could have prepared her for what, or rather who, was sitting under one of the poolside umbrellas: none other than David Webster, but in the guise of Van Vebstriche!

He smiled. 'Leezie Meeller! So ve meet again, isn't it. And in such vundervul circumstancis, no?'

She took his outstretched hand. It felt cold and clammy. She'd rather have put both of her hands round his pigging neck!

'Great! You remember one another from last year,' said Robbie. 'Van Vebstriche is one of our family's oldest friends. He's just popped over from Amsterdam on business for the weekend. Hope you don't mind, but he'll be sharing the bangers with us.'

Lizzie said nothing. Jeez, what do you say in a situation like this? Oh, er, Robbie, your great friend here is actually an impostor who has repeatedly tried to kill me for about a year. Perhaps he might consider drowning me as his next trick, or poisoning my sausages! No she'd have to watch her back and be vigilant for a couple of hours, see what developed.

'Vell, Leezie, I vunder what it is you a aving to be getting up to zinze ve are last meeting eh? Up to no goot, I'm sure, like all ov ze teenagers. Robbie tells me zat yo are aving ze awful accident but all is vell now. Zat is goot.' Then he added a little more sinisterly, 'Sometimes it is ze hurt inside vich is verse, no?'

He went back to reading a book, which looked as if it had come from the Axenthorpe library. He knew well enough that she was fine.

Getting proof of who he was and his unending disguises and what he was up to was Lizzie's seemingly insurmountable problem. If only she could trap him with the last stone, he would be prison-bound, and this was all she could work on. He really did deserve whatever was in store for him!

Finally, he got up from his chair, put the book he was using for research under his arm, said a general goodbye and without looking in her direction left the pool area. She watched him disappear behind some trees, then reappear some distance along the gravel road that led to the Highwayman's Perch cottage.

Her concentration was shattered when Robbie suddenly bombed her from the opposite side of the pool, leaving her completely saturated. She took off her glasses, ran to the edge of the pool and returned the compliment. When she surfaced she had jumped up above him and with both arms locked on the top of his blonde head, gave him a severe ducking. When he'd come up he was coughing, spluttering and laughing. Lizzie Miller, scared of the water…!

The vicar had arrived back at the church from a local meeting that had been held at Axenthorpe at about three. Francesca had told him that Lizzie had done her first stint and what a great help she'd been. He thanked her and disappeared into the vestry, adding as he went that unless anything ultra urgent cropped up in the church, he wasn't to be disturbed. Francesca said fine by her, and that she in turn had to nip to the post office and she'd leave him to it.

Martin Leonard locked the vestry door. He listened for a couple of seconds and when he was convinced all was silent he walked to the cupboard that concealed the video recorder. He opened the double fronted doors, pulled out the large files and books, and knelt in front of the video machine. There, hanging on the shuttle stop frame control, was a little leather pouch held fast with a thong. With trembling hands he pulled the leather drawstring cord. He carefully upended the pouch and let the contents fall on to his desk. The sapphire slid onto a pile of the latest parish magazines. He collapsed into his red leather-upholstered swivelling chair, rested his forehead on his left arm, and stared at the jewel! The light shafting through the vestry window made it sparkle. How in God's name had it got there?

Maybe it would mean going back to the drawing board, and back to miracles….

He then pushed the video 'play' button and watched on the TV as the picture shuttled quickly in reverse. Lizzie's figure came in to shot. Now we'll see something! He stopped the machine, then reversed it until Lizzie first came into shot. He checked the time on the digital display. Martin turned up the volume on the TV. The noise of shoes on stone and conversations were hollow and harsh but clear.

Lizzie remained in camera shot virtually the whole time. He fast-forwarded the film till he saw her disappear towards the vestry. He rewound and watched again. He saw her lay out her lunch on the pew and heard her say something to herself about washing her hands. He stopped the video machine, zeroed the counter and let the video run again. He heard the footsteps, heard the loo flush and watched as she reappeared again in one minute fifty-eight seconds. Surely that would not have given her time enough to have a good look round, find the hidden video, place the pouch and go to the loo and wash her hands? On and on his thoughts raged!

Lizzie would have to have known where the video recorder was hidden! How? There was no reasonable explanation at all. So really he was no further forward. Well, he was, because he'd got the fifth jewel. Obviously this was cause for yet another celebration!

He switched off the Icon's alarm, took the little picture from the niche and pushed the sapphire into its place. The sky in the background lit up as he did so. Trick of the light, got to be, he thought. However the scene depicted was remarkably sharper with every stone that was replaced!

Robbie's dad deposited Lizzie back home on the dot of nine thirty. She thanked both of them for a great afternoon and dinner. Lizzie surprised herself when she asked if she could see Robbie the following weekend. He smiled and winked, and said he'd phone her. When they had gone, she was quizzed about her afternoon by her parents, and when they were satisfied that everything had gone well (apart from Lizzie intentionally not telling them about Van Vebstriche) they told her about the sapphire.

Jane Miller watched her daughter, noting her reaction when she said how wonderful it was, and gosh, mustn't the vicar be pleased, and why hadn't they told the Axenthorpes before they left, and just – wow!

Lizzie's mum wondered about her daughter. How could she have the brass neck to straightforwardly lie to her?

David Webster looked up from the book he was reading, gazed out through the patio windows across the garden and wondered about Miller's ability to trace the stones. God, now he'd missed the sapphire. Things seemed to be going from bad to worse for him!

The vicar stopped writing his sermon for the following week. Divine guidance... Could Lizzie have some special gift that lesser mortals had no chance of beginning to understand? Might she really be able to commune with this devilish Highwayman? He sipped at the cold tea that he'd poured out an hour ago. He didn't notice how bad it tasted. She was always around when something happened. She had to be the common denominator, but he couldn't prove a thing, even with technology on his side!

Had all three of them – Jane Miller, David Webster and Martin Leonard – been able to pool all their information, resources and knowledge together, the sort of conclusion that each of them were coming to would have made total sense. Each had their secrets, admittedly on different levels, and they were never going to be shared!

Eliza's Secret

Tom Bennett was very weak now. She had tried to make his last hours as comfortable as she could. There were constant interruptions from her father getting her to carry out menial tasks in the pub, and it wasn't until half past two that she was able to sit with Bennett for any length of time.

She had to sit very close to him to listen to what he had to say. Tom told her about the secret passage and what she would find there if she had the courage to look, and he'd told her the hiding places of the stones.

She vowed never to tell a soul, and in any case no one ever took any notice of what she had to say because of her humble origins. She was astounded when he told her to look in the false heel of his left boot. When she had finally managed to get the wedge of leather out, a strange and beautiful gem slid into the palm of her hand. He had watched her turn it over and over in her little hands.

'Oh, sir, I can't take this. 'Twould be like stealin',' said Eliza.

'You must hide it. In your room, perhaps. It's an opal from the Icon. I'd rather it stayed missing for the moment,' remarked Bennett.

She wrapped it in a scrap of material and placed it in her apron pocket.

'Go now, Eliza. Maybe it'll bring you luck. The stones up to the present moment have just brought shame, disgrace and death to whoever...' Then he'd lapsed in to unconsciousness again.

The only time that she saw him alive again was when the crowd dragged him from the stable, virtually dead, to the Gallows Oak. But she'd seen that final wink and crooked smile, and it had been aimed at her. How the villagers cheered when his body twitched at the end of the rope until it had gone still!

Eliza had left them to it. She told her father she was going to do some chores in the inn. Instead she went to her room and sobbed her heart out. She opened the scrap of material. The opal lay there in her grubby palms. She vowed never to sell it and it would be a reminder of him, Tom Bennett, Highwayman! She totally believed his story. The crowd had certainly hanged an innocent man!

Above the window of her room lay a huge wooden beam that supported the wall above it. Plaster had crumbled away, and a small hole had appeared where wall met beam. She placed the opal in the material, wrapped it up carefully, and pushed it as far into the hole as it would go. She jammed some straw and earth to seal up the little scar. Next she scratched a love heart on to the beam with a knife. She wrote a capital 'T' with an 'E' etched into the side of the vertical stroke. She'd never forget him. She dated it, and added an arrow to the top left of the heart pointing diagonally upwards to indicate the position of the opal. Anyone looking at the love heart would put it down to a silly girl's dream!

Eliza Mellor, later Smith when she had married, died in the summer of 1870. She became the wife of the new landlord of the staging Inn in Hazelthwaite. True to her word, she never told anyone of the opal's existence. Strangely enough, the beam over the window had never been replaced or disturbed. The window, over the years, had been changed several times. Even with a lot of repair work to the window and room, the secret of the gem remained in the little cavity above the beam.

There had been one year when it had nearly been discovered, as the interior of the post office had been replastered from top to bottom. A particularly careful tradesman, a total perfectionist, was digging about the beam with his trowel. He almost flicked it out but at the last second settled for what he had done and covered the hole completely, this time very thoroughly. He'd been intrigued by the carving, thought it relevant to the general design and age of the room, and left it as a feature! He'd told the decorator that he thought the beam would look good with a matt varnish finish, and this had made the heart with its inscription stand out.

From that day on Lizzie's bedroom had been finished in white emulsion with the beams stained an oak colour, and she liked it from day one when they had moved in. Lizzie had been intrigued by the carving, just as the plasterer had been. She thought it was very romantic. She hadn't given the heart any significant thought, other than realising someone a long time ago had drawn and dated it. She thought she might do the same, one day in the future!

Hazelthwaite Media Star

Hazelthwaite village had become incredibly big news as each stone had been found. TV companies, radio, newspapers and magazines had all fought to get a different angle from anyone who was willing to speak about their thoughts on the subject. Now there was only one jewel left to be accounted for, and once that was found, no doubt the world and his wife would be camped out in the little north-eastern village. Lizzie couldn't believe how many of the articles had so many far-fetched theories and downright lies in them. Some were funny; some just stunned her.

Naturally the local paper, the *Axenthorpe Advertiser*, had run innumerable articles on the Icon, and Danny Grimshaw was becoming a journalistic legend. He tended not to speculate with his stories and articles but took a more mature, balanced stance on the subject matter.

He was almost certain that someone had stumbled on some kind of documentation that had been written by Tom Bennett almost two hundred years ago. This person was perhaps not following tenuous clues but had excellent information, recovering the stones and feeding them back to the church over a period of time to lend a certain mystique to the whole story.

Danny Grimshaw was almost totally correct in his assumptions. However, he didn't once link any of the stories to the supernatural. This kept him well away from Lizzie and any of the villagers. He had interviewed them, as he'd done everyone in the community, to get the younger perspective; but no one gave him the merest hint of what they thought the truth might be.

Unlike the tabloids, which reckoned the truth lay in alien landings and suchlike, he took a serious view, and had no time or truck for their type of reporting. Danny Grimshaw would wait patiently and try to sniff out the real truth.

When Agnes had died, or been murdered, the media had come and gone in a flash; but the return of the jewels had kept the place in a high profile. Everyone loves a mystery! Hazelthwaite had become a personality, every bit as famous as any star of sport or the cinema; and of course the downside of this was tourism. It had always been a popular tourist trap but now in early summer it had become almost unbearable. Lizzie hadn't really considered that she was responsible for the extra attention!

Lizzie had been to Robbie's several times now, and each time 'he' – Van Webstriche – had been there, mean and moody but always correct and courteous. He certainly had plenty of 'business' trips to Britain! She asked Robbie about him, but he only reiterated what a good family friend he was and that he spent huge amounts of time researching the Icon's history. It was mainly to do with his Amsterdam connection in the jewel trade. After all, the Axenthorpe Icon in its day, and most certainly now, was priceless. The stones were magnificent, and the little picture was a national heritage symbol. When Lizzie had quizzed him why it had been so badly guarded in the church if it had been worth so much, he had shrugged and put it down to one of those things that happens. After all, it didn't look much. She thought that it had begged to be nicked and had been badly looked after no matter what time in history!

But seemingly, for the summer Webster in his disguise had a totally legitimate reason for being close to her. She wondered whether he had the guts to ride as the Highwayman again! Nothing would surprise her about the audacity of the man! She couldn't shop him; what would have been her reasons?

The girls sat chatting on the bench round the Gallows Oak one evening after school. They discussed the way the village had been taken over by tourists. Possibly the only good point about the situation was that quite a number of local people were doing casual B.&B. to make some money from the influx of visitors. Even Lizzie thought enough was enough, and wondered whether an end to the quest could become a reality sooner rather than later. Truth was, she hadn't any idea of Bennett's whereabouts, as he hadn't appeared to her and she hadn't felt his presence close to her. Severe doubts began creeping into her mind.

Could he have used up all of his energy? He had told her that he might run out of the ability to appear to her, so perhaps this was the end. She said goodbye to her friends and wandered back to the post office.

Mabel remarked to Amy that Lizzie had become quite moody and insular again, and perhaps she'd had too much happen to her in one year. They left wondering what they could dream up. Certainly the impending visit of Bendy and Donna for the hols wouldn't be much fun with Lizzie in her present mood. Even Robbie hadn't seemed to have had much of an effect on her, although they knew she was quite smitten with him.

Lizzie walked upstairs and paused before opening her bedroom door. She brushed her hand through her hair, huffed and cleaned her glasses, and went inside. The room was darkish with the coming of nightfall. She sat in front of her dressing table mirror, her head resting on the backs of her cupped hands. The light changed in her room and something on her mirror grabbed her attention. There was *writing* on the mirror! You could just about make out words on the glass if you looked at them from a certain angle. What the hell could she do to make them stand out more clearly? She huffed on her glasses and a thumbprint showed on the lens. God that was it!

She clattered downstairs. Her parents were still stocking the shop for the following morning. She raced into the kitchen, filled the electric kettle with water and returned to her room. She plugged the kettle into the nearest socket but the lead came nowhere close to the mirror. She put the kettle on to boil and then manoeuvred her dressing table towards the plug. By now a steady stream of steam was hissing from the spout. She aimed the flow at the mirror. It became covered in steam but left the words, 'Horseshoe Wood midnight T'.

Tonight! Hell! She unplugged the kettle and took it back to the kitchen. She just managed to replace her dressing table back into position when her mum came into her room and said that the kettle was blowing its brains out, and would she like a cuppa?

Lizzie couldn't contain her enthusiasm at the dinner table that evening, and Jane Miller was convinced that something was up. This was a total mood swing from breakfast, or for that matter for the last couple of weeks. She'd thought that Robbie might be a positive influence on Lizzie, but no. Of course she didn't know that Webster was the prime mover and shaker for Lizzie's problems!

Hell at Devils Heights

Lizzie went to bed early. Jane Miller played along with her. Was her shoulder really hurting again? Something at school bothering her? Lizzie replied in the negative to all of the questions: 'Just tired, Mum, okay?'

John told his wife to leave her alone and give her some space. Knowing her, she had some late homework to do that should've been done last week, that sort of thing. Jane raised her eyebrows and sighed. No, Lizzie was up to no good, and whatever was happening, it was tonight! She could read the signs now. Whatever could she be thinking of – and this being a school night! She thought of John's comment, 'Knowing her...' That was the whole point, neither of them knew their daughter at all, that was the truth of the situation. She wondered where they'd slipped up. Slipped up, that was an understatement if ever there was one!

The church clock had struck ten thirty, and although it was early, Lizzie had to risk going now, so that she'd be in good time to walk up to Devil's Heights by midnight. She wanted to be up there soon at Horseshoe Woods to get a good hiding place. As far as she was concerned, the road up to Axenthorpe was out for her, and she really wasn't relishing the forest path, where she'd been spooked several months before.

By 10.40 she had negotiated the treeline and was well on her way up the path to the Heights. Jane Miller knocked on her door at quarter to eleven to bid her goodnight. There was no answer. She entered Lizzie's room. 'The little devil's gone,' she whispered to herself. She looked about the room for some sort of clue. 'Come on, Lizzie, you've missed something I know it,' she said. Her eyes skimmed the room. The carpet, yes, there was the clue. Lizzie's dressing table legs were not positioned in the original impressions on the carpet. She'd moved it – why? The mirror...it had been rubbed, and fairly recently. There was something still there. She looked carefully. 'Need some more light,' she said quietly. She brought the bedside lamp over. The remaining letters said, 'Horse od idnigh 7.

The words she understood and could fill in: 7, not a clue!

She heard her husband coming up the stairs. God, if he was to find out that Lizzie wasn't in her room!

'Goodnight, Lizzie,' she said.

'Make sure the bugs don't bite,' she heard him say automatically.

'Fancy a hot choccy, love?' she said, closing an empty bedroom.

'You read my mind,' he smiled.

As she popped two sleeping pills in to his cup, she looked to heaven and asked forgiveness from the Almighty. Grasping the two mugs, she went back upstairs.

When he'd fallen asleep, which hadn't taken long, she dashed downstairs, put on her outdoor clothes and made her way into the courtyard. Which way? It didn't really matter – the wretched girl was only going to one place; however she did have a one hour start.

The wind had got up and clouds scudded across the sky, dappling the light from the moon. She heard the garden gate bang. Well, that had been secured earlier so she'd gone the same way as before but this time heading right towards Devil's Heights. She pushed through the broken fence panels at the end of the garden. The torch beam marked out the path before her. Why hadn't she walked up on the Axenthorpe road? It would have been so much quicker. She could've hidden if vehicles approached. Why take the forestry route, when Jane knew she hated it? But this wasn't her daughter she was following now! This was… she shrugged.

Lizzie made the Heights in record time. She hadn't thought twice about using the path, or her fear of the woods, just concentrated her efforts on making the top undetected. She'd had to negotiate a courting couple in a car, had disturbed a family of foxes on the prowl, and had been momentarily shocked when an owl had swooped over her head. She had arrived at the top, slipped over the road and was now making her way along the path that led round the ring of trees, as she had done before. In fact the many ramblers who had recently visited the area had worn the path away to such an extent that two or three people could walk along it side by side.

She stopped dead in her tracks when she heard a horse whinny. She listened. A couple of cars passed along the Heights road, their lights lancing into the darkness. She ducked down for fear of being spotted. Very gently she pushed her way through the dense mat of ferns and bushes, swearing when she felt brambles brush her arm and face, and then she broke cover by a large tree trunk into the inner circle of the wood itself.

The 'Highwayman' was there, sitting astride his horse. She moved forward.

'I got your message,' she half whispered.

He turned. 'Good, Lizzie, I knew you'd crack the code,' said Webster.

Lizzie froze. '*You!*' She spat out the word.

'Oh yes, Lizzie love, it's me,' he announced.

'How did you do it?' she said.

'You wouldn't believe my skills in burglary, Lizzie… and your cottage, well…' He smiled. 'So you answer to the Highwayman, do you, Lizzie? I don't begin to understand how you do it, but you do, else you wouldn't be here now,' he growled.

The clouds cleared from the face of the moon and its light reflected off the pair of pistols pointing at her.

'The last jewel, Lizzie, the opal – where is it?' he said in a confident voice.

'I don't know what you're talking about!' she shouted, tears filling her eyes.

The first pistol shot rang out. A spurt of grass and earth erupted close by her feet. She fell to her knees, saying over and over again that she didn't know.

Jane Miller was just crossing the road when she heard the pistol shot. Christ! He was going to kill her, execute her! She screamed out to Lizzie that she was coming. Webster fired again. The horse reared up. He mouthed an oath and spurred it in to a gallop. He passed Jane Miller as she ran into the woods. She threw herself to the side and rolled out of the way of the flailing hooves. He snarled at her as he galloped past. Jane got up and ran to her daughter's assistance. They clung to one another. She pulled Lizzie up. Both were sobbing.

Webster reined the horse round and galloped back into the woods. Lizzie's face registered her disbelief as horse and rider thundered towards them. Surely not! Webster was bearing down on them at full gallop. They both dived away in different directions, but at that very instant, and for a reason that Jane Miller never understood, Webster's horse reared up and threw his rider so heavily to the ground that he was immediately rendered unconscious.

As Webster galloped into Horseshoe Woods, the Highwayman had urged his horse to suddenly appear between Webster's mount and the Millers.

Webster certainly couldn't believe such a disastrous turn of events!

Jane Miller certainly didn't believe what she saw. Why would the horse do something like that at the very last second?

Lizzie's sigh was one of relief. She could actually see what had happened!

Lizzie looked round and saw Tom Bennett, smiling. He uttered something like, 'Exciting here tonight, eh Lizzie? I'll see you soon,' and he and his horse disappeared.

In all of the to-do, Webster had recovered from his fall and run off. Jane Miller looked at her daughter. Lizzie eyed her.

'Now you see why I've been the way I have. He's been back some time, but I couldn't tell anyone because he was called Van Webstriche and was guest of the Axenthorpes,' she sobbed.

Jane's last remark to her daughter as they made their way down the road to Hazelthwaite was something along the lines of, 'If the police don't do their job this time, I certainly will!'

The Final Escape

Webster ran for all he was worth to the Highwayman's Perch. Several times he stumbled, cursed the ache in his side, the result of falling from his horse. When he staggered into the lounge the two men who confronted him needed no explanation. One of the men hit him hard in the side that he was holding.

Webster grunted in pain and sank to his knees. The following kick, aimed at his stomach, knocked out what little breath he had left in his lungs. His bent head then took the full force of the well-dressed man's foot.

'Get him in the chopper fast. He's wasted far too much of my time and money.'

The man walked to the door and flashed his torch a couple of times across the garden in to the night. Seconds later, they heard the sound of an engine whine and rotor blades start to beat the air rhythmically. Leaving the patio doors open, the two men dragged Webster to the helicopter. They bundled him inside and without any conversation at all the pilot lifted off, spun the helicopter round and headed for the coast. The night goggles he wore allowed him to fly low along the pre-arranged course.

After one hour of flying the pilot radioed the shortest of messages to the ocean-going luxury cruiser, and after receiving manoeuvring instructions made a smooth landing on the stern helipad. The boat was registered in the Cayman Islands and belonging to Axenthorpe Holdings. It made for a northern French port before making passage to its home marina somewhere in the south of Spain.

For the first time in many months Lizzie was now safe from the psychopath, Webster; but obviously she wasn't to know of this fact!

The police enquiry into the Webster affair was thorough to the point of being more like the Spanish Inquisition. Some detective had mentioned the word, and Lizzie remembered that this was the term she had forgotten from school.

The 'inquisition' had involved Lord and Lady Axenthorpe, Robbie and anyone who had been close to Lizzie and Webster. The whole story had hit the youngest Axenthorpe hard. After all, several times he had reassured Lizzie that Van Vebstriche, as he knew him, was a top bloke. He felt awful! As far as he was concerned, Lizzie would be finished with him. He'd be lucky if she'd speak to him again. All the things that had happened to her that had come out in the 'inquisition' made him realise how little he knew about her and how incredibly interesting she was. But that was in the past for him now…

The police still couldn't make head or tail of Jane Miller's stories about pursuing her daughter. Why hadn't she told her husband? And were there family problems? And God, so much dirty washing came to the top of the basket the more they ferreted around! Even John had some pretty stern words with his wife. There had been so much deceit, and all he'd been told to do was put up with it: 'You'd never understand!' *Understand*? Didn't he support his daughter after the first shooting? Put up and shut up… really! Understanding was wafer-thin at that present moment of time, not to mention his feeling a total twit for being so easily suckered by his wife.

Lizzie…well, Lizzie blamed everything on Webster and trying to do things for him. He'd threatened her family, especially her mum, and offered to burn down the post office. She'd found nothing for him because his research had been wrong, and the only thing she'd really found was how to make a sore shoulder worse. On his behalf she'd broken into people's property, but not – and she stressed *not* – in order to take anything.

Most of all, she realised how easy it was to lie, and she certainly continued to do this, big time!

People had come forward to talk to the police on the night Lizzie was shot at, saying that they'd heard the sound of engines, which could well have been a helicopter. The sounds had been heard in the small hours of that particular morning, yes, but nothing else. The Axenthorpes, however, confirmed this by saying that Van Vebstriche had had several business associates fly in to see him from northern Europe. No flight plans had been logged with the civil aviation authorities at the time, and the way things seemed to be panning out this was just another nail in Webster's coffin. Now they saw how much they'd been taken in by him, and how sorry they were!

When the several days of intense police pressure were over, Lizzie and her family were left on their own, well, apart from the bunfight with the press, who were impolitely told to get lost by John Miller. Lizzie heard her dad on the phone use some quite uncharacteristic agricultural language to them. It all added up to 'Leave us alone, go away!'

This phase of Lizzie's life had come to an end. She had to settle down now, they said, and look forward to a quieter and well overdue summer holiday.

From the time her best friends Bendy and Donna had left her after Christmas, until the beginning of the summer holidays, when they were to return, Lizzie had been in touch with them constantly. She had told them everything that had happened, with the odd omission, of course! Although their parents were still a little at odds with one another with their daughters going to visit with the North of England's answer to Beryl the Peril, they were pleased for them to go.

Bendy and Donna having a friend who had become a celebrity for all of the wrong reasons tickled them to death. The two girls thought that as soon as they hit Hazelthwaite in the hols, it would be rock and roll all the way! For Bendy, that would include bread rolls, sausage rolls, great pigging great caramel doughnuts and anything else she could stuff down her gob! Her comforter, as always was food – loads of it – and her build-up to the holiday had forced her 'diet' back to start the next day, then the next...and so it went on.

Donna was less excitable, and although she was looking forward to her stay, she thought the change in Lizzie at Christmas and the tone of her letters and phone calls to them were ever so slightly distant, in every sense of the word! Still, who knew what the future would bring? Things might be terrific.

★

They arrived at exactly the same time as the previous year, and the squealing and yelling had been the same. Lizzie had rushed out to meet them and had dragged them upstairs to tell them all her news. Her news outweighed their measly crumbs about fifty to one, but they let her blabber on and on, managing the odd interrupted sentence here and there.

Donna finally brought up the subject of Robbie. 'Well, Lizzie, what's he like? You said last year you had no time for blokes because they didn't like you. Seems like this guy's made quite a way into your...' she said, and pointed to Lizzie's heart.

Bendy exploded with laughter. 'Hope you mean her heart,' she giggled.

Lizzie clubbed her over the head with her pillow, and after that a pillow fight raged. So much stupidity and laughter could only be brought under control by Lizzie's mum, who called them down for tea.

Bendy walked to Lizzie's window. She viewed the darkening village green, the Gallows Oak in full leaf, the sinister Devil's Heights and said, 'You've got it all here, Lizzie. You're so lucky. I suppose, with Mabel and Amy here as your friends, we don't figure much in your life now. We're too far away,' she sighed.

'You're closer to me now than ever, even though you're both still in London, Bendy,' Lizzie whispered, 'especially your fat belly.'

Bendy gave it a wobble and this time the noise was hysterical from all three of them.

After dinner they walked across the green to meet Mabel and Amy, who were already at the Gallows Oak. As the sun dipped lower into the western sky and the shadows lengthened, Hazelthwaite settled down to enjoy a beautiful warm evening. The smell of barbecued food drifted across the green, and they all looked at Bendy, who told them she'd started her diet. The pub car park was full and cars had been parked along the edge of the verge. From all round the village, sounds of chatter and laughter rose and fell. Who'd have believed that such a charming place could have gone through so much trauma in the last year or so?

Lizzie and her friends sat there quietly taking it all in. A perfect end to a perfect day, and Lizzie hadn't had too many of those recently. Perhaps everything was changing for the better. She hadn't thought about Tom Bennett or David Webster for quite a while, and although while chatting with the girls earlier the latter's name had been brought up, it was only mentioned in passing.

Bendy and Donna were sharing the same room they'd had before, when Bendy had been so frightened by the Highwayman. She vowed this year, no matter what happened – noise, blinding flash, whatever – she would *not* be going to look out of the window at the dead of night. The curtains would remain firmly closed together!

The problem was that Lizzie's mum had left the top of the sash window slightly open but in a locked position to let what little fresh air there was circulate into the room. It had been remarkably hot and stuffy for about a week, and with the two girls sharing the room a little ventilation, she thought, would not go amiss. The curtains were also wide open to let the moon light in.

Bendy looked unsure when they'd entered the room but Donna said she'd sleep in the bed next to the window just in case a thunderstorm brewed up. Amy had earlier mentioned the possibility of a 'thorm' due to the conditions. Bendy thought that was all she needed. Still, it might make for a bit of unpredictable excitement!

Both Lizzie and Bendy woke immediately when the first crash of thunder echoed round the basin of Hazelthwaite. Lizzie heard her mother call to her and she replied that she was okay. Then Lizzie heard her reassure Bendy and Donna. Bendy replied, but Donna slept through the thunder, and Jane Miller's call. The long flashes of lightning lit their bedrooms and the thunder roared. Lizzie sat by her window watching Hazelthwaite as if it was being lit by huge strobes. After the third set of flashes she turned round and found Tom Bennett sitting on the end of her bed.

She let out a little moan.

'Can't you stop doing that appearing trick?' she half whispered, just as another enormous peal of thunder rumbled across the valley.

'Like to keep you guessing,' he replied in hushed tones. 'I see your friends are staying with you again… hardly seems possible a year has slipped by,' he continued taking off his tricorn hat. The black bow that tied his long, dark hair came to rest over his left shoulder.

'Listen, Lizzie…' he paused for what seemed an age… 'I've something important to tell you.'

She listened intently, as his voice seemed to be fading.

'Speak up!' she said, in far too loud a voice.

From her room, Bendy heard Lizzie mumbling away. Bad dreams, she supposed.

The Highwayman cleared his throat. He seemed hesitant, almost frightened of what he was going to say. 'Lizzie, I've a sort of confession to make to you,' he finally said.

'For goodness' sake, spit it out,' she replied again, far too loudly for her own good.

This time Bendy could actually make out the odd word or two. Perhaps she ought to check on Lizzie, see if she was okay. After all, Lizzie had come to her aid last time. She climbed out of bed and tiptoed to the door. She didn't know why she did this, as Donna seemed dead to the world.

Opening her door quietly, she made her way to Lizzie's door and was about to put her hand on the door handle when she heard Lizzie speak again. Bendy pressed her ear to the door and strained to hear every syllable.

'What do you mean, you don't know where the last one is? Tell me about the girl… just before you were hanged. Christ, I've come this far for you to tell me that… I don't believe it!' said an obviously angry Lizzie.

Then there was quiet.

'Don't give me that, Tom Bennett, you must have some clue!'

Then she was quiet again.

'Oh, leave me to it indeed! Where do I start to look? Oh, you passed out… How convenient, and anyway she'd have done God knows what with it – maybe even sold it!'

'Sorry, I didn't mean it like that. I know you were hurt...look I'll do the best I can. When will I see you again?'

The conversation seemed to cease, as Bendy didn't hear Lizzie speak again. If she was having a dream it had seemed very real. She supposed that if you were talking in your sleep you would have a one-sided conversation. She'd ask Lizzie at breakfast. Bendy crept back to her bedroom, slipped through the door and slid under the covers.

From across the other side of the room and from under her covers she heard Donna say, 'Bendy, where have you been?'

'The loo,' she whispered, 'I thought you were dead asleep.'

'Even you flush the loo! What was Lizzie prattling on about?' Donna continued.

When Bendy had related the one-sided conversation to her, Donna told her to say nothing to Lizzie in the morning, and if she didn't promise she'd say awful things about her. Bendy made a pursed lip under the bedclothes, then stuck her tongue out at her friend.

'And don't stick your tongue out at me, Bendy,' said Donna, smiling.

The thunderstorm passed through at about three in the morning and when dawn broke it was going to be another beautiful day.

Lizzie lay in bed with her hands linked behind her head supporting her neck. If Tom Bennett's story was true and this girl Eliza had taken the jewel, she could have hidden it anywhere, and as she said to him last night, she could have sold it. He felt sure that she wouldn't have sold it!

Eliza, she thought, now where would she be able to find out anything about the girl? As she lay there, a plan started to form in her mind. The first part of Lizzie's plan would involve all the girls. After all, five heads are better than one, and as they wouldn't know what she was really after, she could make up some sort of research project for them all to do, during some of the long summer days.

Mabel and Amy arrived about ten. They let themselves in at the judas gate and joined the girls around the table in the courtyard. Amy remarked how pretty it was now, and how quiet it was here in comparison to the rest of the place, which was incredibly busy with literally busloads of tourists coming to view the celebrity village. Jane Miller brought them out Cokes and an overgenerous plate of differently filled doughnuts that Bendy eyed with a wicked gleam.

'For God's sake, Bendy,' said Donna, 'you've just had breakfast, you're gross!'

'It's hols, so knickers!' With that she sucked out a large amount of caramel filling from one of the cakes. 'Wicked!' she cooed. Lizzie winced.

'I thought we might find out about a little of the village history,' she suddenly piped up.

All four girls stopped in mid bite, then swallowed hard (in Bendy's case, choked) and gawped at her.

'Does this history thing involve boys and mucking about?' asked Bendy.

'I'm being serious,' said Lizzie, looking at them.

'Amy, feel her forehead, pet,' said Mabel.

Amy said, 'You don't mind us being ever so slightly suspicious about your motives, Lizzie, as your grades in history were the pits. If I remember, you got...'

'Okay, okay. It was just a thought, only we all complain of boredom,' said Lizzie.

'It's the hols, we're supposed to be bored,' said Bendy getting stuck, literally, into another cake.

'What were you thinking of, pet,' said Mabel, winking at the others.

'Oh, maybe do some research on special places in the village and surrounds, interesting people, stuff like that,' Lizzie replied.

Bendy followed the caramel doughnut with an apple-filled one. Her upper and lower lips and general mouth surrounds were now totally covered with sugar and bits of filling.

'Parish registers, censuses, the graveyard, Axenthorpe Hall library,' said Donna. 'Those would be the things you'd need to look at.'

'Robbie's eyes,' said Mabel.

'*Oooh,*' they all replied at the same time.

Bendy's '*oooh*' resulted in her coughing with her mouth full, and apple doughnut being splattered freely over the girls, the table and a hanging basket, such was its force!

After they'd worked out what and who they were going to research, Lizzie (totally pleased the way things had gone) left them the interesting things to do while she went off to the church to look through the parish register and hunt around the graveyard for any 'interesting' information.

Mabel suggested that perhaps when they completed their local history of the area, the vicar might display their findings in the church. Lizzie couldn't have cared less what happened to it.

If they pooled their knowledge after a week or two spent rooting around and something shed some light on the history of Eliza, she'd be happy. In fact, that was all Lizzie was interested in. They thought they would focus on people of the local area, as a general history could be an enormous undertaking from about 1800. Lizzie suggested fifty years earlier, and they had said fine. And so the girls set out on their various tasks to put together a local history of a cross section of the population of Hazelthwaite that would span about two hundred and fifty years. The girls had absolutely no inkling of an idea what their friend Lizzie was up to.

Understanding from a Love Heart

Lizzie's mum took Bendy and Donna into Axenthorpe to access the *Advertiser*'s archives and then to look in the local library. Amy and Mabel were given the task of researching from Lord Axenthorpe's private library. They had to phone and book a reservation, which had proved to be no problem, but it would have to be done the following day.

Lizzie had walked down the gravel path to the church porch and explained to Francesca what she would be doing. The vicar allowed her to look through the past records of births, marriages and deaths, but the books were on no account to leave his desk in the vestry. Martin Leonard still mistrusted Lizzie.

When Lizzie opened the door she saw the ledgers stacked neatly in two piles. She assumed that her task wouldn't take long. After all, she was looking for an Eliza who had lived in the village all her life. Well, people didn't travel far in those days. Probably, even to have travelled to Axenthorpe would have been an achievement, what with the rough roads and expense and danger of travel.

Now, how far back would she need to go? The early 1800s seemed to be a good starting point. Hadn't the girls mentioned 1803? She couldn't remember just what the reference had been about, but that was as good as anything.

She worked down the lists of names. However, she soon realised it was going to be a little more difficult than she imagined because of the handwriting styles, writing that had faded over the years, damp marks and water staining that had disfigured the books over time. Poor storage in damp cupboards had taken their toll on the old paper. The books also had a terrible fusty smell about them that got on to your hands.

Lizzie's finger gently followed each of the entries down the left-hand side of the page. She finally came to an entry under the name of Smith. Benjamin Mark Smith had married a Mellor, Elizabeth May. So far this girl was the only person whose entry might fit the bill, as she might have had her name shortened to Eliza. Uncanny they both had the same Christian name and virtually the same surname. Lizzie didn't have any other name, just plain Elizabeth, which she hated. Married in 1815. She looked for other clues. She found her birth date, 1792, so that would have made her about twelve or thirteen when she had tended Tom Bennett and showed him what kindness she could the night before he died.

Lizzie sat back to think. She was going to try and put herself in the position of a girl virtually the same age as herself and think what she might have done. Lizzie looked at the book again. She traced her finger through some more of the entries. There it was: Died, August 16th 1870. That would have made her seventy-eight, a fair old age in those days.

Married name, Smith. 'Jeez!' she hissed. 'Oops, sorry,' she continued, looking to the heavens and remembering where she was. 'Surely Agnes Smith couldn't have been, no, granddaughter... great-granddaughter?' Lizzie stopped again; she couldn't work out the dates fast enough. This was too much to take in.

That hadn't been too bad. She idly turned back the pages and looked at the years 1800. Her finger moved down the page from about 1750. When she arrived at the 1780s entries for births, the twins William and Thomas Bennett stood out like sore thumbs. She couldn't believe it! Wait a minute! She rushed out of the vestry, almost knocking over a group of OAPs who had come to view the floral exhibits.

Lizzie looked down the list of vicars on the board outlined in gold. There it was – she knew she'd recognised the name: William Bennett, Rev., 1803–1804. He had had hardly any time as the vicar here, she thought.

Lizzie retraced her steps to the vestry and shut the books. She'd seen enough. She thanked Francesca and asked her where she might find the headstone of an Elizabeth May Smith. Francesca told her roughly where the family grave was situated.

Lizzie trod carefully across the plots, most of which were tended neatly with cut grass and fresh flowers. She bent down to read the inscription.

To our beloved 'Eliza' who will be sorely missed
Died peacefully in her sleep.

A strange symbol had been etched in at the bottom of the tombstone. It looked like a capital 'T' with an 'E' beside it. What made Lizzie gulp was the year-old grave of Agnes Smith. Lizzie noted how well tended it was. She wondered who kept it so tidy. Now all she had to do was wait to see what the others had found out.

Lizzie wasn't at all surprised when Bendy and Donna returned with next to nothing. The library and the *Advertiser*, although being helpful, just didn't have the specific information on 'interesting' people that they were after.

Mabel and Amy had scoured the information for 1800 and thereabouts, and although they'd found out about registers from that time mostly it concerned what Lizzie had already unearthed. There was no one of real interest at all, it seemed, living then in those parts, apart from the Highwayman, and the event of his hanging. They hadn't accessed any information about the girl, 'Eliza'. Perhaps this was where the quest ended – where the adventure that had included reality and the supernatural ceased. Lizzie looked at the girls glumly. They weren't sure why she was down.

Lizzie and the girls continued to pursue the history of Hazelthwaite through its inhabitants from 1750 to the present day, but the information they unearthed was fairly ordinary. They managed to take examples of a cross section of life that did include Elizabeth Mellor, but the girls never twigged that this was the person who Lizzie was so interested in!

All of the information was conscientiously typed up on word processors, as they all had access to some sort of computer in their houses. Bendy and Donna used Lizzie's laptop, while Lizzie laboriously used her father's computer. More often than not Lizzie would curse, but when stared at with that 'we don't approve look' from her friends, say, 'Well, you should hear the language on the school bus!' Bendy confirmed what she said and added it was bad, if not worse, in London, but that didn't mean that they needed to follow like lemmings! Lizzie told them flat that she'd say what she'd like especially when she was blitzed with idiotic error messages, spelling errors and grammar underlinings!

However, by working on the odd afternoon a week or when the weather was poor and there wasn't anything better to do, they finally produced a quite presentable piece of work. This was much to the surprise of Mabel and Amy, who tended to take things for granted. This piece of work had been taken seriously, and they had actually wanted to do it as well as they could. Lizzie had said they sounded like a couple of teachers. Mabel and Amy *wanted* to be a couple of teachers! Lizzie had raised her eyebrows and given her glasses a huff and a polish, swept a hand through her hair and said her ambition was to be as lazy as she could. All of them had thumped her with pillows, bringing back a twinge of pain in her shoulders.

But it was to be when Bendy and Donna had gone home to London a week before the summer holiday came to an end that Lizzie put the final piece in the jigsaw. It had looked certain that the Icon would never have the last stone pushed into its frame. Lizzie dwelt on this for days after they'd left.

Tom Bennett hadn't appeared to her, and the information on Eliza Mellor had been pushed to the back of her mind. The last person she had thought about was Robbie Axenthorpe. So one could imagine Lizzie's horror when one Saturday morning she heard her mother say, 'Just go on up, Robbie, I'm sure Lizzie would be pleased to see you!'

Lizzie was still in bed. She looked worse than a sight. Hair all over the place, breath like a sewer outflow, not a hell of a lot on and Robbie was coming up the stairs. The fifth stair squeaked...

Ooh! She panicked, rolled over the bed and caught her foot in a loose sheet at the end of the bed, which meant she lay upside down in a heap covered with Winnie the Pooh duvet around her. He was just about to open the door when her hand clicked the key in the lock.

'You are up?' said Robbie. He'd been well briefed by her mother in a whispered conversation about her present state of unreadiness. The fact of her not being up and the shock of his arrival, and the fact that she'd sent him up might result in her never speaking to her mother again!

Robbie had of course realised the mileage in this.

'Gimme a couple of mins,' wailed Lizzie, trying to dress, wash and clean her teeth all at the same time. 'I was just about to come down for breakfast. Why don't you pop down yourself and get mum to make you a coffee?' she shouted, stalling for time. Pause. *Mother, I'll kill you,*' she whispered to herself.

"Kay,' said Robbie. She heard him laughing as he went down stairs to the kitchen. She then heard more laughing as her mother and Robbie proceeded to chat about her. If mother starts to show him the baby snaps, I'll…

Finally, twenty minutes later, she made her entrance. Robbie decided not to have a third cup of coffee but said some toast would be good. He added, much to Jane Miller's delight that he thought Lizzie's baby and toddler photos were a wow, and he really liked the holiday one where she was dressed up like Posh Sp… Lizzie looked at her mother daggers. She in turn gave a pursed-lips kiss back.

'Well,' she said, 'what have you come for?'

'Will sorry do?' he answered. 'I've kept clear because I thought that you would still be angry with me. Hate me. I'll go if you like.'

Lizzie didn't answer. The look said it all and she leaned over and gave him a peck on the cheek.

'You look great,' he smiled, 'it's amazing what toothpaste around the top lip does for you.'

Lizzie shut her eyes. She wiped her mouth with the back of her hand. Oh God, how *embarrassing!*

He laughed again. 'Just coddin',' he said. 'Go for a walk?'

'S'pose,' she answered.

Her mother called from the top of the stairs, 'Your room's respectable, Lizzie.'

The two of them went upstairs. 'Nice view,' commented Robbie. 'Could do a great cricket commentary from here.'

Lizzie eyed him and shrugged.

'You'd have to be a pillock to be interested in cricket,' she answered.

'Thanks,' he replied, 'And here's me thinking you were quite keen last year.'

'Only mildly,' she said in reply. 'Well, my interest was limited. Your brother's rather dishy.'

Robbie laughed out loud.

He looked round the room. It certainly didn't look like the bedroom of a tomboy, like she made herself out to be. His eyes took in the Winnie the Pooh bedclothes and matching curtains and cushion covers. He smiled. Then his eyes travelled back to the beam across the window.

'Who wrote the inscription in the beam?' he asked.

'Dunno, it's been there forever. Well, you can see the date,' Lizzie replied.

'A love heart with a "T" and...' he stopped. 'Don't know what the other letter is, eighteen something can't quite make it out. Funny how the arrow goes up to the far side and not down. Got no feathers, either.'

Lizzie's eyes widened. Of course – that was it! She looked at Robbie, then the arrow, then the T. Jeez, the other letter dug in was an E: T and E, Thomas and Eliza. So the little girl just might have had a crush on someone who she'd only met for a few hours, or who'd shared a great secret with her that she'd never disclosed. God, she couldn't get rid of Robbie quick enough!

A swift walk to the Gallows Oak and the promise of a phone call for later and she'd seen him off. Good riddance as well! She'd play a bit harder to get than a few pleasant words. In fact, she felt a twinge of conscience, and slipped him a personal text message a couple of hours later. It was personal enough for Lizzie to give her glasses a huff and a polish after she'd sent it!

She had waited until the house was quiet that night before she started to gently pick away the plaster at the corner of the beam.

She used a small screwdriver, and bit by bit the powdery substance fell from around the beam. Only once did she have heart failure when she thought a whole lump would fall but it stayed in place until she'd carved a triangular gap.

The church clock struck half past one in the morning. The gap now stretched back several inches. She gently pulled some straw and two hundred years of dust from the hole. Then she felt the tips of her fingers touch something soft. Gently, she inched the little package towards the mouth of the gap she'd carved.

A small grubby piece of material was sitting in the palm of her now trembling hand. She walked to her bed and sat on the duvet. She pulled the bedside lamp closer and with nervous fingers opened the material to reveal the opal. The last stone of the Axenthorpe Icon had been recovered, and this time she hadn't had to get wet, be scared or be quizzed by anyone!

She had to thank a girl of about her own age who'd had the good nature to help someone in trouble and then learn to adore them in a such a short time – adore them to the extent of taking a massive secret to the grave. Smart, though, to leave enough of a clue, be it ever so obscure, just in case one day…

How builders that had worked on the room since the opal had been hidden hadn't stumbled on it was a miracle. Lizzie used the pot of interior filler to cover the hole she had made, but not before she'd inserted a little note of her own.

It simply said,

Thanks Eliza for keeping your secret,
I'm sure you won't mind me
Righting a terrible wrong
Love, Lizzie.

She wrapped the note in Eliza's material and gently placed it back in the hole. As she covered the gap with the white filler she wept. This time the tears came for the right reasons.

Sexton eats an Opal!

Francesca Golightly looked after Agnes Smith's grave. There was no dark secret about this fact, and Francesca had nothing to do with her family at all. She did it because no one else was able to.

So it was that Lizzie decided to give Francesca the privilege of finding and returning the final stone to the vicar. Lizzie loved the way Francesca embellished the story of her find. She made it almost as exciting as the real thing had been!

Lizzie had watched the days when Francesca would go and clip the grass and put fresh flowers in the ornamental pot by the grave's headstone. It worked out, more or less, every other Wednesday. So, early one school morning, Lizzie nipped in to the graveyard, put the opal by the pot of withered flowers and left for school, full of excitement about what was to follow.

When she'd come home, brimming with expectation, to what had been a quiet and ordinary day in Hazelthwaite, she was deeply agitated. She didn't want her mother to suspect anything, so she went about normal things that she would do after school. After eating tea, she told her folks she was off to see Mabel for an hour and wouldn't be late.

Lizzie left by the garden path and slipped unnoticed into the graveyard. She made her way to Agnes' grave. It was looking spruce and clean. The grass was newly clipped and fresh flowers were in the vase. The gemstone was nowhere to be seen...disappeared into thin air. What the hell had gone wrong?

A couple of days later, when she'd arrived home from school, again extremely depressed, her mother had told her an extraordinary story. Apparently Francesca had come in to the shop full of it!

Sexton, the church cat, had been rushed off to the vet's with a mystery illness of some kind. He couldn't eat and was really poorly. The vet had operated immediately, and in the contents of his stomach he'd found a huge opal. The vicar realised that it was the jewel from the 'Icon' because of its shape. Cat and stone had been brought home, and both were doing well! The vet assumed that the daft cat had thought the opal was something good to eat, and had swallowed it whole and suffered the consequences! Francesca had come to tend some grave or other, oh, Agnes Smith's, she thought, just in time to save the cat's life, otherwise it would have died and been buried with the stone inside it. How the stone got to be by the grave was an absolute mystery, yet again...

Lizzie smiled. That cat was an absolute bloke!

★

'And although we shall never know the story of how these gemstones were returned,' droned the vicar...

Lizzie walked to the Gallows Oak with Mabel and Amy. Again, they eyed her suspiciously, and once more she told them to get lost in no uncertain terms!

When they'd said their goodbyes, Lizzie sat on her own idly looking across the village green and Devil's Heights beyond.

She suddenly felt chilly.

Tom Bennett dropped from the branch he'd been sitting on and stood before her. Yes, he was handsome, she thought. She fully understood why Eliza had fallen for him all those years before.

'Congratulations, Lizzie, you've done well, especially working out the fate of the last stone!' he said with his usual crooked smile.

'Thank you. You know you had a real admirer in your last twenty-four hours,' she replied, returning the smile.

'Oh, I don't know about that,' he said, pushing his tricorn hat back and scratching his neck.

Lizzie was silent for a minute or two.

'I don't want you to go,' she said, tears welling up in her eyes.

'Well, my time has come. You've righted my so-called "wrong", Lizzie dear. I did tell you that you were "Chosen"...' He stopped, as he could see she was distressed.

She looked up with renewed interest when he went on. 'Just suppose Lizzie–' and he'd been saving this up for a time like this, when he knew that she'd be upset, 'that I'd lied to you. There might be something you could do for me in the future, how would that sound to you? We seem to make a good team. What with my brains...'

He was stopped in mid sentence by Lizzie reaching up on tiptoe and giving him a peck on his cheek with her lips which were met by a rather cold sensation, 'and my charm and bloody good looks,' she giggled.

In a flash he'd gone. Lizzie was left in front of the Gallows Oak, laughing.

'I love a liar! Takes a good one to know one, Tom Bennett!' she screamed, spinning around not knowing in which direction he'd gone.

Bennett watched her run back to the post office from about five hundred feet up. He smiled the crooked smile, reared his horse up in the sunset, then galloped silently through the air in the direction of his home at Greywater Scar. A kiss from the Chosen one, now that was something to cherish until the next time they met!

Lightning Source UK Ltd.
Milton Keynes UK
28 July 2010

157481UK00001B/10/A